GOLD FEVER

THE CLIPPER SHIP "FLYING CLOUD" from
Gleason's Pictorial Magazine, 1851.

GOLD FEVER

SAN FRANCISCO

1851

Ken Salter

REGENT PRESS
Berkeley, California
2013

Copyright © 2013 Ken Salter

[Paperback]
ISBN 13: 978-1-58790-240-6
ISBN 10:1-58790-240-0

[E-book]
ISBN 13: 978-1-58790-241-3
ISBN 10: 1-58790-241-9

Library of Congress Control Number: 2013935952

Cover Design: Paul Veres

First Edtion
First Printing

To Order Books of for Further Information contact
REGENT PRESS
regentpress@mindspring.com

Manufactured in the U.S.A.
REGENT PRESS
www.regentpress.net

California Gold Rush Journal

TABLE OF CONTENTS

California Gold Rush Journal
LIST OF ILLUSTRATIONS

From the Author's private collection, some of which were donated to Le Musee du Nouveau Monde in La Rochelle, France.

15. "GREAT FIRE IN SAN FRANCISCO," from *Gleason's Pictorial Magazine*, 1851.

16. "SAN FRANCISCO FIRE OF MAY 3-4, 1851."

17. "MAP OF BURNT DISTRICT OF MAY 3-4 FIRE, 1851."

18. "SACRAMENTO CITY, CALIFORNIA," 1851.

19. "STEAMER DAY," 1851.

20. "CHINESE MINERS IN CALIFORNIA," 1851.

21. "WASHING WITH A CRADLE," "WASHING WITH PAN," and "SLUICE AND TUNNEL, TIMBUCTOO."

22. "A FRENCH MINER," from *Mountains and Molehills*, by Frank Marryat, 1855 (*author's collection*).

23. "A CALIFORNIA CABIN," from *Gleason's Drawing Room Companion*, 1851.

24. Photos of a French Bear's Grease Pot and B. Lefevre Pomade Pots dug in San Francisco (*museum donation*).

25. "CHINESE GAMBLING HOUSE" c. 1851.

26. A trade card for "MRS. WINSLOW'S SOOTHING SYRUP."

27. "CHINESE RESTAURANT," San Francisco.

28. "HANGING OF JENKINS ON THE PLAZA," 1851.

29. "FIRE OF JUNE 22, 1851."

30. "DIAGRAM OF BURNT DISTRICT OF JUNE 22nd FIRE."

California Gold Rush Journal

INTRODUCTION

Berkeley, California – February 2013

The miners came in forty-nine
The whores in fifty-one
And when they got together
They produced the native son
— FROM A MINER'S DITTY

In 1848 Yerba Buena was a sleepy, backwater trading post with 2,000 inhabitants living in tents, shanties and adobes.

In 1849, John Marshall's gold discovery reverberated around the world and the gold rush was on. Individuals lucky enough to be in California provisioned themselves with food, tents, supplies, and miners' tools and headed for the rivers of the Sierra Nevada in search of gold. They panned the gold-laden river gravels with considerable success. Reports of their successes and abundant riches became a staple news item in the European and American press. The promise of new found riches and escape from poverty in Europe and South America was not lost on poor farmers suffering failed crops and a dreadful recession. It was not lost on European governments either as a way to colonize and profit from the rich lands of California or to rid themselves of their political and social undesirables — socialists, revolutionaries, republicans, prostitutes, and political activists as well as the poor they couldn't feed.

While the exaggerated reports of gold to be picked up along the river banks excited the poor, it also stimulated unscrupulous promoters to devise schemes and set up undercapitalized joint ventures and mining societies to offer transport to California for shareholders in exchange for mortgaging their lands and inheritances to buy shares of stock in these ventures.

By 1850, most easy to mine gold was gone. Yerba Buena, now named San Francisco, had become a bustling, muddy, windy, raw and dangerous town with over 2,000 saloons, 700 abandoned ships and a permanent population of 25,000 emigrants — gold seekers, merchants, whores, thugs, professional con artists and boatloads more arriving weekly.

By 1851, San Francisco had suffered from major fires, land speculation, lawlessness, and political and police corruption and had become a State in the Union after the rout of local Mexican and *Californio* militias. With the ratio of men to women at 100-1, the new California Legislature passed a significant law affecting the status of women. The new law was designed to attract marriageable women to marry the legion of single miners and to settle permanently in the state. The law provided that a woman's earnings and any inheritance she might receive would remain her separate property and not be subject to a husband's or father's control as was the case in most countries in the world. Word of this new right was not lost on Europe's mothers with marriageable daughters, widows, adventurous women and Jezebels. Women risked their health, security and sometimes their life in the perilous six month sea voyage from Europe around Cape Horn or the mosquito and disease infested crossing of the Isthmus of Panama by dugout pirogue and mule. Still they flocked to California to snap up the rich miners and merchants or to make their fortune in other ways.

It is estimated that by 1851 there were over 100,000 men seeking their fortune in the river beds and banks of the Sierra Nevada river systems from south of Mariposa, California to southern Oregon. With so many miners seeking to find and control the best gold bearing gravels and more arriving daily, disputes and rivalries were inevitable.

Many American miners felt the gold should be theirs alone and pressed the California Legislature to impose a $20.00 (one and one quarter ounce of gold) per month tax on foreign miners. The tax stimulated anger and feuds pitting American and English speaking miners against the non-English speakers — Mexican, Chileans, Chinese and the 25,000 or more French who banded with the Spanish speaking foreigners to contest the tax and defend their mining claims against the "Yankees," who sought to expel them.

Our story begins in January, 1851. Pierre Dubois, chief clerk to a Paris notary, is ordered to go to San Francisco and find evidence to exonerate a rich client who lent his name and prestige to a fraudulent mining society that sent four boatloads of impoverished emigrants to San Francisco with promises of two years support only to find themselves stranded on arrival.

— *Ken Salter,*
Berkeley, California

California Gold Rush Journal

CHAPTER ONE

Le Havre, France — January 1851

MY BOSS, A WELL-CONNECTED "NOTAIRE" IN PARIS sent me, his chief clerk, to Le Havre by a fast coach at the behest of his client, Jules Favre, a noted lawyer and liberal statesman. Favre had become associated with La Californienne Mining Co., which claimed to own gold bearing properties in California. Apparently, Favre, who had a reputation for honesty and integrity, feared he might have been snookered by the company's promoters who'd sought his prestigious name as "avocat" and principal lawyer on La Californienne's board of directors.

I was charged to go Le Havre and investigate Maitre Favre's concerns. We had learned that three or four members of the mining company, who had sailed to San Francisco on the Company's first ship, the "Le Jacques Lafitte," in November 1849, had just returned from the mines and were in Le Havre. I was to track them down, get their story and gather evidence to exonerate Favre.

My briefing file contained newspaper clippings detailing how the directors of "La Société des Mines D'Or de la Californie," had been arrested in early 1849 for fraudulent promotion and sale of worthless stock for a similar mining venture. I also reviewed several letters written from San Francisco by Etienne Derbec, a former typesetter for the "Journal des Débats." His letters, published by his former employer, painted a bleak prospect for success in the mines. Derbec asserted that most French mining ventures in California were doomed to failure because they were under capitalized, the would-be miners were not prepared for the harsh conditions in the placers, and worst of all, the easy to mine gold had been picked up by the hordes of Americans and foreigners who'd raced to California shortly after the news of the gold strike spread like wildfire in 1848.

Upon arrival in Le Havre, I directed my coach to the harbor master's office. His chief clerk, a beady-faced and dour individual dressed all in black, read my letter of introduction and announced with a sneer, "This is no matter for the harbor master."

"I beg to differ. We ask only to see the passenger lists for arrivals from California for the last week. Our clients have made a long, hard trip and need our assistance."

"It is still not our concern," the beetle repeated.

I dropped two silver coins on the counter and watched how deftly they were palmed and disappeared into the beetle's side pocket. He motioned to a subordinate to assist me. The young, pimply-faced clerk led me to a large mahogany desk with tilted top designed to receive ledgers. He flipped pages on a large, leather bound log book until he found the entries I sought.

Joseph-Antoine Ban Mayer, on my list of officials sent by Favre's Company on its first ship, had taken first class accommodation back. The other names on my list, Louis Magne, Charles Tavernier, and Jules Jacob, had returned in steerage, the cheapest, least desirable accommodations for a long passage around Cape Horn. The ledger indicated they had all arrived three days ago. I would have to hurry if I was to catch Ban Mayer. He had the means to escape this bleak, unappealing port town.

"Where can I find the best accommodations in this god-awful cold and windy town?" I asked the pimply-faced clerk.

He gave me a stunned, startled look. "What do you mean?"

"After days on the road, I want to treat myself to the best food and accommodations your town can offer," I said dropping a bronze coin on the ledger book.

"The most expensive?" he replied daftly. I nodded yes. "That would be the Hotel de l'Empereur or Les Trois Cygnes," he said eyeing the coin.

"Which is the closest?"

"Les Trois Cygnes. It's near the Bassin du Commerce. The Empereur is on the other side of the square," he said eyeing the coin longingly and hoping for another.

I grabbed my small notebook and made for the door. I hailed an elderly, well-dressed gentleman with top hat and gold handled cane.

"My good sir, I'm a stranger to this town. How can I get to Hotel de l'Empereur?"

He assessed my traveling garments from top to bottom before replying. "It's not far from the quay. Take the bridge and follow the road to the Bassin du Commerce and turn left. It's at the end of the basin." I bowed my thanks and sprinted for my coach.

Twenty minutes later I walked into the sumptuous lobby of the hotel. The reception desk was manned by a short, stolid man dressed in Napoleonic livery. I suppressed my desire to laugh at this pretentious, ridiculous little man dressed like a toy soldier.

"Good-day, I have an urgent message for the Chevalier Joseph-Antoine Ban Mayer from his lawyer in Paris. Please tell him I'll await him in the bar," I said pointing to the polished hardwood bar with brass rails.

"The Chevalier left strict instructions that he not be disturbed."

"I am sure he will reward you for making an exception. It's worth a lot of money to him if he acts quickly," I lied while fishing out several silver coins to give the clerk.

I did not wait for a reply. I made my way to the bar with its oversized painting depicting a glorified pose of Empereur Napoleon I. I was banking on Ban Mayer's curiosity to bring him out of seclusion. He had been one of the figureheads of the first expedition along with a former mayor, two mining engineers, a head accountant and others.

I ordered a half bottle of Bordeaux red wine which the mustached bartender with long, black sideburns poured for me. The bottle had an applied, glass seal with the words "Chateau Lafitte/ 1845" embossed on the seal. The aroma of black cherries, vanilla and subtle mix of spices assaulted my nose as I took a first sip. Lovely I thought both of the wine and the large portrait of Empress Josephine.

My bliss at the texture and character of the wine was short-lived. The pounding of boots behind me broke my reverie. I turned to face an irate man in his sixties dressed in formal black attire with white cravat and a medal attesting to his being "Chevalier de la Légion d'Honneur" pinned on the left breast of his dinner jacket.

His ruddy face and bushy eye brows gone gray stared at me from behind a monocle attached to a gold chain. "And who are you?" His clipped, curt tone betrayed his military past and belief he was an officer addressing an inferior under his command.

I returned his critical stare eye-to-eye to let him know I was not the least bit intimidated. I took another sip of wine before responding. "I work for lawyers representing Maitre Jacques Favre, head lawyer for La Californienne Mining Co. My name is Pierre Dubois. Maitre Favre has charged me with responsibility to determine why your venture failed," I replied coolly while deliberately misrepresenting my authority.

"Damnation! I am ruined and Favre and the rest of the crooks had the gall to pay themselves a five percent dividend on their shares while we froze our ass in San Francisco with no support," he shouted jabbing the air with his finger and letting the monocle dangle on its chain.

The mention of a dividend before any gold was recovered was surprising. It suggested the promoters knew the venture would fail and decided to cash out early or use the dividend as bait to attract more investors and capital. "Are you sure a dividend was actually paid and not merely authorized," I said sipping my wine.

"Do you take me for a fool? Of course the dividend was paid while I was in San Francisco. The mail may be slow, but with so many ships bringing newspapers and periodicals, we were never more than a couple of months behind events in Europe. They used the new capital to open sales offices in Belgium, Switzerland, Holland, Germany and elsewhere to solicit even more money to enrich themselves rather than provide us with the support we needed to run a successful mining venture. We were had, lock, stock and barrel," he said shaking the monocle at me.

"What caused the venture to fail? You seemed to have resourceful directors and mining expertise aplenty to exploit the gold placers."

"Bah. Nonsense. Not one of them had any practical experience or knowledge how to run a gold mining operation. Bunch of desk jockeys, even the mining engineers. But that's not why we failed. When we arrived in San Francisco, there were no company agents to meet us as promised. No launch to take us and our luggage and equipment ashore. No accommodations. No transport to the placers. No company owned gold claims. A complete fraud," he stammered, face flushed and irate.

"So what did you do?" I asked.

"We had to fend for ourselves. Those of us with resources paid to be taken ashore. Our trunks and equipment were impounded until customs clearance. We had to find lodgings and figure out how to get home from that god forsaken place teeming with rabble and the scum of the earth," he barked.

"What of the rest of the passengers?" I asked.

"They were stuck on board until the French Consul arranged for them to come ashore," he said without sympathy.

"Did you get to the mines eventually?"

"Of course not! With no logistical support or capital there was no way to proceed. A complete waste of time and money. I lost a year of my life to get there and home, not to mention the outrageous prices I had to pay for unsatisfactory food and lodgings," he growled. "Now if you'll excuse me, I have a dinner engagement." He did an abrupt about face and marched off.

I finished my wine and was glad I had not wasted any on the pompous old soldier. I ordered my coach to take me to Les Trois Cygnes hotel. I had no desire to bump into the Chevalier again. He provided some useful information, but little to exonerate our client who certainly knew of and profited from the five percent share distribution. Clearly, all who sailed on the first ship had been duped to take passage on a lost cause. The promoters knew it when they were paid a dividend with no earnings in gold. Was Favre building a case to sue the other directors and promoters to show he, too, was duped to lend his name to the venture?

Lots to mull over after a hot bath, a sampling of oysters, mussels, langoustines and a grilled lobster. Nice to know that innocent or not, Favre would be hosting me in style.

California Gold Rush Journal

CHAPTER TWO

Le Havre, France — January 1851

After breakfast and posting my report of my meeting with the Chevalier to my boss in Paris, I directed my coachman to an area of cheap watering holes, flea-bag hotels and flop houses. If my assumption was correct, the three steerage passengers would be holed up here awaiting funds to travel home or working to pay their transport. If I could locate one, I might well find all three. After five months at sea, they would know each other well. But, I had no physical descriptions, only names and a hometown.

I instructed my coachman, Georges, to buy rounds of drink in the most popular drinking establishments and make inquiries after the three I sought. If he came up empty handed, he was authorized to hire some of his new drinking buddies to help him find our voyagers. I told him to say I sought to interview the three on their California adventures for pay. Georges, my coachman for the last two years, liked this kind of assignment. His engaging smile, Auvergne accent, easy way of talking, and folksy ways with a glass in his hand allowed him to fit easily into working class bars where my Parisian dress and polish would evoke suspicion and silence.

I repaired to a more upscale bistro frequented by ship's officers and settled into a booth to read newspapers, sip local white wine and wait. It took Georges two hours to find his first mark, Louis Magne, an Auvergnat from Aurillac. Magne was working in one of the area's many rooming houses where poorly paid sailors and other down on their luck folk could rent a straw mattress with one blanket in a large dormitory for a few sous with no charge for fleas or bedbugs. Magne's establishment also ran a soup kitchen for its residents.

Magne was taller than most French. His broad shoulders, rugged features and calloused hands attested to a life of physical labor, while his hazel eyes, dimpled, boyish face, shock of auburn hair and beard and easy grin suggested a more gentle side to his nature. He looked to be in his early thirties dressed in work trousers and a red flannel shirt.

As it was near noon, I ordered a carafe of white wine, three dozen oysters and the bistro's special fish stew for the three of us. The "soupe de poissons" with white fish, clams and mussels was surprising good. After Georges' introductions I suggested we eat before talking about Magne's experiences.

Magne attacked his meal as if it were his last. His big hands spooned his soup like he was shoveling coal into the belly of a steam engine, stopping only to take a long swig of wine and crunch big crusts of black bread into his soup. Georges kept ladling him more soup and kept his glass full while we scraped oysters from shells and popped them greedily down our craws. The repast finished, I ordered tumblers of Calvados and cigars. On signal from me, Georges excused himself to feed our horses.

"Tell me a little about yourself. What made you decide to go to California?" I said.

Magne drew deeply on his cigar before responding. "We were just poor farmers trying to eke out a living raising oats and rye and grazing a few head of Salers for their milk. We made it into cheese to sell at the market in Aurillac in the Cantal. My father was doing poorly after the hard winter of '48. I wanted to marry my sweetheart, Leontine, but we had no money to rent our own place. My parents still had to feed my three younger sisters who had no dowry for marriage," he said stopping to take a large gulp of Calvados and another pull on his cigar.

"How did you learn about La Californienne's mining venture in the middle of the Cantal?" I asked.

"Well, everyone was talking about the gold in California and how you just had to walk the bank of a river and pick it up. I saw an announcement in our paper about a special bank for emigrants going to California. The bank offered to loan money to pay passage to California and the gold placers. The bank said it would loan money against our farm, but my parents were afraid to do that. The farm was all they had. My sisters and I wanted to get married, so we sort of ganged up on our parents and pressured them. It seemed the only way to get out of our poverty. Father was failing in strength, so it fell to me to run the farm. It fed us, but nothing more. I guess we were desperate and selfish." Magne said with chagrin.

I ordered another round of Calvados and we both paused to relight our cigars. "What finally tipped the balance in your favor?" I asked.

"An acquaintance also wanted to go to California. He told me about a French mining company that provided passage to California and would lodge and feed its miners until they got rich. I went to town to see for myself. The company's broadsheet was posted outside city hall. It was four pages long and seemed to answer most of my parents' objections. It said buy 9 shares of stock for 100 Francs each and the company would give you free passage to the company's gold and silver mines in California and provide a stake for two years of supplies until we got rich," Magne said with emotion.

"Was that the broadsheet entitled 'Le Californien' dated August 29, 1849 for the company called 'La Californienne' that claimed to own gold bearing properties in California?" I asked.

"I don't remember the exact date, but it must have been about that time because I was on their first boat that sailed in November, 1849."

"How did you get the 900 Francs to go?"

"I took the broadsheet home to show my parents and sisters. Father was dubious. He said it sounded too good to be true and it didn't really matter because we didn't have 25 Francs let alone 900. We had to pay the blacksmith to mend our plow, pay the veterinarian bill and buy seeds for Spring planting." Magne paused to drain his tumbler.

"I told him we could get a big enough loan on the farm to buy the shares and enough to hire someone to help with the farm for the two years or less I would be gone. When I returned with our fortune made, we could repay the loan, father and mother could retire, my sisters and I could marry. We wouldn't have to live hand-to-mouth anymore wondering if disease would kill our animals or too little rain would wither our crops."

"So, your father agreed?"

"Not at first. Mother was the first to weaken. She knew it was a long shot full of risk if I failed or died in the process. She'd never seen the sea and was deathly afraid my boat would founder and sink trying to round Cape Horn. The papers were full of stories of riches to be made, but also of ship wrecks and details of a lawless country full of uncouth heathens, Indians, bears and crazed fortune seekers." He paused to relight his cigar.

"Yet, she had two daughters of an age to marry and a third who'd be ready when I returned with their dowries. Farm life was hard on her and the prospect of retiring to help look after grandchildren had a lot of appeal. So, in the end, she joined our efforts to persuade father. Our pressure was relentless. I argued that if I wasn't on the company's first boat, the gold would be all gone while we dithered. Father finally gave in. He reluctantly agreed to sign the loan jeopardizing the farm he'd inherited and worked all his life," Magne said sadly.

"So, you mortgaged the farm for two years, bought the shares and sailed on the 'Jacques Lafitte' with the company's first expedition," I summarized.

"Yes, foolishly I did. I calculated it shouldn't take long to put aside the 1,200 Francs to send my parents to pay off the loan. That's only $240 American dollars or 15 ounces of gold. I'm a hard worker. I thought I could also make enough to buy my own farm, marry and see my sisters happily married with money left over. Of course, I was wrong," he said with remorse and looked enviously at his empty tumbler.

"It took me a month to get my stomach used to the boat's pitching, the rancid salt meat, wormy biscuits, sour wine, hard Dutch cheese and lack of fresh vegetables and fruit. We might have been poor farmers, but we ate well. How I miss our Cantal cheeses, Salers and Saint-Nectaire!..."

I interrupted. "Tell me about your arrival in San Francisco," I wanted to keep him focused and not listen to maudlin regrets.

"Hah, that was the kicker. They told us we'd be lodged in San Francisco until the baggage and mining equipment cleared customs, then we'd go as a group to the company's mines. Our ship was anchored in the bay that was filled with abandoned boats. We had to watch as other ships arrived and the sailors jumped ship and raced for the mines. We knew something was wrong," he said as his voice rose in anger.

"The captain and the heads of our expedition were soon arguing furiously with the customs officials who came on board. Finally, a small launch came to our ship and took our head men to the long wharf. We thought another boat would come for us. But none came. Some of the bolder passengers got fed up waiting and demanded that the ship's first officer take them ashore in the ship's long boat. He told them there was no one from the mining company to meet them and no arrangements for transport to shore or lodging. He could signal a private boat that ferried passengers, but we'd have to pay the ferry man to row us ashore. Most of us had spent our cash on shore in Valparaiso on food and lodgings after the frightening passage around Cape Horn. A few paid their passage to town, but the rest of us were stuck."

"How did you get ashore?" I asked.

"After four freezing days of bay fog and lousy food, the French Consul came on board to speak to us..."

"Who was that?" I interjected.

"His name was Patrice Dillon."

"What did he tell you?"

"He told us our mining company had no local representatives and had left us to our own devices. He said he would arrange for us to be brought ashore and lodged until our goods cleared customs, but we'd have to work to repay the consulate's expense and accumulate a grub stake to go to the placers."

"What did you do?"

"He told us there were plenty of jobs for skilled carpenters, masons and building laborers as the city was expanding daily and rebuilding from a recent fire. Carpenters and other skilled workers could earn $10 to $14.00 a day and living expenses in town would run about $4.00 a day if we were careful. Few of us had those skills and were told we would have to work as laborers on the wharves and in the warehouses and earn $6 to $8.00 a day. If we skimped, we could save $3.00 a day but it would take several months of saving to get to the mines. His assistant made a list of passengers and their skills."

"What did they do for you?"

"As I was strong and fit, I got work for the customs house

hauling goods off ships and storing them in the customs warehouses by the wharves. Once they cleared and duty was paid, I carted them to the owner's lodgings for a fee and a tip. I learned fast that those with money could do anything and got richer by the day. So many ships were arriving with cargo, that there was no warehouse space most times. The cargos were sold aboard by auction. Often the goods were sold at a loss when too much of the same stuff flooded the market."

"That's interesting. What items were in over supply?" I asked.

"Well, most mining tools and clothes and staples like beans and flour and salt pork. Prices had been real high at the beginning as everyone needed them to take to the mines," Magne replied.

"What sort of goods commanded high prices?" I asked.

"Well, most medicines, toiletries, bottled wines and liquor, and fancy foods in tins, like anchovies, sardines, truffles, capers, pickles and the like in sealed bottles brought the best prices."

"Were you able to get to the gold fields eventually," I asked.

"It took me and some friends over three months to get supplies and transport. We made for Marysville and then for the Yuba River where we knew there were some companies of French miners at a place called French Corral. Since we couldn't speak much English, we headed there," he said while I ordered fresh cigars and his tumbler refilled.

"It was mid-summer and hotter than hell. We'd met a few French in San Francisco who'd made their fortune and were returning home rich, but most of the miners were barely making $6.00 a day panning or working rockers together. It was just enough to live on but little or no profit. Food and supplies had to be brought in by mule and cost double the price in town. Worst of all, there was no easy gold to be had," he said as he took a deep drag on his new cigar. I nodded for him to continue.

"We lived like the Yankees on pancakes, salt pork and beans. We slept in tents and worked 10 to 12 hours a day shoveling what we'd dug up in the river bed into rockers to screen for the gold. The water was freezing and the sun unmerciful. We shared a bottle of cheap brandy on Sunday after doing our housekeeping. We kept hoping to strike a rich pocket of gold despite the weariness of our daily routine. Every once in a while, someone would find a big nugget or small pocket and we'd all celebrate, hoping we'd be next. But me and my buddies only managed to find small flakes and grains. We knew if we didn't make a strike before the rainy season in October or November, we'd have to pack it in and return to the city to work as laborers all winter just to get a grub stake for the next year. Already, groups with money were hauling in machinery to crush the gold-bearing quartz outcrops they planned to flush out with pressure hoses. We knew our methods were ineffective and limited," he said with a sigh.

"Why did you decide to return to France?" I asked.

"We knew we'd never get rich this way without a lucky strike. I worried about my family and the loan to repay and if we lost the farm, it'd be my fault. I'd finally got a letter from my fiancé saying that father was doing poorly and both my parents were worried sick about the loan. Leontine wanted me to come home. The hired hand wasn't working out and the farm was suffering. She was willing to live with us in our already crowded house and help with the farm, if I'd only come home," he paused to drag on his cigar and looked longingly at his empty tumbler before continuing.

"The letter gave me an idea. I had to pay $4.00 to the Mexican who brought it to the camp from Marysville along with the supplies he packed in. That's a quarter ounce of gold. Everyone is envious of those getting letters from home. Most couldn't read or write and need others to write for them. I decided to quit mining to see if I could earn my gold as a letter courier. I started to take letters from the mining camps along the Yuba River on Mondays to post in Marysville and return by Saturday with mail for the camps and spend Sundays as a scribe for those who couldn't write. I soon had enough profit to buy a mule so I could return from Marysville with supplies to sell as well as the mail," he said pausing to pour a glass of water from the carafe on the table.

"Was the new venture profitable?" I asked.

"Yes, to my surprise and much easier than working in the river. I undercut the prices for staples brought in by the Mexicans who worked for merchants making high profits. I brought real French wine and cognac in bottles that was not watered down or mixed unlike most of the brandy and rye whiskey sold to the camps. I also brought French delicacies I knew the successful miners would buy — small pots of foie gras and paté from the Périgord, sardines in tins from La Rochelle, Dijon mustard and small pickles in glass containers, cherries soaked in marc and plums in plum brandy, all the luxuries from home."

"Where did you find these luxury goods?" I asked out of curiosity.

"Marysville was founded by a successful Frenchman and named after his wife. There were several French merchants who were happy to sell goods to me at discount to get mining trade. I was soon averaging $75-$100.00 a week in profit and saved $700.00. That's nearly 3,500 Francs after two months work including the little I made mining and on the sale of my equipment and mule. The rains came early, so I collected a big sack of mail to post in France on my way home. I took the steamer to Panama, crossed through Panama in the rain and mud and picked up a French boat in New Orleans."

"Since you'd earned enough to repay the loan with interest, why did you book steerage on your ship home?"

"I wanted to save every sou I could to keep my promise to my sisters and fiancée. That's why I took the job here, so I could earn money for the trip home without touching our nest egg," he said proudly.

I took out my wallet and counted out several 50 Franc bills from Favre's expense money and handed them to Magne. "Will this get you on the next coach to the Auvergne?" I asked.

Magne's eyes looked ready to pop at the sight of my largesse. "Yes Sir, more than enough," he stammered.

"Good. Then get you gone. I appreciate your candid and forthright account of your California adventure. I'm pleased it didn't end in the loss of your farm," I said as I waved him to go.

I watched him dash off in the direction of the coach station. I stayed to write an account of my interview that pertained to the failures of the Californienne Mining Co. to meet their obligations to their shareholder-miners and dispatched Georges to get my report on the late afternoon post to Paris. The Calvados had me yawning. I decided to treat myself to a late siesta at my hotel in anticipation of another scrumptious sea food dinner later. The oysters and grilled homard from the previous night would be hard to beat but fun to try.

California Gold Rush Journal
CHAPTER THREE
Paris, France — January 1851

Georges reported that he could not find the other two returned miners. I decided after an early English breakfast of poached eggs, bacon, smoked salmon on toast and a pot of strong coffee that we should return to Paris and see in person where the investigation was headed given what I had learned. I would miss the fresh seafood and delicious local wines and spirits Le Havre offered, but not the bone-chilling wind and ominous dark skies threatening a gale or worse as we bumped over pot holes on the road to Paris.

After a late night arrival, I did not make my appearance at my boss's law office until mid-morning. He was in a foul mood and threw a hissy fit at my late appearance. My two reports lay on his large cherry wood desk. He motioned me to one of the two Voltaire arm chairs facing him. He threw me a piercing look from behind gold-rimmed spectacles as he picked up my two reports from Le Havre.

"Was this really the best you could do to exonerate our client?" He barked in his high-pitched voice that echoed in his cavernous office with portraits of his ancestors glaring down at me from the wall and bronze statuettes of hunters and the hunted on pedestals behind his desk. Impeccably dressed as always in his brown three-piece suit with gold watch fob and neatly folded kerchief as adornments, he tapped his fingers impatiently on his massive desk waiting for my reply.

"The Chevalier has probably already instructed his lawyers to sue all the directors including your client. He's one of the first to return and probably scents a killing to be made in the courts if he can attach the company's promotional capital before news spreads that there's no gold being mined and the shares are worthless," I said.

"I fail to see how this helps my friend, Favre. Your job was to find exonerating evidence. Why did you not try to persuade the Chevalier that Favre was not complicit in promotional fraud?" He growled.

"The Chevalier would have none of it. You will recall he referred to all the directors as crooks," I said pointing to my report.

"Yes, so you stated. But you made no effort to argue that Favre was duped just like him. We must have exonerating evidence. He's no longer young and must prevail in this matter. We want you to go to California and do a full investigation…"

"What? No Way!" I exclaimed. "I'm not going on a fool's errand. San Francisco and back is a year at sea and who knows what I'll find there. For all we know, they're all either stranded there or on their way home. Better to wait in Le Havre and debrief those who return," I said trying vainly to keep my voice calm.

"All told, four of the Society's ships have sailed to San Francisco with hundreds of emigrants sponsored by the Society. The last ship sailed in July, 1850. It's quite possible the later groups were successful and what happened on the arrival of the first ship was an unfortunate misunderstanding," he said.

"Not bloody likely," I retorted in English.

"That's precisely why we need you on this mission. You

speak English and can interview the local officials and consult records in their language. You are unmarried and free to travel. Maitre Favre has assured me that you will be handsomely rewarded on your return."

"And if I refuse?"

"Out of the question if you value your position," he said with a hard edge of finality.

"I see. May I have the day to mull it over and decide what support I would need for such a venture?" I stated evenly. I was furious, of course. Never nice to be bluntly reminded you held a losing hand and despite your competency, you could be dismissed and discarded like a broken marionette.

"I'll see you first thing in the morning," I said curtly. I picked up my leather satchel with my writing materials and headed for a small bistro in the Latin Quarter where lawyers, notaries, and their cronies did not frequent. I ordered a half bottle of Veuve Cliquot champagne, lit a cigar and pondered my future. I was still hot under my collar at the threat to fire me. The first glass of champagne helped calm me and focus on my future. To stay in Paris in these unsettled times had its own risks. My boss was a staunch royalist who despised the socialists and republicans who had overthrown King Louis-Philippe. He considered them all dangerous anarchists. I had to play along with his sympathies as a condition of my position as head clerk. I would never be treated fairly despite knowing more about commercial, real estate and probate succession matters than he did. By my second glass of champagne I was feeling more positive about my options.

My boss hob-nobbed with and drew his clients from the upper class rich. Many, like Favre, became his "friend." I supervised all the pleadings and agreements with a staff of two assistants. If he chose to fire me, he could slander or blackmail me with other notaries. That would assure I'd be effectively barred from working for the more established firms. I had no desire to work for a reactionary boss or change occupations. Despite my talents at thirty years of age, there was no way for me, without capital, to become a notary in Paris with my own practice. If I married here, I would be stuck under by boss's thumb forever.

By my third glass of the widow's bubbly, my decision was made. I'd go to San Francisco, but with certain conditions. Favre's offer to reward me on my return was hollow, unacceptable and unenforceable. If I'm to do his dirty work, I want to be paid up front. I needed to squeeze the client for as much advance money as possible. I might decide to stay in San Francisco if I could be my own boss, but that would take capital, lots of it in the expensive boom-town depicted by Parisian journals. I would also need a paid assistant and a companion for the long voyage.

After a light lunch my plan took shape. I doubled back to our stables to speak with Georges. We slipped out to a small bar frequented by coachmen and stable hands. I ordered a carafe of red wine and the best cigars the bar could offer. I told Georges of my decision to sail to California on the Favre matter.

"I'm going to need an assistant for the work in San Francisco. I thought you might be interested in the job," I said after we were comfortably settled in the obscurity of a back booth.

"Gar…that's a big order ain't it. You gonna give up the comforts of Paris for a year at sea?" He replied flipping the ball in my court.

"Would you be tempted if I could get you triple your present wages paid in advance, say for eighteen months and work only while in San Francisco?" I said baiting the hook.

"Hum…no work on the boat and I would draw me wages for the trip both ways — right?"

"Yes, but you'd have to learn English on the trip over. We'll need to speak with the Yankees and other foreigners when we get there," I said.

"You gonna find a nice little English doxie to teach me an' keep my bunk warm on the long, hard trip?" He retorted with a mischievous smile.

"You're quite capable of finding one or more on your own. Imagine being on a ship with bored married women, tarts and widows with daughters looking for husbands. With your charm and blarney, you'd be lucky to get to San Francisco without some serious claw marks on your pretty-boy face," I said teasingly.

"What makes you think I won't jump ship an' head for the placers once we get there?" He said knowingly. He'd undoubtedly learned a lot in Le Havre.

"Well for one, your wages earned on the trip will be kept in a trust account under my control for your safe return or investment in San Francisco if you decide to stay there," I replied with a "gotcha" smirk.

"What about pocket money?" He protested.

"One month's salary for the trip. Any more, you'll have to win at cards. A second class cabin and all expenses paid," I said holding out my hand. With only a slight hesitation, he shook on the terms. "When do we leave boss?" He asked with a big laugh.

"As soon as I can arrange passage, secure passports and negotiate terms with my boss. Keep mum until it's in the bag. You'll need a seaworthy travel trunk and clothes for all climates. Good rain slickers and boots for foul weather for a start. Send the chits for payment to me. Now, I've got to see about booking passage and some other matters." I left Georges with the carafe of Rhone wine and headed for the ship booking offices on the Seine.

As to be expected, there were long lines of anxious folks waiting at all the booking offices. One featured a barker promising quick passage and success in the gold fields. All posted alluring broad sheets extolling their services and ships for San

Francisco. I went straight to the head of the line of the booking office with the most stylishly dressed clerks. "I represent a very important government official who must be on your next ship so he can take his post in the Consulate in San Francisco," I bluffed in an authoritative voice to the annoyance of those waiting patiently in line. "Lead me to your director," I added.

"Yes, of course. Right this way sir," he replied.

The director's desk was piled high with folders spilling their contents. The paunchy little man with a pencil thin moustache was shouting cabin rates to a harried assistant. "Yes?" He barked.

I gave my boss' name and indicated I was here to negotiate immediate passage for the staff of the Consul General in San Francisco.

"And who would that be?" He replied with a dubious look.

"Consul Patrice Dillon, of course. With so many French emigrating, he urgently needs additional staff to process the new arrivals."

"Not possible," he shrugged. "We're fully booked for the next two months," he said.

"That won't do. They have to be in San Francisco by mid-May at the latest," I stated.

"Even our fastest ship takes at least five months. Only American Clipper ships can get to San Francisco in less than four months," he retorted.

"Fine, then book us on the next American Clipper," I said.

"You must be kidding! Voyage with uncouth Americans…"

"Our clients have to deal with American officials all the time. You've been reading too much sensational fiction," I said cutting him off. "When is the next Clipper sailing?"

"The 'Flying Cloud' will be in Le Havre in a week or so. She's delivering tea to England from China and will deliver more cargo here. But she sails to New York before going to California…"

"Perfect," I said interrupting again. "Time is of the essence, as the English say. We'll need one first class cabin for two and second class accommodation for a single man. What is the tariff for both legs of the journey—Le Havre/New York and New York/San Francisco?"

"Uhh. I don't know. This is most unusual...err...irregular. I'll have to make enquiries," he stammered.

"Fine. I'll send a staff member round tomorrow. Give the messenger the booking confirmation and statement for the tickets and I'll have a bank draft delivered. Our client in the foreign ministry will hold you accountable for making this booking a top priority. We would not want our client so upset he might consider revoking your lucrative license, would we?" I said with a hint of menace. "Of course not. The booking will be confirmed by noon tomorrow," he said meekly.

"Good day then," I said as I made my way past the impatient minions in line who eyed me with contempt for having pulled rank.

I bought copies of the leading Parisian dailies containing the shipping news and latest sensational news of the California Gold Rush. I took a cab to the Left Bank and a brasserie near where my girlfriend, Manon, works as an under-chef in a local restaurant. I ordered a fine-champagne cognac, a Cuban cigar and took a secluded side table to read the news and wait for Manon to finish her shift.

I was chuckling over a report that a French ship was rumored to be transporting over 15 million dollars in gold to France from a successful mining venture in northern California, when I caught a whiff of Manon's presence. As usual, she had exchanged her flour and sauce-stained cook's apron for a stylish wool tunic and dress short enough to reveal her well-turned ankles.

Her subtle perfume with hints of cinnamon and spices

teased my senses as she bent over my shoulder to buss both cheeks and whisper in my ear, "Cheri, I wanted to go to Le Havre with you so much. It's not fair; you get to have all the fun while I slave in the kitchen," she said in her most seductive voice, then laughed.

"Ahh. You may get your wish. I have to choose either to go to San Francisco or get fired. Which should I choose?" I said gravely.

Manon's dark eyes flashed. "Cheri, don't joke with me. Are you serious? You're going to San Francisco? What about me?" She asked petulantly.

"Well, I've booked a first class cabin for two. All you have to do is say yes sweetly and I'll consider it," I teased.

She beckoned my head to her luscious, full lips, then bit my ear playfully and whispered, "You don't take me, I kill you. How about that," she said tossing her lustrous mane of dark curls and gold hoops so she appeared to shimmer in the reflected gas light.

We both laughed. I ordered a bottle of champagne and brought her up to date on my adventures in Le Havre and the boss' ultimatum. By the time we'd finished dinner and another bottle of bubbly, we were both planning what to pack, what merchandise to buy for resale, and what we'd need for Manon to start her own restaurant in San Francisco.

California Gold Rush Journal

CHAPTER FOUR

Paris - Le Havre, France — January 1851

I arrived to work early to prepare agreements necessary for our trip. I drafted a power of attorney authorizing me to investigate the activities of the La Californienne Mining Society in Favre's behalf, an authorization to draw funds for the investigation, salary and wage agreements for Georges and me at triple rates for 18 months, and the cost of first and second class round trip ship fares. I estimated the fares at $5,000.00 or 25,000 Francs on an American Clipper ship. I calculated our daily expense needs for six months at around $25.00 day for first class lodgings, meals and travel expenses. All payable in advance. All drafts were on my boss's letterhead with signatures required for my boss and his client.

My boss arrived earlier than usual and motioned me to his office. "Well, what have you decided?" He demanded.

"I am willing to go only if my trip and investigation are adequately funded in advance. I will need round trip tickets for me and an assistant, plus a substantial sum for living, travel and investigation expenses, as well as 18 month's salary for me and wages for my assistant at three times our current rates paid in advance," I said evenly.

"Over my dead body! That's highway robbery," he shouted.

"Not really. There's no guarantee I will ever get to San Francisco and back alive. So, it's really over my dead body. You can tell your client he's paying life insurance when it comes to my salary," I stated calmly.

"Well, maybe I can sell my client on a double salary, but there's no need for an expensive assistant to sit on his ass for 12 months at sea," he barked.

"I beg to disagree. I have spoken to Georges, our coachman. He's outgoing and loquacious. He will be able to locate and speak with the rough and tumble miners and other foreigners who wouldn't give me the time of day. He can go places in a dangerous city just as he did for me in Le Havre to locate Magne. He, too, will risk his life at sea for 12 months and have to navigate the dangerous streets of San Francisco where all are armed to the teeth and prepared to shoot or stab first and ask questions later." I handed him a newspaper clipping from yesterday's press and pointed to the article on street violence by rowdies and criminals in San Francisco. He read it quickly and his only comment was, "Hrrump."

"I have inquired about passage. The most efficient vessels appear to be American Clipper ships built for the China trade and the Gold Rush. They are a bit faster than our French ships. One is docked in London and will be in Le Havre soon. I propose to be on it. It will give Georges an opportunity to learn English and the ways of Americans during the trip. We'll both have to deal with them in San Francisco and the mining camps," I stated frankly.

"Here are the necessary agreements and papers that need to be signed and funded," I said and handed him the papers I had drafted.

He perused them quickly. "Outrageous! He will never go for this. So much money in advance and no guarantee you will be able to exonerate him from this mess. He'll reward you handsomely if you are successful. But I couldn't recommend this. Perhaps double salary and wages and half the amount you request for ground expenses," he whined.

I was sure he had breakfasted with Favre this morning and was authorized to fund the trip. I anticipated his anger and tight-fisted nature to haggle costs. I hoped he knew little of Yankee Clipper ships. One recently set the record for the fastest sailing time from New York to San Francisco around Cape Horn in just over three months. I counted on a shorter voyage than the 5-6 months by French ships. It would give Manon and me more time and capital to set up my business and Manon's restaurant. I figured he was posturing to save his client money and higher fees for himself.

"I'll tell Georges there's no deal," I bluffed.

"I didn't say that. I have authority to pay you double salary and wages, the ship's fare both ways and ground expenses in San Francisco not to exceed an advance of $3,000.00 or 15,000 Francs."

Good, I thought. We're more than half way home. "I'm not sure Georges will accept the offer. Perhaps if Favre paid his necessary outfitting for the trip, he might be mollified. We'll both need sea trunks, foul weather gear, traveling clothes for winter and the tropics, medicine chests, gold scales and a host of other items that will be much cheaper here than in San Francisco. Our client should expect to pay these items in advance as they are necessities," I said.

He paused several moments with a pained expression before replying. "I'm not sure. How much are we talking about," he said peevishly.

"I don't really know. Certainly our client should see the necessity of this demand which will save him money and us lots of time in San Francisco trying to find goods that can be purchased here. It's your job to sell the deal. We'll miss the Clipper if we tarry. The booking agent said they're fully booked for two months on French ships." Ball in his court.

"Alright, I'll authorize the deal to get the investigation going quickly," he said with a pained expression. Tightwad I thought. Wait until you get the bills for the equipment and supplies I planned to buy. He would scream bloody murder when the invoices were on his desk while we celebrated our departure aboard ship with a nice stock of Champagne and a small cask of Armagnac for the voyage. If he were more prescient, he'd realize his chief clerk had flown the coop. He'd have to replace me as he wasn't capable to do most of my work himself.

I prepared a payment voucher for the Clipper tickets and decided to take it to the booking office myself. I took a cab to Manon's restaurant and signaled her that the trip was on. She blew me kiss and did a little pirouette showing some nice leg to demonstrate her pleasure. She planned to leave work claiming cramps from her monthlies after finishing the lunch preparation. She'd spend the afternoon assembling our traveling kits, while I initiated the process to secure passports.

The shipping office was even more crowded today. I waved to the snooty, overdressed clerk and marched directly to the manager's office. His desk was an advertisement for disarray. "I've brought you payment vouchers from my firm for the Clipper ship tickets," I said, then picked up a cigar from a box on his desk, clipped the end and lit it with a match.

He winced as I blew smoke past him. It was clear he was not happy to see me instead of a minion he could bully. "So, where are the reservations and tickets?" I pulled out my watch on its silver chain while I awaited his response. It was 15 minutes past noon.

"I'm sorry. There are problems," he said sheepishly.

"Spit it out. What problems?" I commanded.

"The Clipper has only five cabins — all first class. We could confirm one cabin for two with great difficulty for your consular staff. There are no second class cabins. We didn't know. Normally, we book only French ships with three classes of accommodations."

I tried not to show my surprise that the Clipper carried so few passengers. They must be making their money on cargo. "You'll have to get them to bump one male passenger so our male staff member can share a cabin."

"That's another problem. Three cabins are booked with important merchants and their wives. The fourth cabin is retained for a woman joining her family in New York. She will share only with another woman," he said giving me a hang-dog look.

"When's the next Clipper due to arrive?" I asked.

"We don't know, but it could be quite some time according to the English booking company."

"You say the woman is going to New York and not California?"

"That's my understanding, yes."

"So we have two cabins confirmed from New York to San Francisco after the stop in New York?" I gave him a hard look and blew smoke at him.

"Yes, but…"

"The French Minister will not be happy, but there is a solution. The consular official's wife will share the cabin with the woman going to New York and the male employee will share the consular official's cabin for the first leg of the trip." Manon would not be any more pleased than I with the arrangement. Maybe Georges could make a quick conquest and change the woman's priorities. We'd have to wait and see. Going first class should console Georges for not getting triple wages. The cabin passengers would dine with the captain and ship's officers, so the food and wine would be better than he could expect in second class. He'd just have to make himself scarce when Manon and I wanted to be alone.

"What is the Clipper's name and when does she sail?" I asked.

"She's called 'The Flying Cloud' and she's due to arrive in Le Havre in about five days time."

"There will be considerable personal luggage and several chests of consular supplies to be carried as cargo to New York and on to San Francisco. What are the tariffs?"

"I'm afraid they're quite steep compared to French ships. We were quoted $1.00 per cubic foot and $65.00 a ton for merchandise."

"I'm not sure of the exact size or weight of the consular supplies yet. Book us for a ton and bill it to our law firm along with the tickets with this voucher," I said. My boss would have a fit over the cost of our transport and the goods billed to his client. I enjoyed spending his money liberally.

"Have the tickets and cargo voucher ready first thing in the morning. We'll have to hurry to get everything to Le Havre in time."

"Very well," he replied.

My next task was to book fast coaches for us and our gear to leave as soon as we had passports for New York and San Francisco. I spent the rest of the day purchasing articles of clothing, medicines, a portable bar and glasses in a small chest, books and maps on California, wine, liqueurs, dried fruits, canvas tents, gold scales, sea worthy cargo chests and a host of other items I could bill to the boss' account.

My next stop was the "mairie" where I pulled rank to get to the head of the line with the clerk who processed passport applications. After completing the 3 applications using a power of attorney for Georges and Manon, I handed them to the clerk with an envelope containing two 100 Franc notes to speed the processing. After peeking in the envelope, the clerk assured me the mayor would approve the applications and they'd be ready for pick-up and delivery to the prefect's office for finalization first thing in the morning.

After coordinating tomorrow's tasks with Georges, I met Manon for a late dinner at her favorite bistro. Her mop of dark ringlets was sprawled over sheaves of papers, so she did not see me arrive. "Occupied my dear?" I taunted.

"Ah Cheri, so much to do in so little time. I am so worried I will forget something important and you will scold me," she said, her dark eyes flashing and with a teasing smile. "Here, you look for yourself at these receipts while I order some wine." She waved to the waiter who had been ogling her pleasing figure out of the corner of his eye and snapped to attention. Her commands sent him scurrying.

I quickly scanned the pile of receipts for French luxury goods she'd bought based on what I'd learned from young Magne's experience in Marysville and the Yuba River mining camps. She'd done an excellent job buying merchandise we could sell at good profit as well as what she'd need to outfit a bar/restaurant. We'd be pressed for time to get everything done. Georges and Manon would pack our merchandise and we'd be on our way as soon as I had tickets, passports and money in hand. We'd have 3-4 weeks at sea to figure out what more to buy in New York.

We both slept fitfully at my apartment after making love for what was probably the last time in Paris. Manon took the news she'd have to share a cabin with a stranger better than I expected. We'd be together for the longer, more difficult voyage to the New World, she pointed out. She was happy to leave France where a woman couldn't own her own business or be on equal footing with men. She had no intention to play second fiddle to anyone, including me.

She possessed all the qualities I sought in a woman. She was intelligent, assertive and demanded to be treated as an equal in all decisions that mattered. She had a burning desire to make something more of herself than the limited options patriarchal French society and law offered its women. Her provocative good looks and riotous sense of humor that first attracted me to her, now kept me enthralled the more I knew her.

Things moved more smoothly than anticipated the next 2 days. The tickets and cargo reservation were ready and in order. My boss coughed up the $3,000.00 expense advance, bank drafts for double my salary and Georges' wages and the countersigned memos authorizing me as Favre's exclusive agent to investigate his mining Society in his behalf.

I left Georges to transport our sea chests full of merchandise and supplies to deliver directly to our ship for loading. Manon and I took a faster carriage to Le Havre with our personal trunks when I secured our passports.

I learned on arrival that our Clipper ship planned to sail in two days. We sent our sea trunks directly to the ship while we enjoyed our new freedom, prospect of adventure in the New World and all the comforts Hotel l'Empereur could provide for two new emigrants-to-be.

1850 French newspaper Ad for "La Banque Des Emigrans"
(*museum donation*)

Bearer Share Certificates for "LE NOUVEAU MONDE"
and "L/AURIFERE" mining companies.

Du Dimanche 5 au Lundi 20 Août 1849,   Ce Journal paraît deux fois par mois.   1re Année. — N° 1.

LE CALIFORNIEN

Journal de l'Industrie et du Commerce français
DANS L'OCÉAN PACIFIQUE.

ABONNEMENTS.

	Paris.	Départ.	Étrang.
3 mois	2	3	4
6 mois	3	4	6
1 an	5	6	8

Renseignements de midi à 4 h.

AVIS IMPORTANT.

Toute demande d'abonnement qui n'est pas accompagnée d'un mandat de poste ou d'une valeur sur Paris, sera considérée comme non avenue.

(AFFRANCHIR.)

Tirage : 40,000 Exemplaires.

ADMINISTRATION : RUE RICHER, 30, A PARIS.

LE CALIFORNIEN publiera les nouvelles les plus récentes et les plus exactes concernant la Californie.
Nos relations incessantes avec les villes des deux Amériques et ses rapports périodiques avec des correspondants particuliers attachés aux divers consulats, donnent à ce Journal le privilège exclusif de mettre le public au courant de tout ce qui intéresse le commerce et l'émigration.
Le Rédacteur en chef, M. Auguste LACOSTE, ancien marin, — qui a accompli et publié un VOYAGE AUTOUR DU MONDE, —
donnera gratuitement des renseignements positifs, non seulement sur la Californie, où il a séjourné,
mais encore sur les ports et les comptoirs du globe.

PARIS, 4 Août 1849.

La découverte des terrains aurifères de la Californie a produit en Europe les sensations les plus vives et les plus opposées. En moins d'un an, l'esprit public, ému des récits contradictoires qui arrivaient d'Amérique, est passé de l'engouement à l'indifférence; l'opinion, avec cette mobilité qui déjoue les calculs de la sagesse, a couru d'un pôle à l'autre; la faveur a fait place à l'oubli! La destinée des grandes choses, de toutes les découvertes appelées à modifier les conditions physiques ou morales de l'humanité, de provoquer parmi les peuples de soudaines contradictions, d'exciter tour à tour les sentiments les plus contraires, l'admiration et le mépris. L'histoire en fournit de nombreux témoignages : le même enthousiasme accueillit, au XVme siècle, la glorieuse conquête de Christophe-Colomb, et, cependant, plusieurs années s'écoulèrent sans que les trésors du Nouveau-Monde, contestés au mépris de l'évidence, fussent, pour les Espagnols, un appât de nature à vaincre leur incrédulité. Cette fois encore, à propos de la Californie, la fait aura donné raison à l'expérience et vérifié cette loi bizarre qui consacre l'éternelle succession des termes contraires. Mais ces nécessités historiques, — issues de la fatalité, — ces réactions inévitables, soit qu'elles s'opèrent dans les faits ou dans les idées, ne peuvent entraver longtemps la marche naturelle des choses et conservent toujours un caractère essentiellement transitoire. Dès que l'erreur est vaincue, l'effet du bon sens reprend son empire et la vérité nouvelle entre dans sa période de développement.

Ainsi, la question Californienne, après avoir traversé ces diverses phases, marche rapidement à sa solution. L'importance des dernières nouvelles reçues de San-Francisco, l'authenticité des rapports émanés des agents officiels des gouvernements français et américain, expliquent ce résultat. Avant peu d'années, la Californie jouera dans le monde commercial un rôle considérable. Elle attire, des pays les plus éloignés, les hommes d'audace et d'intelligence; bientôt elle absorbera les forces vives des nations commerçantes de l'Europe, et l'on voit se manifester très clairement les symptômes de cette fièvre, dont la recrudescence se fait sentir depuis plusieurs mois aux Etats-Unis.

A la faveur de ce mouvement général, l'émigration tend à se régulariser. Les aventuriers et les spéculateurs ne suffisent pas dans un pays nouveau, aux violentes sans les idées, ne peuvent entraver long-violences d'une civilisation naissante. Des hommes cupides ou frivoles traversent une contrée sans y jeter les germes d'une organisation durable. Ils dévorent au lieu de produire; ils épuisent, pour satisfaire leurs aveugles passions, le sol le plus fertile, et disparaissent avant de rien fonder. Seuls, le commerce et l'industrie remplissent une mission véritablement civilisatrice. La Californie devra ses rapides progrès à leur double et féconde action.

Chassé d'Europe, où les agitations révolutionnaires entretiennent une crise sans issue, le capital est irrésistiblement entraîné dans la voie des spéculations lointaines. Au moment où il s'y attendait le moins, la Californie lui offre tout à coup un débouché avantageux; aussitôt, et comme s'il ne lui restait pas d'autre espoir, il l'envahit avec violence. Ce résultat est logique, inévitable; avant de se condamner lui-même à périr de faiblesse et d'inertie, le capital veut chercher son salut dans les hasards d'une entreprise intelligente. Son intérêt, ainsi que la nécessité, lui font une loi de son énergique résolution. Quels aveugles préjugés ne tomberaient pas, en effet, devant ces deux éléments essentiels du succès, qui, à des titres si différents, conspirent en même but? La Californie, par les bénéfices qu'elle promet, aussi bien que par les désastres qu'elle conjure, est réservée à un magnifique avenir.

Pour diriger ce grand mouvement d'émigration qui emporte nos travailleurs et nos capitaux à quatre mille lieues de la France; pour aplanir les difficultés et préparer le succès de ces vastes entreprises, les compagnies s'organisent. Leur rôle d'intermédiaire est d'une très haute importance : les capitaux, livrés à leurs propres ressources, perdus dans leur isolement, s'agiteraient en quelque sorte dans le vide et resteraient frappés d'impuissance. Il leur faut un centre d'action, un terme synthétique, un moteur commun, où l'on voudra s'agréger, qui, de toutes ces forces éparses, sache faire un puissant faisceau. Le travail lui-même, cet élément primordial de la production, a besoin, sous peine de demeurer stérile, d'un représentant actif et dévoué. Grâce à elles, l'exploitation des terrains aurifères atteindra, par la concentration des forces et la simplification des moyens, ces résultats merveilleux dont l'imagination peut à peine se rendre compte, et que les efforts isolés, même dans les plus heureuses conditions, ne sauraient jamais atteindre.

La Californie, nous devons l'autoriser aujourd'hui cette affirmation, va prendre une importance extraordinaire. Par les compagnies, elle représentera bientôt la plus grande partie de la richesse publique. Comme toutes les grandes choses dont le succès consacre et justifie la vogue, elle absorbera complètement l'attention, déplacera les fortunes et provoquera dans les mœurs une heureuse révolution. Elle aura sa Bourse, ses coulisses, ses cafés, ses gazettes. Elle représentera, au sein de notre civilisation décrépite et agonisante, un monde mystérieux et nouveau.

A des intérêts de cette nature, il faut un organe sérieux et indépendant. Si nos forces ne trahissent pas notre volonté, le Californien remplira dignement ce rôle. Animés du sentiment profond de la justice et de l'égalité, nous nous posons comme conciliateurs entre le capital et le travail. Nous défendrons avec un entier dévouement tous les droits méconnus. Les compagnies dont la moralité ne fera pas un doute, trouveront en nous un défenseur ardent et désintéressé. Nous signalerons hardiment au mépris des âmes honnêtes cette tourbe d'écrivains faméliques, aux gages d'une presse vénale et corrompue, espèce de coupe-jarrets littéraires qui guettent, embusqués aux carrefours de l'industrie, l'heure favorable pour demander aux passants, — la calomnie sur la lèvre, — leur bourse ou leur honneur. Nous serons, enfin, pour les chercheurs, dont les intérêts sont sacrés à nos yeux, non seulement un conseil, parfois utile, mais encore un ami toujours dévoué.

Telle est la mission que nous nous sommes imposée. L'avenir dira comment nous l'aurons remplie.

A. LACOSTE.

DE L'ASSOCIATION MUTUELLE.

Les travailleurs, — aussi bien que les capitalistes, — ont un intérêt immense à l'exploitation des terrains aurifères de la Californie. Il est donc pour eux de la plus haute importance de se placer, pour produire, dans une condition normale qui les protège à la fois contre les dangers de l'isolement et les exigences du capital. Comment les travailleurs doivent-ils prendre part à l'exploitation ? A cette question, le bon sens public a déjà répondu : par l'association. L'association est l'unique moyen de faire participer les travailleurs aux bienfaits des grandes entreprises industrielles. C'est un fait acquis. On ne conteste plus aujourd'hui la valeur de ce principe, définitivement consacré par l'expérience, et les efforts de tous les conservateurs sincères tendent à assurer pacifiquement son application.

Les avantages de l'association, en ce qui touche surtout aux entreprises lointaines, périlleuses, sont d'une telle évidence qu'ils saisissent spontanément les esprits droits et réfléchis. Que peuvent, en effet, dans les opérations de cette nature, des travailleurs isolés, dépourvus de capitaux, et possédant à peine la somme indispensable aux frais de leur passage? Ils sont réduits à l'impuissance par la misère et l'isolement. Quel serait, à son tour, le rôle du capital, si le travail se fécondait pour son action? Il périrait de sa propre inertie. Tout puissants lorsqu'ils sont unis, ces deux éléments tombent, — dès qu'ils se séparent, — frappés de stérilité. C'est une loi nécessaire et dont les conséquences sont inévitables.

L'association mutuelle du capital et du travail porte dans son sein le secret du succès :

Elle met les travailleurs à l'abri des dangers qui menacent, sur une terre lointaine, les hommes isolés.

CONSERVES ALIMENTAIRES.

Maison du savant Economiste APPERT,

Auteur de l'Art de conserver indéfinimont fraîches, naturelles, agréables et saines les Viandes, Gibier, Légumes, Truffes, Pâtés, Fruits, Lait, etc., et disposés de manière à être aussi facilement emportées en voiture qu'à bord des navires.

MÉDAILLES D'OR AUX EXPOSITIONS DE 1827, 1839, 1844. — RÉCOMPENSES NATIONALES DE 2,000 ET 12,000 FR.

Rue Folie-Méricourt, 4, près le boulevart du Temple, à Paris.

[Tableau des prix des conserves — non reproduit en détail en raison de la densité du texte]

Il suffira d'envoyer une traite acceptable sur Paris, et l'on expédiera. — Les boîtes sont d'un litre environ. Rapportée intacte, une boîte bombée serait remplacée ; mais toutes les conserves de la Maison APPERT subissent, avant d'être livrées, une épreuve qui garantit leur conservation. Les boîtes avariées par le bombage ne restent jamais à la charge de l'acheteur.

MINES D'OR. — LA CALIFORNIENNE.

Conseil de Surveillance.

MM. RENOU DE BALLON, représentant du peuple à la constituan'e.

EREYMAND, représentant du peuple.

GAILLARD, maire de Saint-Grégoire (Charente-Inférieure.

Conseil des Mines.

MM. JARROUX, ingénieur des mines.

BERLEUR, ingénieur civil.

MESLIN, architecte de Paris.

La CALIFORNIENNE étant la seule de toutes les Compagnies anglaises et françaises qui soit propriétaire de terrains aurifères en Californie, pourra, sans entraves, en exploiter les Mines d'or. — L'acte de vente est déposé chez Mᵉ Thion de La Chaume, notaire, 3 rue Laffitte, à Paris. — Les premiers travailleurs, organisés en association mutuelle, partiront du Havre, le 30 septembre prochain, sous la direction de M. GAILLARD, membre du Conseil d'Administration, navigateur expérimenté, qui a séjourné plusieurs années dans l'Inde et dans les deux Amériques. — Le passage est gratuit ; seulement chaque associé-travailleur doit souscrire et acquitter huit actions de cent francs, dont les trois définitifs ne lui seront remis qu'après l'expiration de son engagement. — Un médecin, un pharmacien, un aumônier désigné par Mgr l'archevêque de Paris, accompagneront l'expédition. — L'émission du capital de CINQ MILLIONS, représenté par 50,000 actions de 100 fr., sera arrêté après le prochain départ, et les actions délivrées ultérieurement ne donneront part aux bénéfices que la seconde année.

Conseil Judiciaire.

MM. JULES FAVRE, avocat, représentant du peuple.

WALKER, agréé au tribunal de commerce de Paris.

Consignataires.

MM. PELLEVOISIN, SULZER et Cⁱᵉ, au Havre.

J. J. CHAUVITEAU et Cⁱᵉ, à San-Francisco (Californie).

Directeur-Général.

M. CH. ROCHEGRANGY.

Les actions donnent droit, 1° à la propriété des terrains aurifères ; 2° à un intérêt de 5 0/0 ; 3° à un dividende de 75 0/0 dans tous les bénéfices. D'après les bases consciencieusement établies, une action de 100 fr. doit chaque année doubler son capital, et chaque associé travailleur peut aussi, après dix années d'engagement, avoir la certitude de réaliser tant par son travail que par la mise de fonds, une fortune honorable, et réparer les pertes qu'auraient pu lui faire éprouver les dernières révolutions politiques.

La Compagnie délivre des actions contre des marchandises propres à l'exportation, après qu'elles ont été vérifiées et acceptées par les commissions nommées par le conseil de surveillance. La Compagnie a fait l'acquisition de dix machines par le système d'amalgamation, bien supérieures aux machines américaines et à celles employées dans les mines d'or de la Russie et de l'Amérique méridionale : car elles recueillent en même temps, par la combinaison d'un double lavage et de l'emploi du mercure, tous les grains d'or, pépites et paillettes contenues dans les terrains aurifères, sans en laisser échapper la plus petite parcelle, tandis que dix machines mises par cent hommes même inexpérimentés, donneront plus de résultats que quinze cents habiles laveurs.

La Compagnie a passé des contrats pour de grands approvisionnements de pain et de biscuits de mer incorruptibles par le procédé de M. Alxard, et la maison Appert doit le ravitaillement en conserves alimentaires.

La Compagnie assure l'existence à chaque travailleur, ainsi que tous les objets qui lui seront nécessaires pendant la durée de son engagement de dix ans.

Les documents que la Compagnie a reçus de M. le ministre de l'Intérieur des États-Unis, et de M. l'ambassadeur de France à Washington assurent à l'entreprise toute sécurité et un succès complet, la crise commerciale qui pèse actuellement sur l'Europe ne s'étant pas fait ressentir en Amérique, et ces contrées n'ayant éprouvé aucun bouleversement politique.

Le paiement des actions (de 100 fr. chaque) se fait en bons sur la poste de Paris, ou en traites à vue sur les principales villes de France. Les fonds provenant des actions sont déposés à la Banque de France.

Les demandes d'actions et d'inscriptions de travailleurs étant très-nombreuses, il est important que les personnes qui veulent partir, celles qui, sans partir, veulent participer aux bénéfices de la première année en prenant des actions, s'empressent d'écrire immédiatement.

S'adresser, pour souscrire et pour toute demande de renseignements, à la Direction générale, rue de Trévise, 44, à Paris.

POUR NEW-YORK ET LA CALIFORNIE.

L'AGENCE AMÉRICAINE, rue Notre-Dame-des-Victoires, 44, près la Bourse, à Paris, a toujours des navires en charge pour les États-Unis et la Californie.—Fournit aux émigrants des passages aux prix les plus modérés. — Renseignements sur les États-Unis et la Californie. — Expéditions pour l'Amérique.—Envois d'échantillons par bateaux à vapeur et de marchandises pour l'Angleterre, tous les mardis.

Brevets d'invention pour tous les pays : bureau spécial pour cet objet. Capitaux procurés et conseils gratuits.

DÉPART DU HAVRE POUR SAN FRANCISCO.

Le magnifique paquebot américain de 4200 tonneaux NIC-BIDDLE, capitaine Caulkins, partira le 10 août fixe.

Les aménagements de ce vaste et élégant navire présentent aux passagers toutes garanties de confort. La dunette est très spacieuse et l'entrepont est d'une hauteur sans pareille.

Les marchandises de toutes provenances, importées sous pavillon américain, sont admises au simple droit.

M. DUBOIS, ex-tapissier des théâtres nationaux, demande de l'ouvrage, soit à Paris, soit dans une ville de province. Il se transporterait, au besoin, dans les châteaux ou maisons de campagne, et accepterait du travail de gré à gré, à des prix très modérés.

S'adresser rue du Croissant, 8. (Affranchir.)

RÉDACTEUR EN CHEF, GÉRANT : A. LACOSTE.

IMPRIMERIE CENTRALE DE NAPOLÉON CHAIX ET Cⁱᵉ, rue Bergère, 20.

"LE CALIFORNIEN"

California Gold Rush Journal

CHAPTER FIVE

Le Havre/At Sea — January 1851

After a leisurely breakfast, Manon and I braved the wind and rain to take a cab to the docks in search of our ship. Even the horse drawing our cabriolet had its head down in the eye-stinging weather. The driver pulled onto a central wharf and stopped beside a magnificent ship with three towering masts.

"Here she be," our driver said from behind the flap of his greatcoat.

"Wait for us here, we won't be long," I said as we struggled into our foul weather gear purchased for the trip. We dashed for the lowered gangway which bobbed up and down with each wave that splashed the dock. As we neared the top, a hand reached out for Manon but not me. The sailor indicated to follow him and led us to a doorway under the deck on the stern. Inside the passage, we removed our rain hats and slickers and placed them on wooden pegs to drip.

The sailor led us to a small dining room. "Wait here if ya please. Lt. Jones be whichya in a jiffy," he said.

The compact dining room featured a long fruitwood table with shiny patina and several chairs at intervals. The table, firmly anchored to the floor, was encircled with an inch high, rounded wood barrier and holes 2-3 inches wide at each chair interval. The sideboards and liquor cabinets had higher barriers to keep bottles and glasses from rolling off as the ship pitched at sea.

Our musings were interrupted by the appearance of a tall, lean, ship's officer in an impeccably smart uniform bearing three chevrons on each shoulder. His blond hair, straight nose and blue eyes suggested an English or northern European ancestry. His broad, welcoming smile focused on Manon.

"I'm Third Officer, Peter Jones, at your service. Welcome aboard on behalf of Captain Richards and the rest of the crew. I'm acting Purser until we sail. And you folks are?" He said appraising Manon who'd just released her mop of curly black locks from her scarf.

"Pierre Dubois, envoy to the Consul at San Francisco," I fudged. "And Mlle. Manon Rousseau, my companion," as we shook hands.

"His fiancé actually," Manon added with a possessive look at me that dashed any hope for a shipboard romance for the now self-conscious officer. "I'm quite upset that I must share quarters with an unknown woman and not with my man. I truly hope you can do something about it," she said giving him a piercing look.

"I'm terribly sorry. We're a fast cargo ship and until a few months ago carried only five passengers in three cabins. Because of merchant demands on our China run, we remodeled the three cabins into five. Beyond that, we have no flexibility. I hope you understand."

"Yes, as long as you understand our need for time together and privacy. You can, I assume, confirm that Pierre and I will share the same cabin on the longer trip to San Francisco," she said evenly.

"Of course," he replied apologetically.

"Good, then we'd like to inspect all the cabins so we can decide which one will be suitable for us from New York to San Francisco," she commanded.

Lt. Jones led us down a narrow, somber passageway off the dining room and stopped at the first door. He lit a hurricane lamp and we surveyed the room. Two bunk beds occupied the right with two buckets by the ladder to the top bunk. A small vanity with two small drawers and tiny shelves took up the left side. Two enamel wash basins and a water pitcher in recessed holes sat atop the vanity. Above it, a small mirror was fixed to the wall. Above it — a shelf with six inch netting to keep objects from falling ran the length of the small room. There would be room for only two small sea chests and only one person could walk between the bunks and vanity at one time.

Manon looked at me with raised eyebrows, then said mockingly to Lt. Jones, "And this is what you call first class and charge twice the rates of other ships?"

He blushed under her criticism. "I'm afraid so. There was more room with just the three cabins. The ship is built for speed, not comfort. The officers' cabins on the other side are even smaller. Only the captain has a large cabin. I'm truly sorry," he said averting her steely glare. When Manon is not pleased, she lets you know it with both barrels.

"Show me the other cabins," she ordered.

All the cabins were configured the same except one had slightly more room due to the curvature of the stern above. "My fiancé will take this one," she said pointing to the largest cabin, "and you'll reserve it for us for the trip to San Francisco. You'll put me and the other woman in the adjacent cabin with the water closet between," she said tapping her foot.

"Yes, of course," he replied. I chuckled. The Lieutenant was starting to realize who was really in charge of accommodations. Manon had worked as a cook for a pair of snooty English diplomats in Paris before working in restaurants. She was used to giving orders in English.

"Have your sailors bring our personal trunks to our rooms at once," she ordered. "Now, show us the sitting rooms and library."

"Sitting room?" He stammered.

"Yes, where we can read, play cards and converse during the day and after dinner. Surely, you don't expect us to sit in our stuffy, cramped cabins twiddling our fingers when we can't be on deck. Do you?" She said, her dark eyes flashing like lightening on a metal rod.

"I'm sorry, we don't have such a room. Passengers usually stay in their cabins when the weather's bad," he said shakily.

"That just won't do. You'll instruct the cook staff to clear up promptly after breakfast and lunch so the dining room can serve as a commons room until needed for dinner service. You'll find some comfortable arm chairs so we can read in comfort. We expect the first class service we've paid for," she said, her steely gaze boring an imaginary hole in his crisp uniform just below the heart.

"Uh, I'm only the third officer. The captain will have to approve…"

"See that he does. If you can't arrange it, I will. You're going to have a very unpleasant crossing to New York if your guests are uncomfortable," Manon warned.

We waited until our trunks were installed in our cabins before donning our rain gear. The rain had eased as we carefully made our way down the slippery gangway. Our cabman was napping inside the cab and cheerily returned us to our hotel. After seeing our cramped quarters we would share apart, we decided to live it up on our last night in France.

We dined early like the English so we could spend the better part of our evening in the big four poster bed we would sorely miss in the days to come. For starters, we shared a bottle of vintage Champagne at the bar with two dozen No. 2 "fines claires" oysters. In the dining room, we began with a lobster bisque soup and a bottle of 1849 Chablis. For our main course, we chose grilled "homard," a cousin to a lobster, with a side of Chanterelle mushrooms lightly sautéed in olive oil and then smothered in butter. We finished with crèpes à l'Armagnac and half a bottle of 1845 Chateau d'Yquem dessert wine.

The next morning we breakfasted only on tea and toast to prepare for the ship's departure and a normally rough winter crossing of the Channel Islands between France and England. I had crossed from Calais to Dover several times on business and knew how rough the sea could be. We'd need to eat sparingly until we got our sea legs and tummies settled.

The clouds remained ominous, but the rain tapered off and was followed by a brisk breeze that would aid our departure. As our cab splashed along the quay, our Clipper ship looked transformed. She bobbed at her lines like a sleek lioness poised among a herd of water buffalo. She was as long as the French ships moored fore and aft of her, but little more than half their width and so elegant compared to the others. Built for speed in all wind conditions, she would try to set a new record for the Atlantic crossing.

We met Georges who assured us that our cargo was securely stowed and our cabins assured. First Officer, Swen Peterson, a tall, stalwart Danish American with a red beard, gray-green eyes, and spit and polish uniform greeted us. "The Captain invites you to share a glass of Champagne with him, the ship's officers and the other passengers before we sail," he said escorting us to the dining room.

Captain Richards motioned Lt. Peter Jones to serve us Champagne. Lt. Jones avoided our gaze as he passed round glasses. His hand trembled as he poured the bubbly too quickly in Manon's glass and it fizzed over onto the highly polished teak floor.

Captain Richards, a trim man in his fifties with chiseled features, well-honed body and a wrestler's handshake winced at his third officer's gaffe, but said nothing as he turned to Manon and smiled. "I've heard from Lt. Jones that you've already toured our Spartan accommodations. While we can't enlarge them, we'll make every effort possible to assure your comfort. Your welcome suggestion regarding use of the dining room as a commons room after meals will be implemented," he said graciously and kissed her hand.

Georges and I appraised the other persons in the room while Captain Richards offered the peace pipe to Manon who rewarded him with a winning smile. Three other civilians, who I assumed were passengers, stood at the other end of the table. The middle-aged couple dressed in English tweeds whispered together in hushed tones and a demurely dressed woman in her early twenties eyed Manon with an openly curious expression.

Georges lost no time crossing the room to introduce himself to the young woman, who we learned was called Nelly Swanson. She seemed pleased with Georges' attention as she bobbed her head attentively to his inquiries. She played with twists of her light auburn, shoulder-length hair as she sipped Champagne and struggled to reply in her hesitant, high school French. Georges' attentions and the wine gave her cheeks a rosy glow.

The other couple, Jonathan and Rose Steinhart, was on their way to Marysville to open a new branch of Adams Express Co. to serve French miners and merchants in the northern placers. The other four passengers were arranging their cabins and planned to appear for lunch, which would be at 1:30 P.M. due to our imminent departure.

Manon and I decided to watch the Clipper's departure rather than fuss with cabin issues. Georges busied himself helping Miss Swanson with her trunk and settling in. We were happy he was making progress gaining her confidence. Wharf hands on the quay released the huge ropes securing the ship and our sailors scurried up our rigging to the spars like monkeys to unfurl sails to the barked commands of First Officer Peterson. Captain Richards stood by the wheel manned by a ship's officer with two stripes on his chevrons, who we assumed was Second Officer Pedigrew. The top sails suddenly caught the wind and we sliced away from the wharf, followed buoys marking the channel and soon were heeled over on a starboard tack in open sea. We gained more speed as more canvas sails were unfurled. They billowed and strained, the rigging twanged and the ship's joints creaked and protested alarmingly.

Manon's tresses were blowing past her face and we both gripped the rail tightly as the wind picked up and the coast of France receded quickly into the gray gloom that was Le Havre. We hung on for dear life as the ship dipped and rolled in the shifting wind. First Officer Peterson grabbed us both by the arm and wrestled us over the pitching deck to the door leading to our cabins. "Best to stay inside until we get through the Channel Islands and gain open sea. We're in for a bit of a blow, but we'll make good time on this tack," he said before dashing back out the door. We stumbled our way to our cabins.

Georges was green about the gills and holding one of the buckets by the bunk in a death grip when I entered. He proceeded to barf up his big breakfast as the ship began to pitch and roll in earnest. When he reached the dry heaves stage, I peeled his fingers off the bucket and handed him another. Bracing myself carefully each step, I managed to dump the nauseating concoction in the water closet next door.

I heard groans from Manon's cabin. I knocked gently and asked if she was alright. The door opened a few seconds later and Manon slipped out. She, too, was queasy, but her roommate was deathly seasick and the smell of puke in the tiny cabin was making Manon more queasy by the minute. As it was the same with Georges, we decided to put the two together to share their misery. We struggled mightily to push and shove Georges into Manon's cabin and heave him up to the upper bunk. Miss Nelly was oblivious to our efforts. She was sprawled sideways, moaning on the lower bunk with her head aligned with her bucket.

I led Manon back to my cabin, propped her up on the lower bunk with a wash basin handy in case she became sick. I braced myself on the floor with my back to her bunk. The ship's bells rang for lunch. My stomach was settling, but I wasn't hungry. I asked Manon if she could eat anything; she shook her head no.

I was curious to see which passengers had a stomach for food. Only the Captain and First Officer were seated at the table, breaking bread into a hearty soup. Both seemed surprised to see me and inquired politely after my roommate. "He and Miss Swanson are sick as dogs in her cabin," I said casually as if they were already an item. There wouldn't be much to romance for the next few days in any case.

The two ship's officers showed no surprise the two were together. Peterson rang a bell and a cook's assistant, a gangly fifteen year old, tow-headed boy with measles scars appeared and was instructed to provide clean buckets to Manon's cabin and clean the adjacent water closet. Peterson rang the bell again and the ship's cook appeared. "Sammy, looks like you've got only one customer to cook for. Jimmy's gone to freshen a cabin. See what Mr. Dubois would like to eat, then bring us our steaks," Peterson said.

"I'll just have some soup and tea, please. I also want to take a pot of tea and crackers back to our cabin," I said to the cook. Addressing the ship's officers, I said, "I wondered what those holes in the table were for. Are they water bottles?"

The Captain laughed and handed me a bottle with an unusual form in that it had no base to stand upright. "We call 'em torpedo sodas; as you see, they fit neatly in the hole and can't tip over. We like to carry our own water. They're heavy, so we stack 'em in the prow for ballast until we need 'em," the Captain said.

"Interesting. So, they're made not to stand up," I observed while reading the embossing on the side of the root beer amber colored bottle, "KEACH/BALT."

"Some fancy restaurants in New York serve 'em in silver holders. When we take on drinking water in Shanghai, you never know what you're getting. Clean, pure spring water cuts down on sickness, so we take our bottles with us and throw the empties when we dock," the Captain said.

The three of us chatted about the improving weather as they ate their juicy Charolais steaks they smothered in "Perkins Steak Sauce" from a large bottle that slid across the table several times. I learned that they were determined to make port in New York in under three weeks to set another speed record. Apparently, all the Clipper captains had running bets on which ship was fastest.

I took Manon her tea and a tin of biscuits the cook promised would settle her stomach. She was sitting up in her bunk and had discarded the porcelain wash basin. She threw me a brave smile.

"How's the tummy?"

"It's been happier. How long will it take to get used to this rocking?" She replied.

"A day or so," I said optimistically. Some passengers would probably stay queasy much of the time unless the wind diminished, which the ship's officers didn't expect in this winter season crossing of the Atlantic. "Cook says to eat these biscuits and drink this tisane to settle your stomach."

Manon gave me a look of disbelief, but did drink the herbal tea and nibble a couple of English biscuits. I climbed to the top bunk and we spent the rest of the afternoon and evening bracing ourselves in our bunks as the wind howled outside, our ship creaked and groaned, and we sought to calm our stomachs with each lurch and roll of the ship.

California Gold Rush Journal

CHAPTER SIX

At Sea / New York – January 1851

The extreme rocking ended sometime in the night. By morning our ship rolled in a steady cadence and seemed to be surfing the waves. Manon poked her head in her cabin to see if she could fetch a change of clothes, but backed out quickly holding her nose. We ignored the ship's bells calling us to breakfast and exited onto the deck above our cabins. Our Clipper was surfing moderate waves. With a steady wind blowing from behind and all sails billowing, it felt like ice skating loops on a frozen pond. A sailor handled the wheel. The air was rain-fresh and exhilarating after our stuffy cabin.

The Captain and First and Second Officers were finishing breakfast and nodded as we arrived. Only one other passenger made it to breakfast. A sallow-faced man in his mid-forties introduced himself as Robert Gaillard, a wine merchant. He stated he was traveling to San Francisco with a cargo of wines and spirits for his associate's store. His rumpled outfit and puffy eyes attested to a rough first night at sea. He volunteered that his wife, Giselle, was still seasick. Sammy proposed poached eggs and fried ham for breakfast. We settled for fresh baked bread and tea after watching Gaillard struggle to wash down his ham with black coffee. A change in wind would send him to commune with his wife.

Manon asked Jimmy, who served both as cook's helper and cabin boy, to clean up George and Nelly's cabin and give them fresh buckets. Manon charmed Sammy into letting her tour his galley. I stayed to chat with Gaillard.

"How is your business in San Francisco?" I asked.

"It was great at first. My associate, Raoul, is Chilean and one of the first merchants to arrive after word of the gold strike. He brought a stock of Chilean wine and some of my French wines and cognac from Santiago and made a lot of money. Many of the early miners came back to San Francisco rich and spent their new fortunes generously on liquor, gambling and women in that order. However, the bay soon filled with ships bringing American whiskey, rum, inferior brandy, gin and cheap wine that could be mixed and watered and sold in a bottle with a paper label as a vintage wine to the unsophisticated. Competition became tough and profits plummeted." He paused to shove away his plate and take a swig of coffee.

"What's the remedy for that?"

"Well, that's why we are going to San Francisco. With more and more French and Europeans coming to the city as miners and merchants, they'll demand quality wines and cognacs because they know the difference. To assure the integrity and origin of our wines, we are transporting only wines and alcohols in bottles with seals proving who bottled them."

I remembered the half bottle of Chateau LaFitte I had ordered while waiting for the Chevalier in Le Havre. "You mean the little round glass seal applied on the neck of the bottle with the vintner's name?"

"Yes, that plus the vintner's own label. Only the best chateau wines in Bordeaux use the seal as it's more costly to ship cases of bottled wine than barrels which don't have to be packed in straw and can be bottled on arrival." he said with pride.

"That's clever and interesting. I will be consulting with a client who wishes to establish an authentic French restaurant in San Francisco. Do you have a price list for your wines? My client would be most interested in contacting your firm," I said.

Gaillard's flint-gray eyes glinted with pleasure. "Of course, of course, obliged. Perhaps we can arrange a tasting of the better reds when the weather settles. I have a case of sample bottles in the cabin," he said with assurance.

Manon returned from her tour with Sammy, who followed her like a puppy with his first bone. We left Gaillard to plan his wine tasting. We returned to the deck to enjoy the fresh air and steady our legs to the rhythm of the ship's new roll, which had it slicing through medium size waves in a stiff wind. I briefed her on Gaillard's venture and she recounted how she'd reviewed the food menu for the first week and offered to show Sammy how to make a traditional "boeuf berrichon" in a red wine and shallot marinade instead of the planned roast beef and gravy.

At dinner, both Gaillards made a brief appearance. Robert was still gray-faced, and his wife, Giselle, pale and tentative. She was of medium height, with an attractive figure and soft, delicate features. Her most striking attribute was her rich reddish-auburn hair that glinted with ruby-red highlights when the whale oil lamps backlit her chignon. She gave us a weak smile and headed for her cabin clutching a pot of tea and a tin of Sammy's biscuit cure as soon as the platter of filet of sole arrived.

It took two days of uneventful but steady sailing before the last couple made an appearance at table. Jacques Vincent was a swarthy, ruddy-faced, smartly dressed man in his late thirties. His younger wife, Odile, was a blue-eyed, blond with heavily rouged cheeks and a large bosom which she proudly displayed in a form-fitting satin dress with a daring décolletage. Vincent claimed to be a haberdasher dealing in men's clothing and accessories and introduced his wife as his assistant.

At his wife's introduction, Manon whispered in my ear, "bet she measures the trousers and what goes in them," and pinched my thigh under the table while all eyes noted Mme Vincent's girlish laugh and little bow of recognition which threatened to pop her large breasts out of their bindings.

The reactions were interesting. The ship's officers hid their reactions in their large napkins. Georges smiled his appreciation at the display and the more reserved wine merchant and his refined wife seemed shocked. The banker and his wife pretended they were not looking, only talking to each other.

Georges exited with a tray of food for him and Nelly Swanson, who chose to dine in her cabin. Georges' gentle and constant wooing was taking hold. Miss Swanson did not ask Manon to rejoin her in the cabin and Georges moved Manon's trunk into my room and his next door. When I asked Georges how his English lessons were going, he gave me a big wink.

Captain had Third Officer Peter Jones pour red wine at table and made a toast to Sammy's new cuisine. He threw Manon an appreciative smile. The wine merchant pursed his lips after tasting the non-vintage red Bordeaux Superior wine the Captain had ordered decanted. While the cuisine improved from boiled chicken, potatoes and cabbage the previous evening, the wine was quite ordinary and the cheese plate following the main course contained mostly hard, Dutch cheeses with little taste. The English double cheddar and blue Stilton needed a big, well-aged Gigondas or Givry wine from the Rhone valley to complement the French marriage of wine and cheese. Hopefully, our wine merchant would come to our rescue.

We profited from strong steady winds and moderate swells for the next few days. Captain Richards was pleased as our ship made record time. All passengers, even Nelly Swanson on Georges' arm, spent considerable time promenading the decks after our morning and mid-day meals.

The sea gulls and other shore birds had abandoned us for the better pickings of fishing boats and whalers. Our faithful dolphins continued to entertain us with their antics. Two or three pairs would race alongside our ship, then suddenly cross our bow with a burst of speed and artful elegance. At other times, they would race each other and suddenly spring into the air, roll over completely and dive gracefully back into the sea. The next acrobat would try to outdo the previous performer by executing an even more daring roll over.

The Steinharts kept mostly to themselves. He paced the deck nervously puffing on his pipe and watched the sailors scamper up the rigging and along the yard arms as they unfurled or reefed sails. His wife monopolized the wing back chair the Captain placed in the dining room to read or knit. We felt they thought themselves, as bankers, socially superior to the rest of us as they chose not to mingle with their inferiors. They did condescend to play whist with the wine merchant, Robert Gaillard and his wife, Giselle, to break the monotony of our days.

Manon spent an hour a day teaching Sammy the simpler elements of French cooking — how to disguise aging meat and poultry with tasty sauces, to bake scones and croissants, to make crepes and other simple dishes to spice up our boring daily menu. He willingly agreed to buy all the spices and ingredients Manon needed to expand his repertoire for the longer leg of our voyage once we reached New York.

Georges and Nelly avoided the other passengers whenever possible. I hoped he was learning English with lots of pillow talk.

I read books on California and English common law cases. I noted in my journal what I learned from the ship's officers about New York City and Americans in general. I tried to generate ideas for how to kick start my own notary and legal practice in San Francisco to take advantage of the needs of the large French population migrating to California.

Jacques Vincent tried to establish an afternoon gambling parlor on the dining table to play twenty-one, monte and other card games for modest stakes. No one took the bait to gamble with him or his "wife," Odile. She continued to display her ample cleavage in an array of revealing dresses with plunging necklines.

It became apparent that Vincent was more gambler than haberdasher and Odile's décolletage a prop to lure their marks. They spent their afternoons playing twenty-one with each other or solitaire if alone.

The first and last quarrel with Captain Richards occurred shortly after the men's queasy stomachs settled. The Captain announced that we could not smoke in the dining room or in our cabins for reasons of safety. All the men enjoyed a good cigar with brandy after dinner and it was usually too slippery or dangerous to be on deck after dark given the amount of wine we consumed with the evening meal.

Vincent railed about being denied to smoke while he played cards in the dining room and both Steinhart, the banker, and Gaillard, the wine merchant, protested vehemently the prohibition to smoke in their cabins where each had a stash of excellent cigars and French liqueurs.

"Your prohibition is grossly unfair and restrictive," complained Steinhart. "I mainly smoke only a pipe," he groused.

"It's for everyone's safety," the Captain replied evenly.

"We've been smoking safely all our lives," Vincent piped in.

"You haven't been smoking at sea where a sudden rogue wave or rough seas could send everything flying including your cigars or pipes or a lighted match. That's why all the whale oil lamps on board are firmly anchored to walls," the Captain answered.

"We paid for first class accommodation and would be allowed to smoke after dinner in a sitting room on a French ship," Steinhart said acidly.

"Well, you're not on a French ship. You can wait for one in New York if you want. I'm Captain of this ship and you will follow my rules or else. If we find or smell evidence of smoking in your cabin, we'll confiscate your stock and put you off at the first port of call," the Captain retorted.

Steinhart's face flushed crimson and he stormed out of the dining room. I stayed out of the spat. Manon and the other women don't smoke. Men were accustomed to smoke in a male only parlor after dinner. All the women seemed pleased with the rule as smoking in our small dining room would have polluted the room with layers of smoke and smell with no way to clean out the foul air in rough weather.

Ten days into our crossing we encountered bad weather. We were not allowed on deck for two days while the wind howled, the sea roiled and the ship's tall masts with reefed sails creaked and groaned. We slid over mountainous waves, dipped down into their trough and back up again. We shuddered with the ship. No sleep for two nights. When the storm abated and the sea calmed, our queasy stomachs could manage only broth and tea. Cigars stayed in their boxes for several days.

The Captain indicated we were only a few days from New York. The appearance of noisy cormorants diving for fish gave us the first indication land was near. Next came a fish eagle, who hitched a ride on our foremast and showed us a thing or two about fishing.

The eagle would suddenly swoop from its perch at high speed, pluck a fish in its talons, then wings flapping ferociously to gain altitude, soar back to its perch to tear apart its prey as we watched envious of its fresh catch. We were racing through the waves at fifteen to eighteen knots an hour — way too fast to troll a fishing line. We had to settle for salted cod and bream cooked in lard as Sammy had no more eggs for a mayonnaise sauce or olive oil to cook with.

Captain Richards announced at dinner we would sight land the next day and could, with a favorable tide, possibly dock at Long Island by late afternoon. However, we wouldn't be able to go ashore until all passengers and the ship cleared customs. He promised Sammy would be able to purchase fresh meat, vegetables and fruit to celebrate our arrival at port. We'd have two days shore leave while the ship took on fresh provisions and additional cargo for the second leg of our adventure at sea.

The wind turned unfavorable the next day and we didn't make port until early evening. We crowded the dockside rail to observe the beehive of activity on the wharf as black and white laborers sweated in unison to load and unload large, horse-drawn wagons that crowded the quay.

Sammy treated us to breast of duck in a cranberry sauce, mashed potatoes, and ice cream and cookies for dessert at dinner. It helped to compensate for our disappointment at not being able to disembark.

Our sailors had earned extra rations of rum and were soon singing bawdy songs, dancing jigs and clapping to the lively tunes of an accordion and fiddle.

We cleared customs shortly after breakfast the next day. Manon and I hired a cab to take us to a hotel recommended by the Captain. Georges and Nelly decided to spend their last two days together holed up in a love nest near the port.

Our cab made slow progress through streets full of hawkers and vendors touting their wares in Yiddish, Dutch, German, Swedish, Spanish, highly accented English and other languages. Political refuges from Europe and Bolivar exiles from South America exhorted their causes from soap boxes while street urchins darted through throngs of immigrants playing hide and seek with frantic mothers seeking to corral their broods while bargaining ingredients for the evening soup.

Our hotel was in a quaint Dutch-named cul-de-sac that would provide some respite from the hustle and bustle of this boisterous haven for immigrants.

With only a day and a half before we sailed and Georges unavailable, we dropped off our luggage at the hotel and continued on to the upscale mercantile area of the city. We needed to buy more merchandise to sell in San Francisco and convert my letters of credit for expenses and salary into dollars in gold coin which I'd learned were in short supply in San Francisco and traded at a higher rate than gold dust and flakes. Manon bought spices, special flours, dried fruits and mushrooms, cheeses, conserves and other foods she hoped would survive the tropics we had to pass through.

The best part of our New York stay was spent in a comfortable double bed. Holding hands from a bunk bed in a rolling sea has its limitations.

California Gold Rush Journal

CHAPTER SEVEN

New York / Valparaiso — February 1851

While Manon checked with Sammy to see if he'd bought the supplies she'd ordered and set the menu for the next week at sea, I sought out Georges as we slipped out of the harbor.

"So, how was your sweet lass," I asked in English with a conspirator's smile.

"Ohhh. She were fine. A bit clingy, but all honey in the right places. If you knows what I mean," he replied in heavily accented English.

"Then you were lucky she was booked only to New York."

"Yes and no. She's determined to come to California. She wants me to strike up a business we can both work in. Made me buy her an engagement ring and promise to send money for her passage as soon as I'm settled," he replied soberly in French.

"My goodness. The lassie drives a hard bargain. Never thought I'd see you with a ring in your nose," I said tongue-in-cheek. "Are you really going to honor your commitment?"

"Don't rightly know. She's the first woman I've known who takes me seriously. Not flighty, harpy or grabbin' likes most I've known. If California is what they say it is, a rich land for poor immigrants to make something of themselves, then I might just send for her even though she's above my station."

"Won't her family object?"

"She's sure they will. Dad's a money man. Somethin' to do with investin' other folks' money in land and buildings. Mum sent her to an aunt in Paris to learn cultured ways. Now she's supposed to marry into a family what can help her dad's business. Says she don't want to be sold into New York society to promote her family. New York's full of gold fever and everyone wants to go to California — some to mine, some to farm the rich valleys and some just to get paid a decent wage for their skills or labor. Heard a carpenter or mason can make $12 to $14 a day. That's three times what they get in New York. She wants to be part of it," Georges said all fired up. "Says her Dad would stop her if he could. But if I send her a ticket, she promises to come to make a life together."

"We'll I'm happy for you both. Hope it works out. Lucky for me she'll be waiting in New York. I nearly lost a valuable assistant."

"Better this way. I know I don't want to be a coachman in Paris no more. I needs to save me wages and then some before I settle with a woman. Got to figure out what we'd do."

"Have you met your new roommate yet?" I asked to change the subject.

"Yeah. He's pulling things out of his trunk and bitching about the crowded conditions. Family's sending him first class to San Francisco to scout for rich farm land to grow grapes. Dad owns a wine business and is lookin' to become a wine supplier with his own vineyards. Thinks he'll make more money. Seems to be a bit of a lounger to me. Soft hands."

We got our first look at our new passenger, Tommy Rogers, at lunch. He was dressed like a New York dandy — striped trousers, silk shirt with gold cufflinks, vest with ostentatious gold watch fob and cheroots stuffed where a gentleman would wear a handkerchief, cravat with ruby stick pin, and a tall beaver hat that slouched over thick, slick, pomaded hair. He looked in his middle twenties. He kept darting his milky blue eyes from Odile's ample bosom to Manon's cascading curls. His effort to flirt with Manon ended with her dismissive look.

After lunch, the Vincents moved on Tommy Rogers. Jacques invited him to a friendly, low stakes game of twenty-one with him and Odile, who took the seat beside Rogers. She whispered to him about how snooty and unfriendly the other passengers were while granting him a bird's-eye view of her pert, rouged nipples straining for release from her low cut bodice. After letting Rogers win a few hands, Vincent suggested they play for higher stakes and provided brass markers worth one dollar each. By the end of the afternoon, Rogers was slowly losing his stake in markers to Vincent but gaining with Odile who openly flirted with him, calling him "my dear boy," "my shameful rogue," and "my wicked tease."

Captain Richards was not amused by the Vincents' behavior. He announced at dinner that that for the rest of the voyage there would be no gambling in the dining room. Vincent squawked, but retreated on the subject when Odile whispered something in his ear.

The next day the Vincents and Rogers retired to the Vincents' cabin where they could pursue their gambling and other games out of the Captain's view.

We had favorable winds and made excellent time down the Atlantic Coast as we bypassed the Caribbean Islands on track for the coast of South America. Captain Richards confided to me that he was going to try to set the world record for the fastest time from New York to San Francisco. We were averaging fourteen knots and making 280 miles a day compared to broader beamed European boats that averaged only six knots an hour and 130-150 miles a day in favorable wind. He knew we would make excellent time until we hit the tropics around the equator. To get through the light, quirky winds there, we'd have to rely on our slim profile and sharp bow which minimized resistance by cutting through oncoming seas, our multitude of sails to catch the weak breezes, the lack of structures on deck to minimize wind resistance and other technical features in the construction and design of The Flying Cloud by the Bostonian, Donald McKay.

I noticed that he'd taken on more sailors in New York. The ship was teeming with activity as the sails on the foremast and the main mast were constantly being trimmed. "I'm surprised you added more crew, especially if we are going to be in balmy weather much of the trip," I asked.

"Absolutely necessary. The hardest part of our journey will be rounding Cape Horn and sailing up to Valparaiso. It can take some ships three weeks to round the Horn. Winds and currents are fierce there and usually blowing directly in our face rather than from behind. So it's hard to make headway. I'll need every sailor then. The weather will be extreme — stormy, possibly icy or even snowing. We'll have to adjust sail in foul weather twenty-four hours a day until we get through. There'll be little sleep until we're well away from Cape Horn. All of us will earn our keep through this ordeal."

I was surprised at what he said. "From what I've read, most of the sails on French ships were reefed coming around the Horn, so progress was slow. Are you suggesting we'll try to go through this stormy weather under full sail," I asked with a stunned look.

He laughed nervously before replying, "That's the way records are made."

Holy shit! Now I was really rattled. "Won't we be at risk to lose our masts and perish in the sea?" I shouted.

He regarded me evenly, "That's the secret of Clipper ships. They were designed for speed in all kinds of weather. Speed is money to the owners and probably the passengers as well. My officers are the best. We've faced as bad or worse in the South China Sea. We'll come through fine. You'll just have to rely on us."

I noticed that Captain Richards often consulted a book he carried like a priest his rosary. It was entitled, "Wind and Current Charts of the North Atlantic."

"Is that your secret weapon?" I said pointing to his well-thumbed reference book.

"Yes, actually. These "Sailing Directions" contain up-to-date charts that indicate areas of steady winds and calm belts. All American and even some foreign ships use these aids. The charts are updated every year. They are the Clipper captain's bible. If we're going to set a record to San Francisco, it'll be because of these charts," he said patting his book fondly.

I thought what a pity most French captains and cartographers couldn't read English. I thought of the French immigrant ships to California loaded with whole families condemned to six months of foul air, moldering food, sickness, and communicable disease below decks in the cheapest steerage passage who might have survived their voyage if their captain could read the American charts. I had seen plenty of 17th and 18th C. maps depicting California as an island or "terre inconnu," unknown land, which attested to the fact most cartographers were not aware of the early accounts of exploration of the California coast and its friendly bays.

The crew celebrated our passing the equator in a ceremony they called "baptism of the line" by holding mock trials of sailors crossing the equator for the first time. The "judges," dressed as Neptune and other sea gods with white flour in their hair and double rations of rum in their bellies, pronounced "judgment" while, a "priest" baptized them with a bucket of sea water. We were invited to participate in the festivities but declined.

Sammy, with Manon's assistance, prepared a special dinner to honor the occasion. We dined on "paté de foie gras," "gigot de chevreuil mariné," and "cerises en sirop" (foie gras, leg of marinated deer, and cherries in an alcohol syrup) all from our stock of tins we planned to sell in San Francisco,

The Captain offered several bottles of Champagne to begin the evening with canapés, olives and nuts for starters. The wine merchant contributed three bottles of 1842 sweet white sauterne wine to go with the "foie gras." The little glass seal on the bottles was embossed with the year and "Sauterne." I offered several bottles of 1838 red Burgundy wine, labeled "Les Hospices de Beaune" to complement the meat dishes and we finished the evening with champagne, brandy and cigars on deck in the humid air.

For several days our sailors were aloft in the rigging of our masts adjusting our sails to tease the fickle breezes into them. Our speed dropped to 4-6 knots and the ship's officers constantly tried to coax more speed out of our massive sails, which provided us some shade but little relief from the blistering heat. We spent most our time on deck as the humid heat penetrated our cabins. We were all wearing our lightest clothing and praying for blessed rain to cool us down. When it came, it was warm and not refreshing. The crew rigged tarps to capture fresh drinking water and store it in barrels. At the Captain's suggestion, we brought our soiled, sweat-soaked garments on deck to wash in the sweet rainwater. All the women, even the attractive, shy Giselle Gaillard and the snooty Rose Steinhart, allowed the the rain to penetrate to their bodies and reveled to be able to wash their hair. The men stripped to their trousers and lathered their bodies, beards and hair with soap as well. All normal modesty was set aside out of necessity.

We were no sooner clean and refreshed than confined to our torpidly hot cabins as a storm bore down on us with crushing ferocity. Thunder-like canon balls at close range assaulted our ears, the ship's sails strained and all the moving parts of our ship pleaded for mercy as the storm raged for three sleepless nights. When we were allowed back on deck, there was a chill in the air. Captain Richards said we had raced past the last of the tropics in the storm and the weather would turn more and more cold and unsettled as we neared the bottom of South America and sought to pass by Cape Horn.

We were all fatigued and grumpy, but happy for the change in weather. We exchanged our summer clothes for winter wools as the wind was now nippy. We saw seaweed in the water and could hear the sharp cries of penguins in the night. It was too cold to remain on deck after dinner even though we had daylight until 9 P.M. Our ship fought fierce south west winds and mountainous waves as Captain Richards struggled with all sail on to pass east of the Malvinas so he could tack with the wind to assault Cape Horn on a run rather than fight head winds. After a day of endless tacking, we managed to slide by the Malvinas on their eastern shore. What a bleak sight — no trees, no trace of green, just arid rock.

Captain Richards wasn't joking when he said he would not reef our sails to appease the winds of Cape Horn. By looping east of the Malvinas and the Tierra del Fuego passage, he was able to assault the Cape on a tack instead of head on while we cringed in our bunks and his swarthy sailors fought howling winds, sleet and ice to cling to the spar lines to adjust sails when needed at Officer Peterson's command.

Georges and Tommy Rogers were wrapped around their buckets. Manon's efforts to disguise the ship's salted meat and poultry with sauces after the tropics were on hold. Impossible to navigate the corridor to the dining room or keep anything on the dining room table, so we existed on Sammy's tea, hot buttered biscuits, hot lentil soup and those wonderful bottles of fresh carbonated New England mineral water in the torpedo shaped bottles embossed with the bottlers' names, "Boyd's," "Keach," and "Gardner" from Baltimore that Jimmy brought to our room. These odd bottles with their refreshing water came in a variety of pleasing colors, root beer amber, violet, dark green, apricot yellow, and even dark puce. Manon remarked that it would be a shame to throw away such pretty bottles when we made port.

The seas were still roiling but calmer after we made it around Cape Horn, rounded Tierra del Fuego and picked up south west winds that would push us to Valparaiso, Chile. We were allowed back on deck despite the bitter cold winds and rain squalls. We could make out the majestic spikes of the snow and fog enshrouded Chilean Andes as we sailed up the coast. Fresh food was long gone and the salted meats almost inedible despite Manon's efforts to make them palatable with various curry spices. We preferred the hearty lentil and pea soups that had been our savior when the dining room was closed and pasta with black olives and olive oil that Manon had Sammy purchase in New York as a precaution against spoiled meats and poultry.

As we moved up the long, craggy coast of Chile, we were joined again by playful porpoises that raced our ship and crossed our bow in games of tag. We also spotted spouting whales and were serenaded by the high-pitched cries of gulls that followed the ship to fight over Sammy's droppings over the rail after each meal.

While we spotted other ships that sought to hail us, Captain Richards ignored their offers to parlay or exchange goods for fresh food. He was hell bent on his quest to set a record for speed.

Captain Richards announced at lunch that we would make port in Valparaiso by early evening as we had favorable winds and seas. The first indication we were near was a lighthouse blinking to mark the entrance to the harbor. We could see patches of green by houses on the slopes of hills surrounding the harbor. We were surrounded by rocks on both sides as we neatly slipped into Valparaiso Bay. The bay was not big, but was well protected from the elements of sea and wind. It was strange but exhilarating to experience the calm of the bay and the sight of 150 ships gently bobbing at anchor after our recent ordeals.

We dropped anchor close to the wharves piled with supplies. As the only ship to arrive that day, customs formalities were dispensed with quickly. The officials stared in awe at the sleek lines of our ship. One official cried "Madre de Dios" when Captain Richards informed him how many days at sea we were from New York to Valparaiso. Apparently, we had set the world record for that leg of the passage and were on track to set the record to San Francisco. Captain Richards warned us that we must be ready to join our ship as soon as she finished taking on fresh provisions. He ordered Second Officer Pedigrew to escort us ashore and to our hotels so the captain would know where to find us. It was apparent he was determined to go for the world record for New York to San Francisco.

California Gold Rush Journal

Chapter Eight

Valparaiso / San Francisco — March 1851

Officer Pedigrew dropped us off at Hotel de la France which was close to the main road to the port. Manon wasted no time charming the owner to secure a large bungalow at the rear of the property for the two of us. The other passengers would have to fight over available rooms in the hotel. Our bungalow was replete with large veranda, sitting room with dining table and a bedroom with double bed. The bungalow served as a honeymoon suite. A carafe of Chilean red wine with two glasses and bowl of summer fruits had been thoughtfully left on a small, hardwood table on the veranda.

Manon flashed me a devilish look. "So, cheri, you wanna go have dinner with all the others or perhaps stay here with me?"

"Let's have a picnic on the big brass bed," I suggested hopefully.

"Not so fast big boy. I had to persuade the concierge we were on our honeymoon to get this little palace. Why don't you have Georges bring us some food and a bottle of champagne from the restaurant recommended by the hotel?"

I duly requested Georges to bring back a "late" supper for us and leave it on the veranda. When I returned to our lodging, Manon greeted me from a large wicker chair on the veranda with a glass of red wine in one hand and a ripe pear in the other. She had loosened her dark curly locks which fell down the back of her light cotton chemise now transparent in the reflected light of the whale oil lamp. Her shapely breasts pushed against the gauzy fabric. Her dark eyes moved seductively from the goblet of wine to the pear dripping its juices where she had taken a big bite.

"So," she said. "What about my dinner?" Her toes wriggled a little dance of anticipation.

"All in due time, my precious temptress," I took a sip of her wine, then a bite of her pear, put both on the table, scooped her in my arms and deposited her on our big brass bed.

"Are you going to ravish the fair maiden?" She said rolling her big black eyes seductively.

When other appetites finally roused us from our heavenly double bed, we found Georges had left a bottle of now tepid French champagne and set a loaf of bread, two slices of "paté maison" garnished with small pickles in the French style, green and black olives, and sticks of celery on one plate and two servings of breast of duck "à l'orange" garnished with string beans and tiny "pommes frites." Both plates were covered with large napkins and a note said, "Enjoy your picnic. G."

After demolishing our meal, which included Manon teasingly licking her plate like a spoiled kitten, we resumed our roles as honeymooners. It finally ended with a pillow fight and tickling contest until we both gave in exhausted and exhilarated to be on land, in each other's arms, and away from our dreadful cabin aboard the Flying Cloud.

We toured the merchant arcades serving the port. After a visit to the post office to send an interim travel report to Paris, we sampled wares in the "mercado." The Chilean wines were surprisingly good. The light "vino blanco" white wines were crisp and fruity and the "vino rosso" reds full-bodied with deep cherry and cinnamon aromas. We ordered several cases delivered to our ship. I sampled and purchased several boxes of excellent cigars. Manon bought fresh and dried fruits, spices, nuts and other items to add variety to the next leg of the voyage.

Georges caught up with us at the end of the afternoon as we were enjoying a plate of fresh shrimps, "papas fritas" and a pitcher of Chilean "vino blanco" at a charming restaurant with outdoor tables and dramatic views of the mountains ringing the port and the seaside villas. We were feeling mellow as we sipped our wine, tapped our fingers to the syncopated rhythms of the Chilean guitar player who crooned love songs in a sultry voice.

I had tasked Georges to check out the bars and bistros frequented by the sailors to learn the latest news from California from returning sailors and miners.

"So Georges, what's the latest news from California?" I asked.

"Lots of unhappy Chilenos. They say the Yankees discriminate against them and force them off their claims at the placers. They're all armed to the teeth and prepared to shoot all foreigners who interfere. The Yankees say the gold is theirs."

"What about the French miners? Any info about the ones on La Californienne's ships?"

"Nothing specific. But the Chilenos say the French are treated just like them. They don't understand the Yankees who call them "Les Keskydees."

Both Manon and I guffawed, then laughed 'til tears rolled down our cheeks. "Les Keskydees? You mean they don't know what anyone is saying?"

"Yes. That's why they hang out with the Chilenos and Mexicans. Nobody understands what they say. The Yankees passed a law saying all foreigners got to pay $20 a month to mine. Chilenos are furious, so many came home. Can't make any money.

Everything's so expensive. Sailors say don't bother to go to the mines. Too many damned Yankees and crooks, they say."

"Any word from the Captain about when we sail?"

"Pedigrew says Captain wants us all on board at daylight. Plans to sail on the morning tide when last of supplies loaded. He says he'll have a coach at the hotel at 5 A.M."

California Gold Rush Journal

CHAPTER NINE

Valparaiso / Chile / San Francisco — April 1851

Manon cast a last, lingering look through sleepy lids at our love nest as Officer Pettigrew hustled us into the carriage. Our luggage would follow. He informed us that we would take breakfast aboard the Flying Cloud and she would sail on the tide around 8 A.M.

"Why then must we be rousted out of bed at 5 A.M.?" Manon glowered at Pettigrew.

"Captain's orders," he replied stone-faced.

I try not to pick a fight, especially a lost cause, before I've had my morning coffee. Manon's used to rising early in Paris and ready to do battle whenever she believes she's being treated unfairly.

"It's all about the bloody record, isn't it? Doesn't trust us to be on time, so he sends a flunky to corral us like we were kids playing hooky from school. Right?" Trying to bait him, she taps her foot furiously.

"Wouldn't know, M'am. Just following orders."

Needless-to-say, we were a tired, sorry, bleary-eyed lot when Sammy announced he was serving scrambled eggs and fresh croissants for breakfast. A look around the table confirmed we'd all been burning the candle at both ends in our short land stay.

Our baggage arrived and was deposited in our cabins while we broke our fast. Our majestic ship swooped past the host of broad beamed ships bobbing at anchor from a host of nations. The wharves were crowded with onlookers watching our swift, full sail exit from the harbor. Back to the motion and roll of our Clipper now slicing through the waves with a brisk northeast wind as the coast of Chile with its friendly inhabitants faded from view. At least our next stop would be San Francisco.

While Manon consulted with Sammy on his French cooking lessons and menu planning, I pigeonholed Georges for a chat on deck.

"Did you write to your sweetheart about the lovely Chilenas making goo-goo eyes at you in town?" I teased. Manon and I had noticed that the port area and even the commercial areas we visited teemed with an interesting assortment of local ladies available for hire. Many were very attractive with luxuriant dark black hair, beautiful black eyes and tawny skin. Their approach was so different from Parisian prostitutes. They coyly asked potential clients, "Would you like to come with me to my house?" We saw several leading sailors and even ship's officers to their apartments, always on the first floor of houses and tenements.

"Don't mean nothing. Just a little sport before a long fast. She were a live wire. Made me take her to a club with guitar music, singing and dancing afore she'd take me home. Now I've to listen to bloody Tommy Rogers carping about how he's losing his dad's money and she's all over him like glue to keep him gambling. If you knows what I mean."

"Any other info that might be useful to us?"

"Our sailors what was takin' on provisions said almost all the flour along with lots of fruits and grains in California comes from here. The luxury goods all come from Europe."

This intelligence would be useful to Manon and would

validate my purchases of merchandise for sale if I didn't have too much competition. Time would tell. Captain Richards beamed his pleasure. Our Clipper was splitting through moderate waves at 14 knots an hour with a stiff wind billowing all our sails. Sammy regaled us at lunch and dinner with new recipes learned from Manon. We couldn't get enough fresh fruits and vegetables from Chile's rich heartland. We feasted on "pavé de boeuf au Roquefort, escalopes de veau à la viennoise," "foie de veau en aspic" and "gigot" with Yorkshire Pudding (steak filet with a Roquefort cheese sauce, veal scaloppini, beef liver in aspic, and leg of lamb with Yorkshire pudding) at our evening meals with rich Chilean red wines to wash it down. At lunch we were treated to "croquettes de morue, filets de maquereaux au vin blanc, huitres et moules marinières" (croquettes of cod, baked mackerel filets in white wine, oysters and mussels in a white wine bouillon) and special Chilean white wines to complement each menu. Even our wine merchant was pleased with the quality of the Chilean wines he had never sampled before.

It was pleasant sailing and everyone was in a merry mood until the wind died abruptly as we approached Callao on the Peruvian coast. The weather had been turning increasingly warm, but with refreshing breezes, we had been comfortable trading fall attire for summer cottons. When the wind stalled, we became immediately uncomfortable.

Captain Richards spent most of his time nervously pacing the deck and barking orders to First Officer Peterson, who relayed changes in course to the helmsman and to the sailors aloft on the spars by bullhorn. The Captain fretted over his 1850 edition of "Sailing Directions," while he tried to ferret out where the feeble, fickle breezes were hiding. The sailor in the crow's nest scoured the horizon by spyglass for telltale signs of waves pushed by wind as our speed plummeted and the blazing sun and stifling humidity started to punish us.

Our cabins became intolerable ovens where we couldn't sleep or bear to be. The first to crack was the banker, who berated his wife for eschewing her high collar dresses for ones with low neck lines that insulted his sense of decorum while we all sought the elusive shade of sails on deck.

"Rose. For god's sake cover up. I won't have you displayed like a strumpet for all to gawk."

"I can't take it anymore. I'm hot and miserable. You and your goddamn plans to open a bank in an uncivilized country inhabited by savages." She glared at the rest of us with a look that included us in her view of the uncouth.

"I am your husband and you'll obey me or else." He raised his hand as if to strike her, his face flushed with rage.

"You wouldn't dare strike me. I'd have the Captain put you out of our cabin for the rest of the voyage. He's a gentleman and you're a crazed fool for dragging me from a comfortable life in Paris so you can fiddle accounts and use the gold of others thinking you'll get rich. From what I've learned, the Napoleonic Code and all its provisions allowing men to dominate their wives ceased to exist the moment we left France on this ship. We're on an American ship where American law is in force. I believe I'm free to do as I damn well please."

"Shut your mouth. I won't have you discussing my business in public. Go to the cabin at once."

"Hah. Call this sad lot of dreamers and losers a public," she gestured to the rest of us who were dripping sweat and uncomfortable like her. She ambled over to the rail, casually picked up a bucket of sea water and poured it over her head while giving her husband a disdainful look. She then sauntered over to a coil of rope in the shade of our sails and seated herself like a queen of the hill.

Steinhart stared at his wife in disbelief and with mounting fury. What had been a cotton dress with deep décolletage was now a wet wrapping molded to her well-endowed body and revealing its attractions in unabashed detail. Her husband stormed down the deck towards the entrance to our cabins and disappeared into the inferno below.

Manon whispered in my ear in English, "Oh la la. Zee snooty banker got zee black eye, non?"

I chuckled. "He got more than a black eye. He lost the fight. She's gonna wear the pants now. Just wait and see."

"Good for her. You treat me like that, I kill you slow and nasty. Feed you to the sharks. How you like that?" She said tongue-in-cheek, then flashed me a whimsical smile from behind puckered lips. We both laughed. Since the ship was at reduced speed, sailors off duty had caught a large, white shark with ferocious teeth. Manon's alluded threat was as fearful as the ocean predator we would eat if Sammy had the stomach to cook in this infernal heat.

Sammy surprised us again. That evening while we were still lolling around the deck after the dinner bells chimed, Jimmy brought us small bowls of soup for us to sample. Sammy called it shark fin soup, a dish he learned while the Flying Cloud was picking up tea in China. The sample was delicious. We braved the hot, muggy dining room for more.

After the delicious soup, Sammy served pan fried shark steaks with a garlic lemon sauce. As the white wine was not chilled, we drank it mixed with sparkling mineral water taken on board in Valparaiso. These bottles had bases and were embossed "Taylor & Co./ Valparaiso / Chile." As the drinking water on board was starting to taste rank, the refreshing carbonated soda water hit the spot.

While Captain Richards coaxed our sails to exploit weak and fragile breezes to maintain 3-4 knots where other ships would stall, the crew labored on a promise of double rations of rum in San Francisco and other inducements to get us through the tropics and in position to pick up north westerly trade winds from the Pacific.

When we finally left the tropics behind, we all cheered the Captain and his crew, except the Vincents. Our gamblers had beseeched the Captain, as we approached the equator off Guayaquil, Ecuador, to allow us to take our mattresses on deck to sleep. The Captain refused pointing out that we would be in his and the crew's way as the ship maneuvered 24 hours a day to maintain headway. He confided to Manon that he was concerned for the safety of his attractive female passengers, who while on deck in the torpid heat, had been the subject of speculation and lust by some sailors.

At long last, we picked up brisk, cool breezes from the trade winds and resumed our race against the clock for San Francisco. The dynamics of the limited interpersonal relationships among the passengers changed along with the weather and the prospect of soon sailing into San Francisco Bay.

The banker's wife, Rose Steinhart, made a move to ensnare Captain Richards with her charms to spite her husband. She now came to dinner in dresses that emphasized her mature figure and ample bust. Failing to land the married Captain despite a gallant effort, she settled for First Officer Peterson, who was unmarried. They were soon spending time together in Peterson's small, but very private cabin when he was off duty while her husband fumed.

I learned from Georges, who now had Tommy Rogers crying on his shoulder, that once Vincent had all of Roger's money and a signed promissory note for an additional $2,200.00 enforceable in California, the alluring after gambling sessions with Odile on the Vincent's lower bunk, while Vincent smoked a cigar on deck, had abruptly ended. The Vincents now shunned him. Odile then set her sights on Georges, but despite missing a roll in the hay on a regular basis, he resisted her. So, she carried on brazenly with the ship's third officer, Lt. Peter Jones, who shared a cabin with second officer, Carson Pettigrew. Rumor had it she serviced them both.

Manon and Giselle Gaillard, the wine merchant's wife, became fast friends. Giselle, like Manon, wanted to make something more of herself than a bookkeeper for her husband's wine business. Bored with card games, Manon taught English to Giselle. They formed an afternoon study group that included Georges and sometimes me when they were stumped by the irregular grammar. As we neared the end of the voyage, all three could communicate basic needs and ask intelligent questions in the language of the New World. Giselle's husband, Robert, courted my favor once he learned that Manon and I aspired to establish a quality French restaurant in San Francisco. We passed many pleasurable moments sampling his wines.

The weather grew increasingly colder as we sailed north. Captain Richards seemed more and more excited as he consulted his log books and hinted he would soon have an important announcement for us.

A hand-written invitation to join the Captain for cocktails before dinner was delivered to our cabins while we lunched. While there was no mention of formal dress, we all dressed in our best, least soiled, and most presentable attire. At the cocktail, Third Officer Jones served champagne chilled in ice buckets of very cold Pacific sea water.

"I'm very pleased to inform you that tomorrow we will enter San Francisco Bay and drop anchor at our destination...," we interrupted him with whoops of joy, clinked glasses and shouted hurrah "for he's a jolly good fellow." "I am further pleased to announce that you have shared in a historical first. By my calculation, we will have sailed 17,597 nautical miles from New York around Cape Horn to San Francisco in the record time of eighty-nine days and twenty to twenty-three hours depending on tomorrow's winds at an average speed of 8 knots. I thank you humbly for all the hardships you shared to make this record possible. I propose a toast to the fastest ship in the world, to the Flying Cloud, who has earned her name."

We drank, ate and partied well into the night. Next day at cocktail time we sliced into San Francisco Bay between narrow headlands under full sail to an incredible sight. The Bay was full of hundreds of anchored ships, most clearly abandoned. We dropped anchor near a very long wharf and waited for customs officials.

"VUE DE SAN FRANCISCO" in 1850, an engraving.

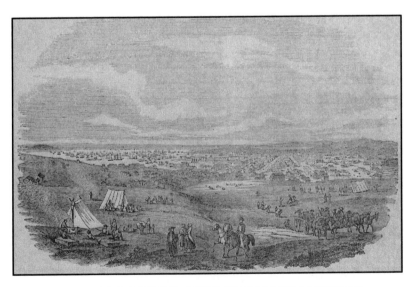

1851 VIEW OF THE CITY OF SAN FRANCISCO.

"PORTSMOUTH SQUARE, SAN FRANCISCO,"
1850 lithograph.

"THE EAST SIDE OF PORTSMOUTH SQUARE," Spring 1850.

"COLORED POPULATION —
Greaser, Chinaman, and Negro," in 1851.

"STREET SCENE IN SAN FRANCISCO," 1851
(*museum donation*).

1849-1850 Street Map of San Francisco
(*museum donation*).

Street Map of San Francisco (*museum donation*).

California Gold Rush Journal

Chapter Ten

San Francisco — May 1851

We cleared customs quickly as we were so few passengers. Captain Richards arranged for our transport to shore. We carried small satchels with necessary clothes only. We would have to return to the ship for our trunks later.

It was a very cool evening with low clouds threatening rain. We literally wobbled along as we sought to exchange our sea legs for land legs as we looked around us in amazement. At the shore line, ships had been run into land and converted into rooming houses, stores, warehouses, jails and even gambling dens.

We had an address of a hotel run by a French woman on Dupont Street on the northern fringe of the commercial heart of the city. We stumbled our way across Montgomery Street and then up Commercial Street with its mix of banks and gambling dens in the diffused light through windows from red brick and wooden buildings and from open doors of smoke filled gambling palaces.

We arrived at a large square, marked Portsmouth Square, which was still bustling with activity. Many of the buildings were large, two-storied gambling establishments that appeared to be chock full of oddly dressed gamblers. I could recognize the dress of Chilenos with their colorful ponchos as they milled about the square; there were Chinamen with long braids, baggy trousers, and skull caps chattering excitedly in their strange language, dark skinned Pacific Islanders, Caucasians in various states of dress and undress, bearded, scruffy men in flannel shirts, dirty trousers, and worn boots plus others. All were males and their varied attire included a large knife sheathed in a buckskin holder dangling from a leather belt on the side and a large revolver stuffed into the waist.

We didn't tarry. The sight of Manon traipsing along with Georges and me created considerable vocal, leering interest among so many womanless males. We ignored the cat calls and companionship offers directed at Manon as we quickly crossed the square and on to Dupont Street to L'Hotel de l'Alliance. Accommodations were Spartan at best. Georges was given a mattress and one blanket despite the chill night air and would spend his first night on land in a small room with three other men at $1 a night each. Manon and I were offered a small garret room not larger than our ship cabin. It contained a bed with a sheet and duvet, a coat tree, a small vanity with mirror, wash basin and pitcher of water, and one chamber pot. Our room rented for $3.50 a night and the WC was down the hall on the floor below next to a large closet containing a bath tub. Hot water was extra and could be obtained only during the day when the maid did the rooms.

We dumped our satchels in our uninviting rooms, and retraced our steps back along Dupont Street to a friendly looking bistro whose outdoor slate in French offered fresh oysters, rabbit or venison stew, and a cheese plate for $3.50. Only three of the eight tables were occupied, all by French speaking clients whom we ignored. The choice of wines was limited to house white and red.

We ordered a pitcher of each and the three course meal.

Any celebration would have to wait. The mussels were saltier and fatter than those in Le Havre but the venison and rabbit ragout were quite tasty after the rancid, over salty ship's fare at the end of the voyage. Georges and I celebrated our arrival and first meal with one of my good cigars and a large snifter of Cognac while Manon stuck to red wine. Our modest meal, wine and after dinner "digestif" came to $16.00 or an ounce of gold dust at the going rate.

After I paid our tab in freshly minted $5.00 gold coins, the proprietor proposed a breakfast of fresh baked croissants and baguettes with coffee in the morning in an effort to lure us back on the morrow. As I didn't want my change in gold dust, we agreed to apply it to our next day's breakfast. Manon wanted to return in the morning to query him on who supplied the rabbit and venison and who baked the croissants and bread and at what cost.

We tumbled into our makeshift beds and slept soundly until first light when the sounds of carts and their drivers shouting and cussing reluctant horses and donkeys through muddy streets interrupted our reverie. Manon tried to block out the raucous, unwelcome noise first with her pillow, then mine to no avail. It was too early for breakfast, so we opted to ignore the rude awakening and initiate our new bed in a way we couldn't in the bunks of our cramped ship cabin.

As it would be up to a week before our goods cleared customs, we decided to visit the town to learn what we could of commercial opportunities and the fate of the men and women sent on the La Californienne's company boats. I tasked Georges to visit merchants and bars along Dupont Street to see what he could learn after a breakfast of buttery croissants, soft boiled eggs and coffee. Manon threw the proprietor a charming smile and he happily agreed to answer her food supply and cost questions.

I left her there and headed back to Commercial Street

where many French and American banks were located. As I had several thousand dollars in gold coin to protect, I stopped by Adams & Co., a New York bank that advertised it bought gold dust and nuggets from miners and merchants for $14-16 an ounce. A shaggily dressed miner in a stained, once red flannel shirt, dirty trousers stuffed in scruffy high boots and tattered hat was ahead of me in line. The clerk had finished weighing gold dust and flakes from the miner's poke.

"We can give you $140.00 for your ten ounces, Mr. Hanford," the clerk said off-handedly.

"What yer mean $140? That's out right crookery. I may be an untutored miner but we all knows gold is worth $16.00 an ounce. You owe me $160.00 an that's a damn fact."

"Our terms are quite clearly stated on the board at the entrance. We buy dust, flakes and small nuggets for $14 to $16 an ounce. Your dust isn't pure, there's some black sand and mica mixed in, so it's not worth $16.00 an ounce," the clerk stated authoritatively.

"You're a bunch of damn thieves an you know it. Pen pusher cheats the lot of you. It's back breakin' work in icy cold water an' a hot sun beating on you with naught but flapjacks an' beans to sustain a man. Now you want to take the sweat of my labor for less than it's worth. Merchants, bars and even whores don't quibble. They weighs it and give you $16.00 an ounce for goods and services." He was now shouting and waving his hat with menace.

"Let me get the manager, sir," the clerk said eyeing nervously the big revolver tucked in the client's leather belt.

"Manager be damned! You shovel my gold into my poke, and be quick about it. I'm not doing business with cheats."

The clerk's fingers trembled as he scooped the miner's gold dust and flakes back into the large leather pouch on the counter. The miner scrutinized the operation with one hand on the handle of his large revolver. The clerk was careful to get every speck of gold in the poke, then pulled the strings tight. The miner snatched his poke and stomped out the door.

I informed the clerk that I bore letters of credit and wanted to open an account with a bank manager. I had no intention of discussing my business or showing my gold coins at a teller's counter with prying eyes following every move. The clerk led me to a door marked "Horace Bidwell, Asst. Manager." Bidwell was a short, beefy, red-nosed man dressed in a suit his belly had outgrown. I tendered him my letters of credit. He seemed surprised they were drawn on a Paris bank.

"I understand there's a shortage of gold coinage in San Francisco. I've heard that some folks are actually melting and minting gold slugs and selling them in $5 and $10 denominations to meet the need for coins and that in fact there's only 80% gold in the slugs," I stated from what I had learned from Pierre-Louis, the proprietor of "Les Bons Amis" bistro where we had supped.

"Why yes, that's so," he said, a dumfounded look on his face.

"Good. I have brought from New York $2,500 in $5, $10 and $20 gold coins which I wish to sell at a premium. Say $2,750."

"Well, ugh, that's highly unusual. I don't think we can do that. We can of course open an account for you in the amount of the coins," he said haltingly.

"That's too bad. I would have preferred to do business with an American bank, but I'm sure the French bank across the street will be delighted to pay a premium for the coins they can resell to the gambling houses and other establishments," I said as I picked up my letters of credit on the desk.

A bead of sweat on Bidwell's brow threatened to run down his face. "Ugh…I'm not authorized…ugh let me ask the bank manager," he stammered. He rushed out of the office and dashed into another office. He returned shortly. "Our manager says he would be willing to pay you the ten percent commission you're asking for the coins if you establish accounts with our bank," he said with a defeated look on his face.

"Good. Then take me to your manager and I'll make arrangements with him directly." The bank manager, John Hopkins, was a tall, suave looking man impeccably dressed in a suit and tie from a fashionable New York men's clothing establishment. He set up accounts based on the letters of credit, credited my new checking account with $2,750.00 in exchange for the gold coins and offered me free storage in their basement vault when I informed him I had another $2,000.00 in gold coins to store. I asked and noted his recommendation of a printer and the location of the French Consulate. He handed me a large cigar in a glass tube sealed with red wax as we parted with a clap on my back and "Feel free to consult me anytime" handshake.

California Gold Rush Journal
CHAPTER ELEVEN
San Francisco — May 1, 1851

After leaving the bank, I ambled back through Portsmouth Square on my way to my lunch date with Manon. I was curious to see the interior of the gambling palaces and the behavior of the participants without the distraction Manon would cause. The tallest of the establishments was emblazoned with the name "EL DORADO" in huge letters across the façade of the three story building in brick. To the right of it, was a longer two story, building with balconies on the second story and dormer windows poking out of the roof with its sign announcing "PARKER HOUSE." Each palace featured a barker in top hat beckoning the milling crowd in front to enter.

On a whim, I chose to enter the "EL DORADO." First glance sufficed to answer why they were called palaces. One entered into a grand salon about twenty meters long that was brilliantly lit with French chandeliers. The walls were adorned with paintings of nudes in the style of Goya's the Naked Maja and large gilded mirrors reminiscent of opulent chateaux on the Loire. At the far end several musicians on a raised platform played gay dance music and polkas.

Gamblers and gawkers crowded around dozens of gambling tables and two roulette wheels. So chock-full, it was difficult to move through the cigar puffing throng. The gamblers were a motley crew: French in tall beaver hats, Chilenos wearing their broad hats and ponchos, Chinese in round silk and silvered skull caps and baggy pants. European and Yankee dandies stood elbow-to-elbow with scruffy miners in unwashed flannel shirts, dirty wool and homespun trousers stuffed in tattered boots and slouch hats they'd probably used for pillows, sailors, and Mexicans pulling on long dark cheroots. All were armed to the teeth and focused on the gambling tables where professional gamblers stacked and restacked silver dollars, gold coins, and brass markers in play.

I squeezed through the horde to where I could observe play on a green table featuring faro, a game popular in Paris. In addition to the slickly dressed professional gambler turning over the cards with flair, a buxom young woman hung on the arm of a European player while the gawkers around the table peered intently at her daring décolletage which caused some onlookers to suck in their breath as her breasts rose and surged in her bodice each time she leaned her elbows on the table or twisted to whisper in her companion's ear. I learned later she was the house's employee hired at $16.00 an evening to keep the players confident and betting and the crowd entertained.

I watched as the professional gambler with a large stack of gold and silver coins in his corner called for bets, then turned over cards for the bettors. The object is to guess the value of the cards the professional gambler deals and has probably marked. The cards are neatly packaged in a mahogany box with a painted tiger as logo.

Amazingly, despite steady losses for most of the gamblers, no sooner was a chair at the table vacated than another player occupied it. I made my way out of the smoke filled palace, past the large mahogany bar and across the way to the post office which had a long line of folks hoping the latest ship arrivals brought letters from home. I needed to send a report of our arrival to our boss, but would send Georges to deal with the post. Hopefully, he could use his charm to make a friend of a postal clerk to allow us to by-pass the long lines to receive mail and expedite letters to and from his "fiancée."

Manon had invited me to meet her at a small, intimate restaurant called "Café de Paris" where she was to meet Giselle Gaillard from our ship. The two women were trying to figure out how they might work together. As I strolled along Dupont Street in the direction of Broadway, I was impressed by the number of French merchants already engaged in commerce. Wine and alcohol merchants, hair dressing salons, dress and hat shops, bars and cafes, restaurants, boarding houses and hotels, bread and pastry shops proudly announced their wares and services on freshly painted signs in French. I even noted a French doctor and boot maker, but spied no lawyers or notaries though I knew from passenger lists on mining company boats that many had come to San Francisco.

I was surprised to see Manon and her companion wearing everyday bonnets that hid each woman's glorious head of hair. Their bonnets bobbed excitedly as they chatted intently. I knew a plot was brewing when Manon spotted me and winked.

"Ah cheri, you are spying on us, yes?"

"No, but there is mischief in the air. I never thought to see you disguised as a "haus frau." I said pointing to her new bonnet.

"But this is for you, cheri. All the men look at me from top to bottom, and when they see no ring on my finger, they make very crude suggestions and offer lots of dollars for my services," she said with a wicked grin and toss of her bonnet.

I thought of the attractive young woman flirting and displaying her wares for an ounce of gold in the gambling palace. Winsome women must be in short supply and in high demand.

"I believe you have earned yourself a pretty gold ring this morning," I said with a low bow to both ladies.

"Yes, even I had to brush off would-be Romeos and I am clearly married," Giselle piped in displaying her expensive wedding band set with a large emerald. "The milliner where we bought our bonnets said that until recently there were very few women for all the men in town and just two classes of women — married or prostitutes. She said even the women who work in the gambling houses will sell themselves if the offer is high enough," she said suddenly shy after her bold assertion.

"We think it will cost you more than a gold ring to keep your Manon respectable, non?" Manon said with a giggle and laughter.

"I think we should order a bottle of champagne and ask to see the menu while you ladies fill me in on your scheming and my role in your plans." I motioned for the waiter to bring menus and the wine list.

While we dined on fresh oysters, a seafood salad and "calamari fritti" in the Italian style, Manon and Giselle revealed their planning. The girls were going to partner with me to establish Manon's cherished new restaurant and catering service. Manon would set the menus, cook initially until she could hire or train a cook to her liking. Both would develop contacts for fresh food sources and emphasize what was in season locally. Giselle would have access to her husband's wine at wholesale prices and hopefully with a period of grace to pay.

While we licked our fingers over the remains of our "millefeuilles," pastry desserts offered by the proprietor, a jovial, balding Frenchman from Rouen, I popped the key question, "And what is my little role in your project?"

They looked at each other sheepishly, then broke into girlish laughter as Manon nodded to Giselle to respond first. "You are to be our benefactor," she said stifling an urge to giggle.

"Manon couldn't resist a laugh. "Cheri, tu seras notre Papa Sucre," she said in French."

"Ah so, I'm to be your Sugar Daddy. How nice! My way of paying for your now highly appreciated services," I riposted tongue-in-cheek.

"Yes and you get to protect us from all these over-sexed men, non?" Manon said laying on the charm and shaking out her curly black locks from her bonnet. "You like the special privileges you get for free, yes?"

I chuckled to myself. I would need more than a revolver and Bowie knife to protect these two from all the potential predators lurking in this lawless city. "You ladies hold all the high cards. I submit." They both laughed and gave me a "we knew you would" look of mission accomplished.

We spent the rest of the afternoon looking for a suitable house to rent where we could live upstairs and use the ground floor for an office, a kitchen and possible store to sell our goods still awaiting inspection aboard The Flying Cloud. We were horrified to learn what the lodgings we thought we needed would cost if available. Two-room suites in office buildings without kitchens could be rented on a monthly basis for $150.00 a week. No houses such as we desired were available anywhere in the commercial center and would rent for $1,500 or more a month. The only thing available was a small cottage on a sandy, hilly lot well away from the commercial center at $350.00 month.

We also inquired about a suitable commercial location where Manon and Giselle could prepare and sell food as caterers. The few sites offered were prohibitively expensive and poorly situated. San Francisco real estate had been the object of intensive speculation since 1849. The established merchants had bought their lots and built with borrowed or family capital or newly made fortunes in gold. That wasn't an option for us. Hundreds of merchants and new immigrants were arriving monthly and driving up prices as they sought to establish themselves. We would have to stay in our hotel until we could execute plan B.

We celebrated Manon and Giselle's new partnership that evening at the French restaurant in the Hotel de la Fraternité where Giselle and her husband lodged. It was located on Kearny Street between Bush and Sutter Streets. The owner, Pierre Simeon, agreed to uncork some of Robert Gaillard's special wines without charge, so he could join us in tasting the special vintages waiting in the hold of The Flying Cloud. Pierre prepared a celebratory meal for the partners. We munched squab on toast and home-made duck paté with white Loire valley wines as starters, then roast chicken stuffed with minced pork as the main course with a Sancerre red wine and a vintage Gigondas from the Rhone Valley. Pierre offered us a chocolate cake for dessert which we enjoyed with champagne to finish off our evening.

Walking back Kearny Street to California, and then up to Dupont Street to avoid hangers on, riff-raff and cutpurses Georges had warned us congregate around Portsmouth Square at night looking for easy or drunk marks, we decided on the elements of our new plan that would occupy us in the coming days.

"INTERIOR OF THE ELDORADO" Gambling Palace in 1851.

"SAN FRANCISCO BEAUTIES —
The Celestial, The Senora, and Madame" in 1851.

California Gold Rush Journal

Chapter Twelve

San Francisco – May 2, 1851

After an early breakfast at Les Bons Amis bistro, Manon and Georges set out together to order business cards for me and Manon's new partnership with Giselle and a long list of errands including a trip to a jeweler to buy a wedding band for Manon. I set off to revisit The Flying Cloud to see when we might expect our goods to be transported to the Customs House.

I hailed First Officer Swen Peterson who was directing a crew of sailors to load a heavy safe onto the ship's launch while another group of sailors stood guard with rifles. He agreed to allow me to return on the launch with him in order to speak with Captain Richards.

Captain Richards invited me to take a coffee with him in his cabin for privacy. Sammy served us coffee and warm hot cross buns and threw me a round house grin signaling his pleasure to see me.

"Captain, I have a favor to ask." He nodded for me to continue.

"We have been unable to find suitable living and business accommodations in or near the commercial center. Prices are outrageous and well beyond our modest means. We have commercial goods to sell and Manon and Giselle Gaillard want to start a catering business and build it into a restaurant eventually. I thought perhaps we could purchase one of the smaller, abandoned ships in the harbor that have suitable officers cabins, crew quarters, a large galley for food prep and adequate space in the hold to accommodate our goods and rental space for other merchants. Do you think such a plan is feasible?"

"Yes. While many of the earlier arrivals are rotting badly due to neglect, there still are some of the smaller vessels that are sea worthy and would provide a few years service still."

"What sort of ship would you recommend?" I asked delighted with his response.

"Well, if it was me, I'd probably choose one of the English brigs. They were well-built and the officers' cabins generally well appointed. They've only two masts and required a much smaller crew than the barks with three masts. It's a shame they are being sold for their lumber. I heard the "Eliza" was being offered for $3,500.00 from the harbor master. She might be just the thing you need."

"Would it be possible to hire your launch and some crew to look at the Eliza, that is if you're not too busy."

"Actually, I'd like to look her over with you. We're stuck here for the moment and I'm bored. Several of our sailors jumped ship to try their luck at placer mining. My junior officers are interviewing sailors wanting to return to New York. They're a sorry lot. Worked their asses off in the mines and have nothing to show for it. In fact, if you buy the brig, I'll have them sail it to the pier to check their seamanship."

Captain Richards had First Officer Peterson prepare the launch for us. They would be taking on lots more gold for transport to New York but they needed to empty the hold of our goods first. The Eliza was out in the bay anchored in the lee of Yerba Buena Island. Captain Richards had the launch crew grapple a line to her deck and then two sailors rappelled up the rope to the deck. They lowered a rope ladder which we climbed to board the ship.

While Captain Richards checked the bilges for leaks and the state of the ship's sails and rigging, I inspected the officers' quarters. The Captain's cabin was double the size of Captain Richard's quarters on the Flying Cloud. The rest of the officers' cabins were four times more spacious than the hermit's cell we slept in for three months. The galley was big enough for three persons to work in. The dining room was roomy and well appointed. There was even a wine cellar with empty bottles. The forecastle had sixteen bunks and screws for additional sailors to hook hammocks. It was thumbs up for the accommodations.

Captain Richards pronounced the Eliza seaworthy for sailing to the wharf. Much of the sail was rotten due to rats and exposure to the elements..

"Will I have to buy sails to move her?"

"No. I'll put the new hires to work sewing sail to make a workable set for one mast. We need to keep them busy and away from the temptations of the city. We'll house them on the Eliza if you buy the ship."

Captain Richards dropped me off at the harbor master's office. I learned that he had a power of attorney to sell the Eliza for her owners in London. He promised he would find space on the long wharf to dock her though it wouldn't be cheap. I was sure he'd do the deal as he was probably getting a hefty commission on the sale and could gouge me on the wharf rent.

Next stop was my banker, Adams and Co. where I secured a bank draft for $3,500.00 payable to the harbor master who I had agreed to meet early on the morrow.

Georges met me at a prearranged café for a quick bite of lunch. My business cards would be available next morning. Manon was off with Giselle after a successful shopping spree.

After a late lunch, I made my way to the French Consulate located at the corner of Jackson and Mason Streets. Ignoring the long queue of supplicants, I strode straight to the head of the line. The pudgy, hoarse-voiced official was waving his arms wildly and berating a sorry looking woman who looked to be consumptive. I barged past him and on to an officious looking young man busy cleaning his nails at his desk.

"I am an investigator for the principals of La Californienne Mining Society. I have come from Paris to meet with Consul Patrice Dillon. He should be expecting me. I need an appointment to see him tomorrow so I can leave for the placers as soon as possible to assist those members who are destitute."

The young official flicked shut the blade of his "Laguiole" pocket knife before replying. "That's most irregular. The Consul is a very busy man. It normally takes a least a week for an appointment after a written request is submitted and approved," he said dismissively.

"Emile Beauchamp? That's your name is it?" I said pointing to a name plate on his desk. "I'm afraid I will have to report your insolence and delay of my mission to the Foreign Minister when I return to Paris," I added waving a letter with a large wax seal past his nose.

"Err…perhaps I should take your letter to the Vice Consul. Consul Dillon is not here this afternoon," he stammered, his face flushed and clearly alarmed.

"The letter is highly sensitive and confidential. My instructions are to give it only to Consul Dillon. Perhaps you'd like to reexamine the Consul's appointment calendar with the Vice Consul before I file an official complaint," I said throwing him a steely-eyed, piercing look.

Beauchamp scuttled off hurriedly. After a brief consultation with another consular official in a private office, he returned and handed me an engraved appointment card with a

2:30 P.M. appointment penned in a shaky hand. I chuckled to myself. The scared pup had forgotten even to ask my name. I plucked a quill pen from the inkwell on his desk and printed my name on the appointment form, then wrote it again on a slip of paper and handed it to him.

"Perhaps you should enter my name on the Consul's appointment ledger so he knows who he is to meet," I said as he blushed beet red at his gaffe. I dropped the quill on his desk and watched him wince as a large blob of black ink spread on the highly polished desk as I took my leave.

Manon and Georges were very excited at the prospect of living on our ship and quitting our cramped quarters in the hotel. We deferred any celebration until it was a done deal.

Manon did flash me a devilish smile as she flaunted her new gold ring set with a big cabochon emerald. "So cheri. You like my new married look, non? It goes nice with my new bonnet, yes?"

I didn't dare say what I really thought. "I am surprised you went for an emerald. A black stone would complement the fire in your eyes so much better." I hedged.

"Yes, but we have new status to maintain now we own a boat, non?"

I had no retort for the clever lady. So, I just nodded my head in agreement. You don't win many arguments with Manon once she knows what she wants.

After a simple dinner of local mussels and trout, we spent the rest of the evening planning our move.

California Gold Rush Journal

CHAPTER THIRTEEN

San Francisco — May 3, 1851

The harbor master was delighted to get his check and tender a bill of sale. He probably thought I was a sucker and knew I wasn't a sailor. He must have doubted I could get the Eliza to the long wharf anytime soon because he agreed to provide a berth in the middle of the long wharf for $250.00 a month starting May 1st. He was surprised when I plunked $250.00 in $10.00 gold coins on his desk and asked for a receipt for May's rent. I then informed him that Captain Richards of the Flying Cloud would be sailing my ship and planned to berth it within the next two days. The harbor master's smile evaporated. He had to figure out how to make room for our ship on a crowded wharf.

I sent Georges to the Flying Cloud to inform Captain Richards of our successful purchase and a request to accelerate the preparation to move the Eliza and allow Manon and Giselle to accompany his crew to inspect our ship. My next stop was at the customs house to lobby for a quick inspection of our goods still aboard the Flying Cloud and permission to transfer our merchandise to the Eliza. After showing the bill of sale, I was begrudgingly informed that customs would consider my requests.

After a quick lunch, Manon and Georges headed to the wharf to meet Captain Richards and I headed for the French

Consulate. Consular Officer Beauchamp gave me a sour look as I strolled past him with a little swagger to my step. Consul Dillon had me wait a good half hour before deigning to have me led into his plush office.

He was tall and suave looking and dressed for lunch at the Tour D'Argent Restaurant in Paris. He looked up at me from behind gold spectacles perched on his aristocratic nose, then at my calling card fresh from the printer and gave me a hard look. "What can I do for you Mr. DuBois? I don't have a lot of time to spend with you," he said dismissively.

"I see your staff did not inform you of my mission. I'm here to conduct an investigation into why emigrants of La Californienne Mining Society arrived in San Francisco destitute," I said evenly and handed him my authorization signed by Jules Favre, chief lawyer for the society.

"Ah yes, a sad affair," he replied tapping his fingers as he read my power of attorney. "Sorry if I seemed a bit put off, but I had no idea of who you are or why my staff booked your appointment."

"I'm afraid your Mr. Beauchamp made a snap judgment about me and my mission and deemed the matter too trivial to be of interest to you," I said giving the young official tit for tat.

"Then why did he give you an urgent appointment?" Dillon said letting a quizzical frown pinch his face.

"Simple. I suggested Jules Favre had important contacts in the Foreign Minister's office and might be inclined to have him recalled and sacked for impeding my investigation that affects the reputation of some highly placed individuals and will undoubtedly lead to distasteful and distracting litigation."

Consul Dillon raised his eyebrows and regarded me warily. "It seems that the chickens are coming home to roost on this matter."

"Yes. Fraudulent promotion and abandonment of innocent

emigrants doesn't have a nice ring to it, does it?

"No, but there are other considerations that must be factored in. The French government wants to encourage emigration to California. That is our present goal. Gold aside, California is rich in natural resources — fertile valleys, abundant wild life and fish, towering forests, plentiful water, protected harbors, a mild climate and most importantly no significant population. Now with gold fever to excite the imagination, we can encourage emigration here as well as we do in Algeria to establish our presence here to develop commerce and ultimately see some of the wealth of the land return to France," he said smugly.

"So the ends justify the means?"

"That's not what I'm saying. The discovery of gold has accelerated the process. Emigrants from all over Europe are flocking to California and many who are successful in the gold fields will bring their riches home. Many have already returned to France wealthy men. Our French merchants in San Francisco are selling French goods and our merchant ships bring goods and emigrants. That's our real mission here: develop commerce and assist our people to establish a French presence here."

"Even though we're not wanted here by the Americans?"

"That's a different issue. There were Russian outposts on the California coast for their trappers and Spanish missions and ranchos before the Americans even heard of California. Sutter was Swiss and encouraged sailors and people from the Sandwich Islands to work his fields, vineyards and tend his cattle. But gold has changed all that."

"Is that why the United States sent its military to oust the Spanish and declare California a state?"

"In large part it was the gold, but gold fever in New York and New Orleans is as strong as it is in France. American emigration won't stop. They've been absorbing Europe's poor for

over a hundred years with the promise of free land to homestead and pushing westward relentlessly. Napoleon stupidly
sold off our Louisiana to the Americans for a pittance just to finance another losing war. And American settlers from our former territories on the Ohio and Mississippi Rivers have been
streaming westward in increasing numbers since news of the
gold strike. Even many of our own trappers from Canada came
to California before the discovery of gold."

"Were they successful in the mines?"

"Yes, very. For example, many French were in northern California when word of the strike reached them. They deployed
immediately along the Yuba and Feather rivers and many were
very successful when the gold was easy to mine and plentiful.
One of the most successful was Charles Covillaud, who with
partners hit a rich gold vein. He bought property, married an
American girl and established the town of Marysville which he
named after his new spouse."

I recalled the story Louis Magne told me. "This is the same
town where you sent the first group of emigrants from the La
Californienne Society who arrived on the "Jacques Laffitte?"

"Yes. Once I was able to get them off the ship and on the
way to the mines, we sent them north to Marysville where
there was an established French presence and from there they
could join other French miners on the north and south forks
of the Yuba River where they could be supplied by the towns of
Nevada City and Grass Valley.

"I was able to interview some members of the first party to
arrive here. They stated there were no company representatives
to meet them and they were left to fend for themselves. Is that
accurate?"

Dillon paused before answering as we were approaching the
heart of my inquiry. "Yes, there was no ground support. The consulate had to advance the needy ones funds to disembark with

their gear and arrange transport to the mines as I have indicated."

"And most of the steerage passengers who had borrowed money by mortgaging their houses or inheritances for the trip were forced to borrow money from the consulate and do menial labor on the docks or in town until they could repay the loan and save enough to support themselves for a period at the mines, correct?"

"That's true for some of the emigrants," he hedged.

"I was told that was the case for all but a few. Was I misinformed?"

"Well now that I think about it, you're probably right. It was quite some time ago and there have been thousands of arrivals since." I decided to not quibble over "probably right" and shift focus to what might help Jules Favre.

"What about the leaders of the mission? I believe the head was a former mayor of a French town and there were civil mining engineers and other professionals to lead the emigrants to the placers and direct the mining. Did they not make some effort to keep the group together for the joint venture?"

Dillon laughed and appeared to lighten up. "A ship of fools leading poor lambs. When they learned there was no ground support, they headed right for the booking offices to secure passage home."

"Do you think they had no prior knowledge they would have no ground support?"

"I'm sure they wouldn't have undertaken the rigors of the voyage had they known the true facts. Even with ground support, their mission would have flopped. The mining engineers had limited experience with placer mining or how to extract gold from quartz veins and the poorer passengers, who were from rural farming communities for the most part, had even less idea of how to mine or the hardships they would have to endure once they reached the placers."

"Did they tell you that the mining society had represented in its prospectus that it owned gold and silver properties in the Sierra Nevada the emigrants would work and they'd be supported with food and shelter for up to two years until they made their fortune?"

"No. That's a new one and I've heard a lot of tall tales. When the offer is too good to be true, it's not."

"Did any of the expedition leaders offer to help their fellow countrymen get to the placers?"

Dillon guffawed. "Not only did they do nothing to help, they berated us and claimed it was our fault for not informing them in advance of the true conditions awaiting them in San Francisco. The mayor threatened to have us all recalled and held accountable for his lost time making the voyage and his personal expenses. It was lamentable."

"Was it any different with the next three ships the society sent?"

"No, not really, except we were better prepared to handle the situation. The second ship like the first had an expedition leader and a doctor and other professionals at its head. They, too, were ignorant of the situation and thought the first group would have laid a red carpet for them to follow. We rented a boat to convey the passengers who still wanted to try their luck at mining up to Sacramento and then on to Modesto or Marysville where they could reach French mining camps since hardly any could speak English. The third and fourth ships had no leaders; they were just loaded with emigrants. We told them what the situation was. There were good jobs for carpenters, masons, carters, lumbermen and fishermen in and around the city. Some French had come in search of rich farming land and were now expanding their crops in the fertile valley between San Francisco and San Jose to meet the food needs of the cities and the miners. Most with needed skills, including farming and animal husbandry, forsook mining and went to work for wages."

"Was it the same with the other mining societies that sold shares in joint ventures and lured would-be miners to emigrate?"

"Yes, indeed. We've been swamped with misinformed and unhappy emigrants who were led to believe they would be able pick up gold nuggets along the banks of rivers. It's been pretty much the same with all the societies that raised money by selling shares to the innocent or the greedy. 'L'Espérance, Le Nouveau Monde, L'Aurifère, and a host of others like 'La Californienne.'"

"Has the situation been reported to the Foreign Ministry?"

"Of course, the government is fully informed."

"Then why is it not stopped?" I said incredulously.

"It's not within our power stop the emigration. Mining societies raise capital and encourage exploitation of the placers. If there is some fraud, it will have to be settled in the courts," Dillon said with a big smile that signaled the interview was over.

I had most of the useful information I needed for my report which certainly wouldn't exonerate the boss' client, but wouldn't hurt him either unless he had worked actively with the society's promoters. I could argue for a stronger government response but to what avail? The government wanted poor folks and trouble makers to emigrate abroad. So, I opted for a graceful exit instead. I would need to work with Consul Dillon as long as I was here, so there was nothing to be gained by burning my bridges prematurely.

"I really appreciate the time you've spent with me and my client will be pleased to learn that the first ship's sad experience was not the same as the later ships. I will need an affidavit signed by the consulate covering what we have discussed. I trust that won't be a problem."

Consul Dillon hesitated a flicker of a second. "Why don't

you draft your report and I'll review it for accuracy. When we're agreed on the language then we can affix the consulate's seal."

A clever, cautious reply but expected. I preferred to write the account in any case so all the relevant issues were addressed. I would have to balance criticism of the society with praise for the Consul's efforts to assist the emigrants. That would be the price for the seal. My boss would be irate that I could not provide exoneration here, but events here didn't prove fraud on the part of those leading the expedition. Jules Favre had lent his prestigious name as lawyer to the incorporating documents and the prospectus. His defense was in Paris and depended on how much he knew or ought to have known of the fraudulent scheme to sell shares to mine non-existent properties in California.

I planned to delay sending my report as long as possible by haggling for the consulate's seal and it would go by the slowest French boat I could find. I would go to Marysville and visit the French mining camps in search of the society's expedition members who had decided to mine. Meanwhile, we had businesses to start and not more than six months to become profitable before my boss cut off our funds.

After leaving the consulate, I headed back up to Dupont Street, found a hole-in-the wall café and installed myself at a back booth with a carafe of white wine and large cigar to write a draft of the document I would eventually submit to Dillon while our interview was fresh in my mind. We had arranged a special dinner at Pierre-Louis' bistro, Les Bons Amis, to celebrate purchase of the ship and the women's new venture. Pierre-Louis knew some hunters who'd promised him a wild boar and a brace of pheasants for our gala.

California Gold Rush Journal

CHAPTER FOURTEEN

San Francisco — May 3 & 4, 1851

Pierre-Louis outdid himself preparing our celebratory meal despite Manon having turned down his offer to run and expand his bistro. He wanted Manon to help with menus and serve as hostess to attract a more cosmopolitan clientele from among the bankers, speculators, real estate moguls, and moneyed crowd of nouveau riche. Like most of the businesses along Dupont Street run by the French, the owners and help didn't speak English and their clientele was mostly French with some Belgians, Chileans and Mexicans on occasion.

Pierre-Louis arranged to have the wild pig roasted on a spit by some Chinese he knew for a portion of the animal. On Manon's advice, he basted the pheasants in olive oil, then added sliced potatoes and cabbage and let it bake slowly. We splurged with vintage reds from the Rhone Valley. We were all excited by our prospects. Manon and Georges loved our ship and our new spacious quarters. Manon was already scouting for ovens she could install in the forecastle. The ship still had some seasoned wood for the cooking stoves and Manon had a long list of supplies she needed. She had sweet-talked Captain Richards to accelerate the preparation to move her ship in the next two days.

Georges also was pumped at the thought of moving into an officer's stateroom after sleeping on the floor of the hotel with three snoring, noisy, inebriated roommates who usually slept in their boots. He was making noises about sending for his sweet Nelly now that he had private quarters. He'd started pestering Manon for a commitment that Nelly could help in her catering business until they figured out what they wanted to do. He had been inquiring about travel to San Francisco via Panama.

A few glasses of wine washed away Giselle's normal reserve. She, too, was loudly and gaily celebrating her new independence to work for herself which was guaranteed in California by the new legislature but not in France. With so many single men in the state and a dearth of women to marry, the legislature had wisely decided that all assets a woman owned prior to marriage and earned during marriage would remain her separate property. This revolutionary change in a woman's legal status was designed to attract rich women and wives for the young, single miners and encourage couples to settle permanently in California.

Once the news hit Europe, it prompted a wave of female emigration. Mothers with marriageable daughters, widows, adventuresses, and Jezebels were now arriving in San Francisco in droves to snag a successful miner or businessman. Giselle's husband, Robert, didn't appear too happy at his wife's exuberance for independence, but he wisely decided to grin and bear it.

Our appetites sated on the delicious meal, we were now enjoying after dinner drinks and cigars when we heard a loud hue and cry from the direction of Portsmouth Square. Probably just a ruckus between drunken gamblers and a gang of Sydney Ducks, mostly ex-cons, who had emigrated from Australia to mine the pockets of the unwary on the streets of San Francisco.

The frantic pealing of Church bells brought looks of concern. All diners and even Pierre-Louis rushed outside. There was a large plume of heavy black smoke being billowed by a blustery wind from the Clay Street side of Portsmouth Square. As we watched in horror, the site of the flames exploded and shot fire and shrapnel in all directions. Almost immediately several wooden roofs were alight and the wind driven fire was moving swiftly toward Commercial and Sacramento Streets and the heart of the downtown business district. The clanging of fire wagons was drowned out by the loud popping and crackling explosions in the wake of the fast spreading fire. It looked unstoppable.

"My god," cried Giselle. "It's going burn our hotel. What can we do?"

"Best stay right here and be prepared to run for your life if the wind shifts," cautioned Pierre-Louis. "I've seen this kind of fire before and there's no way to stop it with water hoses or bucket brigades. The fire brigades will need to blow up houses and shops in its path to keep it from spreading and maybe light a backfire. But the wind is very strong now and subject to shift at any time. The fire could turn back on us, so be prepared."

Looking at Manon and me, he warned, "Better go down the street to your hotel and gather up valuables you don't want to lose." To Robert and Giselle, "You two better stay here until the fire is out. The streets near the fire will be too dangerous to travel. If the Ducks set the fire, they'll be busy looting; they'll harm or rob anyone in their way."

While Manon, Georges and I dashed to our hotel to gather valuables, Pierre-Louis ordered all cooking fires extinguished and his safe dragged to the bistro's cellar. Dupont Street was a blur of frenzied activity as the residents scurried to and fro with sacks and even wheel barrows loaded with goods as they deliberated where to run if the wind changed. We rejoined our friends at the bistro and hunkered down to await events.

As the night wore on, we could see the inferno spreading

like a giant red octopus. Tentacles of fire were approaching the long, central wharf. Bush, Sansome and Washington Streets were roaring furnaces. The wind would not abate. We heard the gambling houses and the Adelphi Theatre on the Clay side of Portsmouth Square crumble one by one. Horses in burning stables shrieked in frenzied fear while others bolted wildly through the streets seeking refuge. It was bedlam.

Pierre-Louis was a steadying influence. He laid his loaded, double-barreled shotgun on the bar counter next to a box of cartridges. His cook and waiter were both armed with pistols and knives. They were ready to confront looters and protect their clients. We considered returning to our hotel, but were counseled against it. If we fell asleep in our garret, we would be trapped by fire if the wind shifted. Pierre-Louis had the dining tables cleared, rounded up some blankets and we tried vainly to sleep on the tables or in our chairs while Pierre-Louis and his staff took turns standing guard.

By daybreak the worst was over. The horrendous sounds of buildings exploding and cries of grief and fear had given way to a disconcerting calm. The wind had died only to be replaced by a wet fog. After a breakfast of hot coffee and stale bread, we decided to tour what was left of our city. If the long wharf had been destroyed, we had no place to berth our ship.

The Clay Street side of Portsmouth Square was now reduced to steaming ashes. The lavish gambling parlors and theatres were gone. Only a few rooming houses on the west and east side of the square remained standing. Desperate owners and employees raked still smoldering ashes trying to recover their gold and silver before the scavengers arrived. One chap found a lump of molten, misshaped gold coins and quickly shoveled it into a bucket which he quickly covered with a layer of ash.

The entire downtown, merchant area was completely destroyed; even the brick buildings had succumbed to the inferno when super heated flames attacked their roof beams and wooden balconies. Scorched printing presses, wood stoves, metal bed frames and a host of other fire blistered objects were all that remained. A silent, sober army of merchants toiled with rakes and shovels in the rubble while others tore their hair and wailed. All was lost. Most would be wiped out unless they had ample capital reserves or lines of credit with which to rebuild. If not, they'd have to sell their lots for passage home.

I, too, was concerned about my gold coins in the basement safe of Adams & Co. While Manon and I surveyed the damage down Washington Street to the bay, Georges did reconnaissance of the banks along Commercial Street. With all the tall buildings burned to the ground, we could see that at least part of the Central Wharf was still standing and some tall ships still berthed on it. As we arrived at the bay line amid the charred rubble of all the dockside warehouses and their contents, we were astonished to see our Eliza berthed on the wharf about a hundred yards from the bay shore and the Flying Cloud bobbing gently behind her. Sailors were busy emptying the hold of the Flying Cloud and transferring the cargo to the Eliza.

We hailed First Officer Peterson who was shouting orders for the line of carters to hurry with their loads from one ship to the other. He paused long enough to indicate with a wave of hand we should make our way to Captain Richards' cabin.

Captain Richards greeted us with a roguish smile. "Nice piece of work, aay?"

A queen bee could have started a new hive in my open, bewildered mouth. "I don't understand how you got the Eliza here," I stammered.

He chortled. "Piece of cake. When the fire broke out, we knew by the direction of the strong wind that the fire would sweep down to the wharves and consume them if action was not taken promptly. We sailed our launch to the wharf and warned the ships berthed on her to put to sea or risk being set on fire. Before long, almost all ships that could sail were anchored a safe distance away in the bay. We then organized the desperate folks remaining on the wharf into a work gang. We tore up the planks of the wharf from where they connected to land and on back far enough to make a fire break to save the wharf. Once we saw the fire couldn't jump to the wharf, I ordered the launch back to the Flying Cloud with instructions to raise anchor on the Eliza and sail her to the wharf where you see her; we sailed our ship in and docked her behind so we could transfer cargo. We wanted to get a good berth before the others returned."

"Brilliant," I managed to mutter.

"So, Captain, how long will you stay with us?" Manon asked.

"Just long enough to transfer cargo from one ship to another and get us loaded for the trip home. We've been stuck here far too long and with the fire, who knows how functional the customs folks will be. They'll take care of their own skins before getting any work done."

I finally grasped what he was doing. "So you are transferring all the Flying Cloud's cargo to the Eliza and not just our goods. Customs will have to clear the cargo from our ship rather than yours."

"Yes, I'll notify the harbor master if I can find him. The claim will be of necessity. Almost all the dock warehouses have been destroyed. There's probably no empty space to unload and store for customs. They'll have no choice but to inspect aboard the Eliza. You should be able to charge premium rates for goods stored in your hold."

"We are deeply indebted to you Captain for your foresight and quick action to save the wharf and get our ship moved here. How can we ever repay you?"

"Have your wine merchant friend break out a case or two of his good red wine for our trip home. That'll go nicely with the delicious recipes Manon taught Sammy. Sammy will exchange the wine for some food staples you'll need to tide you over until you can get supply lines going. Fortunately, we've stocked more than we will need to get to Valparaiso and can sail as soon as the last gold is secure in our hold."

Manon was beaming with pleasure and stayed to hobnob with Sammy while I returned to the Eliza to locate our trunks and personal affairs to set up house. This was going to be an exciting and perhaps difficult time in the aftermath of the fire which had consumed just over twenty square blocks of the downtown commercial center including the customs house and its warehouses.

"GREAT FIRE IN SAN FRANCISCO,"
from *Gleason's Pictorial Magazine, 1851.*

"SAN FRANCISCO FIRE OF MAY 3-4, 1851"

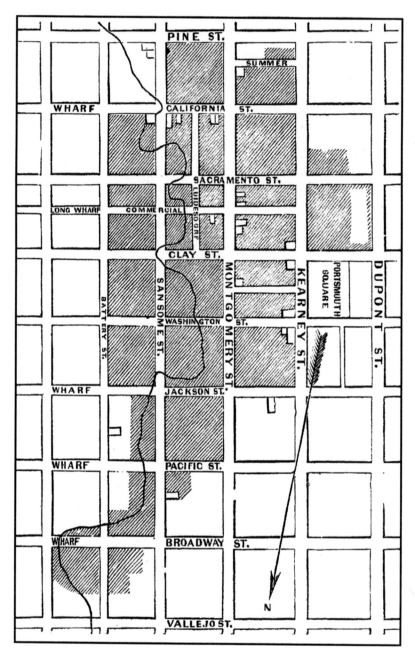

"MAP OF BURNT DISTRICT OF MAY 3-4, 1851"

California Gold Rush Journal

CHAPTER FIFTEEN

San Francisco — May 4, 1851

Manon was beaming after her consultation with Sammy. He'd agreed to supply her kitchen with enough staples to cook for us and start her business. After all the cargo was loaded, the Flying Cloud's sailors wheeled over two barrels of Chilean flour, a hogshead of molasses, a small barrel of cane sugar and one of rice, two damme-jeannes of olive oil, three dozen fresh eggs, assorted spices and other staples.

Georges showed up with the welcome news that Adams & Co.'s offices had been spared the fire. Next a frenzied Giselle arrived in tears. In between sobs she announced that her husband's co-owned wine store had burned with all its contents. Her husband was distraught and feared they were ruined. His Chilean partner, Raoul, had been living in an apartment above the store with his girlfriend, Teresa, and now they were homeless. Giselle was sobbing so hard, Manon had to comfort her until she could continue her story.

When Giselle regained her composure, she told us that she and her husband's hotel had been spared the inferno, but they were afraid to stay there. Destitute and homeless, desperados stalked residents to rob them. Some shopkeepers were keeping their stores shuttered out of fear of continued looting.

At this news, Georges piped in, "I heard it were the Sydney Ducks what started the fire. They says one of the Ducks was seen leaving a paint store on Clay Street opposite the Plaza, then whoosh it went up in smoke seconds later. The fire went ragin' with all the paint and oils in the store, then the whole building exploded and spread the fire to everything nearby."

"Did they catch him?" I asked

"Dunno, but they know for a fact that the Sydney Ducks was real busy lootin' and robbin' most of the night. So, they're sure it was the Ducks what set the fire. The guy what told me said no sooner did a merchant run to help fight the fire or leave with valuables than a group of Ducks looted his store."

"Are you sure none of the Ducks were arrested?" I asked in disbelief.

"Was too much going on I heard. Most of the police, firemen and residents was tryin' to fight the fire and other folks lookin' to save themselves and their valuables. Heard some fellows got themselves set on fire trying to go back into burning houses. Some was rollin' in the muddy gutters cuz their clothes was on fire."

"Good lord. We were right to stay off the streets last night. Looks like mob rule is the order of the day. No wonder you guys are scared," I said pointing to Giselle.

"How did they stop the fire?" I asked Georges.

"Dunno. Heard it burned until about 7 A.M. and finally burned itself out. People was going crazy all night. One fellow shot his brains out when his house and business went up in smoke. They say another man shot and killed a Mexican woman for no reason and another killed his wife and kids, then his self 'cause they was ruined."

"What about the Ducks. Did the fire burn any of them out?" I asked

"That's what's worrying some. They say a big part of

Sydneytown burned and they're afraid of revenge by the Ducks.

"Let's hope they stop these maniacs before they turn on us just because we are foreigners.

"It's apparent that we face a lawless period where the gun is king and the mob rules," I said to no one in particular.

"Do you think you and your husband would like to rent one of the officer's cabins on our ship?" I asked Giselle. "We'll probably all be safer here than in town until the governor sends some troops to secure the city. At least we can pull the gangway up at night."

"An' we could get a guard dog, too. Maybe one that can catch rats and earn his keep, non?" Giselle said.

"An' let's get some shotguns to defend our ship," added Georges.

After conferring with Manon about renting the officer's cabin to the Gaillards, we sent Georges with Giselle back to her hotel to find and discuss the offer with Robert.

After they left, Manon and I seized the moment to review our situation and her business plan.

"I think perhaps we should rent all the officers quarters to people we plan to work with. But that means cooking for them, what do you think? Do we really want so many people living here?" I said.

"Yes, better to have Giselle here because we have to do food prep early. Now Robert has no store to sell his wine, we can sell it from the boat, yes?"

"How do you mean?"

"We put up our tent in front of the ship in the morning an' we have two stands — one for breakfast and lunch snacks I make with Giselle an' in the other one we sell wine by the glass to the sailors, dock workers, and passengers who take the ferry to Sacramento. Maybe Robert wants to sell also by the glass. He'll make more money that way. We use the Paris bistro glasses, you know the heavy ones that don't hold too much wine.

Robert can make a list of his wines and he can also sell directly to restaurants." Manon said in an excited rush.

"Who's going to sell the wine by the glass?"

"Well, I think maybe Robert's partner, Raoul, could sell wine at the stand. He knows the wines an' he needs a job, non?"

"And, it would provide a male presence at the stand to keep unwelcome paws off the cooks," I noted with a bemused smile.

"Yes, an' maybe Raoul's girlfriend like to work too. She could help in the kitchen, fetch supplies and if she's pretty, maybe sell at the stand."

"Sounds like you are planning to rent the last officer's cabin, well?"

"Well yourself. It makes sense, no? We start early so this way we have all the staff here. Tents get set up an' workers on the wharf don't have to stop at a bistro or look for a baker. We provide tasty snacks for breakfast and lunch and they wash it down with Chilean wine, yes?"

"What sort of gourmet snacks do you have up your sleeve?"

"I talked to Pierre-Louis. He knows hunters. They're gonna provide me with wild meat and poultry. They hunt deer, antelope, wild pig, pheasant, quail, turkeys and rabbit. We make patés and sausages for sale and for sandwiches. An' we make a hearty soup with lentils and meat. All fresh an' very tasty. We prepare the evening meal with the best meats and fowl for us. With our "table d'hôte" we rent our cabins at a higher rate for room and board, non? Dinner from 8PM to 10PM and then lights out in the dining room; smelly cigars on the poop deck, yes?"

"You certainly are a clever cookie, Manon. Won't it be too much to work early for the morning trade and do a dinner for seven or eight people?"

"Not really. We do all the cooking in the morning. We reheat for dinner. That's why I think of Raoul's girlfriend. If they stay here, we have extra help in the kitchen and with clean-up after dinner, non?"

"Let's hope our friends like to wake up early to work. Giselle and Robert never were the first ones at breakfast on the Flying Cloud were they?"

"You, too, cheri. No lounging around in bed when Manon has to start work. You have to get the kitchen fire going, while I prepare food, yes? How the English say it, 'What's good for the goose, good for the gander,' eh." Manon was shaking her finger like a momma scolding a bad boy.

Another round lost. I could only hope the others were willing to get on Manon's early morning wagon. No place here for a Lazy Thomas. By the time Manon finished the rest of her marching orders for her new business, Georges was back with Giselle and a cart with their personal belongings. We helped her stow her affairs in her cabin.

"Pierre, Robert is delighted to have us move to the ship. It's where his wine is stored and where I'll work with Manon. He's very concerned about Raoul and his friend, Teresa. They must find a place to stay. Do you think they could bunk in the crew's quarter's until they find a safe place to rent? They're willing to pay. The store is gone but Raoul has some money in the bank and can get a letter of credit for a new shipment of Chilean wine and start a new business." Giselle's pretty hazel eyes pleaded. Manon gave me an "I told you so" look.

While Manon excused herself to change to go to town with Georges and a cart to buy fresh food at the farmer's market over by the Mission, I quickly laid out Manon's business plan and the Chilean couple's role if they were in agreement.

Giselle gave a great sigh of relief. "Oh, I'm sure they would love to join our venture. It's so traumatic to lose everything in the fire. They only have the clothes on their back. I'm sure you'll like them. They'll be relieved to have a place to stay with us and a job. Will they get the remaining officer's cabin? They'll be so happy to have a safe haven."

Manon suddenly and dramatically reappeared. "What you think, huh?" She did a pirouette, then a deep bow and hearty laugh. "Every ship need one more sailor, yes?" We all cracked up. Georges was laughing so hard he was choking. Manon was dressed like an American sailor. Long bell bottom trousers over soft boots, rough, loose fitting cotton shirt with blue and red scarf around her neck. She'd somehow managed to contain and stuff most of her lush, curly black mane into her large sailor's cap and the rest hung down her back in a tight pigtail. Funniest of all was the handle of a knife peeking out of a boot and the big caliber marine's pistol stuck into the front of her black belt.

"What a pretty sailor boy," I said. "You'll have to be careful not to be Shanghaied onto someone's boat," I said tongue-in-cheek. She would be subject to arrest for wearing men's pants if someone saw through the disguise.

"Pretty good, huh," she retorted. "Mess with me an' I shoot to kill," and her flashing black eyes meant it. I realized we'd need to spend some time doing target practice off the stern to make good her threat, though a sharp boot knife in a chef's hand would be dangerous deterrent to an aggressor.

Manon danced off in her new disguise with Georges to shop for food while Giselle and I unpacked boxes of kitchen goods, the tents and goods we'd bought to sell. Customs would have to get moving if they wanted to nail us for our goods. Manon's business plan called for retail to start at the foot of our gangplank next day with wine by the glass.

Manon and Georges returned with the cart overflowing with fresh vegetables, a side of deer, 6 chickens, sacks of potatoes, milk, bottled mineral water and large bottles of spring water for cooking. She and Giselle fired up the galley's stoves. Georges returned to town to fetch Robert, Raoul, Teresa and their goods. Our ship was going to be a beehive of activity for the next few days.

California Gold Rush Journal
Chapter Sixteen
San Francisco – May 5, 1851

Manon poked me hard, then whipped off the duvet and attacked my toes. I moaned as the clammy cold morning air sent a shiver through me.

"Come on lazy bones. You gotta fire to light in my kitchen. No coffee for the lazy."

"I'd rather light one in your bed. Can't we start our chores a little later?" I muttered still drowsy and missing my sweet dreams.

"Hey Buster. This is not Paris with bars and bistros to make your coffee and serve croissants. We gotta work hard to make a living. So get a move on." She gave me a little buss on the lips and pointed to our bed. "Tonight if you're a good boy." She left me to struggle into my cold clothes and big sweater.

We'd had a late night celebrating our new digs and plan to inaugurate our new enterprises. Raoul and Teresa showed up for dinner dragging suitcases of newly bought clothes. Raoul was tall, suave and sported a nicely trimmed Van Dyke goatee. He had a winning smile to go with his tawny colored skin and long-ish black hair tied in a bob. He was in his early thirties. Teresa had attractive, Spanish features — milky blue eyes, blond hair worn in a pony tail, and skin the hue of light olive oil. Her ample figure would assure male interest despite her attempt to hide it in loose fitting garments. She looked to be twenty four or five. They were both outgoing with eyes that sparkled when they laughed. They both appeared ambitious and pleased to work with us. Teri, as she liked to be called, and Manon hit it off immediately.

Needless-to say, all the men had drunk too much of Robert's good, heavy red wines long past midnight and my head was as heavy as a lead bonnet this morning. Still I managed to light the stoves so Manon could heat the large pots of soup she had made yesterday as well as start the dark roast Mexican coffee I needed to face the rigors of our first day's business on the wharf.

Robert and Raoul also had been rousted from their beds and together we struggled to lower the gangway to the wharf and put up two large tents alongside our ship. We rolled empty barrels down the gangway and set them up with large planks across to make tables. One tent would serve as bar and wine shop and the other a canteen. Teri arrived with welcome mugs of dark black coffee. She then helped Raoul prepare the bar. Giselle organized the Canteen under Manon's supervision while I fired up two large braziers with cooking stove coals — one for hot coffee, the other for Manon's hearty meat and lentil soup. We were almost done when a gangly, pimply-faced youngster arrived with fresh baked baguettes, hearty bread and a tub of butter from Pierre-Louis' baker.

Manon chalked the day's menu on a large slate she placed on an artist's easel:

BREAKFAST MENU

Bowl of Hearty Meat Soup, Bread & Butter, Mug of Coffee *$1.00*

Buttered Bread with Paté & Mug of Coffee .... *50 Cents*

Bowl of Hearty Meat Soup .... *75 Cents*

Glass of Red or White Wine .... *50 Cents*

Mug of Coffee .... *25 Cents*

> ## Lunch Menu
> Venison Sandwich and Glass of Wine ....…… $1.00
> Meat Pie and Glass of Wine ....….............……… $1.00
> Bowl of Hearty Soup with Bread & Butter ....….. $1.00

As Raoul and Teri were used to measuring gold dust, flakes and the array of silver coins and bits in circulation, they set up our gold scales and handled payments. There were already several clients slurping soup and dropping bread bits in their bowls when I left to visit the mayor's office to secure a permit to sell on the wharf.

I learned from Consul Dillon that on April 9, 1851, the California Legislature passed a tax law discriminating against foreign miners. In addition to paying for their mining claims, foreign miners had to pay $20.00 a month for the privilege of extracting California's gold. The $20.00 a month tax also applied to non-U.S. citizens who wished to sell goods from a store or like us on the Central Wharf. Dillon advised me to pay the tax until the anti-foreigner clamor died down and the tax could be lowered or repealed. With the burning of the business district by the Australian Ducks gang and the loss of millions of dollars of uninsured inventory and property, it was no time to test Yankee animosity.

The mayor of the town was newly elected and was nominally in charge of the police. As the police were notoriously corrupt, even the Yankees avoided them and knew better than to rely on them for help.

City Hall was a hornet's nest of angry merchants seeking redress for the loss of their businesses. The new mayor was probably enjoying a late breakfast with his mistress or one of the ladies for hire in the best bordellos on Dupont Street. He'd left his minions to deal with the mad hatters while the police played cards for drinks and cigars.

My appearance drew immediate police interest. No doubt I looked an easy mark for a bribe. When I declined the offer to pay $25.00 for the selling permit and chose to wait in line for access to a clerk, the police dropped me and resumed their game. While waiting my turn, I tuned in to the buzz of excited chatter about the new Committee of Vigilance.

Apparently, Sam Brannan had this morning published a list of the Committee's members. One fellow ahead of me was reading out some of the nearly two hundred members to his companions. They were awed that almost all of the movers and shakers of the city were on the list.

After I'd forked over my blood money payment of $20.00 for the selling permit, I bought a copy of a local paper to read the news for myself at Les Bons Amis with more strong coffee and a cigar. The Committee's members included most of the town's most respectable, rich and prominent citizens who'd lead the vigilantes. The Committee was going to send death warnings to suspected crooks and all criminals were ordered out of town. Those who stayed would be hanged immediately if caught red-handed. They planned to board incoming ships at the Golden Gate to look for "criminal types" among the passengers. Those who could not prove they were "decent and honorable" were to be shipped back to where they came from. The rule of the Committee was to be "if they don't look right, git."

The whole business gave me the shivers. California was now a State in the Union and supposed to be bound by the U.S. Constitution's Bill of Rights which included protection from unlawful search and seizure, and the taking of life, liberty or property without due process of law. If the Committee of Vigilance decided I and my companions didn't "look right" according to the new demeanor test, could they tow our ship off the wharf and force us to set sail for France or Chile?

Why wasn't Governor John MacDougal sending federal

troops to quiet things down or warning the Committee it could be prosecuted for taking the law into its own hands? I shared my concerns with Pierre-Louis.

"Lots of angry merchants who lost considerable fortunes support the Committee because there is no effective rule of law in the city. If they let the Ducks off after torching the town, then they'll blackmail all the businesses to pay them protection money. You pay or we burn you out. Things have gotten out of hand so maybe it's not such a bad thing," he said.

"Aren't you afraid they'll turn on all foreigners like us," I said.

"Not really. The Yankees need foreign businessmen. They like our wines, liqueurs, food, and even our French accents when we speak English. They especially like our women. All the best gambling houses on the Square employ sexy French wenches to attract clientele. When they choose to, they can charge two or three hundred dollars for a one night stand with a newly rich miner or an established merchant or banker. I've heard tell of some of these ladies who serviced clients regularly when not working the tables or bar. Some even posted the hours they'd receive clients on their doors. A few have even married rich Yankees and others have made a fortune on their backs in a year and have returned home very rich."

"And with the new legislation allowing women to keep their earnings and inheritances, women looking for rich husbands are arriving in droves. But most miners go bust, don't they?" I added.

"Especially now the easy to mine gold is gone. It's really a rare lucky hit and mostly miss for the new arrivals. Most go bust and have to work on the docks for months to earn steerage passage and slink home with their tails between their legs like whipped curs. They're not going to get a wife here. Gonna be a lot of disappointed women arriving with so many bankrupted merchants and no place to stay after the fire. They'll have to find work or go home."

"So do you think the Committee's actions were necessary to protect merchants like us?"

"Yes, and if asked to, I'll join. Without law and order we will have nothing at the end. If the wind had turned, I have no bistro and lose everything. Hopefully, the Committee will run the rats out of town and we won't have another arsonist destroying our businesses."

Food for thought. I was glad we were on a ship. We needed to learn how to sail it into the bay in case there was another fire. Georges was right, we also needed to have an arsenal on the ship to repel thieves and possible rapists given the three attractive women in residence. I thanked Pierre-Louis for his assistance to Manon. He had arranged for me to be escorted by his Chinese food preparer and busboy the next day. Manon needed to establish a reliable source for fresh fish and workers to slow roast the wild game we would get from Pierre-Louis' French hunters and trappers.

On the way back to our ship, I visited the baker and prepaid delivery of bread for the rest of the week. I was surprised to see the level of activity in the burned out section I had to cross. Carts were lined up and being loaded with still warm rubble. A small army of laborers worked shoveling, raking and sifting debris. Others were cleaning and stacking reusable bricks and other building materials. Clearly, those with the means meant to rebuild as quickly as possible. Surveyors were placing stakes and contractors were studying plans.

Sailors were still loading The Flying Cloud. First Officer Peterson was in a heated argument with two bearded men in dirty ship officers' uniforms. The two were complaining loudly that both the Flying Cloud and Eliza usurped their places on the wharf. Peterson wasn't backing down.

"You fellows lost your wharf spots when you fled the fire. We stayed and saved the wharf, so we have priority. The Flying Cloud will sail tomorrow, so her space will be available."

"Yeah, but it wasn't with these ships. You guys came on your launch, not in your ship; so your argument is all bull shit," the tallest and grubbiest of the two yelled.

"If we hadn't saved the wharf, there wouldn't be anything to tie up to would there? The harbor master authorized both our ships to use these moorings, so if you're smart, you'll anchor next to the Flying Cloud to have the space tomorrow and put your other boat wherever it'll fit," Peterson countered.

"We paid our rent for May, so the space is ours," the shorter, paunchier one asserted.

"How much did you pay?" I piped in.

"What's that got to do with it?" The tall one snarled.

"Well, I was by the harbor master's office this morning and they said with the fire the old rents were no longer valid now that most of the warehouses had burned. Everybody has to negotiate the new rent and get a reallocated space. I had to pay $250.00 month for this space," I said pointing to the Eliza.

"Son of bitch," said the tall one biting on my hook. "Bastard's raisin' rents just like that to profit from the fire."

Peterson threw me a sly smile then added, "In that case, you boys better get your boats tied up any where they'll fit. Sounds like everyone's been dealt a new hand. Waiting for a spot tomorrow may be too late."

They both took off at a fast clip for their painters. We watched them row furiously for their sloops. They'd have to tie up way down the wharf as all the spots near us and close to the entrance to the town were already taken.

I thanked Peterson for his help. He said he'd arrange for a more compatible ship to dock near us and close to shore. He knew the captain of a ship used as a warehouse who would jump at the chance to get dock space so close to the entrance to town. I told him we would have letters for Valparaiso and New York to send with him. He would send a sailor for them in the morning. I knew the harbor master wouldn't move us. We were probably paying twice what the others paid.

I checked with Manon. She was making soup for the next day. It was nice and warm in her galley compared to the wharf where a cool breeze was undermining a weak sun.

"I sent Georges to get more meat. We sold all our soup and sandwiches and lots of wine. We'll need much more bread to-morrow. Since we sold all our food, maybe we should put out other merchandise for the afternoon. Georges can help you sell when he gets back. Giselle or Teri can help with set up, non?" She flashed me a winning smile. Finally, she was her own boss and had a money-making business.

"I'll send Georges back to the baker when he returns. What's for dinner?" I asked as I scooped up the sandwich she had saved for my lunch.

"You men just think about your stomach and how to get hard working women into your bed, right? Dinner will be a surprise. Now go make us some money and we'll see about the romance part later," she said with wink and a shooing motion. I laughed and threw her my most enticing smile.

Giselle had opened most of the wooden boxes containing the merchandise we had brought to sell. We lugged a selection down the gangway. Giselle and Teri arranged the merchandise while I marked prices on the slate. The table soon displayed a selection of gourmet food items in glass containers and little faience pots with black stenciled labels: Dijon mustard from Louit Frères, Bordeaux and Maille in Paris, paté with truffles from the Périgord, bottles of French olive oil in liter and half liter sizes, small French pickles, French truffles in dark glass bottles sealed with cork and wax, sardines packed in olive oil in tins from La Rochelle, capers in distinctive deep green bottles from Bordeaux, and small flasks of Cognac and Armagnac that would fit nicely in the pocket of a traveling cloak.

We didn't have long to wait for customers. There was a steady stream of well-dressed-men and women making their way to the ferry landing for passage to Sacramento, Benicia and Stockton where they could find hotel and boarding house space. As most carried little luggage, we assumed they were fire victims. Not knowing what they would find at their destination, many splurged on our luxury food items that I had marked up at six to one over cost. Several even opted for Robert's expensive wine.

Manon surprised us with a fabulous dinner offering: omelets with chanterelle and "cèpes de Bordeaux" mushrooms she'd brought from France dried and brought back to life by soaking. We'd all had a busy and successful day. Our hangovers forgotten, we celebrated again, but turned in early. Manon crooked her finger at me and flashed a wicked smile. I followed her to our cabin like a dog getting his first bone.

California Gold Rush Journal

CHAPTER SEVENTEEN

San Francisco – May 6, 1851

Manon cuddled into my arms and whispered in my ear, "So, cheri, maybe you get up and bring your Manon a nice hot cup of coffee in bed, yes?"

She laughed at my antics to climb into my frigid, stiff clothes. The air was clammy-cold and I could see only swirling fog out our porthole. There was no sign of life from our friends. I lit the lamps and then teased an unwilling stove from coughing smoke to providing a flame. While I waited for the water to boil and lit the woodstove in the dining room, I reviewed our account book. Manon's food table grossed $120.00, the wine bar made $75.00 not counting Robert's wine, and my gourmet food table added $110.00 to our coffers. Our net was $175. We'd nearly made our May rent in one day and Manon would try to double her food sales in a week. After delivering Manon's coffee and receiving a really sweet smile, I banged on all the officer's cabins. "Time to rise and shine and get those doggies movin," I chimed to groans from within.

It would take some time to change our nocturnal habits to complement the need to rise early as food providers. In French we say "l'avenir appartient à ceux qui se lèvent tôt," or the "the early bird gets the worm," sums it up. As I couldn't visit the Chinese quarter until early afternoon, when Wah Fong finished his shift for Pierre-Louis, I prepared rent notices to the owners of the cargo in our hold from The Flying Cloud. Who knows when customs would get around to releasing it. I would have Georges chat up the other boat workers to find out what they were charging clients to warehouse goods by the ton and square meter.

I let Georges and Raoul hassle with the gangway and tent set up while I prepared letters to Valparaiso and New York ordering more merchandise and wine. Raoul had letters for Chile, Robert for France and Georges for his girl in New York. When the sailor from the Flying Cloud arrived to retrieve them, I sent him back with a venison paté Manon made the day before and was now cool enough to slice along with a thank you note and our blessings for a safe passage back to New York. It would be a shame to lose all the gold stashed aboard as cargo to a Cape Horn storm.

Robert had visited most of the remaining restaurants and wine merchants in San Francisco to offer his wines at wholesale now he had lost his shop. Neither he nor Raoul had capital to rebuild their store. I counseled them to hold on to their lot. Once others rebuilt, their land would be worth more, and be easier to secure a loan to build or sell. Meanwhile, they could sell from our ship and wine bar.

Manon and I had discussed whether to rent bunks in the forecastle on a weekly basis given the shortage of rooms after the fire. Given the initial success of her wharf side food sales, we wisely decided to forego the extra income for security reasons. We didn't want to leave the gangway down in the evening or deal with the problems due to arise when unhappy folks are bunking in close quarters with strangers.

After lunch, Georges and I set off for Pierre-Louis' bistro. Some merchants had already cleared their burned out lots and started to rebuild. Carpenters and masons were unloading large wagons overflowing with lumber and barrels of nails. The lumber yards and saw mills were located on the fringes of the town unaffected by the fire. The wood they called "redwood," was new to me. The builders swore by it. They said it was termite, bug and rot resistant and much easier to mill than oak or other hardwoods. Apparently, there were vast redwood forests in the north of California and Oregon.

Wah Fong looked like most of his fellow countrymen whom the Yankees called "Celestials." Wide pantaloons bagging from behind, adorned his slight frame; a round hat like a skullcap fit close to his scalp and his black, shiny hair was plaited in a long queue. His coal-black eyes engaged us and he greeted us with a friendly smile.

"I takee you visit China town," he said in his pidgin English and gave us a deep bow of respect.

"Thank you for helping us," I replied and offered my hand to shake.

He seemed startled I would treat him as an equal, but gave me a limp handshake to go with a broad smile. I knew the Chinese had been badly treated by the Yankees who judged them a lowly, barely human sub-species much like the Southerners considered their slaves — alright to screw, even rape their women, but shun them as social inferiors. Like the French and Chileans, they didn't socialize with Yankees who were their clients. Georges had recounted how some Chinese men, who were addicted to gambling, had been set upon in Portsmouth Square by some drunk Yankees who'd cut off their pigtails. He'd even heard that some Chinese miners had been shot and killed by Yankees who pushed them out of their claims in the placer mines.

Fong, as he like to be called, led us down Dupont Street to upper Sacramento Street to an area of the city called "Little China." There were still a few distinctive structures made of brightly painted wood with curved roof beams brought over in sections from China and reassembled, but most buildings were a hodge-podge of poorly constructed tenements and store fronts.

The streets reverberated with a din of strange, high pitched voices as the Chinese jostled each other for traction on their muddy streets. Barefoot water boys lugged huge, sloshing pots of water at the end of a shoulder yoke. Ducks, geese and chickens hung from metal hooks in food shops. The air was thick with smoke from cooking fires and swirling incense. Shoppers and merchants yelled at each other to contest prices and haggle wares. The streets teemed with men dressed like Fong with an occasional exception of a man in expensive silks.

"Where are the women?" I asked

"China man no likee his woman out of house," he replied.

Georges whispered in my ear, "That's because most of 'em work as whores."

I gave him a surprised look, "And how would you know that?" I teased.

"Learned it from the sailors and dock workers. At's where they have to go. Chinese and Chilean whores the only ones they can afford on the little they make. Some even say Chinese women built different down there, if an' you knows what I mean."

"Really, I'm surprised that a man of the world like you would believe that."

"I'm not sayin' it's true; it's just what some say. Wouldn't know meself," he said testily.

Fong indicated an alley and we ducked into to it. Our noses were assaulted with an array of smells — joss sticks, soy sauce, scented soap and a sweet, cloying scent Fong identified as opium. I caught a glimpse of an interior courtyard where men labored stirring hot tubs of clothes while others used large flat irons to press and iron European shirts and pants. The wooden sign over the portico was in Chinese characters but it was clearly a laundry.

We made another turn into another alley and were suddenly witness to the flesh trade Georges had mentioned. A middle aged Chinese woman spied us and took us for willing tricks. Fong said something to her in their language, but she was having none of it. She tugged us towards her establishment.

"You like lookee-see an' doee. My China girls velly nice." She dragged us into a cramped anteroom where four sparsely clad girls no older than thirteen or fourteen preened for us. The lead girl opened her silk robe to show us her small budding breasts rouged like her pale cheeks.

The girl grabbed Georges and made a move to pull him past a large silk screen that must hide the entrance to their cribs. Georges was saved by the arrival of Fong with a couple of local enforcers. The girls cringed and the Madam started a harangue that would have put a harridan to shame.

We made a hasty exit back to the alley. As we moved deeper into this strange jumble of warrens, we were propositioned again. Some establishments actually displayed their girls in windows wearing very short shifts and posing suggestively. We passed several sailors and laborers being escorted to and from these establishments. I was astonished to see a young Caucasian girl in her early twenties leading three sailors.

"What is she doing here?" I asked Fong. He gave me a sheepish look. "White girl velly high status for rich China man. She like to smoke gow pipe too much. Now she have to work for new master. She no bring sailor to parlor houses, she no get smoke opium pipe.

"You mean she's his concubine and lives here?" I asked hardly believing my eyes.

"She just like slave girls work in cribs. She slave to the pipe, so do what boss man say."

I was amazed at this perverse and strange world just a few

blocks from where we had rented rooms and eaten on our arrival. As we continued our walk through Little China's labyrinth of twisting alleys, I peeked in another courtyard where Chinamen sat at long trestle tables twisting tobacco into cigars and stuffing them in wooden molds.

The smell of the opium dens and cries of the sex trade barkers offering young slave girls for 75 cents to a dollar gave way to strong, pungent smells of searing meat, hot chiles, soy and other savory cooking scents. Fong pointed to a restaurant decorated to look like a Chinese junk.

Fong spoke excitedly to a small, jovial faced man with an enormous paunch and lively eyes who could pass for the nephew of the gilded plaster of Paris Buddha on a pedestal by the counter. He beckoned us to sit in a large booth. No sooner were we seated than a very attractive woman in her late teens arrived with a tray filled with a large tea pot, small porcelain tea cups, soup bowls decorated with red dragons, white porcelain spoons with the same design and a large, steaming bowl of soup with noodles, bits of chicken and stuffed pastry squares that looked like Italian ravioli.

"You drinkee tea and enjoy Won Ton soup. Fong bring fisherman to see you." That said, Fong disappeared out the door. Our host spoke to the pretty waitress with dark almond-shaped eyes set in a heart-shaped face and she served us a green tea and ladled out the delicious smelling soup. Her lustrous black hair was piled on top of her head held in place with large tortoise shell combs; her dark red, high-collared, form-fitting dress had Georges' eyes popping as she sauntered back to the counter with the empty tray. The long slit up the side of her dress revealed a tantalizing glimpse of firm calf and smooth thigh as she did her slow, teasing walk.

We sipped our tea and slurped the savory soup until Fong returned with two wiry, bronze-skinned Chinamen in their early thirties. Their long blouses and pantaloons smelled of sea salt and sported bits of fish scales. Their long queues were neatly tucked into fishing caps. They bowed and Fong introduced them in his pidgin English as owners of several small boats that fished the bay and along the coast. They moved here from Monterey when the Gold Rush created a demand for fresh seafood for the burgeoning Chinese population and the numerous noodle eateries in "Little China."

By Fong's prearrangement, we sampled an array of fabulous fish dishes: small bay shrimps in a spicy black bean sauce, black bass, sturgeon and salmon poached whole and served with delicious sauces, deep-fried calamari and shrimps, oysters on the half shell, scallops in a lemon-butter sauce, steamed mussels and clams, fresh sea urchins and the most delicious shellfish I have ever tasted: abalone pan-seared in oil.

Fong assured me all of these fish and crustaceans could be provided most of the year. In addition, there would be a tasty local crab and more varieties of salmon available in the Fall when they returned to the creeks that spawned them. We spent a good hour haggling over prices and terms of delivery with Fong as intermediary as none of the fishermen spoke a word of English.

I arranged to buy the shell fish by the bucket and the larger fish by size to be delivered daily to our ship. Manon wanted to expand her soup repertoire with a hearty fish stew and a shellfish bouillabaisse. Fong assured us that there was an abundance of mussels, clams, oysters, as well as good white fish that could be provided on a daily basis. We prepaid the first delivery for the next day to show our good faith and I had Fong secure me a fresh abalone in its large shell from the restaurant's stock to share with Manon. I paid the restaurant owner for our food and let Georges give the waitress a sizable tip.

We wound our way through more tortuous alleys as we

made our way back to the docks. Along the way we passed stalls selling fresh vegetables, coolie clothes, herbal medicines and lots of carts selling bowls of hot noodles, rice cakes and doughy balls filled with savories Fong said were called "dim sum." As we got closer to the port area, most of the businesses focused on the sex trade and opium. Prices for girls started at 50 cents and one Chinese barker announced boys under sixteen could have a girl for 15 cents if it was their first time.

As I was curious, I asked Fong if we could visit an opium den. He shook his head. "Owner no want trouble. Better only go to smoke gow pipe. Maybe some other time." When we popped out of the Chinese quarter, I thanked Fong for his help and slipped him a ten dollar gold coin in appreciation. He skipped back into the warrens of "Little China" with a broad smile and little wave good-bye.

Our next stop was a grubby, smoke filled bar on Russian Hill not far from Union Street. We asked the burly barkeep with an eye patch for the two hunters we sought and he pointed to a table at the rear. Our two French Canadian hunters looked up at us and motioned us to a pair of wobbly stools. Both were dressed in soiled leather pants and long sleeved jerkins with leather fringes and numerous grease stains. Their unkempt beards were more gray than black and their salt and pepper moustaches stained from chewing tobacco. Their slouch hats perched jauntily over unkempt hair. Francois, the smaller, wiry one with a necklace of bear claws said something in almost incomprehensible French. Bernard, the taller, beefier one with a scar from his left eye to where his cheek became beard nodded and took aim and let fly a long line of black spit at a cuspidor before stuffing another plug of tobacco in a mouth filled with rotting teeth.

I motioned the bartender over and ordered a bottle of wine and two more glasses. The uncorked bottle he brought had seen better days and the sour, acidic wine was hard to swallow with a straight face after the luscious meal we'd experienced in "Little China."

Bernard assured us in his heavily accented 18th C. French that they could provide a steady supply of larger game: deer, antelope and wild pig. They hunted the woods surrounding Mt. Tamalpais on the northern side of the bay entrance, slaughtered their kill and had an arrangement with a Frenchman to ferry the meat to San Francisco's French restaurants. Bernard boasted he and Francois directed a band of eight former French and Russian fur trappers. They and the Russians hunted the big game with .50 caliber Plains rifles and the others hunted with shotgun the marshes and flat lands around Richardson's Bay for wild duck, geese, quail, pheasant, partridge, turkey and jack rabbit.

I pointed to his distinctive necklace. "And do you hunt bear as well?" I asked.

"Yes, we hunt black bear, brown bear, Grizzly bear, beaver and even mountain lions but not for meat. We sell the skins for clothes, rugs and decoration and the paws and gall bladders of the bears and lions to the Chinaman who makes aphrodisiacs and special concoctions for the rich."

"What about the bear fat? Do you sell it too?" I asked.

"No, several of us have taken squaws for wives. They do the butcherin' and cookin'; some of them like the fat and use it in cookin' but not us."

"Would you be willing to provide us with a keg or two of bear fat when it's available along with our meat and poultry?"

"Sure. We just feed it to our dogs or leave it for the buzzards and crows"

They had nearly finished the bottle of wine and I quickly brought our business to a conclusion before I had to entertain more toasts with another bottle of what was now mostly vinegar. We agreed on a steady supply of game birds to be delivered to our ship and larger, butchered game to be delivered to

Pierre-Louis' bistro for him to have roasted — a quarter for him and three quarters for us. I dropped two twenty dollar gold coins on the table to cement the deal and establish our credit. On the way out, I slipped the barkeep a five dollar gold coin. I asked him to buy our hunters a couple more bottles of wine and keep the change.

The trappers from Canada had been in the wild for many years, moving from French Canada, down to the Pacific Northwest and some on to Oregon and California as they decimated the beaver population to supply fashionable top hats and other clothes in vogue. They were unaware of the latest craze among the European dandies who slicked back their long hair with a pomade of scented bear's grease. We had considered buying French Bear's Grease to sell here, but were less sure of its market than the gourmet foods. In Europe, most of the bear fat came from Russia and was expensive by the time the French perfumers processed and packaged it for sale in attractive blue and white porcelain pots with scenes of bears and hunters. I had in mind to find a local druggist willing to process and sell a bear grease pomade in partnership with us.

My head was bursting with ideas to make business as we returned to our wharf and ship. The fog which had lifted during late morning was now stealing back in on the wings of a cold wind out of the northwest. The tents were stowed signaling another sell out day for Manon's business. I was surprised to see a large male Tabby cat sitting like royalty at the top of the gangway and eyeing me suspiciously. I knew Giselle fed food scraps to the many stray cats orphaned by the fire, but didn't expect one in residence.

As we were the last home, it was time to pull up the gangway. Georges found Raoul to help him and I pointed to the cat who had moved from the gangway to the door to the dining room. Raoul indicated the cat was Giselle's. Just then, Giselle appeared on deck and the cat immediately headed for her and affectionately brushed his head against her skirts purring happiness. I hoped he could look a rat in the eye and do more than say "Boo." Giselle had named him "Gamelle Boy" for the way he shooed off competitors to protect the food scrap bowl for himself.

Manon and I retired early after dinner so we could review in detail the arrangements I had made and she could plan future menus. She was particularly curious to see "Little China" for herself.

"So cheri, you gonna have to take your cute sailor boy for a tour of the town. Maybe he gonna get better offer than fifteen cents, yes?"

"I'm sure a rich China man would love a slave boy to play with. Your first offer would probably be an opium pipe for free."

"But if sailor boy wanna try the gow pipe to see opium den. You gonna rescue him, yes?"

"Of course, but first sailor girl is going to have to build her wharf business and her Pierre has to do some work for to justify his salary."

Manon gave me a pouty lip smile, then crooked her finger and pointed to our bed. "Sailor girl hafta have a little fun if she gonna work so hard, non?"

California Gold Rush Journal

CHAPTER EIGHTEEN

San Francisco – May 7, 1851

Manon prepared the albalone for lunch for the two of us. She swirled a dollop of olive oil in a hot skillet until the oil started popping, then dropped the abalone she'd cut in half in the pan to sear 30 seconds only on each side the way she cooked calamari and small squid. The result was heavenly. The tender abalone sliced like butter and its silky texture and nutty flavor was unlike anything we had tasted before. I'd opened a bottle of Cheverny white wine that I'd chilled in the cold bay waters by dropping it over the side in a wooden bucket and hauling it out after half an hour.

"Manon gonna like cooking in San Francisco if her cheri brings home such nice surprises," she said sipping her wine. "An' what a beautiful shell. Maybe clever boy figure how to make me nice jewelry, yes?"

It had taken lots of grunting and more than a few choice cuss words to pry open the seven inch, almond shaped shells whose interior looked like mother of pearl and shone opalescent in the sun. Manon was right, we need to find someone who could fashion earrings, necklaces and even buttons with the exquisite shells.

"Maybe we should see if Giselle and Teri have some ideas about jewelry design. Meanwhile, let's order lots of abalone and stockpile the shells. Imagine the Yankees stuffing themselves on fried oysters, potatoes and eggs and thinking they're eating delicacies."

"Yes, while the clever Chinese are eating abalone, calamari, shrimp, mussels, scallops and delicious fish. Manon, the sailor boy, wanna eat in Chinese restaurant. Maybe she'll learn some new tricks, yes?"

"You're already the best cook on the wharf, but I'm glad there's no Chinese competition here yet. They probably could sell their noodle and Won Ton soups much cheaper than we sell our soup."

"Yes, but Yankees like good meat in their soup. What Manon sells is very tasty an' wait 'til they taste her bouillabaisse. Nobody makes a fish soup better than Manon, yes?"

I chuckled. She was a great cook, still we had lot's of competition on the Central Wharf. Now things were normalized after the fire, the wharf was crowded with stands like ours hawking vegetables, drinks, and discount merchandise for would-be miners going to the placers. Despite the competition, we had two distinct advantages. First, Giselle and Teri were both very attractive salesladies. While Giselle was more reserved, patrons loved her French accent and always chic appearance. No bonnet necessary behind her stand. Teri was more outgoing. She bantered with her bar clients and wasn't put off by the crude offers she had to fend off on occasion. Giselle wanted Teri to wear a wedding band like Manon wore when off the ship. Teri adamantly refused. She was single and as she said, "who knows when a rich, handsome Yankee might make an offer of marriage she couldn't refuse."

As she saw it, Raoul had the benefit of a woman in his bed without a commitment on his part. He, like many latino men, liked having a woman in his "casa chica," but once he made his pile, he'd return to Chile, marry into upper class society and put his wife in the "big house" to raise his kids. Teri, like Manon and Giselle, wanted to stay here, where as a woman, she had more freedom than in Chile

Our second advantage was our arrangement for regular deliveries of fresh meat, poultry, fish and shell fish of the best quality. Other stands sold fish and cooked food but quality was often lacking. What fish was available was hit and miss depending on the weather and available bait. The food stands relied on local, California beef from former Mexican, now Californio, ranchos in the Santa Clara Valley that raised their cows for their hides and not their rather tasteless, stringy meat. Wharf cooks used lots of hot sauce and spices to disguise their products but they couldn't compare in taste and quality to our more expensive offerings.

In preparation for our trip to the placers, I had asked Georges to establish a contact with someone in the Post Office at Portsmouth Square. He learned that since the fire destroyed most of the businesses on the square, the five postal clerks were swamped with work and patron complaints. It took them days to sort incoming ship mail alphabetically by addressee. As more and more ships were arriving weekly, they were overwhelmed. Patrons had to wait in long lines for hours at a time to check for mail. Those who could afford it, paid stand-ins by the hour to hold their place in line. Prior to the fire, street merchants sold coffee, newspapers, and snacks from kiosks around the square, but with the frenzied activity to rebuild the gambling palaces, this system was disrupted.

Georges presented my offer. We had secured passenger lists for not only the four ships from the La Californienne Mining Co., but lists supplied by the French consulate for many other French emigrant ships as well. Consul Dillon had sent most

French gold seekers to Marysville and from there they joined other French mining the Yuba and other northern rivers. This was the area we planned to visit. We offered to sort the French mail and deliver it to the French who'd left for the mines. Any undelivered mail would be left with Ricard, the local agent.

Another Frenchman by the name of Anselin had run an ad in April in the French page of the Daily True Standard announcing he would leave for the placers on April 26th and take letters to miners in the Marysville area. He was paid $1.00 to $2.00 a letter and took 233 letters with him to deliver to M. Ricard at the L'Hotel de France de Marysville, who was an agent for letters.

Anselin departed before the fire. Since then the mail situation was chaotic. None of the American clerks could speak or read French and had difficulty even reading a foreign addressee's name. They had snapped up our offer. We had about 750 letters to sort and match against passenger lists and other criteria. We asked Robert to do the sorting while we made additional preparations.

Due to a scarcity of warehouse space after the fire, cargo ships were arriving daily with no way to unload and store merchandise in their holds. As a result, cargo was sold by auction on condition the buyer removed it promptly. As we had spare storage, I was able to buy 500 cases of good quality wine, 50 casks of French and Spanish brandy, and 50 casks of Sugar Islands rum to sell through our wine bar. The buys guaranteed a good supply for a few months.

The addition of the brandy and rum to our repertoire was significant as drinking toasts was the common bond between strangers. Any reason for celebration, a letter received, sealing of a deal or a decision to buy passage to return home called for a toast or even a round of drinks for anyone present.

We were also afraid of a repeat of the May 3rd fire. We organized a volunteer fire brigade for the wharf before leaving for the placers. The wharf had been saved by quick thinking Captain Richards. His crew and other volunteers quickly removed decking timbers to separate the wharf from the shoreline. We rigged a series of large bells on poles to sound a fire alarm and purchased crow bars, saws and axes to store in a locked shed near the beginning of the wharf to be used in case of fire.

In addition to the letters, we purchased boxes of cigars to transport to the placers with the rest of our travel gear. We figured our arrival at the mines with sought after mail, brandy and cigars would loosen tongues for our investigation.

We booked passage on a side paddle steam boat renamed "El Dorado" after she sailed to San Francisco from Chile with a load of miners. She was one of many paddle wheel steamers to leave from the end of our wharf on a regular basis for Sacramento. The first American steamboat, "The Senator," had made a fortune for her owners after she left Boston, rounded Cape Horn for San Francisco and made her first run to Sacramento on November 5, 1849. As the sole steamboat to navigate the bay and rivers to Sacramento, she could charge $30.00 per passenger and $35.00 per ton of cargo. In the first 12 months before the arrival of competing paddle boats from South America, she made $600,000.

Manon prepared a satchel full of goodies for our trip and we celebrated my departure by retiring to our bed early. When Manon was sure I'd had more than my fill and finally ready for sleep, she whispered in my ear, "That's gonna have to last you 'til you come home, Big Boy. If Manon hears you were a bad boy while Manon works her tail off for you in the galley, she's gonna make your life very miserable. Better bring the satchel back full of money and not souvenirs from bawdy houses." She bit my ear harder than usual for emphasis. It would be our first time apart since we'd left France.

Our steamboat belched black smoke into the early morning bay fog as we boarded. Most passengers headed directly to the bar on their deck to order a whiskey to ward off the chill while we settled for black, bitter coffee. The boat settled into a thumping rhythm as the stokers filled the boilers and we made headway against the ebbing tide flooding past Alcatraz Island and out to sea. It was too cold to go on deck, so we huddled on an oak bench with a view of the bay ahead. Spumes of spray splattered our window as our bow split through the chop of moderate waves as we entered San Pablo Bay.

Manon's goodies drew conspicuous envy as we laid out our picnic lunch on our bench — slices of duck paté, and salmon in aspic to spread on a fresh baguette delivered to our ship this morning. A nice bottle of Bordeaux Superior helped to warm our insides as we munched our gourmet lunch. Some passengers snacked on stale bread and tins of smelly mackerel and sardines while others tried the lumpy, potato heavy clam chowder and stale crackers offered by the boat's bistro. A large group drank their lunch at the bar.

The weather was foul and the bay choppy as we reached the Carquinez Straits and made our turn into the small bay and delta leading to the Sacramento River. Eventually, we turned north into the wide, fast flowing river and steamed for Sacramento. It was early evening before we arrived and docked. The town was still trying to recover from a rainy winter that saw the river flood the wharves and much of the low lying town. There was still mud everywhere. We chose to pay for a carriage ride to our hotel which was fortunately spared the flooding.

Given the muddy conditions of the roads and the slewing of the carts hauling goods from the wharves to the overland trails leading to the southern mines, we opted to continue our voyage to Marysville by boat as long as possible. As the river was still swollen, we booked passage on a small sloop that could accommodate our goods and several passengers, but had no cabins or shelter other than a canvas rigged to provide some shade and minimal protection from rain or the elements. Fortunately, the weather was fair with a petulant sun peeking through the ground fog of the valley.

Our boat had to tack back and forth across the river at angles to make headway up the still swollen Sacramento River. It was slow going and we were glad we still possessed leftovers from Manon's goodie bag.

The sloop had no bar or food service, so we passed a bottle of Spanish brandy to our fellow travelers of which there were five. Three brothers with strapping broad shoulders and youthful exuberance from Maine wanting to try their luck at the placers, a short, sallow-faced Bostonian dressed in heavy tweeds carrying papers for Adams Co. Express, and a dapper looking dandy from New Orleans whose forced smile and feral eyes announced trouble for gamblers and wealthy widows alike were our traveling companions.

As it would have been selfish of us not to share our food, I suggested we all pool our resources and do a picnic lunch. I laid out three slices of Manon's paté and the remainder of our salmon on a hogshead of flour carried as deck cargo for Marysville. To this the others added a bag of walnuts, a tin of tuna and one of anchovies, two bottles of labeled red wine, a box of crackers, and a tin of biscuits. Our offer of brandy met with unanimous approval and worked as designed to loosen tongues and the picnic was sufficiently enticing to put all in a good mood.

I was curious about the Bostonian's role with my bank. "We travelled with a couple of bankers bound for Marysville on our ship from New York. I am sure you must know of them. Jonathan and Rose Steinhart."

The Bostonian snickered and swallowed his urge to gloat. "Oh yes. The Steinharts. Such a waste. Not cut out for the rigors of California. He made a muck of the company's start up. Couldn't deal with the rough and tumble element from the mines. The ones that made their fortunes. I'm on my way to deliver the bad news. He's sacked and I'm the new interim manager," he exulted.

"What about his wife?" I asked.

"Hah. That one. The Man-eater," he said with malice. "Took one look at Marysville and her ladyship was on the next boat back to Sacramento and on to San Francisco. Not good enough for her highness. Rumor has it she's on the make to snare someone above her station who'll return her to Europe a rich divorcee. No better than the other Jezebels if you ask me."

I had planned to visit Adams & Co. Express while in Marysville, but was now reluctant to witness more putdowns after what he'd suffered on the ship from his wife's infidelity. I turned my attention to the dandy.

"And what brings you to Marysville, if I may ask."

"Curiosity, mostly. Just want to see how folks extract the gold and what they can do with it."

"So, you're a tourist and potential investor?"

"You might say that. And what about you and your friend," he said pointing to Georges. "You here on business or to do with the mines?"

"We're French journalists. Here to report on how the French miners are doing for our paper," I parried.

"Yeah. Figured you must be professionals by the looks of you. Like to know where you got the good tasting food. I'll pay the place a visit when I get back to San Francisco."

"A hole-in-the-wall stand over by Russian Hill," I lied. No way I wanted to see this disingenuous predator near our three women or our ship. I wouldn't be surprised to see him lightening the gold pouches of all who crossed his path. He was bad news.

The three brothers were naive and poorly informed about what to expect once they got to the placers. Perhaps what they lacked in knowledge could be compensated by hard work and luck.

By mid-afternoon we reached the point where the Feather River flows into the Sacramento River. We entered the Feather River which would lead us to Marysville. It, too, was also swollen, muddy and swift flowing. It would be slow progress tacking back and forth but probably better than getting stuck in the muddy coach tracks. The captain, a taciturn, no nonsense sailor announced we would soon arrive as we sailed off the Feather River and into the Yuba River on our right. Marysville lies on high ground in between where the two rivers merge into one. We docked in early evening and hired a coach to take us and our luggage to the L'Hotel de France de Marysville.

"SACRAMENTO CITY, CALIFORNIA," 1851.

"STEAMER DAY," 1851.

California Gold Rush Journal

CHAPTER NINETEEN

Marysville and The Northern Mines — May 7, 1851

Wed selected M. Ricard's hotel because he was the local post office agent for letters for miners in the northern placers along the upper Feather River and both forks of the Yuba River. The hotel lacked the charm of our Sacramento hotel — no covered veranda overlooking the town where one could stretch one's legs or enjoy an after dinner cigar and drink while watching the sun set or the stars twinkle. The rooms on the second and third floors were accessed by a staircase on each side and overlooked the bar and lobby below. I was pleased to see the lobby sign posted in large letters, "No Gambling or Solicitation Allowed."

As we had arrived late and tired the night before, we had supped in the hotel's small restaurant. After Manon's creations, the fare though cooked for a mostly French clientele, was more suitable for a Franco-American café — omelets, beef stew, onion soup, and fried meat dishes garnished with boiled potatoes or pasta. Desserts were pies made with syrupy fruit preserves and lots of sugar.

We'd tour the town later in the day to find more palatable fare. While Georges chatted up the clerk handling the mail consignment, I sought out Maurice Ricard to learn what he knew of the people on our lists and apprise him of my interest in the fate of the mining companies and their members. He was having coffee at the bar and I joined him.

Ricard was a portly, affable man in his fifties with a firm hand shake, receding pepper-brown hair and inquisitive eyes. He built his hotel in Marysville because he knew the town's founder, Charles Covillaud, a fellow Frenchman from the Department of Charente, France. As Ricard recounted, Covillaud had left France in 1841 for New Orleans to make his fortune in the New World. He made his way up the Mississippi River to St. Joseph, Missouri where with a partner, Claude Chana, he ran a general merchandise store supplying goods to the increasing number of pioneers and settlers going west in caravans. In 1846 Covillaud and Chana pulled up stakes, joined one of the caravans and set out to get to Oregon or California before the onset of winter and snow could prevent them from crossing the Sierra Nevada.

"He was real lucky," Ricard said pausing to light one of my cigars. "It was a real bad winter that came early trapping one group they refer to as "The Donner Party" in the impassable snow. Charles made it through the pass just before the blizzard hit. Many in The Donner Party froze to death and some say they even ate the dead to survive until a rescue party could save them."

"How did Covillaud wind up in Marysville?" I asked. I wanted to shift the conversation to my inquiry, but sensed he intended to take his time to tell his story before he'd be receptive to my concerns.

"Some fellows are just born lucky, I guess. He made his way down the Yuba River and settled near here. There were a lot of French Canadians in the area who were hunting along the rivers now the Russians had given up and ceded their fort on the coast. He was one of the first to hear of the gold strike on the

American River in January 1848. Figured if there was gold in the American River, there should be some in the Yuba as well. He, with several friends, tried their luck at prospecting. Bingo! In June 1848 he struck it rich. Hit a rich vein of gold and invested it in land including what's now this town."

"You mean he bought the land for the entire town?"

"Sure did. His holdings included almost all the land between the confluence of the Yuba and Feather Rivers. It was a strategic starting point for miners to go up the two rivers. He wrote me he had an architect drawing plans for the town. Claimed it would be a little Sacramento — a supply point for men and supplies going to the northern placers. Offered me a free parcel and loan guaranty if I'd come and build a hotel which he said would be profitable and essential to the development of his town."

"And you did what I would have done, you were on the next ship to San Francisco," I added enviously.

"Yes, with the bad conditions in France my hotel was going nowhere. I was excited by the Gold Rush but too old to endure the rigors of mining. Charles offered me a timely opportunity to start over. I sold everything and headed for California. By the time I got here, the wharves and warehouses were in and merchants were buying land to build. Charles loaned me the money to build and you see the result."

He beamed his pleasure with the result. I passed on the opportunity to complain about the so-so menu in the restaurant. We were in a remote area and he probably was trying to cater to less discriminating taste buds or preparing them for cuisine at the placers. "I heard the town was named for his wife."

"Yes, in 1848 he married Mary Murphy, a survivor of the Donner Party. He told me in France he wanted to make his fortune and marry a young woman. Voila! He found her here. So he named the town after his American wife. Luck just follows

Charles like a golden rainbow."

"So has business been good for you?" I said inching towards what I wanted to know.

"Yes. A lot of French pass through here. So, they're happy to stay with us until they can secure transport to the mines. There are several French merchants in town as well, so they're comfortable and can communicate their needs.

"So, perhaps you remember a young miner named Louis Magne. He took letters and supplies to the mines before he returned to his family farm in Auvergne."

"Sure. He was a nice kid. Like so many we see on the return trip, he was homesick and an unlucky prospector. If he hadn't made some money taking letters directly to the miners, he'd have had to work an extra six months or more to earn passage home. We do see a lot of unhappy folks on the way back."

"The post office in San Francisco commissioned us to bring letters from home to the French in the northern placers as delivery is disrupted and chaotic since the recent fire wiped out most of the commercial district. Consul Dillon kindly provided us with passenger lists of names of most he sent this way. We were hoping your mail clerk could assist us by reviewing the list of addressees on the envelopes. That way we could deliver mail as we travel from here to the diggings on the Yuba and on to Nevada City and Grass Valley. Undelivered letters would be returned to your hotel agency."

"Well, I think that might be possible. You say Consul Dillon authorized you?"

"Yes, he's had complaints from Paris about the fate of several boat loads of emigrants he sent on to this area. He wants us to locate some of the emigrants and report to him on their wellbeing," I said hoping my version of authorization wouldn't be challenged as I didn't want to reveal who I worked for or why.

Ricard paused to puff up the fire in his cigar. "Well, I suppose Augustin could look at your lists. He handles the mail consignment agency for the postal service."

"That will be very much appreciated and help us with our mission. Any tips for us for our journey?"

"Well, for one, you should take as many supplies from here as you can and a waterproof tent. Tracks are still muddy and food may be scarce in some camps and three times the price if you can find it. So you'll need pack mules if you go by horse. Stage won't go to many of the smaller camps, so you'll have to pack in," he said eyeing my business attire and the dubious prospect of me riding a horse.

"What about risks? Indians? Bears? Thieves?" I asked evenly.

"Well, animals and Indians will attack for food after a tough winter. Not much threat from thieves but you better be well armed. Probably need to hire a guide who knows the lay of the land. A hunter or trapper would be your best bet. Also, there have been some altercations."

"What sort of problems," I asked with concern.

"Well, I'm sure you know all about the fuss over the Miner's Tax if you're working for Consul Dillon." I nodded yes. "Well there have been some disturbing new developments. Bunch of unruly Irish miners tried to run French miners off their claims near the camp at Mokelumne Hill in the southern mines. Our miners responded by hoisting our tricolor flag and refused to be intimidated. That provoked the Irish who attacked and killed one miner and wounded several others. Governor ordered the militia to restore order. Consul Dillon is trying to negotiate a settlement."

"A settlement?" I said choking back my indignation. "What is there to settle? Why aren't the Irish claim jumpers being strung up like the Vigilantes propose in San Francisco to the gang who fired the city?"

"From what I've heard, the Governor wants a political settlement. The Yankees don't like foreigners mining 'their' gold and he wants to keep this incident from becoming a catalyst for armed conflict between Yankee and foreign miners."

"Yes, but the Irish are not Americans or citizens of California anymore than the French. It doesn't make any sense."

"Well, there's a big Irish emigration at the moment because of crop failures in their country. They speak English which most foreigners don't, and like the English, the Yankees mingle with them and don't consider them outsiders like us and the Chileans and Mexicans."

The "English" I'd heard spoken by Cockneys and the Irish working the British docks was hardly recognizable as "English" even to educated Brits and as non-comprehensible as some of the French dialects still spoken by villagers in rural France. But why quibble with Ricard? If the Americans considered them allies, then that's what they were. "Do we need to be concerned that Americans and their allies will be hostile to us?"

"Well, I don't know. The incident at Mokelumne Hill has got tensions running pretty high even up here. Visitors from the southern placers tell various versions of what happened or more rightly what someone told them happened. French and American miners up here don't like each other and stick to their separate camps. Who knows what the Americans have been told. One misunderstanding, a false rumor or a group of drunk miners looking to settle a score could light the powder keg. Everyone is armed to the teeth and on edge."

"I'm grateful for the information and your candid assessment. We'll be wary and cautious. I agree we need a local guide who knows where the French are mining. Not a good moment to arrive unannounced in an unfriendly mining camp. Where could I locate a reliable guide?"

"Probably should inquire at Le Bar du Prospecteur. That's

their hangout when they're in town. Barkeep there, Raymond, can refer you to a good mountain man."

I thanked Ricard again for his help and suggestions. Before heading to the stables where Georges was arranging for horses and pack mules, I dropped off a box of cigars and a few week-old newspapers for Ricard at his bar.

Georges had arranged to purchase two horses and three pack mules. Georges' stallion was a magnificent black animal with white markings — sleek but muscled form, large eyes full of pride and willful resistance, flaring nostrils gauging my approach and sending me a tail swishing warning not to approach. Georges was rubbing his horse down and trying to spoil it with lumps of sugar. "Ain't he a beaut," Georges announced like a proud Papa. "Yours is over there," he said pointing to nondescript gray mare with sagging belly and soulful eyes.

Georges had obviously splurged on his acquisition but I said nothing. After so many years of tending to horses reared to draw heavy carts and carriages, he had earned the right to a spirited horse of his own. I only hoped the horse would adapt to its new role as leader of our pack over soggy ground. I noticed several wooden mule pack saddles piled in a corner. Georges was reluctant to leave his new horse, but I needed him to help me settle on a guide. On the way to the bar, I filled Georges in on what I learned about the troubled relations on the placers.

The Bar du Prospecteur was quite a change from bars in San Francisco and Sacramento — no billards, gambling tables or nudes on the wall and no women serving drinks and sizing up potential clients. Its main feature was a large mahogany bar with brass foot rails and a spittoon every three feet. Smoke obscured most of the light from the whale oil lamps on the walls. Six scruffy mountain men sat on hand-hewn chairs alternating sips from big schooners of beer with shots of whiskey from large black bottles. Two played dominoes and the others cards.

All six puffed on clay pipes like coal-fired locomotives climbing a grade. No one gave more than a curious glance at our arrival.

As this was a drinking man's bar, we followed the lead of its patrons and ordered English beer bottled in ceramic bottles with paper labels and wax seals. Raymond, the barkeep, placed shot glasses next to our glass schooners and set down a large black glass bottle with a simple paper label reading "Jameson's Finest Rye Whiskey." He poured us each a shot of whiskey in a small shot glass with a tiny handle. I motioned for him to join us in a drink, but he nodded no.

"I don't drink while I work or wouldn't last to the end of my shift with our clientele. I will take one of your cigars for later if you can spare one," he said looking at the five cigars sticking out of George's vest pocket. "What brings you to the Prospector Bar?"

"We're journalists on our way to visit and report on French mining camps between here and Auburn. Maurice Ricard at the hotel referred us to you. Said you'd be able to recommend a guide for us from your patrons."

Raymond stopped wiping glasses to scan the room. He motioned with his steel-gray eyes in the direction of the two playing dominoes and whispered "either of those two would do well. They've been hunting both forks of the Yuba for several months supplying the camps with fresh meat. Once they've made a pile of gold dust, they head back to town to drink it and pay for the girls at Fanny's house. They room upstairs. Been here over a week, so they should be short of funds soon. I'd try them first." We took our schooners, shot glasses and bottle of rye whiskey over to their table.

"Mind if we join you? We've got a business proposition to discuss," I said.

Each man gave us a scrutinizing look, then motioned to the vacant two chairs at their table. I pointed to their empty shot glasses and our bottle. "Join us for a drink."

Both men set down their clay pipes with bowls shaped with rustic faces like on the prow of ships, filled their shot glass, threw down the whiskey in a well-practised motion and followed it with a slug of beer. After brushing his mouth on his leather sleeve with fringes, the tall, slender one dressed in buckskin like an Indian scout said in a thick Canadian accent, "What's on yer mind?"

"We're journalists doing a tour of the northern placers and need an experienced guide from here to Auburn."

The burly, black-bearded one dressed in a red wool shirt, dirty breeches, and high boots piped in, "we work as a team. You take both of us or find someone else." The one in buckskin nodded his agreement, then poured another round of whiskey for him and his buddy and dumped the spent contents of his pipe into the spittoon at his feet.

Georges broke the silence. "Can both of you hunt as well as guide us to the French camps?" They both laughed heartily and nodded yes. "Then one can hunt while the other guides and guards our troop. Right?" Both nodded yes. "Then we need you both. We'll have fresh game and fowl to eat along the way and you boys can sell what we don't eat to the camps we visit. "

Georges' concern for his stomach sealed the deal. We agreed on a per diem wage of $10.00 each and they would hunt and roast our main meal over our campfire each evening. They would supply guns, ammo, tents, mules and horses to accommodate their needs. We'd provide the other necessities. We cemented the new relationship with Cyrille Beauchamp, the one in buckskin, and Jean-Louis Bertrand, the one in the wool shirt and bandana around his neck with another round of drinks and they agreed to meet with Georges the next day to organize our expedition.

California Gold Rush Journal

CHAPTER TWENTY

Marysville and The Northern Placers — May 1851

We spent the morning buying provisions and equipment suggested by our hotel keeper and others. Georges secured a list of mining camps where the mail clerk thought we'd find miners we were looking for. He even consigned a few letters for delivery where he knew we'd find the addressees. We'd set our rendez-vous with our Cajun guides for late morning and hoped to hit the trail after a light lunch.

Cyrille and Jean-Louis were waiting for us at the stables. They were packed and ready to go to my surprise given the amount of whiskey they'd consumed the day before. Both were dressed in the same clothes they'd worn at the bar. I wondered if they slept in their boots. We'd surely find out soon.

Two smallish Indian Pinto ponies without saddles were tethered to stable posts, two scruffy mules stood loaded with gear and another two mules wore empty pack saddles. Cyrille had added a leather belt around his dirty breeches from which hung a Bowie knife and a machete in leather sheaths. Jean-Louis had added to his buckskin outfit a holster containing a .50 caliber Colt pistol and a sawed-off double-barreled shot gun he'd slung across his back on a leather strap. Four long-barreled Plains rifles, axes and powder horns poked out of their mule packs. Several jugs of whiskey hung from the pommels of the mules' pack saddles.

Our guides were armed and dangerous. I'd noticed that most stage coaches carried an armed guard as well as a driver usually armed with a six-shot pistol. The guard's weapon of choice was a "scatter gun," just like Jean-Louis carried. The cut-down shotgun barrels allowed the shooter to scatter deadly shot in a wide pattern more likely to wound pursuing bandits and their horses than normal shotguns or rifles. While Georges and I each had two-shot French pistols, we would be no match for the likes of our companions. Hopefully, they'd defend us and not rob us for the gold they knew we carried.

Cyrille took one look at Georges' magnificent stallion and shook his head. "Not the best horse for mountain travel. Better suited for a race track," he observed. He just guffawed when he saw my sway-backed mare. "If game is scarce we can always eat horse meat, though dat one gonna be tough to chew."

Even though Georges and I were dressed in riding attire, our guides' evaluation of our horses and puny weapons clearly marked us as city slickers unsuited for mountain travel. I pointed to two dogs tied to a hitching post outside. The brown and white Brittany was clearly a hunting dog, but the larger one looked to be a cross between a bulldog and a wolf. "Do they come with us?" I asked. "Of course, 'Sac à Puces,'" pointing to the Brittany, "points and retrieves game birds, and 'Lupo' is our guard dog against surprise attack from Indians, wolves, wild pigs and bears on the trail," Jean-Louis said.

The thought that "Lupo" would be on guard duty while we slept helped calm the shivers running down my spine. His many ear and facial scars suggested he was a veteran fighter. It was clear we were totally unprepared for what we might face on the trail and needed both men and their dogs. Our guides argued that we forbear lunch in a bistro and get started immediately. We could eat our freshly purchased rolls and black bread with cheese at a stop en route.

Cyrille produced a tattered, grease stained map and indicated we would exit the stage coach road to Grass Valley shortly after leaving Marysville and follow the Yuba River on its south side heading east toward the mining camps of Smartville and Timbuctoo on the south side of the river. The northern route along the river would be easier going but with the river still swollen with runoff, it probably had no safe crossing. By following the river's south bank, we had a better chance of finding game but it would be slow slogging. They knew a safe place to camp for the night, but we had to get moving to arrive before dark.

After about a mile and a half on the muddy, pot hole studded coach road, we swung left onto a track leading to the river which was roaring but out of sight. The track became less mud and more gravel as we arrived at the Yuba River. One look confirmed Cyrille's concern. No way we could cross this raging torrent. Rushing water crashed against large boulders sending spumes of spray as it sought the narrow channels between the obstacles.

I couldn't imagine how one could mine the river in such conditions. Jean-Louis responded to my concerns, "No one can work in the river when it's raging. Large groups of miners work together to divert the river upstream so they can dig the gravel beds or work pockets of trapped water and gravel. Often it leads to disputes with miners downstream who may lose water to wash the gravels in their claims or be flooded by the diversion. Most miners want to be upstream from any diversions and work small tributaries, the river banks or side gravels. You'll see when we get nearer the mining camps."

True to Jean-Louis' prediction, we saw no one trying to mine the river our first day. We reached a small plateau where they proposed to camp. As Georges and I with our pack train moved slowly and cautiously along the river bank, Cyrille took

"Sac à Puces," flea bag in French, a black powder Plains rifle and shotgun and traipsed off into the heavy brush and hilly forest land between us and the coach road. While we set up our tent, Jean-Louis took an axe and began whacking and trimming young, ten foot saplings which he dropped in a pile.

After clearing a perimeter and getting our campfire going, Jean-Louis planted the bases of the poles he'd cut in soft earth. They formed a circle with the notched tops fitting together and secured with strips of rawhide. Then he unfurled a roll of deerskin hides that had been sewn together and tied them to the poles. The end result was a large Plains Indian style teepee. Lupo immediately stationed himself by the door flap while Jean-Louis stowed their gear and sleeping rolls inside.

After putting more wood on our campfire, Jean-Louis had us stow all our goods from our pack mules and our tack, but not our saddles in our tent; then he tethered the mules in between our tent and their teepee with the four horses inside the circle of mules.

"Why not tether the animals where they can crop the fresh grasses?" I asked.

Jean-Pierre laughed at my suggestion. "Because in the morning you'll be walking to Auburn and carrying your packs."

"What?" I stammered. "Surely with Lupo guarding, no bear is going risk attacking our animals."

Jean-Louis just shook his head. "Indians, not bears," he said.

"Indians? Surely you must be joking. What would Indians be doing in this desolate spot."

"Waiting for you to fall asleep tonight so they can steal our animals and anything else they can get their hands on."

"How do you know?" I asked incredulously.

"A party of Indians has been tracking us for the last two hours. They were probably hunting like Cyrille until they saw bigger game — us. "

"Surely, they wouldn't risk attacking us with the dogs and all our guns," I said in a nervous voice.

"They'll wait until near dawn and try to catch us asleep; when Lupo sounds the alarm, they will silence him with arrows and may do the same with you two as you as you emerge from your tent groggy and befuddled by sleep. They know you carry only two-shot pistols, inaccurate under the best conditions, but useless in the dark. They'll have you shoot at noises and phantoms until your four shots are gone and rush you or keep you hunkered down in your tent while you try to reload in the dark. Meanwhile, they'll steal the horses with ease while we are confused by the sudden attack and slip back into the forest as silently as they came."

"Why won't they be deterred by you and Cyrille?"

"They know we have superior weapons, so they will try to keep us pinned inside our teepee. I might get one or two by poking the scatter gun outside the entrance flap and firing in the dark, but they'll still get our horses and probably some of the less stubborn mules and that's the object of the raid."

"So what do we do?" I asked with trepidation.

"We let them know we expect their attack and are ready for them. They know the forest, work by stealth and cover of darkness. We have to take those advantages away. First, we have to build fires around our camp, so we can see them if they choose to attack. Second, we use your saddles and the mules' pack saddles for shields and we defend ourselves behind them with the long rifles and shotguns. Once they realize we plan to spend the night waiting for them, they will probably move on and not risk a suicide attack. They're not armed like the Plains Indians with rifles and tomahawks. They have only bows and knives. So let's get to work. There's a lot of wood to be chopped and drift wood to be collected before dark," he said as he passed out the axes.

Georges and I were huffing and puffing with the unaccustomed effort of chopping wood under Jean-Louis' direction when Cyrille arrived in camp with two wild turkeys and a plump partridge hanging from his belt. He held up six fingers and Jean-Louis nodded his understanding. Cyrille had spotted six members of a Maidu hunting party. He dropped the partridge in a kettle of hot water boiling in the camp fire and joined us in preparing our perimeter defense.

Cyrille took over the wood duties while Jean-Louis deftly removed the partridge's feathers and internal organs and put it to roast on a metal spit alongside a pot of coffee. I fetched more river water and broke out the remaining bread rolls and cheese to add to our meal. There would be no whiskey or wine tonight. We'd have to rely on frayed nerves and strong, chicory-laced coffee to keep us alert through the wee hours of the morning. Fortunately, we also had the eyes and ears of two dogs to alert us.

While engaged in meal preparations with Jean-Louis, I used our time together to try and learn why the local Indians were so hostile to us.

"It's very simple," Jean-Louis said. "The California Indians, the Ohlones, Modocs, Yuroks and Maidu, were peaceful before the arrival of the gold seekers. The Ohlones harvested oysters and clams around the bay, fished and gathered acorns to make their flat bread. The Maidu and other Indians in this area fished the rivers for salmon, hunted deer and game birds and met for yearly powwows with other tribes to exchange goods, marry daughters and engage in athletic competitions.

"With the arrival of so many emigrants heading into the mountains and ripping up and diverting their rivers, cutting their forests, and hunting their game, they needed to survive; they, like the Plains Indians, had to fight when their traditional tribal lands were invaded and settlers sought to claim them as their own."

"Are you saying the Indians owned the land?" I asked

Jean-Louis gave me a sad smile. "That's part of the irony and their downfall. They don't believe in land ownership with titles and mortgages. According to their beliefs, no one can own the land. They are privileged to hunt and fish and gather the fruits of the land and must respect it and all its creatures. Then the Yankees arrived. First, the settlers moving west across the prairies in increasing numbers, building forts and homesteading the best and most fertile land. Killing off the buffalo the Indians needed to survive and trying to hem them into reservations so the settlers could take and homestead their ancestral hunting grounds. Now the Yankees have come to California."

"Chinese and Sandwich Island fishermen now harvest the Indians' oysters, clams and fish. Miners from all nations have invaded the valleys shooting the animals and game birds Indians rely on for food and skins for protection against the elements. Some miners have tried to trick the Indians to work for them for trinkets and cast off clothes and tools, even whiskey, which they don't tolerate well. Most Indians are proud and resent the coarse miners only interested in the yellow rocks and sands that are of no value to Indians."

"Is that why we are being stalked? Because we are hunting in their forest?"

"Yes, for the Maidu who lost their hunting and fishing grounds around Marysville to miners and settlers. It's complex. Cyrille and I worked and lived side-by-side with Indian trappers in Canada and the Louisiana Territory. They sold us skins and we supplied them with weapons and supplies needed to hunt. We treated them fairly and there was mutual respect. We weren't there to strip their forests, homestead their ancestral hunting land or run them off the land. We were even offered squaws for wives and bed partners out of friendship."

"And there were only two of you," I added.

"That helped. But in California the Yankee miners and most foreigners consider local Indians to be uncivilized savages and heathens. The braves usually go naked and the squaws wear only short straw mats hung from a belt that cover their sex and and buttocks. They are considered less human to many than Southern States' slaves and John, the Chinaman. As a result, Indian villages and camps have been raided, women raped and braves summarily shot."

"So, all white men are their enemies,"

"Sadly so. They feel justified in stealing horses, food, weapons and anything else of value from the invaders who have uprooted their way of life. Normally, they are nomadic, moving from stream to stream to fish and gather acorns in the fall to see them through the winter. Their need to fish after winter has brought them in conflict with the miners who are working claims and camping all along their rivers. Many miners, especially the Yankees, shoot them on sight believing 'the only good Indian is a dead Indian.'"

I just shook my head. How sad indeed. In France, we have the notion of "the noble savage," from the works of Chateaubriand, Rousseau and others. These romantic notions couldn't stand up to man's greed for gold and fortune at any cost. After Jean-Louis' explanation, the hand writing was on the wall for the California Indians, who like the Plains Indians could not or would not assimilate or be ruled by the white man. They had seen the virtual enslavement of their fellow tribes by the white friars at the Missions. They would be pushed into starvation or exterminated. They had no protection in the new Constitution of the State of California, just as the enslaved Africans were excluded from the liberties and protection of the United States Constitution. It changed how I felt about our imminent encounter. I did not want to fight or have to kill an Indian even in self-defense.

After finishing our perimeter defense, we ate our evening meal. While the roasted partridge was delicious, my stomach was in knots at the prospect of defending our camp. Cyrille lit our perimeter fires and we hunkered down behind the saddles and waited with our backs to the roaring river and our rifles and shotguns aimed at the clearing any attackers would have to cross.

I woke with a start from troubled dreams. Cyrille handed me a steaming mug of coffee. "They've gone," he said. My heart would stop fluttering eventually.

California Gold Rush Journal

CHAPTER TWENTY-ONE

Marysville and The Northern Placers — May 1851

We were all relieved our Maidu Indian stalkers had slipped away to search for other game. I was stiff and sore from a night wrapped in a blanket on river gravels and both my rear end and the inside of my thighs ached from yesterday's unaccustomed saddle. Our bread was gone, so Georges and I ate biscuits from a tin and our guides polished off the rest of the partridge with their dogs whining their disapproval.

We set off in a damp, clinging river fog shortly after dawn to the unseen reverberation of water pounding boulders and rushing down rapids. It was slow slogging as our horses picked their way cautiously along the slippery track. By late morning the fog had dissipated and we could see our way and the river. Cyrille had warned us we would have to ford several small feeder streams today.

The second stream feeding into the river was wide but not deep. Here we got our first glimpse of mining. A group of six Chinese were working two wooden rockers which looked like a baby's cradle beside the stream. One worker shoveled gravel into the rocker, then poured buckets of water over it while a second agitated a handle to shake the cradle back and forth.

The rocker works as a simple screening device. Gravels dumped into the hopper end have to pass through a sieve, a sheet of metal perforated with small holes. Larger gravel rocks are trapped in the hopper and the finer black sands and bits of gold drop into a lower sluice chamber. The wooden sluice descends at an angle and has riffle bars across it to trap the heavier particles of gold while the lighter sands and earth are washed away. The two Chinese not working the rockers shoveled gravels and water into buckets and carried them to the rockers.

After my tour of "Little China" it was strange to see these six Chinese dressed in the same long black trousers and tunics as those in the city. These miners worked barefoot and the long, braided queues of the two kneeling and rocking the cradles touched the ground. All six wore strange, wide-brimmed straw hats. After an initial alarm at our arrival and brief hesitation in their work, they nodded and resumed their labor.

We skirted their mining operation and continued on our way past a string of freshly caught trout hanging on a line between two scrub oaks. Jean-Louis explained their presence this far down from the major mining camps. They had been run off their claim further up river and were trying their luck in this remote spot where American miners wouldn't bother them. Indians wouldn't bother with them other than perhaps to barter for their fish as they were poor and had nothing worth stealing.

By late afternoon we arrived at an encampment of Chilean and French miners. They were hard at work digging river gravels which they dumped into long wooden troughs ten to fifteen feet in length. The troughs called "Long Toms" operated on the same principle as the rocker, except they were angled into flowing water to wash the gravels. Instead of just one sieve there were several. Three miners shoveled gravels into the Long Toms while one miner was occupied removing rocks so the finer particles could reach the series of riffles to trap the gold. The fifth miner removed the gold flakes and pebbles. The remaining fines were collected and separated from the heavy black sands by use of a wooden "batea" or metal gold pan at the end of the day.

We decided to camp here for two nights. Cyrille and Jean-Louis planned to arise before dawn and hunt for large game to feed us and sell the rest to the miners. I suggested a communal meal for our first night and offered to share our two wild turkeys along with a jug of French brandy from La Rochelle. The offer of fresh meat and drink was heartily accepted by one and all.

Normally, the miners celebrated only on Sundays when many went to a larger mining camp upriver where itinerant merchants sold liquor and supplies and often a gambling tent or two could be found. Those who remained at camp mended clothes and boots, cooked bean and lentil based soups to reheat during the work week, washed clothes, wrote letters home or updated journals and read months old newspapers when available. They also weighed and divided their gold and stashed it in tin cans buried under their sleeping cots. This ritual was celebrated with glasses of wine or liquor if available. A fastidious few even bathed in the icy-cold river water.

The camp had no permanent structures. The miners lived two to four persons in large tents on elevated ground so rain would run off to the river. The principal furnishings inside each tent consisted of a large, hand-made table and a few three-legged stools. Some had small traveling chests for clothes, books and personal items but most hung possessions from wooden pegs or nails on tent poles or wrapped them in blankets or bed rolls. Some had oil lamps while others only candles stuck in empty whiskey bottles for light. All cooking, even in rainy weather, was done outside on a hearth under a lean-to . The French miners had built a small, conical bread oven out of fire-hardened mud bricks. They pooled energy and resources to make and bake a goodly number of loaves of thick, dark bread on Sundays to last the week.

I announced that I carried mail for a considerable number of French miners and would post the lists of addressees in the morning with a reward for information on the whereabouts of those on the list. Despite hearing that most miners ate frugally and monotonously, I was pleasantly surprised at my fellow countrymen. They plumed and boned the two large turkeys and made a surprisingly tasty and hearty soup for our main course. In order to feed all twenty-five of us, they added diced potatoes, lentils and pinto beans along with delicious Chanterelle mushrooms and spices they had found and dried previously.

Tent tables were cleared and dragged outside to form a crude refectory table so we could dine together. They added several loaves of their delicious black bread to sop up the savory soup and eat with the hard cheese they kept for rainy days.

Given the occasion and all around good cheer, I opened several round porcelain containers of "Terrine de Paté à la truffe du Périgord." The black transfer etiquette indicated the paté had been made by "B. Laforest, Périgueux, Dordogne." We decided to have our paté and cognac for dessert. The taste of a gastronomic food from home brought tears of joy to some eyes and we spent the rest of the evening singing French songs to an accordion and sharing tall tales.

My posting of names for letters created quite a stir of interest next morning. There were two lucky miners in camp. One received a letter from his family in Nantes and another from a brother in New Orleans who was on his way to the mines via Panama. The five Chilean miners were sad we had no mail for them. I suggested that next time they returned to Marysville for supplies they should speak with Ricard and arrange for a Chilean to bring mail to the mines. While most of Marysville was still a tent city, I had noticed one Chilean merchant and another running a tent bar with draped cubicles at the far end where his Chilena "hostesses" could entertain for a price.

While no one from this camp had come on a "La Californienne" ship, they knew the whereabouts of eight on our passenger lists. Two were working claims upriver where they sometimes bought supplies and a group of six were working sand bars near the large mining camp of Timbuctoo. I gave each informant a clutch of cigars as a reward.

Cyrille and Jean-Louis arrived in camp late afternoon with a four-antlered mule deer, a small doe, and three pheasants slung over the pommels of their pack mules' saddles. They built a big camp fire and after cleaning the birds, put them on a spit they could rotate from time to time. Then, working together with their fine-bladed bone knives they deftly butchered the buck. They cut the loin of one haunch into steaks and put them to cook in iron skillets over the coals of the fire for our dinner. With the other joint, they carved steaks off the loin which they stacked on a plank along with the heart, liver, kidneys, remainder of the two buttock joints, rib racks and front leg joints. The deer skin was scraped clean and tied in a roll. The rest they gave to all the dogs in camp to fight over like coyotes. Lupo went unchallenged for the best scraps.

The savory smell of broiling venison steaks wafting over the camp soon brought mining operations to a halt. Our guides let the encircling group salivate a good while before announcing the meat on the plank and two roasting pheasants were for sale. When the bargaining was over, our guides were richer to the tune of five ounces of gold dust. They had an $80.00 profit for their day's work and an unbutchered doe to haul and sell at the next camp. We traded a box of cigars for three loaves of the miners' delicious black bread and feasted that evening on venison steaks with Dijon mustard in lieu of a sauce. The third pheasant we'd eat on the way to the next mining camp.

We broke camp early next morning and after thanking our hosts, set out to try to make Timbuctoo before dark. The river track was more defined and easier slogging from use, so we made better time. We passed clutches of miners along the route. Most were European but not French, so we nodded and skirted their diggings. Cyrille had gone ahead with the Brittany and Lupo to scout for small game. He reappeared in late afternoon with a brace of jack rabbits and a headless snake hanging from his belt and a large wild boar with fearsome tusks tied on an Indian-style travois pulled by his Pinto pony.

I'd tasted the delicious meat of the wild pig but never seen the animal. "Bravo, Cyrille," I said. "What a monster you shot. Was it not dangerous?"

Cyrille nodded yes. "I get this one before he get me. But was Lupo give me the shot. He stood up to the charge an' when the boar flip him aside, I am ready for clear shot. If I miss, he get me like Lupo," he said pointing to the dog. Lupo had a nasty gash, muddy-red with blood on his right shoulder which Jean-Louis immediately tended to.

Cyrille untied the snake and tossed it at my feet. Unfurled, it was at least a meter and a half long. The snake's skin was marked with a series of diamond like patterns and at the end of its tail were six interlocking horny rings. "Go ahead. Pick it up," Cyrille commanded.

Reluctantly, I obeyed. "Now shake the tail." When I did, it made a sound like a rattle. "Now you have met rattlesnake. You hear that rattle, you stop and back away very slowly. It only makes the sound when it's coiled to strike." He pulled something out of a leather pouch and flipped it to the ground. It was the snake's head — a larger version of the vipers found in France. The snake's fangs looked wicked. "Rattlesnake bite you, you probably die," Cyrille said.

I stared at the snake's two large fangs which curved out of

its mouth. I felt my spine shiver as I imagined the snake coiled, rattles hissing, then the strike through the air and those frightful fangs puncturing my skin.

"Are there a lot of them around here?" I asked with my eyes still glued to both parts of the serpent.

"Yes, they hibernate during winter like the bears. They shed their skin and like the bears are hungry in Spring."

"Do they attack humans?" I asked with trepidation.

"No. They hunt rodents, birds' eggs, and small animals they can swallow whole. They only strike people who're careless and get too close or step on them. The rattle says stay away. So, you better be careful where you or your horse walk."

I could see why Jean-Louis led our pack train with Georges and me in the middle and the mules following. After Jean-Louis finished cleaning and sewing up Lupo's wound, our guides struggled to lift the huge wild pig off the travois and over the pack saddle of a mule. The mule's normally placid temper shifted to anguish and unbridled fear as it kicked and brayed to rid itself of the tusked boar.

"Why is the mule so afraid?" I asked once the boar was tied down on the pack saddle and the fearful mule resigned to its fate.

"It's the same when we hunt bear," Jean-Louis responded. "They know the animal is dangerous in the forest and the smell upsets them. Same with horses with these animals and rattlesnakes. They see or smell the animal and they spook."

I noticed that Cyrille flipped the snake's head into the river and coiled the snake's body in a pouch that he slung over his back.

"Why keep the snake if the animals fear it?" I asked.

Cyrille laughed. "Because snake tastes good." I felt my stomach lurch and tasted bile rising in my throat. My face betrayed my reaction — Ugh!

"We gonna roast it along with the rabbits. You should taste it. Lupo an' Sac à Puces love snake meat. You'll see."

We didn't make Timbuctoo, so we camped by the river where our animals could graze. Our guides struggled to haul the boar up a large branch of an oak tree where it hung by ropes next to the doe.

"Why rope the animals up the tree?" I asked.

"So a bear or mountain lion can't get them," replied Jean-Louis.

I shuddered. The threat from rattlesnakes was bad enough. But bears and cougars were even more frightening as they prowled by night while cold-blooded snakes sought shelter from the cold.

"Will bears and cougars attack our camp?" I asked nervously.

"Not likely," Jean-Louis said. "They will smell our kills but a bear can't get to it and a mountain lion will rouse the dogs if he tries. They don't hunt in packs, so we can easily scare a marauder away.

We ate the rabbits with our black bread and went to bed early. My dreams were full of wild animals chasing me. I was glad to wake at dawn and know we would sleep in a large camp the next day.

"CHINESE MINERS IN CALIFORNIA," 1851.

"WASHING WITH A CRADLE, WASHING WITH PAN,"
and "SLUICE AND TUNNEL, TIMBUCTOO."

California Gold Rush Journal

CHAPTER TWENTY-TWO

TImbuctoo and The Northern Placers — May 1851

Despite my troubled sleep, the night was uneventful. We rose shortly after dawn. Our tent was dripping wet from the river fog. Hot coffee and slices of the miner's dark bread revived my spirits. The morning mist would burn off later as it had since we left Marysville. Georges and I looked forward to seeing a full scale mining operation and locating some of the miners we sought to justify our wages and expenses on our client's behalf.

We arrived at Timbuctoo in late morning. The sun shone brightly as our mule train trudged through the muddy tracks of the mining settlement. The town, if one can call it that, was perched high enough in the hills above the swift flowing Yuba River to avoid any risk of flooding. While there were some permanent structures in wood, it was still mostly a tent city like Marysville. Further up the hill, miners had constructed a number of log cabins.

We stopped at a general merchandise store selling everything from picks and shovels to beans and flour and the pots to cook them in. We learned that there was no post office or agent in the camp. Sought after mail and newspapers arrived from time to time with supply trains, but there was no regular service.

I agreed to post my list of addressees on the store's bulletin board and be present from 1-4 P.M. on Sunday to distribute the mail we carried. As most of the miners working the outlying placers would come to town that day to resupply, drink or gamble, we'd have the best chance to meet those whose mail we carried. The proprietor, a burly, red bearded Scotsman, even offered to provide me with a table and two chairs for mail call. No doubt he thought it would be good for business.

The Scotsman had no idea as to the whereabouts of the six miners we sought to interview. As it was Friday, we decided to set up our camp at the end of the town but closer to the log cabins than the tent encampment that sprawled around the bars that made up the majority of wood structures.

Once camp was established, our guides set about butchering the boar and doe which they planned to sell on Sunday to the highest bidders. They had the foresight to load their second mule with firewood we'd need to cook with. The tastiest cuts would be reserved for our dinners and they planned to cook strips of venison to carry with us on the track to Nevada City. With so many miners strewn around this rich mining region, game would be much harder to find.

As Georges and I were free to do our own thing, we decided to see what attractions the town had to offer. Our first stop was a large tent that served as a bar and sort of social club. The floor was made of roughly sawed cedar planks nailed together to thwart the town's mud. In addition to the cherry wood bar that had been reassembled from sections after being hauled in by mule-drawn wagons, there was a large billiard table in the center and two large, round tables with vacant chairs. There was a newspaper rack full of months old newspapers at one end of the bar. Other than Georges and me, only the barkeep and two scruffy looking muleteers were present.

I ordered a round of boilermakers, a large schooner of beer

with a shot of whiskey, for the two at the end of the bar whose beer and whiskey chasers were long gone. I hoped my generosity would lead to some useful information.

"You boys newly arrived?" The huskier of the two mule drivers said in English with a twangy accent from somewhere in the Appalachian mountains.

"Just arrived a couple of hours ago. A fellow gets mighty thirsty outsmarting Indians and mountain lions along the trail." I replied casually.

"Injuns. You don't say," the slim mule driver with a bushy black beard and slouch hat trimmed with pheasant feathers in the band commented. "Heard tell from some wagon boys that a party of Maidu tried to steal their mules in the night. Said there was a whole pack of 'em they had to run off. Damn no good injuns. Always lookin' ta steal what ain't theirs."

"They must have been the same ones who followed us. How do you know they're Maidu?" I asked.

"Well, them's the ones cause the most trouble from Marysville to Nevada City. The tribe use ta live along the Feather River afore ole Theo Cordua leased the land around Marysville from John Sutter. Theo ran cattle an' built hisself a house an' trading post at what's now south D Street in Marysville. A Frenchie named Covillaud, who'd worked for Cordua, bought out Cordua an' his new wife's brothers' interest after he hit pay dirt in the placers. The Maidu weren't none too happy 'bout all this. So, they took to cattle rustlin' an' stealin' whenever they got a chance. Ain't that right Ned," he asked his husky companion in leather breeches and red plaid shirt. Ned nodded affirmatively.

"Are they warlike?" I asked thinking about the night spent on the cold gravels with a hunting rifle aimed at the perimeter of our camp.

"Well, not really. They got bows an' arrows for huntin' but they caint stand up to our fire power. They're sneaky smart, know the land, an' hard to pin down. Keep movin' camps and rustle an' steal like a bunch of foxes. If they kill a white man, the feds would hunt 'em down an' exterminate 'em like vermin. Reckon they know it too. A lot of 'em been dying from the pox and other diseases I heard." His buddy Ned nodded his agreement.

I could sympathize with the Maidu and had no doubt that their traditional way of life had been disrupted for good. The news they were dying from the diseases brought by the immigrants, for which they apparently had no natural immunity, sounded like a death knell for their race. I kept my thoughts to myself.

"How is the supply business?" I asked.

"Pretty good. Lots of gold coming out of the placers around here. Good for us now that the weather is milder and we can pack in goods on time," said Ned.

"On time?" I asked.

"Goods got to get here by Saturday at the latest, so they can be sold on Sunday when the miners come to town. Miners who make a big strike gonna spend a lot of gold in liquor and having a good time. He wants to eat fancy food and drink champagne. Get a shave and a haircut and pay for a woman. His friends wanna enjoy his money too. An' they spend their own gold gambling, drinking and buying supplies to take back to camp," Horace, the one with the bushy beard, said.

"You'll see starting tomorrow when the miners who have cabins on the hill straggle in. This bar will be packed solid. Them tables will have monte and faro dealers and miners standin' in line to lose their hard earned gold."

"Will some of the miners be here tonight?" I asked.

"Yup. Ones that ain't too far from town will come on in if'n they found some good gold. Only the ones livin' hand-to-mouth will wait 'til Saturday night or Sunday. Best choice of goods will be Saturday an' if the miner wants first pick of the women, it'll be tonight when there's less competition," said Horace. The barkeep who'd been eavesdropping on our parley nodded his agreement.

"Where will the women be?" Georges asked.

"Why right here," said Ned. "They'll be working the bar for ole Thomas here all weekend," he said pointing to the barkeep. "They'll entertain the lucky ones after their shift in a tent set up outside. They'll be more pricey tonight 'cause they know miners or other merchants in town got good gold to pay. So they give better service if ya know what I mean. Some of the real lookers rent a hill cabin and can be purchased for the night, but they cost an arm and a leg. Har, har," he laughed at his joke.

"Is this the main watering hole?" I asked.

"Well, it's the best one that's fer sure. There'll be other fellows set up in tents with whiskey and some will gamble and others bring women what can be had for $5.00 a throw on a cot. Usually, there's a greaser in a big hat an' poncho what brings a bunch of black-eyed women nearly dark as injuns what can be had for $3.00 a throw for ten minutes on Sunday. Gets pretty sloppy by the end of the day, if ya knows what I mean."

After what I'd seen in Little China, I wasn't surprised at this arrangement. Raoul had told me that some unscrupulous Chileans had brought indentured women to serve as low-priced whores in San Francisco. The impoverished women, who had sold themselves to pimps for the price of passage to San Francisco, were forced to service up to 80 men a day for a dollar or two each to pay for room and board. They, like the Chinese, were considered inferior because of their dark skin, mixed Spanish and Indian blood, and inability to speak English or learn their rights. Their tent brothels were located outside the commercial center and protected from interference by payment of bribes to officials and police.

"Where do the French miners hang out when they come to

town?" I asked.

"Well some of the Frenchies come in here to gamble but they doan like sour mash or rye whiskey with beer none too much," Thomas, the barkeep, said in what I took to be a Welsh or north England accent.

"Do they congregate near here?" I asked.

There's a Frenchie what runs a tent bar on Saturdays and Sundays servin' wine an' brandy an' rentin' out gamblin' tables to professional card sharks for a cut in the take. His girls run the bar on the same terms we do here. They're free to contract themselves for a price once their shift's over. One shark even brings along a woman shill what he sells for $16.00 a half hour once the gamblin's over," the barkeep said.

I decided to move on and see what else the town had to offer. I bought another round of drinks for the muleteers and tipped the barkeep with a two and a half dollar gold piece for his information. There were lots of big, empty tents with tables and make shift bars waiting for the throngs of thirsty, bored, foolish and horny miners who'd start trickling in next day. Whoever owned the land and tents on it stood to make a killing on weekends.

We checked out a wood-frame building boasting a hand-painted sign promising "Best Grub This Side of Sacramento." A slate listed the menu offerings: Ham or Bacon & Eggs with Fried Potatoes; Steak & Kidney Pie; Venison Steak with Fried Potatoes; Fried River Trout with mashed potatoes and choice of Cherry or Peach Pie for Dessert. Dinner prices ranged from $2.50 for the ham and eggs to $3.75 for the venison steak and 50 cents more for a slice of glutinous pie whose preserved contents came straight from a can. I was starting to realize how lucky we were to have our guides roasting us fresh, delicious meat every night.

It was clear from our walk around town that we'd have to

wait until Nevada City to get a European style meal. While there may be numbers of French working the placers, they obviously preferred to cook for themselves like the miners we'd dined with at their river camp. The only baker we saw on our tour was a Mexican who specialized in baking "pan dulce," a soft bread with lots of sugar, tortillas, and an insipid, spongy white bread for miner's toast and soaking up egg yolks and molasses. Admittedly, we were spoiled by Manon's creativity and cooking skills, but disappointed nevertheless to find such pedestrian fare in what purported to be a town.

We returned to our camp near dusk to the tantalizing smell of roasting venison and wild boar. Our guides were also boiling lentils and peas to make a savory soup with some choice bits of the wild pig. I fished out of my pack two bottles of Robert's special Bordeaux wine with the applied seals reading "Grand Vin de Medoc" to celebrate the sumptuous meal we would enjoy.

California Gold Rush Journal

CHAPTER TWENTY-THREE

Timbuctoo and The Northern Placers — May 1851

As we didn't expect much activity in town until evening, Georges and I hired a local guide, Peter Damon, to take us on a tour of the placer mining operations. Our two guides, Cyrille and Jean-Louis, sold a portion of their venison and boar meat to local restaurants and set out with their dogs, horses and mules to see if they could bag some more game. Their plan was to ford the river and hunt the opposite bank.

Peter lived in one of the miner's cabins on a hill overlooking the town. We asked if we could visit his humble abode and he readily agreed. He explained that he with his two brothers, like a number of hardy miners, had built their cabin to pass the winter near their diggings and be the first to resume mining when weather allowed in the Spring.

He was injured when the gravel pit he was digging caved in on him and crushed his right arm. His two brothers continued to mine their claim which was producing ten to twelve ounces of gold a week. He welcomed the chance to accompany us to their claim so he could deliver food and supplies and bring to town the week's haul of gold. On Sunday, an agent from Adam's Express would come to town from Nevada City to buy gold and accept deposits to be credited to miner's accounts back home.

The brothers were banking as much gold as possible and forwarding it to their father in Rhode Island for the day their still rich claim was exhausted and they could return home to marry and start their own businesses.

Peter's cabin was constructed of redwood logs with the bark still attached that had been notched at the ends to fit snugly into the notches of the logs forming the walls at right angles. The result was a notched together log box about twenty feet square with an opening for a wooden door and a hearth for cooking. The fireplace was made of large river stones set together with mortar. It ran up the side of the cabin higher than the steep roof so it drew well in winter when the roof was almost buried in snow.

The floor and ceiling were covered with rustic hand-hewn planks. A trap in the ceiling gave access to the attic where provisions could be stored during winter. The furnishings were Spartan. The central piece of furniture was a wooden table with four stools in front of the hearth. Inside the hearth an iron-forged chain with hooks at different heights descended to accommodate several cast iron cooking pots stacked on a kindling box. Two shelves along the wall across from the entryway stored their meager possessions: tin plates, cups and storage bins, two oil lamps, a box of candles, pottery jugs of molasses, whiskey, and other liquids, a pipe rack with several clay pipes, a tin of matches and two of tobacco.

A large gold scale sat in the center of the table next to a family bible. Three shotguns hung on pegs from the roof beams along with three cartridge belts full of shot. Three elevated sleeping pallets filled with fresh straw shared the wall farthest from the fire with three small traveling trunks that served as bedside tables for the brothers.

Outside, they had built an outhouse only a few paces from the entryway, stacked firewood several feet high on both sides of the front door and constructed a small wood shed to keep their kindling dry.

"Are you able to get fresh food and supplies from town during winter," I asked Peter.

"Not often, all the restaurants and all but one bar close down for winter after the first snow. The merchants winter in Nevada City or Grass Valley. It's near impossible to get supplies to us and what does get through is three times what we pay now. We're pretty much on our own."

"What about the French miners. Do any of them stay here during winter?"

"No, they pretty much keep to themselves and don't mingle with us. Most just mine for the season and either winter in a town or return to San Francisco to work for next year's grubstake. I did hear tell of a camp called 'French Corral,' located on a tributary of the Yuba River up near North San Juan and Nevada City where a bunch of trappers have settled and have a permanent camp, but I've never been there."

After our tour of Peter's cabin, we set off on our tour of the diggings. We loaded Peter's supplies on one of our pack mules and set off at a slow pace following the south bank of the river which here was very wide and not as treacherous as some of the spots we'd passed up to now.

All along the bank, groups of miners were laboriously loading rockers or Long Toms with river gravels. We saw miners in gravel pits as high as their heads shoveling bed rock gravels into buckets their pals hauled out by ropes and dumped into the hoppers of their Long Toms.

"Why are there so many miners working so close together? I asked pointing to the line of toilers snaking along the river bank as far as I could see."

"Well a miner can only claim a 10x10 foot plot at a time and he has to work it or lose it. Those are the rules. So when somebody hits a rich pocket, he's soon got company on all sides. The banks of the river along this stretch are narrow enough that groups of three to four or more can dig down to bedrock where the pay dirt is found. Been enough gold found so that nearly every yard of the embankment will be mined. Later, when the river is shallower, they'll extend their digging right into the river bed."

I had to admit it was an impressive sight. An army of miners toiled and probed the nooks and crannies of each river bend where gold could collect. Few talked or paid any attention to our presence. The river valley reverberated with the sounds of picks and shovels striking gravel beds.

It took us over two hours to arrive at Peter's claim. His brothers, Clem and William, were operating a rocker when they stopped to hail us. They'd rented out their Long Tom to neighbors as it needed all three brothers to sift the gravels efficiently. My arrangement with Peter for his services was use of our mule and a hunk of wild boar meat they could boil with their beans to make a soup for the weekend. As they were short-handed, they were determined to stay on their claim and not come to town.

Georges and I left them to visit and exchange goods for gold and continued up the river where the brothers indicated a group of French miners were working. We'd pick up our mule and escort Peter back to town on our return.

The French camp was indistinguishable from other riverside camps. Groups of bearded miners picked and shoveled gravels for their Long Toms. Some toiled in the now hot sun without shirts while others grunted at their work in baggy trousers, shirts with sleeves rolled up, scruffy high boots, slouch hats and large blue bandanas around their necks or arranged under their hats to absorb their sweat.

I introduced myself and Georges as reporters checking on

the progress of French miners in the placers and told them we were especially concerned to learn the whereabouts and success of the miners sent over by mining companies that had abandoned them. Most had not eaten since shortly after dawn and readily accepted my offer to share a picnic lunch with fresh bread from the town and tins of sardines, tuna, mackerel, and paté from the home country. To our delicacies, they added a hard cheese and pan fried crepes they sweetened with molasses and flavored with lemon juice.

Once we'd had our fill and moved on to strong coffee and the box of cigars I offered, I told them about the Sunday mail delivery in town and our interest in talking with members of La Californienne Mining Society.

"That would be me and Jacko," said a wiry young miner with greasy black hair tied in a pony tail pointing to his tall, red-headed companion leaning on a short-handled shovel who introduced himself as Jacques Menager from Chartres.

"We were on the "Uncas" that sailed from Anvers in June of '50. Arrived in the dead of winter and near to starved to death in the fog and rain in 'Frisco.' We were already weak from the voyage — rotting food, rancid water and foul sanitary conditions," said the black haired one who introduced himself as Louis Jugeau from a coastal town in Brittany.

"And we were the lucky ones," the red head piped in. "At least Consul Dillon got us jobs on the wharfs and staked us to get to Marysville so we could start mining with the group here."

"Lucky because he found you winter work and transport?" I asked.

"Well, compared to the rest, yes," said the Breton.

"What rest?" I inquired.

"There was lots of Germans, Belgians, Dutch, and even a Hungarian on the trip over. Consul Dillon advanced us money, but the other Europeans had to fend for themselves. Most were destitute like us on arrival — no place to stay, no money, and no transport to the mines. It had taken our all just to buy our crummy passage," Jacko said bitterly.

"Didn't Dillon help everyone who came on the French ship sent by the French mining society?" I asked.

"No, the Consul announced immediately that there would be no help from our society for anyone not French. Nearly caused a riot with the non-French as they had no consul to bail them out or help them. Dillon only helped us French. Said he had no authority to loan money to citizens of other countries. Some of us pitched in and helped some of the Belgians once we got a job, but most of the others had to sign on as sailors to get food, shelter and passage home," the Breton said.

"Sailors? How could they work as sailors on ships?" I asked with disbelief.

"Didn't have no choice. Weather was nasty and they had no place to go. Some did share what little they had and others sought out fellow countrymen in the city for help, but most knew they'd never make it to the mines. So many sailors had jumped ship, captains were desperate to get crews and not wind up anchored and abandoned like the ghost boats in the bay. So if you were able-bodied they signed you on and figured you'd learn on the wing or with a lash on your back," Jacko said.

I could hardly believe what I was hearing. I could just imagine the desperation of those who had to sign on as sailors to get home. They'd be required to trim and reef sails in foul weather and learn how to survive on the slippery yards and swaying masts or pay a premature trip to Davy Jones' locker. Even here, many of the French miners were from the upper middle class and unused to doing hard, dirty and dangerous manual labor. Only the young, strong and resourceful would last through the long, hot summer to come and even they would need to be lucky to strike a rich enough deposit to pay their way home and have some capital to invest or buy a farm or pay off their parent's mortgage that financed the trip to California.

"Why did you decide to sign on with the La Californienne Mining Society?" I asked.

"Simple choice," the Breton said. "They guaranteed we would be supported for a period of two years. Figured it was ample time to strike it rich. They said they had sent mining engineers ahead to organize mining on the properties they owned and told us we couldn't help but get rich. Didn't find out it was not true 'til the Consul came on board on our arrival."

Jacko bobbed his head in agreement and added, "bunch of crooks, really. My parents gave me my sisters' dowries and borrowed from family to finance the trip. We believed what they told us."

"Who told you?" I asked.

"The company had an office in La Rochelle and they advertised in the local papers. When I met their agent in La Rochelle, he showed me a newspaper called "Le Californien" that reported on their properties. He read me the guarantees and all about the rich gold and silver mines the company owns. My reading is poor, so he spelled it all out for me."

"It was the same for me 'cept I could read it word for word," the Breton said. "Told me they weren't sure when the next company boat would set off, so instead of shipping out of Le Havre like the first two boats, we had to travel to Anvers where they were taking on the Belgians and other nationalities."

"Did the Belgians tell you how they had been recruited?"

"Sure, the exact same way. The company set up recruitment offices in all the major cities, Brussels, Hamburg, Amsterdam and elsewhere. We all fell for the same line. At least we got to the mines. We still have to pay the Consul back and our families. Unless we're real lucky, it'll probably take us two seasons to repay the loans, get home and have anything to show for it but sunburn and calluses. Jacko hasn't written home to tell his two sisters their dowries are gone and they may wind up old maids," the Breton said angrily.

"You guys doing any good with your Long Tom?" I asked.

"Not yet. We're averaging about $5.00 a day per man. That buys food and supplies, but not much more. No point us going to town 'cause we got nothing spare to spend. We keep working on Sunday's hoping to hit richer pay dirt. We figure when there's less water in the river, we can get to some of the gold that's trapped in the pools and under rocks that washed down with the winter rains."

I told the two that I wanted to report their stories in the French press and hoped the French government would pressure their mining society to send money to Consul Dillon to pay for their debt and passage home when the time came to leave. They agreed to sign affidavits I would prepare and notarize by the French consulate in San Francisco on my return; I planned to send them to my boss in an effort to minimize the knowledge of his client. I would lay all the blame on unscrupulous hucksters, who probably working on commission promised bags of gold to their recruits under false pretense. The fact that the society sought to dupe other Europeans as well might create even more pressure to hold the marketers liable and exonerate my boss' client. At least it would be an arrow in the boss' quiver and helped justify my salary. So I hoped!

Since the two society miners couldn't afford to go to town or even take a day off, I left them a tin of paté, a jar of marmalade, a box of cigars and a magnum of French cognac to celebrate their weekend.

While I interviewed the two French miners from the society, Georges did the same with the others in the group. The stories were all similar. They had gone into debt to finance passage to California and the mines and had been promised transport and ground support to the mines by charlatans selling worthless mining stock in shell companies.

We made our way back to the three brothers' camp, retrieved our mule and returned with Peter to Timbuctoo just as the sun was setting.

"A CALIFORNIA CABIN,"
from *Gleason's Drawing Room Companion, 1851.*

"A FRENCH MINER,"
from *Mountains and Molehills*, by Franck Marryat, 1855
(*author's collection*).

California Gold Rush Journal
CHAPTER TWENTY-FOUR
Timbuctoo and The Northern Placers — May 1851

We arrived at our camp in town after dark. Jean-Louis was stirring a large pot perched on a metal grill set in a roaring campfire. The aromas from the pot set our tummies rumbling. They had tried for big game but found none. Instead, they had bagged jack rabbits, quail, pigeons, and partridge. The rabbits were in the pot and the tiny quail roasting on the skewer. After watching the American miners preparing their evening meals of flapjacks, boiled salt beef and refried beans, we had arrived in culinary paradise.

After wolfing down the rabbit stew, greedily tearing apart the succulent little quail and washing it down with vintage Chateauneuf-du-Pape red wine from the Rhone Valley, Georges and I were ready to observe Timbuctoo's night life.

Most of the large tents were now occupied and some even full. We decided to check out first the tent bar where we'd encountered the two muleteers. The bar was packed with a motley group of men who ogled the low cut bodice of the rosy-cheeked barmaid as she poured draft beer in large schooners and filled whiskey shot glasses and set them on the tray of her side kick, a dark-haired beauty with high cheek bones, flashing black eyes and coppery skin that had the males drooling as she walked her walk in high-heeled pumps to serve the two gambling tables.

Both tables thronged with gamblers eager to play red or black on the roulette wheel or twenty-one on the other table. Large sums of money were being bet at both tables. Professional gamblers ran the show. Miners and others without gold or silver coins or paper money from the bank in Nevada City to bet bought gambling tokens from a vivacious, chesty red-head with an Irish accent who weighed gold dust, flakes and nuggets and meticulously inspected the proffered gold for brass filings, mica, quartz and other impurities.

The practice here was to place a generous tip for service or a winning round directly in between the two hefty globes in the barmaids' décolletage. If the tip warranted it, the buxom wench let the high-roller cop a feel.

I decided it was time to move on. Georges was still following every move of the tawny-skinned Senorita and probably imagined himself sampling her charms in a miner's cabin. He was not happy to be celibate and longed for his New York girlfriend. Recently, he had been mumbling a desire to send for her on our return to San Francisco even though he still didn't have a plan for their livelihood.

Our next stop was a large tent where we could hear high-pitched and ribald French spoken. In the center, two gambling tables were crowded with two sets of gamblers playing black jack. To my surprise the far table was manned by Jacques Vincent and his "wife" Odile. Jacques, dressed more modestly than on the ship, was dealing twenty-one to three young Frenchmen in miner's attire. Odile was hanging on the arm of the player with the biggest pile of chips and encouraging him to bet on his hand. The Vincents were so absorbed in their play that neither spotted our arrival.

Georges and I moved off to an angle where we could observe Odile. As on the ship, she wore a form fitting satin dress with daring décolletage. The men gathered around the table followed every subtle move of her luscious and tantalizing breasts as she giggled, leaned forward to allow a glimpse of her rouged nipples, flirted and tossed her blonde hair or rested her bosom on the arm of a player. A ruddy-faced miner in his fifties clenched and unclenched his fists each time Odile's breasts threatened to escape their flimsy binding. Another made a sucking sound each time Odile's breasts surged one way or another.

As I watched the game progress, I was sure Odile was subtly signaling Vincent the value of the cards held by the players. Several of her girlish mannerisms were repeated but in differing poses to the right or left. The players were so intent on trying to win their bets and the crowd so captivated by her antics that the Vincents could cheat with little risk of exposure. Georges was sure she sold her charms for a nice sack of gold when the gambling petered out.

As we had no interest in gambling and there was no other entertainment available, Georges and I searched out a bar that seemed to be dedicated to serious drinkers and took two stools at the end of the bar. Georges soon turned maudlin with the rough-edged brandy we drank with our Havana cigars. I suggested he take a $20.00 gold coin and see if he could secure the favors of the Carmen he had eyed earlier.

"No, that's not what I want. She acts sexy and sells herself just to get the miner's gold. I want to start a new life here with a serious woman like my Nelly. I've decided to send for her as soon as we return," Georges said with resignation.

"Even though you aren't sure what the two of you would do to earn money?" I said.

"I'm afraid if I don't send for her, I'll lose her. Letters are too slow and unsatisfactory. I can't express what I feel in letters and she can't write French well. Her father will make her marry unless she gets passage from me. There'll be plenty of time to figure out what we'll do during the time she's traveling."

"I deposited your funds in New York and can transfer funds to pay Nelly's passage and expenses. It'll make a big dent in your account."

"Doesn't matter. It's our big chance. But, I don't know whether she should come around the Horn or risk the trip through Panama. What do you think?" Georges pleaded.

"Well, there are pros and cons to both ways. Ships around the Horn are slow but expensive for first class passage as we know. They can also be dangerous if the weather turns bad or the provisions spoil. Clipper ship passage is very expensive but two to three months faster. The trip through Panama is the fastest from New York but most risky for a single woman traveling alone. The Chagres River is full of mosquitos and other parasites that transmit dangerous fevers and diseases."

"Yes, I am afraid to have her come via Panama. I've heard from some who came that way that if you get sick, you die. No medical care is available. The natives will just rob you and dump you in the river or leave you in the forest to die."

"She'd have to come with a group of Americans who could protect her. She's not a country girl who's used to riding on mules or fending off aggressive males with a knife," I added.

Georges now looked downright miserable. "I was hoping she could take passage on The Flying Cloud with Captain Richards. She knows the ship and they know her."

"Whether on the Flying Cloud or other American Clipper ship, it would cost you most of your capital." I said soberly. They'd be in a squeeze if she arrived and they couldn't earn their keep except by manual labor.

"I was thinking maybe she could help Manon with the catering business. Her English would be useful in either buying for or promoting the business and helping it expand," Georges said.

"Well, that would be up to Manon to decide. Suppose Manon needed someone to wash dishes, clean the kitchen, peel potatoes and carrots as well as get up at 5 A.M. to light the fires and make the coffee. Is your Nelly going to be willing to start at the bottom?"

"Yes, she'd do it to help even if she only got room and board," Georges quipped.

"How do you know that?" I asked. "She's never done menial work in her life," I added unconvinced.

"We talked about it," Georges said defensively. I raised my eyebrows and motioned him to continue.

"She said she wanted to make her own way in life and knew it would mean working her way up from the bottom until she would be able to use her education to advantage. She even mentioned she'd gratefully work as Sammy's kitchen assistant and clean the ship's chamber pots if it meant she could earn her passage to California. She wants a new life. So do I. We're determined to make our own way. She'll just need an opportunity to prove herself," he stammered and brought his fist down on the bar for emphasis.

I paused to let Georges cool down before replying. It was the first time I'd seen the normally affable and good-natured Georges near losing his temper.

"And what about you? Are you willing to do the same if you have to?" I asked pointedly.

"Absolutely. I don't have Nelly's education. We agreed we'd hire ourselves out as a couple as coachman and governess if we had to. Lots of rich folks in San Francisco gonna need hired help. We'll work together and make our way," Georges said.

I was impressed by Georges' determination. "I will discuss your request with Manon when we return. In any case, you have your cabin on our ship for when she arrives. I'm sure she'll find suitable work," I said with a smile that helped cheer him up.

Next morning I toured the tent city now bustling with activity. More makeshift bars and tables selling food staples and mining gear were in evidence. As miners straggled into town, they were met with fiddlers playing lively tunes for silver bits and barkers touting their wares. Barbers offered to shave bushy beards and to wash and trim greasy hair. A brutish, churlish looking mountain man offered a turn in his small tent with his two Indian women for $2.00 a go.

Our two guides had roasted the rest of the fowl they'd shot and now offered the cooked birds and uncooked remainders of their deer and boar for sale at a table in the shade of a tree. Georges was busy making the rounds of the bars and stalls announcing our mail delivery service for the French and locals. In addition to all the French letters, we'd taken correspondence from Marysville for the town's permanent residents and merchants both for Timbuctoo and Nevada City.

Even before we dragged our table and chairs onto the porch of the general merchandise store where I'd posted our mail call notice, a crowd of scruffy, impatient miners jostled each other to be first in line. Most hadn't consulted the list I'd posted. All assumed I had a letter from home for them. Rather than deal with them one-by-one, I instructed Georges to hold up a letter and call for the addressee by name. We started with the local town folks to cull them out of the throng. As each individual collected his mail, Georges politely asked for a $1.00 contribution to cover our expense of transport.

I was surprised to see four negroes among the locals receiving mail. The barkeep where we'd met the muleteers on our arrival had mentioned that some of the first miners to test the local placers were freed or escaped slaves. They'd come to California once it was settled it was not to be a slave state. It was rumored that the name Timbuctoo was coined by a former slave turned miner who was originally from Timbuktoo in Mali.

As the first letters were picked up by locals, they readily handed Georges the requested fee in silver bits which he dropped in a saddle bag. After the local delivery, we called the names of French emigrants who'd sailed on La Californienne's boats first. There were only seven. Georges told each that for them the delivery was free and the mining company was offering free cigars and brandy after the roll call. Georges would get their story and hopefully learn the whereabouts of others on our lists.

Those receiving a letter jumped for joy and hooted their pleasure; one even impulsively kissed Georges on the forehead. One slim, wiry Frenchman with crumbling boots and mud-dried clothes handed Georges a nice-sized gold nugget when he saw his letter was from his fiancé in Paris. Those who had no mail just shook their heads in disbelief and disgust as they headed for the nearest bar to find solace in cheap booze.

Georges worked his charm on the seven who readily swapped stories for French brandy and cigars. He learned that quite a few who'd come over on the Society's boats were trying their luck further up river at a mining camp called "French Corral." The camp is located on a small tributary of the Yuba River near North San Juan and Nevada City. The camp was founded by remnants of French Canadian trappers and mountain men who'd operated under direction of the Hudson Bay Company. The trappers depleted the rivers of beavers in Canada and the Pacific Northwest and descended as far as the southern mines.

Many decided to settle in California once the trapping petered out and were in place when gold was discovered. One group mined the river near Astoria in the southern placers and another group established their camp at "French Corral." The camp was supposedly named for a Frenchman who raised mules in his corral. According to Georges' informants, the French settlers found rich diggings and were expanding their mining operations on the Yuba River up the San Juan Ridge and as far as North Bloomfield. It was apparent we would need to check out "French Corral" for ourselves.

California Gold Rush Journal
CHAPTER TWENTY-FIVE
French Corral and the Northern Placers – May 1851

We set out from Timbuctoo in a light rain after an early breakfast of toast, scrambled eggs and bacon that Cyrille prepared. Our guides warned us that the river trail would be more arduous as we climbed in altitude. Often, we skirted the river by passing through forests and dales when the river cascaded through deep crevasses and narrow granite channels. We encountered few miners willing to risk the fast moving water.

We were laboring up a hilly incline when Cyrille in the lead held up his hand for us to stop. He slid off his Pinto pony and proceeded cautiously by foot for about thirty feet before retracing his steps back.

"Bear scat," he announced. "We must be wary. A mother and her cub are nearby."

"How do you know it's a mother and cub," I asked innocently.

He laughed. "Simple. See the scat here," he said pointing to a pile of small, freshly dropped turds. "That's the mother. Look here. See how small the scat is. That's the cub."

"Is it a cause for worry?" Georges asked.

"Yes, mother bears are very protective of their cubs. The

cub was born in a cave while the mother hibernated or shortly after. Mama bear will have lost her fat during her winter sleep. She is very hungry now and there is little food. She will be grumpy and ready to fight for food or to protect her cub. She will smell our smoked venison and other food. That makes her very unpredictable," Jean-Louis added.

"Will you shoot her?" Georges asked in an uncertain voice.

"No. We hope not. If we kill Mama bear, her cub will starve to death or be eaten by a cougar. If we wound Mama bear, she will try to kill us to protect her cub. So we must be watchful and try to avoid contact. I will go ahead to watch for signs. If we are lucky, she will hunt fish in the river and we will not meet her," Jean-Louis said.

First rattlesnakes, now hungry bears to worry about and trouble our sleep. We camped on a bluff overlooking the river. After a dinner of smoked venison, Cyrille and Jean-Louis put all our provisions in a rope net and hauled it to hang twenty feet off the ground on an oak limb. We were cautioned not to have any food items in our tent and securely fasten the flap for the night. Georges and I drowned our worries with extra tots of Calvados with our evening cigars. We retired early, but I tossed and turned most of the night. The fear of Mama bear ripping open our flimsy canvas tent and mauling us out of frustration and hunger haunted my dreams.

Next morning the light rain of the preceding day turned into a steady downpour. Our sputtering campfire produced lukewarm coffee and we settled for tinned biscuits for breakfast. Our guides had donned large Chilean ponchos over their regular outfits. The tightly woven wool cloak with a hole for the head served as an efficient, waterproof raincoat. Georges and I were miserable in our uncomfortable rain slickers and boots.

We made slow progress during the morning. Lunch under the branches of dripping oak trees consisted of cold cheese and hard bread. The heavy rain gave way to sporadic but frightening thunder showers. Lightning flashed, then crashed nearby and thunder boomed in our eardrums and spooked our animals. Driving rain and hail pelted us unmercifully during these storms. Finally, we had to dismount and lead our animals over ground now muddy, slick and treacherous.

"You city boys enjoying real mountain life?" Cyrille joked with a laugh. "You like this, den you come back in winter. We show you a real storm in snow and ice."

I now seriously doubted our decision to make for the diggings at French Corral. The thought of a hot bath, clean bed and restaurant meal in Nevada City tempted me to abandon our quest and plead to be taken back to civilization.

"Will we be able to make French Corral by dusk," I asked.

"Not walking in this muck," Jean-Louis replied.

"Maybe tomorrow if the storms let up," Cyrille added with a shrug.

———◆•◆•◆———

Next morning the sun shone brightly and birds chirped pleasantly. Jean-Louis greeted us with a pot of hot coffee and fresh oatmeal pancakes smeared with pungent molasses from Guadeloupe. The sun and hot food revived our spirits. Cyrille had left camp at day break to hunt and would meet our slow moving mule train later.

We descended to the river where trails along the banks were more gravely and less muddy. It was hard, slow slogging never-the-less. Cyrille arrived at our camp as the sun was setting. His pack mule was loaded with a large, hoofed animal that resembled a male deer but wasn't. Cyrille beamed with pleasure and Jean-Louis immediately cut the animal's bindings from the mule and our two guides set to butchering a rear haunch.

That evening we feasted on elk steaks. Jean-Louis made a sauce from dried mushrooms and red wine from the two bottles of Cote de Rhone we drank with our meal. By the time our guides put the stopper on their whiskey jug and we had finished our Calvados and cigars, life seemed worth living again.

Jean-Louis announced about ten o'clock next morning that we should arrive at French Corral around noon. We had been climbing steadily. Eventually, we arrived at a small river valley dotted with miners' cabins on the higher slopes and several larger structures nearer the valley floor. The Yuba River meandered peacefully through this tranquil landscape. It was a dramatic change from the surging river we had been following.

"Why is the river so placid here and wild further down?" I asked.

"You'll see. The miners are diverting and damming the river upstream. The water in the feeder streams and even areas of the river are carried by flumes to supply fast moving water to wash the gravels," Jean-Louis said pointing to an elevated wooden trough descending into the valley from its far end.

We made arrangements for a mail roll call for the following day at the camp's trading post as we had done at Timbuctoo. While our guides butchered the rest of the elk, we made arrangements with a local miner named Michel Corot to tour the diggings upstream and advertise our mail delivery.

As there were well defined trails leading upstream, we were able to travel by horse. As we approached the far end of the vale, I was surprised at the size of the wooden flume which looked like a child's toy from the camp end of the valley. It was built like a railroad trestle with strong, timbered cross-braces supporting the structure of wooden planks designed as a chute to carry water from a higher elevation to its target. The steep descent guaranteed the water would gather speed and power.

"Why is it not carrying water?" I asked.

"Because it's no longer needed. It was built to wash gold out of the sides of the valley. Once the gravels have been all washed, there's no more gold and we must move on," Michel said.

"And leave all this hard work behind?" I said thinking of all the sweat and muscle needed to cut and mill the timbers and erect the flume.

"It's too much work to tear it down and haul it up river. Gravity flows down not up. Further up river, they will build another flume to float the lumber down it to build a dam to divert the river, then use it to carry water to wash the river bed gravels like we did here," he said pointing to the now barren valley floor strewn with a deep layer of gravel and river rock and the river which had lost most of its force here.

We continued our climb up the side of the river until we arrived at another plateau. Here an army of soldier ants worked building a mill race for a large water-lifting wheel. Groups of workers sawed pine and fir trees while others cut them in sections and planed them into rough planks. The water wheel was similar to the large side paddle wheels on the steam ships plying the run from San Francisco to Sacramento. This one had buckets to lift water diverted from the river into the mill race and create a powerful water flow that could wash river gravels once the river bed was exposed. It could also be used as a water pump. Channeled, fast flowing water provided the power to turn the wheel instead of ship boilers.

I was amazed at the scope of the project. "Are the workers hired laborers?" I asked.

"No, we all work in companies and share in profits equally. Much of the remaining gold here is trapped in quartz veins. Winter storms wash out some of the fractured deposits that flow to the river. The old method of shoveling gravel into a rocker or Long Tom is not economical here. We need water power to wash away overburden on quartz deposits and to break the quartz down to get the gold out," Michel said.

"A miner in Timbuctoo told me some miners have ordered machines made to pulverize the quartz. Will we see any on our tour?"

"No, There are none yet though some have been designed by engineers and are on order. They're what they call stamp mills. Metal pistons driven by steam engines pound the gold bearing quartz to dust, then it's treated with mercury which absorbs the gold. When you burn off the mercury, you have the gold."

Michel's account explained why I had seen so many heavy metal containers of liquid mercury stacked like over-sized milk canisters on wagons in the camp. I was glad I would not be around to inhale the vaporized mercury when the final extraction was attempted.

Further along the trail we encountered miners picking into the mountainside. It looked like a futile effort to me. "Why are they attacking the mountain with picks?" I asked.

"They are making holes for dynamite in quartz veins. They will blast the quartz and try to extract larger pieces of gold from the quartz vein that runs through the mountain. The rest will have to wait for a stamp mill and Welsh and Cornish hard rock miners to tunnel the vein," Michel said.

"Why Welsh and Cornish miners? Why can't French miners tunnel the mine?" I asked.

"Quartz mining requires skilled miners and special equipment. Our boys can't do much more than attack an outcropping. The quartz veins run through the entire mountain. The Cornish tin miners have been doing this type of mining for generations with equipment made in England. Even Sutter plans to use them on his lands. Tunneling is risky, dangerous work and takes a big capital investment which we don't have," Michel explained while pointing to the picks, shovels and sledge hammers employed by our French miners.

"So, we have to work the placers with back breaking labor for the spoils and wait for the big boys with capital to reap the profit," I observed to no one in particular.

Michel led us up to a point where we could walk to one of the quartz outcroppings that had been blasted out of the mountain. Several miners were trying to pick apart a boulder size piece of quartz with a small vein of gold running through it. Even I could see the futility of their effort. They'd get a small amount of gold, but most would remain trapped in the quartz. I picked up several small, beautiful quartz crystals with traces of gold to give to Manon on my return. She would be able to fashion distinctive jewelry from them.

We had to lead our horses by their reins up a slippery track of sliding shale to visit the next vale. Here an army of toilers was attempting to impale a series of cut logs with sharp points in the soft river bank. Michel explained they were trying to fashion a channel to divert the river around a bend so they could mine the bed of the river. Working like beavers, they would nail rough hewn planks across the stakes to try to keep the water from seeping out. Other miners were at work building a flume to harness moving water to wash the gravels in a series of Long Toms that waited patiently on the opposite bank of the river.

We'd gone as far as possible with our horses and I decided to return to camp to arrange the mail call for early next morning. Georges stayed behind to mingle with the miners and pick up what info he could about miners we were searching for. Since these miners worked in large companies, we would be able to address the various groups who would take their evening meal together in large log-made mess halls in the camp.

The miners' evening meal was a pleasant surprise for travelers like us, weary from sore rumps and inner thighs rubbing saddles and horses' sides over rough terrain. Each mining company had its own cooks and cookhouse. Miners recovering from sickness or injury fished the river for trout and steelhead. Others scoured the smaller tributaries for crayfish and frogs and gathered edible grasses and legumes. Each group assigned its best hunters to hunt bear, wild boar, deer, rabbits, squirrels and other small game and the host of fowl nesting in the surrounding forests.

We were guests of honor at the tables of three mining companies as a thank you for bringing their mail. We celebrated an "apéritif" with one group who offered river-chilled champagne and plates of homemade pheasant, duck and boar paté with slices of freshly baked bread. We took our first dinner course with a group serving pan-fried trout and "salade des écrevisses," fresh crayfish on a bed of wild salad greens and water cress served with a light, dry sauvignon blanc wine from the Loire Valley. The third group offered a main course choice of "côtes de porc sauvage aux épices," tenderloin of wild boar that had been marinated overnight in an allspice concoction and baked with goose fat or "Faisan Georgette," skillet-fried pieces of pheasant cooked in goose fat with sweetbreads, raisins, white wine, orange syrup, olive oil and aromatic herbs. The main course was served with a pinot noir red wine from the Auvergne in the center of France much to Georges' satisfaction to drink a wine from his home region.

My initial disappointment at not seeing a restaurant or inn at the encampment was easily overcome by our hosts. Who needed a restaurant with moldering imported foods when French chefs could turn out such culinary wonders they offered us from the wilds of the Sierra Nevada. These miners worked hard in grueling conditions, but they ate better than most Yankee city dwellers would ever eat. I was proud of my countrymen for not sacrificing their love of good food and wine and the experience of sharing it together at the end of their long workday. I understood why I had seen no tents or camps along the river.

Our hosts offered us a Spartan but comfortable cabin for the night and we were all early to rise next morning in anticipation of the roll call for mail. The breakfast tables were abuzz with excited chatter in anticipation of a letter from home and the out of date French newspapers and magazines we brought with news of events in their homeland.

We broke our fast for "le petit déjeuner," with strong, chicory-flavored coffee from New Orleans, freshly baked rolls, buns, and dark rye bread smeared with gobs of honey or fruit preserves and jam.

Georges had identified most miners from the La Californienne Society and we called their names first, so Georges could invite them to meet with us after the roll call for news of their sponsor. Many wept for joy on receiving a letter from a loved one and news of home. Others just shook their head in disbelief to see a letter bearing colorful combinations of imperforate stamps with the likeness of Ceres, their name and a delivery address of "San Francisco" or "Dans les Mines de Californie."

Given the reception we had received, we asked no remuneration for the transport of such welcome news. Some volunteered small nuggets from their pokes which I directed to Georges who would need every flake of gold to get his sweetheart to California.

In our short meeting with miners from the Society, I explained that I was investigating the fraud perpetrated on them and would report their hardships first to Consul Dillon in San Francisco, and then to Jules Favre, the principal lawyer for the society during its early promotion who had authorized me to take my investigation to the mines. This met with a rousing cheer from all those assembled.

I asked them to sign petitions I had prepared detailing

their grievances and request for remuneration to pay their debt owed the consulate and passage home. I promised to deliver copies of their petitions to the French government, to Favre for submission to the appropriate tribunals, and to Consul Dillon. Georges wrote the names of miners who signed an "X" for their mark. I distributed paper, ink and pens to the group to write accounts of their hardships imposed by the Society to accompany their petitions. I also offered to take any letters for home with us for posting in San Francisco on our return.

To my delight, every miner present not only signed the petitions but made a list of grievances. Those who could write, penned a letter for home. I assured them my report would list their names, present good health and location at the mines for transmittal to their families. Each left with my business card should they need legal services in San Francisco.

One miner, who had been working the quartz vein yesterday, handed me a small but heavy leather sack along with his letter to post. Inside were several beautiful and multi-faceted quartz crystals; each crystal contained or encased a unique gold nugget. A hastily scrawled slip of paper inside the pouch said, "Thanks for all your help to see we get the justice coming to us. From all of us."

After our successful meeting with so many miners and new leads about who to contact in Nevada City, Auburn, Sacramento and San Francisco, we decided with our guides to leave for Nevada City. Once there, we planned to engage a comfortable hotel, release our guides and arrange to travel by stage coach from Nevada City to Auburn and on to Sacramento where we could catch a steamer home to San Francisco.

California Gold Rush Journal
CHAPTER TWENTY-SIX
Nevada City and Sacramento — May 1851

We arrived in Nevada City in time for a hot bath, quick meal and a date with a feather bed. Our guides were happy with their pay and now were free to hunt full-time and sell their game to the American camps we had by-passed. They would earn more gold than with the self-sufficient French.

After a leisurely breakfast of coffee, Danish sweet rolls and poached eggs, we set out to visit the town. The main street was bustling with activity. As in San Francisco, the streets were lined with planks to keep cartwheels from sinking in the mud. Assorted two storey hotels and boarding houses flanked the main street. Main Street merchants offered a wide range of products and services — hardware, wines and liquors, bars and gambling palaces, banks, stage office, foods and staples, bakery goods, meat and poultry, books, newspapers, tobacco and even a fortune teller.

We booked our passage to Auburn for early afternoon with the local stage company and visited the postal agent's office next to an ornate red-brick firehouse to deliver the letters consigned to us from Marysville.

We had decided to forgo contacting more French miners. I felt we had enough documentation on La Californienne's fraud. In addition, I had letters from other French miners who had been subject to similar manipulation and deceit from their sponsors. They could be used by my boss as bargaining chips to show a pattern of promotional fraud in selling shares if anyone cared at this stage.

Georges was fretting over getting his girl on a ship to San Francisco before her father forced her hand. I missed Manon and was anxious to know how our business was progressing. We were tired and sore from our expedition along the Yuba River.

After an unmemorable lunch of tough, overcooked mutton and potatoes smothered in over-salted, floury gravy, we were happy to board our stage and make our escape from this all-American outpost.

I naively thought our stage coach ride would be an improvement over the time spent in the saddle. While my old mare bumped me along, she was sure-footed and careful where she led. Our stage driver made no concessions to the deep potholes and ruts that characterized the road. Even grasping the leather side holds, we could not prevent bouncing our heads off the stage's roof when the stage went airborne and crashed back to the pockmarked road.

Impossible to read or admire the scenery that blurred past. An old gentleman opposite kept trying to take a nip from his pocket flask but only succeeded in wetting his vest with his whiskey. Georges and the two businessmen opposite him looked green about the gills and ready to lose their lunches at any moment. The two wearing top hats had them smashed out of shape.

Auburn was more French-friendly than Nevada City. According to a local resident we treated to drinks in an Auburn saloon on Main Street, Claude Chana's discovery in 1848 of a rich gold deposit in the ravine that was to be the site of the present town made him a local French hero. Chana, a cooper by trade, had drifted into California like many French Canadian mountain men. He worked for Sutter for a while as a cooper at Sutter's Fort but preferred the nomad's life of a mountain man. After hearing of the discovery of gold at Coloma, he visited the site where Marshall's Mormon workers were picking up gold nuggets from the exposed bedrock of the saw mill race in their spare time.

Already, a group of French trappers and mountain men were using Mexican "bateas," wooden bowls, to pan the river gravels for gold. Chana decided he would look for gold rather than work for Sutter or Marshall. He rounded up three friends, hired a group of nineteen local Indians and six Oregon Indians to do the physical work , and set off to take a mountain short cut to Coloma.

The second night the group camped in Auburn Ravine near Ophir. Chana tried panning the local stream where they watered their horses and found three pieces of coarse gold in his first try. They traveled no further. In three weeks of working the stream, Chana's group found only three pounds of gold using their primitive panning technique that didn't allow them to get into the rich crevasses in the bedrock.

When news of easy gold to be picked up along the Yuba River reached them, they pulled up stakes to try their luck further north on the Yuba River. By September 1849 he had amassed a sum of about $25,000 in coarse gold. He had also learned to mine more efficiently and realized he had probably missed the richest deposits at Auburn Ravine.

In the Spring of 1850, he returned to mine Auburn Ravine but he was too late. A young, discharged soldier from a New York regiment named John S. Wood had also tried his luck in the stream and found gold. He staked his claim and discovered the rich bedrock that on a good day yielded as much as one hundred ounces of gold worth then about $1,500.00 in trade.

As Chana was already rich, he chose to settle in Auburn and was highly thought of. The town was, like Marysville, an ideal location and staging point for miners wanting to access the northern placers and tributaries of the Yuba River or to descend south to the southern placers via Placerville.

We put up for the night in a comfortable hotel on Court Street near the newly and crudely built log structure that served as the town's court house. Our rooms on the second floor afforded us a view to the ravine where gold was discovered and the covered balcony leading to our rooms allowed us to finish our evening with snifters of Calvados and our best cigars. It felt like we were returning to civilization at long last.

We took an early morning stage coach for Sacramento hoping to catch the last ferry to San Francisco. Now with a taste of the pleasures awaiting us on the Eliza, we could only will our driver on as fast as his stage horses could go. Bumps be damned. We were determined to make the boat and arrive on our wharf the next day. I even offered our driver a ten dollar gold coin if we were able to secure suitable river boat passage to San Francisco that evening.

It was evident that he had the coin in mind when he informed the other four passengers that our lunch stop would be brief so they had better order to go as we would proceed as soon as the change of fresh horses could be harnessed.

Georges and I had learned our lesson from Manon about travel and food. We bought fresh rolls and bread, several small rounds of goat cheese, dried fruit, nuts and several bottles of beer in Auburn in preparation for the coach ride and ferry if we made the sailing. We still had a few pots of paté and tins of sardines left from our trip up the Yuba as well. Our fellow passengers were thirsty from the dusty ride and spent their short lunch break at the bar of the coach inn quaffing shots of whiskey and beer chasers with a few nibbles of hard cheese and stale bread.

The old codger opposite Georges and the other three younger business travelers glared their resentment and envy when we attacked our picnic lunch with gusto under their noses. Georges nonchalantly used his bowie-knife to cut slices of spicy pheasant sausage which he lathered with pungent Dijon mustard on his roll; he'd received the sausage as a gift from a cook in French Corral. The rocking and bouncing of our stage coach precluded opening a bottle of wine, so we made do by chugging swigs of our strong Scottish ale in pottery bottles.

As our fellow travelers had taken a snooty attitude towards us foreigners and sought to shun us from the very beginning, we saw no reason to share our delicious lunch. While Georges and I chatted away gaily in French as we savored our lunch, the four Americans twitched their noses and tried to suppress the growling of their considerable tummies.

Our stage coach jerked to a halt in front of the boarding dock at the pier. The steamer "Andrew Jackson" was revving up her boilers for imminent departure but her gangway was still attached to the dock. Our coachman, bless his heart, abandoned his stage and raced wildly toward the ferry shouting at the sailors handling the ropes to the gangway. "Stop. Stop," he cried. The bewildered rope handlers stopped in their tracks.

After a brief exchange with the deck hands, our coachman shouted at us to get on the ship and waved us toward the gangplank. Georges and I grabbed our satchels from inside the coach and raced for the ship. As we scrambled up the gangway, I shouted, "What about our luggage?"

Our coachman was already running for the stage coach with two dock hands on his heels. "Ticket office closed. See the purser. Quick," he yelled as he skidded to a halt in front of the coach. The other four passengers were berating him to take them to their hotels pronto or else.

The hubbub on the dock emptied the steamer's bars. The curious, many with schooners of beer in hand, lined the rails of the two decks to watch the scene play out.

Georges and I pushed through the throng on deck and made for the purser's office. The cubicle was empty. "Merde," Georges mumbled under his breath. We raced for the bar nearby.

The barkeep indicated the purser was on deck with the rest of the bar's clientele. "He done like what upsets his schedule. Every thing strictly by the book. Runs a tight ship an' done like no deviations, if 'an you knows what I mean," the red-nosed bartender said in his heavy Irish brogue.

I handed Georges our hand luggage, dropped a $5.00 gold coin on the bar and invited the two to have a drink on me. "Sit tight and don't leave the bar. We're not leaving the ship under any circumstances," I told Georges in French.

Back on deck, a ship's officer was hollering for the deck hands to remove the gangway and cast off. I could see the coachman struggling with our luggage as the deck hands abandoned him to follow orders. I pushed my way through the gawkers to get to the purser before the gangway was pulled up.

"Stop in the name of the law," I shouted at the purser loud enough for all to hear.

"Who in the name of hell are you to be giving orders on my ship," the beefy man in ship officer's uniform said turning to confront me. His face was beet-red and his beady eyes squinted murderously.

"I am clerk to a Justice of the United States Supreme Court here on official government business. Order those sailors to get my luggage on board and into a first class stateroom at once," I ordered.

"Impossible," the purser retorted pulling out his gold watch from his vest pocket by its long chain. "Ten minutes late. I won't stand for this delay," he shouted waving his thick arms at the deck hands.

The deck hands were frozen unsure what to do. "Hurry lads. Get those trunks on board," I said pointing to the struggling coachman. I flipped two $5.00 gold coins on to the dock at their feet. They were scooped up in a flash as the sailors turned their back on the purser to execute my command.

As the sailors struggled up the gangway with our trunks, I demanded, "What stateroom number?" to the stunned purser still clutching his watch.

"Cabin 45," he mumbled in disbelief at my audacity now my trunks were aboard.

I scooted down the now abandoned gangway and slipped $15.00 in gold coin into our coachman's pocket. He was still out of breath from his sprints and ordeal but gave me a big wink and tipped his hat.

As the purser was still discombobulated by the fast moving events, I gave the order, "Pull the gangway and cast off," just as the angry Captain appeared.

"Who are you to give orders on my ship?" he said in a deep bass voice."

"Not giving orders, sir. Just confirming the purser's order, sir. He seemed to have sent contradictory signals to the deck crew and in the absence of your senior officers, sir, I thought to help out. Sorry if I offended in any way, sir," I said pointing to the purser who now was so furious he could only sputter obscenities and gesticulate wildly.

The Captain, a tall, red-haired Nordic type, cast his piercing gray-green eyes on his hapless purser and ordered him, "Get to your station immediately. You have no authority to order the ship's departure and you know it."

"But sir..." he tried to say.

"When I give an order, you better jump to it," the Captain roared as the maligned purser slunk away and retreated to his station via the bar. The Captain then hollered to the confused deck hands below, "get that gangway up and caste off. Do it now or I'll have your hides."

The sailors scurried like crabs to stow the gangway and release the lines. The Captain stormed off to the bridge muttering to himself about the insubordination of his purser. I was apparently forgotten in the fray. I retrieved Georges from the bar where he and the barkeep were toasting each other in a chummy way.

Our cabin on the top deck was indeed first class. A bottle of chilled champagne in an ice bucket graced a small table with two chairs next to a porthole with a view of Sacramento now receding as our paddle-wheeled boat churned through the muddy river towards San Francisco. The bouquet of fresh red roses smelled heavenly and would provide a romantic touch to our cabin on the Eliza.

Georges and I decided to open the bottle of champagne and fire up our best cigars while we awaited the inevitable confrontation with the purser who arrived to find us firmly situated in the cabin.

"You'll have to move immediately," he bellowed as we calmly sipped our champagne and blew smoke rings in his direction. Not getting a reply, he shouted, "You've no tickets, no booking and no right to a cabin. I order you to leave."

"My dear fellow, you'll do yourself harm if you keep up this useless tirade," I said smoothly as his beet-red face took on a violet tinge. "You yourself authorized us to take this cabin and we have no intention of leaving it. Of course, if you'd prefer us to take this matter up with the Captain, we'll be happy to do so," I added with a twist-of-the-knife smile.

He once again became so angry he couldn't speak. The bulging, purple vein throbbing in his neck looked ready to burst.

"While it's true we were unable to secure an advance booking due to problems with our transport, we are happy to pay for our booking even though we are on official, highly sensitive government business that allows us to commandeer suitable accommodations when necessary. We prefer not to draw attention to the official nature of our business unless forced to do so. Please prepare an invoice for our cabin and we'll submit it for payment," I said dismissively.

"You damn well better pay for this cabin. Bloody government parasites. First you delay our departure. Then order me around and now threaten to not pay for this cabin," he stammered still in his state of flummox.

"You're quite right, good sir. We have offered to pay for our cabin and not bill it to the government given the circumstances of our tardy arrival. Now, if you'll be kind enough to leave us in peace, we have to prepare our report on the lawless state of the northern placers for our superiors. Please book us a table for two for dinner at 8 o'clock in the first class dining room on your way out," I said pointing to the door.

The purser stomped his way to the door and slammed it forcefully as he exited our cabin mouthing a string of expletives. The poor chap hadn't even worked out that we were foreigners and thus couldn't possibly be who I asserted we were.

Once we could no longer hear him, Georges cracked up with laughter and I joined him until tears streaked down our faces. "Gar, what a bunch of baloney you laid down. Snookered him right well, if I don't say so," Georges said.

"That's what's great about this country. A fellow can be pretty much what he wants to be if he can play the role convincingly. We'd both be in irons if we tried our caper on a French ferry," I said.

We finished our champagne and sauntered down to dinner to learn we had no reservations. No surprise there. A $5.00 gold coin to the head waiter secured us a table and a menu featuring Dungeness crab cakes and poached salmon. We were definitely coming back to civilization. The prospect of a night's sleep on the feather beds in our cabin was delectable.

California Gold Rush Journal
CHAPTER TWENTY-SEVEN
San Francisco — May 1851

Our ferry boat docked early in a heavy fog on the Central Wharf and while Georges arranged for transport of our luggage, I made my way to the Eliza. The gangplank was aboard, so I hollered to announce my presence. I was greeted by small, belligerent dog who glared at me as he yapped his warning to the still slumbering inhabitants aboard.

The dog was some kind of piebald terrier with a white body and black spots. His erect ears, refined head and intelligent assessment of me attested he was a good guard dog and not to be messed with despite his small size. After several minutes of non-stop barking, Giselle stumbled out a door from the cabins. She clutched her robe tightly against the clammy, swirling fog. "Qui est la?" she muttered in French.

"It's Pierre," I replied in English.

"Mon Dieu," she exclaimed. "I am so sleepy my English comes slowly."

"Is everything alright?" I asked in French.

"Oui et non," she replied.

Now I was alarmed. "Is Manon okay? Where is she?" I shouted.

"She's okay. She's in the kitchen. I get her," as she found her words in English and quickly retreated back inside our ship.

Something was wrong. Where were the men? The dog had stopped barking. We regarded each other warily as the fog swirled and I waited impatiently for Manon.

"Cheri! Cheri, " Manon screamed with excitement. "Enfin!, at last tu est là," she shrieked in franglais, her combination of French and English when she's excited.

"Where are the men? We need to get the gangway down," I asked.

"Hah! Men. That lazy Robert's in his bed drunk. That no good Raoul did not come home last night. He's staying with a rich woman in town. He takes all of Teri's hard earned money, then dumps her. A rat," she exclaimed. "You meet 'Fido,' yes. Our new dog catches rats. You'll see."

Giselle finally reappeared fully clothed. I had to watch while the two women struggled to lower the gangway. When it was in down and I anchored it in place, Fido trotted down and gave me a good sniff before condescending to allow me to walk up. Giselle retreated back to her room and I joined Manon in the galley. Fido guarded the gangway.

Manon was preparing a Creole Gumbo with fresh oysters and shrimps in the fashion of the classic gumbos from New Orleans. We would be her guinea pigs tonight. If it passed muster, she'd add it to her ever expanding repertoire of catering dishes.

Manon managed to secure some "file," from a client from New Orleans along with some classic gumbo recipes. The "file" consisted of finely ground dry leaves of the Sassafras tree prepared by Choctaw Indians in Louisiana. This essential spice was the secret to authentic gumbos. Manon scalded and shelled large shrimps while I opened oysters. She'd prepared all the ingredients she'd need — 2 quarts of oyster liquor, onion, sprigs of bay leaves, parsley and thyme, butter, flour, salt and pepper and the precious "file."

She explained that the gumbo had to be served and eaten hot off the stove and was not a dish one prepared in advance to reheat. While we finished heating the soupe à l'oignon, and venison stew she'd prepared for sale on the dock, we had a moment to catch up on events.

"What's with Raoul?" I asked.

"He dumped Teri when they couldn't get a loan to rebuild the wine store. Raoul says they discriminate against Chilenos. Is why he can't get money to rebuild. Some Yankees been squatting on their land and selling from a tent. Robert says the bank won't loan because there is problem with the property title and they would have to go to court to boot squatters and clean title," Manon said."

"Is that why Robert is drinking?" I asked.

"Yes and no. He doesn't see any future in San Francisco anymore. It's been getting worse since the fire. He wants to go back to France. Giselle says she wants to stay here. So big fights. He don't work on the ship anymore and gets drunk every night. She don't know what to do."

"Is he pressuring her to go with him?"

"Yes. But she tells me she won't go and he can't make her go. She wants to be businesswoman with me."

"What about Teri?"

"She's real mad at Raoul. He lied to her about needing the money she makes selling on the wharf to pay a lawyer to get his land back. Once he gets the money, he dumped her. Now he stays with a rich Chilena woman who runs a bordello. First she cries, now she says she's gonna kill him and get her money back."

"Oh boy. Sounds like we got a real hornet's nest full of angry women on board. How is Manon doing?" I asked sheepishly.

"She's doing okay now Big Boy is home to help. She's got a big surprise for him, but it got to wait," she said coyly. "Now go set up the tents. We have work to do."

Fido eyed me suspiciously from his guard post as I wrestled with the tent set up. Georges arrived finally with our trunks and we worked together to stow them and prepare the tents for the morning canteen sales. Manon posted her menu on the slate and had me set up and run the bar with Georges until Teri arrived.

Manon shook a finger at Georges, "You sell the wine and booze, but no free samples and no tasting with clients. Understood?"

Georges gave her a wicked smile. "If I make enough money can I have a second helping of your gumbo?" He asked tongue-in-cheek.

Manon raised her eyebrows and gave Georges her look, "We'll see. Won't we?"

Giselle arrived to sell coffee, croissants, sweet rolls, and slices of warm brioche. I was surprised to see her dressed like Teri in a loose fitting wool smock to hide her figure, a bonnet to conceal her lustrous tresses and no wedding ring on her finger. Things must be going bad to worse in her marriage. When Teri showed up with eyes flashing man-eating daggers to run the bar, I decided to take a hike into town to see how the rebuilding of the downtown business district was coming along. Let Georges get a taste of a spurned woman before he sent for his Nelly.

The transformation of the burned out commercial district was amazing. In the three weeks we had been touring the mines, nearly all the charred central district had been rebuilt. The gambling palaces on Portsmouth Square were already open and awaiting early risers and revelers from the previous night. The hotels and banks appeared more solidly built in thick, red brick. Solid iron doors and shutters designed to be fire proof replaced the wooden ones that burned. The buildings appeared somber without the wooden balconies and terraces that had lent so much charm before. Some buildings had huge water towers poised on the roof to flood the premises in case of fire. Everything was grander than before.

As I was curious to learn more, I bought a copy of the Alta California, the only local newspaper to survive the fire, and made my way to Les Bons Amis to take a coffee and learn what gossip I could from Pierre-Louis. As he was busy with tradesmen and deliveries, I sat to read the newspaper.

One of my questions was answered on the front page. Instead of rebuilding the customs house and surrounding warehouses at Montgomery and California streets that burned in the fire, the chief tax and customs collector, T. Butler King, assembled a small army of gigantic, thick-bearded constables armed to the teeth with carbines, Colt revolvers and swords to transfer the million dollars in specie saved from the fire to a new location. King had created a comic scene by standing on the fire charred ruins of the old customs building waving a Colt revolver in one hand and a bludgeon in the other to lead the procession to a new location on the corner of Kearney and Washington streets.

The overkill in security provoked much lampooning. A local wag wrote a song entitled "The King's Campaign; Or Removal of the Deposits," whose ribald verses were sung to great applause in the local saloons. I laughed at the lithographed caricature of the King's procession in the paper. Only in San Francisco I thought. I had wondered why the merchandise in the Eliza's hold had not been inspected to date. Mr. King and his army of clerks were too busy with more important matters.

Another article caught my eye. Ever larger numbers of Chinese were arriving daily as were French and Germans. Even free Negroes were arriving in numbers. According to the paper, the Chinese and Black Americans were "hewers of wood, drawers of water, and would wash laundry and do menial work the white males wouldn't do." The article noted that while the

European emigrants were mostly male, more and more women were arriving looking for husbands who'd been successful in the placers or a business.

"So, my friend. I see the bears did not eat you. When did you get back?" Pierre-Louis asked.

I chuckled. "Just this morning. Gone three weeks and the city's been reborn. Incredible," I said.

"Yes, in San Francisco, time is money. No gambling palace, no profits and no work for the employees. Gold keeps flowing into town, so there's little risk to rebuild if you have capital. So many merchants wiped out by the fire. Others are making a killing. Ships arrive every day with the same merchandise which is sold at a loss. Some merchants buy low and reship the goods back to New York to resell at a profit. It's crazy."

"We've got women problems on the ship. Manon says Robert and his Chilean partner couldn't get a loan on their lot to rebuild and squatters have taken it over. Their women work for Manon and their men are abandoning them. Have you heard about problems with squatters?" I asked.

"Oh yes. Lots not secured against squatters by rebuilding or armed guards were occupied almost immediately by squatters. With so many workers in the area rebuilding and most cafes and food stores destroyed, entrepreneurs set up tents to sell food, liquor and essential supplies."

"Why didn't the authorities shut them down?"

"The Yankees say the best claim to land is possession and use. The mayor says it's a civil matter not one for the criminal courts."

"Surely, you don't mean the practice of squatting on someone else's land is legal?" I said in disbelief.

"It's not so clear cut. Most of the lots in the business district were sold by speculators and promoters. In many cases they just claimed to own the land and sold it quickly to other speculators or merchants eager to build. Clear title to the land is murky."

"I can see now why foreign buyers are at a disadvantage. They wouldn't know the formalities required for proper deeding and recording. No surveys or precise descriptions. So what recourse is there?"

"Well, in the case of your associates, the best course is to negotiate with the squatters. They want the land and are probably willing to pay something for it to avoid lawyers and delays. It would be risky for them to build without some semblance of ownership. No bank will loan on disputed property, especially to foreigners, so I would try to get the best price I could, if it was me."

I would have to mull over the import of Pierre-Louis' sensible analysis. Since my trip to the placers, I was nearly determined to rent a small office and hold myself out as a notaire. Handling issues related to property title and transfer of property was one of my special skills in French law still steeped in the Napoleonic Code. I had started a review of American and English common law principles on the long voyage to San Francisco. With more and more French arriving, there would be an even greater need for my services.

"How has business been?" I asked Pierre-Louis .

"We have more clients but don't make more money. The French quarter here is packed with new immigrants but they watch their pennies, especially the women. I have to offer a special fixed price menu from 6 to 7:30 P.M. to get a steady clientele. They won't pay more than $1.50 a meal and most even go without wine. It's like running a soup kitchen," he said with a sigh.

"And regular customers after that?" I asked.

"Still the same problem. I get a share of the French who appreciate a tasty meal with good wine, but I get few Yankees or other foreigners. I need an attractive waitress who's bilingual.

What about one of your troubled women?"

"Manon and Giselle are happy with their catering venture and they need Teri to run our bar stand now that her boyfriend has spurned her. What about one of the new emigrant women? Surely there should be an attractive hostess among them who needs work."

"Yes, I have lots of women asking to work now, but they don't speak English. I can't afford to pay just for a pretty face," he said.

"I could ask Teri. She may want to leave the ship now that she's separated from her boyfriend. She's attractive, speaks Spanish fluently but her French and English are only basic. Just what's she's picked up since she's been here. Would she be of interest?" I said to be polite.

"I'd prefer a French woman but if she's looking to change jobs, have her see me. It might work out."

I hoped it wouldn't come to that. We needed Teri to run our bar and help with the catering especially now Robert and Raoul weren't contributing to our venture. If I did hang a notaire's signboard to commence my practice, I would need Georges full time and the women could be short-handed. It started to make sense to let Georges send for his girl. With the shake-up on our ship, we'd need her soon. All these musings and others clouded my head as I made my way back to our ship.

California Gold Rush Journal

CHAPTER TWENTY-EIGHT

San Francisco – Late May - Early June 1851

Manon's gumbo proved a huge success the night before. We supped on bay-chilled champagne with Columbine de Crevettes and Paté de Saint-Omer, round shrimp cakes and pork liver paté with plums, for starters. Crab bisque followed and led to the delicious gumbo we wolfed down with several bottles of Richard's Bordeaux blanc white wine. Pity he wasn't there to partake of the fabulous homecoming meal. By the time we finished swabbing the last traces of gumbo from our plates with fresh baguettes and sat with our after dinner drinks and biscotti, we were all relaxed, in a jovial mood and ready for the truth and tell session we all knew was coming.

Georges was the first to take the bull by the horns. "I want everyone to know I am sending for Nelly to join us. Pierre and Manon have agreed we can live on the ship and she'll help with cooking and sales," he said in an unusual hushed tone suitable for a confessional booth. Giselle's cheeks were flushed with the wine and emboldened by Georges' confessional tone. "Me too. I make a big decision," she said in English for Teri's benefit. "I tell Robert I not going back to France with him. It is over with us. He no longer welcome in my cabin. He sleep in town or in front of ship until he goes to France. I have faithful friend in my bed now," she said sheepishly pointing to her big male Tabby cat, "Gamelle Boy." The cat raised an ear on hearing his name, then resumed his snooze in the wicker basket Giselle had placed on a chair near the door.

Teri flashed her steely-blue eyes and smiled for the first time all day. "I also make decision. You treat me like family. Raoul just use me. I stay with you guys an' become Californian where women have rights and done have to take abuse from macho men," she raised her glass and we all cheered her decision.

I, too, was on the brink of a decision about starting a practice but I needed to talk it through with Manon first. Manon and I left the joyous dinner table to celebrate our own homecoming in the privacy of our cabin. The bouquet of red roses set the tone for our overdue romantic encounter.

———◆•◆•◆———

The next few days required the implementation of the various decisions we had all made about our future. After our first frenzied love making, then more tender and drawn out reenactment, Manon had revealed her promised "big surprise." She handed me a set of applications for citizenship.

"What do you think, cheri?" she said with rare timidity at her bold, independent decision.

"I think you will be just the kind of new citizen this state needs. You are hard working, resourceful and bring the enterprising talent the new world needs. I'll be proud of you," I said.

"And what about you?" she asked locking her black eyes on me.

"I want the same thing you do, my love. This country is so full of opportunity and promise. I could never return to France to work in a stuffy notaire's office. Here I can be my own boss. I want to open my own office to provide legal services and business opportunities. I'm convinced it will be successful with all the French here and arriving weekly."

"And what about us?" She asked tenderly.

"I am yours as long as you want me," I said without hesitation.

"Suppose I say you must marry me to keep me. Would you do it?"

"Is that really what you want?" I hedged. We had never discussed marriage and I was surprised she was demanding a commitment. We had agreed that our business ventures together would be on an equal partnership basis but we had both avoided the subject of marriage. We were both independent spirits and I had assumed she wanted it to stay that way.

"You know I can have any man I want here, yes? I get many offers every time I go to town while you're gone. Men willing to give me money, gold, big house if I marry them," she said seriously.

"I'm not surprised. You're beautiful, sexy, spunky and fun to be with. If they knew how well you cook and run a business as well, you'd have a line of suitors as long as the post office line," I said.

"You didn't answer my question Big Boy. Would you marry me to keep me?" She said with a determined look, her hands on her hips and eyebrows raised.

"If you would have me over all the other suitors, I would marry you," I replied quickly not thinking of the implications. I loved her and didn't want to lose her and she was negotiating the price.

Then she dropped the bomb. "Good because I want our child to have a father an' be an American." She watched my stunned expression with satisfaction. "Yes Big Boy we are going to have a baby and Manon doesn't want a bastard child with a part-time papa."

Before I could react properly, Manon seized the initiative. She ordered me to my knees and handed me a simple gold band. "Now is your big chance. You ask me to marry you the American way, yes? No arrangement like between papas in French families."

Who could resist this woman I thought — so remarkable, so self-assured and her ample beauty glowing with signs of her early pregnancy that I had missed in the urgency of our love-making. She wanted me for her husband and the rest was easy.

I plucked a red rose from the vase beside our bed and offered it to her. "With this rose I plead my cause. I would have you to be my wife and the mother of our children. I will love and honor you 'til death do us part. Give me your hand." I put the ring she had given me on the night stand next to the roses. From the pocket of my vest hanging on a chair, I pulled out a small quartz crystal with embedded gold nugget that I had a jeweler fashion into a ring for Manon. I had planned it as a gift from the placers to make-up for our separation, but it seemed perfect for the occasion as I slipped it on her finger.

"Oh cheri, it's so beautiful!" she exclaimed as she twirled her finger to admire the many facets and prisms of light reflected by the whale oil lamp.

"Ah hem. Are you going to keep a guy on his knees 'til you answer his question?"

She looked at me tenderly with tears of joy welling in her eyes. She broke off the long stem of the rose and tucked the remainder into her tumbled tresses by her ear. "Ta rose te dit oui," she said sweetly in French. My beautiful rose says yes.

"How long have you known?" I asked enfolding her in my arms.

"I think we make our baby in Valparaiso. I start to have morning sickness on the boat."

"Then it's truly a love child," I said reminded of our passion and happiness in our honeymoon bungalow after so long at sea.

"Does anyone else know?"

"Just the doctor at the American hospital."

I laughed. "My Manon hasn't wasted any time getting our babe in the hands of Americans."

"Yes. Our child will be born American. And parents will be American too. I get applications for you, too," she said pouting her lips for a kiss to seal the bargain.

"Mother of my child has thought of everything," I sealed the deal.

"No, mother of our child have to plan for everything while papa is running around the country making goo-goo eyes at all the pretty women," she said shaking her finger to scold a naughty boy.

I laughed. And told her of our encounter with Jacques Vincent and his "wife" Odile hanging her boobs on the sucker's arm and signaling Vincent the cards the players held.

"Even Georges was celibate on our trip. Mooning in his beer about losing his Nelly. No time for bad behavior," I said crossing my heart.

"We have so much to do before the baby comes. It's one reason I encouraged Georges to send for his American girl. I'll need more help in the galley. Doctor says we get child for Christmas gift. Nelly can help us with our child and teach to speak good American. Now you have to help Teri. We need her too."

We spent most of a sleepless night cuddled in each other's arms making plans. Things can change real fast when you learn you're gonna be a parent in a few short months.

All of a sudden, I had a lot more responsibility on my plate. I agreed with Manon that we needed to consolidate and confirm our commitment with Teri as soon as possible. Since Raoul had dumped her, she no longer attempted to hide her voluptuous figure from her clients. She wore her blond tresses flowing loose down her back and adorned with a white or red flower to signal she was no man's woman. Her large, loose fitting smocks gave way to colorful, Chilean peasant dresses which accentuated her figure, emphasized her ample bosom, and revealed an enticing glimpse of leg when she bent or swished her skirt. She was selling a lot more from the dockside bar in her alluring dress and we didn't want to lose her.

I invited Teri to lunch in town at Les Bons Amis bistro. It was the first time she'd been away from our wharf operation during the day. I wanted it to be a special treat for her and a chance to discuss her future with us in a more neutral setting. I also wanted her to have a choice between working with us or for a restaurant like Pierre-Louis'.

After the whistles and cat calls as we traversed Portsmouth Square, the male interest in the newly liberated Chilena was more subtle but no less intense in the bistro. She wore a red, high-necked Argentine "tango" dress with a slit up the side that molded her figure and gave tantalizing flashes of well-turned calf and ankle. Her large gold hoop earrings set off her long, tumbling golden locks to perfection. I ordered a bottle of champagne and we each selected oysters on the half shell and a poached fish for our lunch. I had asked Pierre-Louis in advance to make his special chocolate soufflé for dessert.

We chatted animatedly about Manon's announcement to our group that she and I were going to have a child and would be married in a civil ceremony before a California judge rather than a church wedding. That alone would not change our citizenship. To remain French nationals we would have to register the marriage and children with the French consulate. We were ready to submit our naturalization papers and request for a United States passport. Teri was genuinely happy for us and excited at the thought of Manon's child.

After dessert, I shifted our conversation to the situation that had made Teri so mad. "I have learned that Raoul has offered to buy out Robert's share of the lot and wine business for the price of fare back to France. Apparently, Raoul believes with the financial backing of his new mistress, he can buy out the squatters and rebuild the business premises."

"Just like him to screw his partner with the aid of his 'puta' like he did to me," she said knowingly, dark blue eyes flashing murderously.

"How much money did he steal from you?" I asked.

"Everything I make selling his wine and your brandy. $15.00 a day plus my tips. Altogether about $620.00 American money. I'm just lucky he didn't get me pregnant too," she said with bitterness.

"I want you to know that I plan to get it all back for you with interest."

"How can you do that? San Francisco is still a man's town run by men for men," she said with less animosity and renewed interest.

"We let him play his new cards with his 'puta,' his whorehouse madam , and wait until he has his new store. Then we sue him for embezzlement in American law for your $620.00 plus interest of ten percent calculated monthly should amount to a thousand dollars or more before we are through." I said.

"But he'll never pay, I know the bastard. He'll just laugh in my face. Better to cut his balls," she said making a motion with her fish knife that was unmistakable and brought a little shiver of concern from two male diners across the room.

"He doesn't have to pay. Better even if he doesn't. Because we hit his business in the 'cujones,' I said using one of the few words, for balls, a traveler needs to know in Spanish. "We know he has ordered more wine from Chile for his enterprise. When the boat arrives with the wine, I slap an order of attachment on the entire shipment. That makes his shipper mad because he can't get paid until the lien is removed, and Raoul has no wine for his store until he resolves your demands."

"You can really do this?" Teri said as a vindictive smile slowly spread across her face.

"Of course, this is what I did in France and can do here. I plan to ask the judge to allow us to seize his wine at its wholesale price, the price he agreed to pay, to the extent of your claim. Then Manon and I pay you for it and you sell it for us on the wharf. I'll ask for my fees as well and he'll have to pay for any lawyer he hires."

Teri was looking real interested now. "An' he won't have the wine he ordered for his new store, right?"

"That's part of the plan he can't anticipate because he doesn't know the law. I will have the choice of his wine and he'll only get what's left after your judgment and my fees. The longer he fights us or doesn't agree to pay the court order, the less wine he'll get for his store and the madder his "puta" will be to have backed him in the venture. It could take months to get a new shipment of wine and he'll still have to pay for the wine we seize plus storage fees."

"So we have him by his "cujones" an' we squeeze hard, 'verdad'?" She mimed the way she'd do it with both hands while shaking her head in satisfaction.

I was confidant I could do the legal process and get the necessary orders. Executing the seizure would be more difficult and would undoubtedly involve bribes. I recalled the police at the mayor's office when I'd paid for our permit to sell on the wharf. The court's bailiffs would be no less inclined to do my bidding without a lot of greasing of palms. I had to hope that their dislike of a Chilean "greaser" would outweigh any animosity to the French.

Now that Teri was happy contemplating her revenge, I broached the subject that concerned Manon the most. "Manon would like you to join her and Giselle as an equal partner in the catering business."

My words broke through Teri's reverie. "You mean I would not work for $15.00 a day anymore?"

"Yes, you would share equally in the profits from the food and liquor you three will sell. Manon would be the managing partner as it was her business concept and she plans the menus, but decisions about how and where to sell would be made by you three."

"Would I have to put the money Raoul steals from me in the business?"

"No, the business is already profitable and doesn't need more capital. You only have to make a commitment to Manon that you will work in the business full-time for at least three years and help it grow." I paused to light a small cigar while she pondered the implications of the commitment.

"What about the tips I get from customers?" She asked.

"Those are for you personally and not part of the business. You also won't have to pay rent for your cabin on the ship or for your meals as they are part of the catering venture. The same for Giselle now that Robert is out. Manon and I own the ship and we rent storage space in the hold as a separate business. The catering partnership has to pay $200.00 a month as its share of wharf rent plus the monthly selling license. That's all part of the business overhead. If business stays as good as it has been, you three women should each make an excellent profit."

"An' my share of the profit is mine to keep, for real, 'ver-dad'?"

"Yes, it's for real," I echoed her words. "You don't have to make up your mind right now. Take time to think it over and feel free to ask more questions."

"What's to think over? Manon offers me a chance to own part of a good business. No Chilean patron would do that. They all want pretty women to work for them; they make the profit and expect you to warm their bed as well." Teri extended her hand, "I join the partnership," she stated resolutely.

I grasped her hand firmly. "Welcome to the family business," I said happily.

On the walk back to the ship, Teri's step was more resolute. She wore a mantilla over her head and shoulders to frustrate the male loungers. She even smiled at Georges, who'd been tending her stand while we lunched. Fifteen minutes later she was back in her colorful peasant dress and hustling the predominantly male clientele to drink up.

California Gold Rush Journal

CHAPTER TWENTY-NINE

San Francisco — June 1851

Now that Teri was a partner with Manon, I turned my attention to my own affairs. I wrote my boss in Paris a full account of my investigation of the plight of the miners who'd come over on the Californienne Mining Company's ships. I sent my report with all the signed statements and personal accounts of the fraud and its toll on the victims to my boss along with my resignation. I consigned the packet of documents to a group of merchants returning to Paris via the Panama route to New Orleans and then on to Paris. I also sent authorization for my bank to wire funds to a New York attorney for Nelly Swanson to pay her passage and expenses to San Francisco on Georges' behalf.

I informed my boss that Georges and I had decided to remain in San Francisco rather than risk additional damage to our health by return voyage. If he had additional work for me, I now worked as a San Francisco entrepreneur and legal counselor at the rate of $16.00 an hour or $120.00 a day plus expenses. That would be sure to provoke a choking fit and a good rant and rave in the old skinflint. It felt quite liberating to put it in writing. He'd find out soon enough that he'd have no recourse against a new American citizen. I hoped he'd break a tooth trying.

I met with Robert Gaillard who was staying at a cheap rooming house off Dupont Street until his ship sailed for Le Havre. I bought him lunch at Les Bons Amis bistro. He was furious his wife, Giselle, had preferred to separate rather than return to France with him. On Giselle's behalf, I broached the touchy subject of divorce.

"You really need to resolve the legal issues posed by your permanent separation before you return to France. It would be cheaper, easier and much faster to consent to divorce before you leave," I said.

"Nonsense. We were married by a priest in the church and there is no divorce period," he stated brusquely, fingers tapping furiously on the table .

"Despite the church wedding there are many grounds to annul a marriage in the eyes of the church," I stated calmly.

"Why the hell should I give her the right to marry some yokel who struck it rich? She married me and her place is to follow me and do my bidding whether she likes it or not," he said angrily.

"Well, perhaps it's in your interest to consider annulment. What if you want to remarry and have a family once you re-establish your affairs in France? If you don't agree to annul this marriage, you won't be free to remarry but she will," I said evenly.

"What! No way she can divorce me and remarry after her church wedding," he said knocking over his glass of white wine carelessly. I signaled the waiter to stay away while I mopped up the mess with my cloth napkin.

"Unfortunately, you're mistaken. She will be an American and entitled to divorce you in a civil court for abandonment. She will be free to remarry if she chooses. Your church won't accept the American divorce decree, so you will be denied the right to remarry. Not fair to you, but that's the law here." I took a swig of cognac and watched his face turn a deep shade of purple like a beet.

He hastily refilled and drained his wine glass before replying, "Bloody hell. This godforsaken country has undermined all a man's rights. First she gets property rights, now she can divorce on her say; so, no wonder there are so many whores, widows and gold diggers arriving in this unholy place. It's not right," he stammered.

I let him fume a while before speaking. "Right or wrong, there is a way out for you. You consent to her claim of abandonment which will allow for a speedy, uncontested divorce here, and she will give you grounds for an annulment with your church on your return to France."

He pondered my words before responding. "What grounds for annulment?" He said spitting out the words.

"Well, you might try abandonment, but there's no assurance the church would accept it. It might be viewed as a pretext for a consensual divorce which is not allowed. A surer ground would be her refusal to have intercourse in order not to have children." I suggested.

"Well, she has denied me her bed. Isn't that grounds enough?" He said hopefully.

"No, the church will allow separation but not divorce if couples no longer get along or a wife refuses to submit to her husband in bed. Since the purpose of marriage is to secure children and heirs, the couple must first consummate the marriage and engage in sexual relations to produce children. If one party refuses to be bedded so as to avoid having children, then the marriage can be declared null and void."

"So it would be her fault," Robert said with self-satisfaction.

"That's one way of looking at it. Giselle authorized me to provide you with a notarized affidavit stating she refused you her bed because she did not want your child in exchange for your notarized statement that you have decided to return to France and leave her here; and that you agree to give her the remaining wine in the hold of the Eliza."

"What the hell," he yelled. "The bitch refuses to obey her husband and I have to give her my property on top of it. NO WAY."

"You haven't paid for storage fees or worked in the business for some time. You've spent all her share of money from the sale of the wine, so she sees this as fair and equitable." I said hardening my tone.

"Well, I don't think it's fair; it's extortion. It's my property and my money to spend as I please."

"I'm afraid it's take it or leave it. She is generously giving you a basis to annul your marriage and get on with your life back in France. She has to earn her keep here, so there's no wiggle room in her offer. If you don't agree to leave her the wine, you'll lose it anyway. Customs won't release it without her payment of considerable duty," I said exaggerating the truth.

"Christ, come to California and lose your business, your property, your inventory and even your wife who drives in the last nail," he said feeling sorry for himself.

I sensed his defeat and handed him the statement I had prepared for Giselle stating he was purposely abandoning her to return to France and "gives all his remaining property in California" to her. I was purposely vague about the property so as not to give the taxman a reason to take a cut.

He glanced at it briefly, then signed. I gave him Giselle's affidavit refusing to procreate with him and took my leave.

Manon prepared a special meal to celebrate Giselle and Teri's freedom, Teri's turning the tables on Raoul and Giselle's victory over Robert and the patriarchal European system of property ownership. We dined on "croquettes des crabes, coquilles Saint-Jacques, et chevreuil aux champignons sauvages," (crab cakes,

scallops, and roast roe deer in a wild mushroom sauce.) We celebrated our dinner with the best vintages of Robert's wines.

Now that the women's partnership interests were settled, I
turned my attention to finding a suitable office in the newly re-
constructed commercial district. I wanted to be near our Central Wharf where the ferries discharged travelers back from
Sacramento and the various mining districts and towns.

Like my meeting with Robert Gaillard, I used a reserved
back table at Les Bons Amis as my temporary office with Pierre-
Louis' consent. Each morning I bought a copy of the Alta California to read the want ads for rental space and monitor fast
moving events in the city.

The paper's editors made much ado about the continued
lawlessness on city streets, especially after dark. The admoni-
tion of the Vigilance Committee to robbers, cutthroats and
petty criminals alike to flee town or else after the fire had little
effect. Those who fled soon drifted back. The Sydney Ducks
prowled the streets after dark looking to avenge their losses in
the fire and snub the vigilantes. Drunken gamblers and sailors
were easy marks, especially for unscrupulous hooligans lying
in wait.

The most dangerous part of town was away from Nob Hill
in an area bounded by the waterfront, Broadway, Pacific Street
and the steep climb up Telegraph Hill. Whores and their pimps,
thieves, and an array of scoundrels lived here in jerry-built huts
and rough, unpainted wooden shacks. The atmosphere was
thick with the smell of outhouses, smoky fires, and pots cooking with chiles and garlic.

The rough bars in the area used women to entice the mark
to drink liberally, accompany the hostess to the back room
for sex, only to be whacked by the pimp and robbed. Others
drugged the mark's cheap, flavored whiskey to the same effect.
The newspaper estimated that there were currently over 2,000

whores in the city and more arriving weekly by ship from abroad and returning to the rebuilt city from towns and mining camps along the gold bearing rivers where they'd fled after the fire.

The city itself was much changed after the fire and rebuilding. There were no traffic rules or order on the streets. Omnibuses running from Portsmouth Square to the Mission District careened at full speed along the plank toll road and city streets. Delivery wagons and carriages followed course. Even the elegant silver and brass mounted hacks of the rich had to negotiate the race track the streets had become. Add to this mix drunken men on horseback weaving in and out of traffic and woe to the poor pedestrian who was distracted and not prepared to dart and dash for safety.

The streets teemed with newsboys, cigar boys and bootblacks hawking their wares and yelling for attention over the din of drumming hoofs, rattling carriages, carts and huge overloaded drays all on plank streets oozing mud and horse manure. The roar and din of the city streets left a lasting impression on newcomers and residents alike.

The city streets were colorful as well. In addition to "ordinary" foreigners from Europe dressed in the latest styles, one encountered a range of exotic and curious men most had only read about in travel narratives — Moors, Chinese, Arabs, Mexicans, Hindus, Pacific Islanders, Spanish, Russians, African-Americans, Chileans and other South Americans. Most still dressed in their native costumes. In short, the city was full of eccentric characters of all races, religions and backgrounds. Small wonder that the French, who couldn't or wouldn't speak English, were tabbed the "Keskydees" for asking "what's he saying?" all the time.

The newspaper recounted winners and losers in all types of sporting and betting events. A lead column regularly featured the shooting or two a day among gamblers with disputes and knifings over real and imagined slights in the city's countless saloons. Cock fighting locales were duly noted as well as contests between bears and bulls. A local circus featured hammer striking contests, side shows with freaks, booths for throwing balls at Negroes' heads and other diversions.

The paper also announced the arrivals and departures of ships and their cargos. One of the most popular sporting events occurred when the flag and semaphore atop Telegraph Hill signaled a ship had been spotted making for the bay. Gamblers to the core, city slickers bet on when the ship would enter the Golden Gate, slide past Fort Point, what time the quarantine boat would board the ship, the time the arrival cannon would fire, when she would dock and what cargo she carried. Once docked or at anchor, carts, wagons, drays, stevedores, and hotel runners jammed the streets leading to the wharf all hawking their services.

As for cultural activity and nightlife, the fire destroyed both the Jenny Lind and the French Adelphi theatres. Both were being rebuilt but according to the drama critics, the quality of acting and play selection was second rate. The proprietors of the California Exchange, the local stock market, offered their large hall for weekly dances that attracted men and women on the make. Still the major entertainment activity for the male dominated city was gambling or gawking in the numerous, fancy gambling palaces.

My efforts to find a suitable office were frustrating. The owners of the newly erected buildings in the fire zone sought outrageous rents and deposits to try to recoup their fire losses and reconstruction expenses quickly. All the warehouses and offices near the central wharf had burned, so there was little choice in rents unless I settled for a locale not affected by the fire. Even then, with so many newcomers, landlords just kept raising rents.

I had to change my strategy. Instead of chasing the want ads like other would-be renters, I contacted the merchants who still had cargo stored in the hold of the Eliza and owed me monthly storage fees. I offered to trade reduced fees for a part-time office set-up in their place of business. One merchant, Jonathan Delay, bit for the deal. His small shop on Battery Street before Pine Street had just missed burning. He sold pharmaceutical goods and lacked storage area. He let me share the small office at the rear of his store with his bookkeeper.

I arrived at the offices of the Alta California to place an ad for my notary and business management services. Reporters scurried in and out of the editorial offices at a rapid clip. Something was up.

"What's going on?" I asked a pot-bellied man ahead of me.

"Caught red-handed he was. Stealing from a merchant on the wharf. One of them Sydney Ducks. The Vigilance Committee is gonna hang him," the man said with glee.

I moseyed over to the editorial office door to eavesdrop on the editor who was querying an overexcited reporter.

"Just give me the facts," the editor admonished.

"George Virgin returned from the Long Wharf and their boat with about a $1,000.00 in receipts to put in the safe of the shipping company's office at the end of the day. A Sydney Duck by the name of Simpton was waiting for him to leave. When Virgin left for home, the Duck broke into the office and was hauling off the small safe when Virgin unexpectedly returned to the office.

"Was there a confrontation between the two?"

"No, the Duck rushed past the startled steamship clerk dragging the safe and jumped into a skiff he had tied up on the dock and started rowing for Sydney Town. Virgin yelled, 'Stop Thief!' and several boatmen gave chase rowing furiously. One of their comrades was returning from ferrying a passenger to a boat and intercepted the Duck's skiff and slowed him down long enough for the others to catch up and apprehend him.

"Did they turn him over to the police?"

"Yes, Virgin and the boatman, Sullivan, who intercepted the Duck's boat, started to take him to the police but were joined by other citizens including one of the members of the Committee of Vigilance named George Schenck. He persuaded those present to take the Duck, Simpton, to the Committee's offices for trial by the Vigilance members."

"Where were the police?" the editor fumed.

"Schenck had 'em ring the bell at the fire station to call the members of the Committee to conduct the trial of the thief. There was a big crowd drawn by the bell ringing to the Committee's headquarters and hollering for the Duck to hang. That's all we know."

O boy, I thought. This was going to be an exciting next few days. Would the mayor and police intervene? Would the Committee of Vigilance carry out the will of the mob which had been stoked by the daily editorials calling for just such extrajudicial action and lambasting the mayor, police and courts for not convicting any Sydney Ducks for arson to date. The papers also had been lampooning the state's governor for pardoning his cronies who had been convicted of bribery and other offenses.

After placing my ad, I visited the lot owned by Raoul and Robert. It was an armed camp. Three mean looking toughs armed with shotguns prowled the perimeter as "guards." Their companions operated a rudimentary bar with a gambling set-up at the rear of their large tent. All were heavily armed. At the rear of the lot, the squatters lived in smaller tents. I spied two women fussing around a cooking fire. I estimated the gang of squatters at 8-10 in number. By the looks of this bunch of hardened scoundrels, any settlement to regain possession would not be cheap. This group of squatters was not unique. Squatters occupied other lots as well. I suspected it was an opportunistic business for most involved.

Teri threw me a grateful and amused smile when I recounted the scene. No doubt that she was rooting for the squatters all the way.

California Gold Rush Journal

CHAPTER THIRTY

San Francisco — June 1851

I shared my new office set-up with Sophie Benson who ran the store and used the back office to do the store's books. Sophie was a petite, energetic woman in her early thirties. Her engaging smile, large doe-brown eyes and English spoken with a lilting French Canadian accent made her a popular saleswoman for the French cosmetics, perfumes and remedies sold in the store.

I brought her a nice basket filled with French goodies from Manon's galley-paté aux truffes noires, English scones, Colombine de crevettes (black truffle paté, scones and round shrimp cakes), a bottle of rum and two bottles of Robert's vintage cabernet sauvignon as a welcome present for her and her companion, Jonathan Delay, the store owner. She readily agreed to act as my receptionist and relay messages.

She helped me locate Bernard Lefebvre, who had sailed on the Californienne's Company's second ship, the "Gretry," in February, 1850. According to Sophie Benson, Lefebvre and his wife came to San Francisco to establish a French pharmacy. Their drug store was on Washington Street near Dupont Street.

Madame Francoise Lefebvre worked the sales counter of their brightly lit and well-stocked pharmacy. She was modestly dressed and pleasantly plump with bold, friendly blue eyes. Her husband, Bernard, tall and dapper with a waxed moustache and closely clipped black hair, prepared medicines and potions on a counter at the rear. Behind him on specially built shelves, he could select drugs and ingredients from over a hundred French pharmacy bottles with gold and black labels attesting to their exotic contents, remedies and formulas.

I introduced myself as an entrepreneur and partner in Manon's catering business and presented her my business cards. Mrs. Lefebvre glanced at them curiously and said, "How can we help you Mr. Dubois?"

"I would like to discuss a business opportunity with you and your husband," I replied.

The husband threw me a quick glance, wiped his hands on his white smock and joined us in the front of the store. "Are you in the pharmaceutical business?" He asked as his wife handed him the two business cards which he perused quickly.

"Not yet," I replied to peak their interest. "I note that you stock a wide range of cosmetic products," I said picking up a small, attractive blue and white porcelain pot with a blue transfer reading "Parfumerie de la reine des Abeilles-Paris / Graisse d'ours du Nord / Violet parfumeur à Paris." The pot lid depicted two bears fighting each other and the pot base portrayed bears in different poses, walking, trying to climb a tree and with a cub. The pot contained highly perfumed Russian bear's grease which the dandies and high-end gamblers used as a men's hair pomade. The small pot carried a price tag of $4.50.

"Do these luxury items sell well at these prices?" I asked pointing to other pots of bear's grease and similar pots in blue and white faience depicting cows and pastoral scenes containing "moelle de boeuf," a highly scented pomade like the bear's grease but made with beef marrow. Prices ranged from $3.00 to $5.00 a pot.

The couple looked at each other and she nodded to her husband to respond. "They would sell better at a cheaper price, but the ingredients are costly and imported to Paris where the pomades are manufactured. Add to that the cost of shipping to San Francisco and the cost doubles. The customs here imposes a luxury tax on these pots, so they are expensive. We have to stock them along with the pots of creams, tooth paste, rouge, and cosmetics for the ladies. Unfortunately, we make very little profit on these items."

"Could you make a comparable bear's grease pomade if you had a reliable supply of bear's grease?" I asked.

"Of course. The formulas are not complicated. Can you get good quality bear's grease?" Lefebvre asked with growing interest.

"We have an agreement with hunters who provide meat to our catering business. We have an exclusive right to all bear meat and fat with our suppliers. We've been able to accumulate a few pounds of bear fat so far." I said.

"How much do you want for it?" Lefebvre asked too quickly.

"It depends on what kind of a profit sharing arrangement we can arrive at," I said evenly.

"Profit sharing?" Lefebvre croaked, his dapper demeanor and face registering acute disappointment. His wife looked shocked.

"Yes, we are entrepreneurs. We're not interested in selling our bear's grease at wholesale prices or to the highest bidder. Since we have exclusive control of the essential product, we expect to share profits on a 50/50 basis with a pharmacy like yours that could prepare the pomade and package it under an agreed name. You would have exclusive rights to market our California bear's grease and 50% of the profits," I said.

"Really, 50% of the profits is totally unreasonable. We must do the formulation, packaging of pots with paper labels, and the selling which is all the work. Surely, an 80/20 split of profits would be fairer to us. You already have the bear's grease and no more to do," he protested.

"I came to you first because we prefer to promote our fellow countrymen; however, we are business people who plan to stay in San Francisco and become American citizens. We can work as easily with Yankee pharmacists who would probably be thrilled to have a product to rival the expensive, imported pots you sell. There's no luxury tax to pay on California made goods, is there?" I tossed the ball into his court.

He glanced at his wife who lowered her big blue eyes in defeat. "How about a 60/40 split?" He pleaded.

"No, it's an equal partnership or none at all. Any agreement would include all products made with our bear's fat. That would of course include bear's oil as well as other cosmetic by-products," I stated knowingly.

I had learned from Sophie Benson that many pharmacies sold bear's oil in fancy labeled bottles as a popular men's and women's hair restorative. The labeled products she showed me promised all kinds of benefits to the user including a stronger libido. According to Sophie, bear's oil had a greater potential for profit as a patent remedy than bear's grease as a pomade.

Lefebvre registered surprise at my mention of bear's oil. It was clear I'd done my homework. "How soon can you deliver a supply of bear's fat?" He said conceding defeat. He graciously extended his hand to seal the partnership on my terms. His wife followed suit.

"I'll bring a couple of pounds of bear fat tomorrow morning along with the partnership agreement to sign," I replied.

I was so pleased with my morning's work that I decided to treat myself to a dozen oysters on the half shell, a bowl of bouillabaisse and a half liter pitcher of Pierre-Louis' house white wine before returning to my new office to draft the partnership agreement in French and English.

Georges was busy chatting up Sophie Benson when I strolled into my new office after my leisurely lunch. I had asked him to visit his contact in the post office after helping our women with their retail set-up.

"What's new at the post office," I asked.

Georges laughed. "They're drownin' in unclaimed letters. That's what. Even offered me a job to help out. Imagine that," he said tongue-in-cheek.

"I can't see you stuck behind a stack of unsorted mail or listening to irate clients for long," I teased.

"They's so overworked my friend there wanted to know if he could work for us. Hates to be cooped up in that stuffy place like a hen without a nest to lay her eggs. Lousy pay and now they're all squabbling with one another."

"What are they bickering about," I asked.

"Well, they got too much mail arriving an' most of it for the 'Frenchies,' as they call us. Not only on the boats, but they're gettin' lots of letters sent back down from the mining towns marked 'addressee unknown.' An' they're just piling up. They's wonderin' maybe we could do something about it."

"Are they willing to pay for our help?"

"Not so far as I know."

"Do we have any idea how many French letters they have in their dead letter file?" I asked.

"Hear to tell, there's around 3,000 piled up and most of 'em are French.

"Hmmm, could be interesting," I said. "I'm going discuss the situation with the consulate. I think we may be able to make something of this situation if the consulate goes along with my ideas."

Georges left with our rented cart to buy fresh vegetables and meet with our hunters to pick up our weekly supply of meat. I told him to ask for more bear's fat now that I had a deal.

Georges had delivered a copy of my report and the miners' petitions to Consul Dillon and secured an appointment for me with Dillon from the snooty clerk I'd had to put in his place.

Consul Dillon only kept me waiting fifteen minutes this time. Before discussing the miners' complaints, I brought up the situation at the post office. "One solution would be for you to take the letters in the dead letter file and try to locate the addressees or at least send the letters back to France," I suggested.

"Good lord, no. That's out of the question. We've already too much work to keep up with the new arrivals and our government is planning to sponsor even thousands more," Dillon said in a grave voice.

"Thousands more?" I was flabbergasted. "Did you read my report? The gold in the gravels is petering out and most of the remaining gold is locked in deep quartz veins. It will take experienced hard rock miners with special equipment to extract that gold. It's not something farmers and unemployed artisans can do to earn a living," I stated with exasperation.

"I read your report. I've passed on your assessment to the government ministers but it won't make any difference. The government is committed to sending emigrants to settle in California. They're even considering a lottery where the prizes are gold ingots and paid trips to California," he said soberly.

"What! The government is planning to pay emigrants to come here when there is no work for them," I said barely holding my mounting temper in check.

"That's what we are informed. We have no control over government policies," he said with resignation.

"Well, I suppose that means the government will not pay for the return or expenses of the miners who asked me to petition for them."

"Sadly so. We'll probably have to assist many to get from the placers or find work if they have skills. Hopefully, farmers will want to farm and fishermen will want to fish. The land is rich with opportunities other than mining," he said encouragingly.

I handed Dillon my new business card. "In that case, perhaps I can help," I said.

He perused my card and raised his eyebrows to indicate "how?"

"First, my office could handle the dead letter mail for you. You provide me with the letters on consignment and the lists of all arrivals from the ships' manifests that have transported French nationals to California. We match addressee names and write the letter writers informing them that their loved ones arrived but have no present forwarding address. For names not on the arrival manifests, we return the letters with a note indicating we are unable to trace the addressee. That way, they'll all have some news which is better than no news," I said.

"And why would you take on this task?" He asked.

"The consulate would need to publish in the Alta California the names of all the 'missing' persons and request information about anyone on the list be forwarded to my office. You would have to pay me a small fee for providing this service."

"How much?" He replied too quickly.

"Let's say $1.00 per letter or inquiry plus postage." I said not breaking eye contact.

"Hmm. That could cost several thousand dollars," he said peering over his glasses so as to say out of the question.

"First, our charge is minimal and the work gets done. You admit you don't have staff to do it and eventually non-action will catch up to you from irate and desperate French citizens who will complain to the government ministers who'll scapegoat you for allowing the problem."

"How about fifty cents a letter," he said with a straight face.

I laughed at his attempt to bargain. "We will probably lose

money on this. It's a dollar a letter or no deal," I said with a take it or leave it shrug.

"You win. I'll authorize the post office to deliver the letters to the consulate and we'll deliver them to your office."

"You'll need to prepare an authorization for us to act as your agent. I'll prepare the compensation agreement. Staff in my office are bi-lingual and we are prepared to assist any French in need of advice on how to deal with American authorities," I said with a lot of cheek.

We had no staff yet and I was hustling for business. I gave away our services to the consulate at a rock bottom rate in order to get access to their lists of emigrants and authorization to contact the letter senders. I planned to include a form letter with the mailings offering my services as a legal representative equal to the French notaire and detective agency to trace missing relatives and track down those who had deserted their families like Sutter to make their fortunes in the New World unencumbered.

Photos of a French Bear's Grease Pot and
B. Lefevre Pomade Pots dug in San Francisco
(*museum donation*).

California Gold Rush Journal

CHAPTER THIRTY-ONE

San Francisco — June 1851

Manon had been preparing food for her business seven days a week since we moved onto our ship. I offered to take her to the Sunday fancy dress dance at the California Exchange to treat her to some humorous diversion. The newspaper gossip column was full of reports of women dressed to the nines in fancy and often revealing costumes. A French journalist poked fun at the stiffness of the Yankees when they danced their quadrilles, praised the Latin Americans for their grace, and lauded the French for their animation and gaiety.

"It might be fun," I advised. "Watching clumsy males dressed like peacocks trying to keep up with and snag a hot-blooded senorita in a polka or gallop should be hilarious."

"You never took me to "bal musettes" when we were in Paris, so why go to a public dance hall in San Francisco? Soon-to-be-father wants to eye all the pretty senoritas before he gets a marriage license, maybe yes?" She said with a mischievous smile.

"Why would I want to ogle all the fancy ladies on display when I have the funniest and prettiest one all for myself?"

"Hah. You're not gonna say that when your Manon has a big belly and can't get in pretty clothes, are you Big Boy," she said with mock seriousness.

I laughed at her antics. "You'll still be a more interesting woman than all the harpies and gold-diggers. The comic possibilities with your quick wit, sharp tongue and big belly will be endless," I teased.

"Well Big Boy you can still take your Manon somewhere else."

"Sure. Where does she want to go?"

"Big Boy is gonna take Manon, the pretty sailor boy, on a tour of the city. She wants to see Little China and be treated to a special Chinese lunch and other exciting places only men get to go to. She thinks a tour of the city will be more interesting than watching pretty senoritas flirting with sex-crazed peacocks," she said with twinkling eyes.

"Ah. Mom-to-be wants all the pretty ladies and swishy dandies to flirt with sailor boy. What do I do if one hauls you off the street and into his wicked lair?" I said turning the tables.

"Like in the cheap novels, you rescue your Manon from all depraved seducers so your child's not born in a harem or bordello," she said with a flourish as she opened her trunk to select her disguise.

Fully decked out in her bell bottoms, loose mid-shipman's blouse to hide her figure, soft black leather boots and sailor's cap perched jauntily on her head, she was too cute for words.

"When the Chinese see that gorgeous queue draping down your back, they're going to want to take you home, sailor boy."

"That's why you gonna protect me, Big Boy."

We made it to Pierre-Louis' bistro without incident, just a few whistles, cat calls and lots of hungry looks even by passing women. Pierre-Louis escorted us to my favorite back table where we treated ourselves to a half bottle of champagne while waiting for Wah Fong to finish his kitchen shift.

"Where you wanna go boss," said Wah Fong who couldn't

take his eyes off my companion who fluttered her long eye lashes seductively at me.

"My wife's nephew, 'Silvio,' just arrived in San Francisco and wants to visit the town. I thought we could have lunch in one of the best restaurants in Little China and tour the district with you," I said pointing to "Silvio."

Wah Fong hesitated. "Restaurant okay, but maybe trouble in rest of town," he said sheepishly.

"What kind of trouble?" Manon asked before I could reply.

Wah Fong was not used to such directness and tried to beg off answering by giving me a look that said "help please."

"Well? Where do you not want to take me?" Manon said, tapping her boot with annoyance.

"Maybe best we just go to restaurant," Wah Fong said nervously.

"Let's go to the restaurant," I said getting out of my chair and heading for the street in order to avoid the growing test of wills between Manon and our reluctant guide.

Despite Wah Fong's efforts to avoid the seamier locales, there was no way to elude the sex traffic that dominated the area. Wah Fong tried to hustle us quickly through a street with two brothels and their Yankee clients, but Manon was having none of it.

A girl no older than twelve or thirteen called out to Manon, "Hey sailor boy, you wanna lookee-see? Juss 2 bits," she pointed to the area of her pantaloons covering her sex.

"Why would I want to pay just to look," Manon asked Wah Fong so directly he was taken aback.

"Uh, we keep going…," he sputtered.

Manon stopped in her tracks. "No we don't go anywhere until you answer my question," she commanded.

"Ah, Yankee sailor think China girl built different from Yankee girl. He pay fifty cents to see if sex part go north to south like Yankee girl," he said reluctantly.

As we were stopped in the middle of the street, two more girls approached us along with the 12 year-old. None of the girls could be older than fifteen. "You like Touchee-Doee? Only three bits," said a girl with long, strait black hair and luminous almond-oval eyes tugging on my sleeve and pleading with me to go into a parlor house with her.

The youngest girl and another more aggressive girl accosted Manon. "China girl velly nice. You come inside, please. China girl like sailor boy. Special rate for two girl."

Manon gave me a "what the hell" look and a shrug as she let her two girls direct her up the stairs and into the bordello. Wah Fong was furious, but I told him my nephew just arrived on an Italian ship and "boys will be boys," especially after a tour of duty at sea.

Wah Fong fidgeted while I leaned on my walking stick and waited for Manon to reappear. Fifteen or twenty minutes later Manon exited the house and smiled like a conquering general at Wah Fong as he sought to hustle us out of the area.

Wah Fong ushered us through the high arches of a pagoda-like building. He said the large golden characters over the façade meant "House of Divine Seasonings." The interior décor was very ornate with wooden dragons sparring with pot-bellied warriors and mythical creatures painted green and red. "Restaurant velly special. Bring over in many pieces from China," Wah Fong said proudly as he bowed to the owner and they exchanged greetings in their dialect.

Manon whispered to me in a conspiratorial tone, "How much commission do you think he's getting for bringing 'white devils' to eat in this place?"

I restrained my urge to guffaw which would surely give offense. After a lengthy discussion with the head waiter, Wah Fong announced, "Owner offer special meal for honored guests. Start with shark fin soup. Okay?"

Manon shook her head. "I know shark fin soup. What other soups can we have to start?"

Wah Fong looked consternated and upset to call the waiter back for more menu discussion. I suggested we try the delicious won-ton soup I'd eaten at the other restaurant with Georges. After much haggling back and forth we settled on a menu of spring rolls, pot stickers, won-ton soup, hot spicy shrimp, deep-fried calamari, and a house specialty — Mongolian pork. Every dish was delicious.

Wah Fong ate his lunch at a separate table and groused with a staff member.

"So, how did it go in the Bordello," I asked in French now we were alone.

"I told the madam I wanted to buy both girls, but just one at a time. She gave me a big toothy grin and said 'two dolla fifty for two girl.' I gave her two dollars and pointed to the youngest girl. She led me into a backback room partitioned into six cubicles. Inside mine, there was a small cot, a small side table with a basin of water and a used towel. The girl took off her clothes, flopped on the cot and spread her legs before I could tell her not to. It was pathetic. She wasn't more than twelve, yet her thin thighs bore bruise marks inside and out. Her breasts were just little buds. I told her to turn over but she didn't understand."

"Could she speak English?" I asked.

"No, that was the problem. She just kept saying, 'Doee quick, please, doee quick.' She didn't understand anything I said. I took her by the legs and turned her on her stomach. Her backside was also black and blue. I picked up her trousers and smock and motioned her to put them on and pointed to the door. She started to cry like a little girl. I wiped her tears on the dirty towel and sent her out."

"What about the second girl?" I asked.

"She came in right after the first one left. She, too, stripped immediately before I could tell her to stop. She said, 'sailor no like China girl?' I said I preferred boys to girls and she understood. She said 'no boy here. I do for boy.' She got on the cot and presented her rump to me. She said 'doee quick or I get trouble.' What trouble? I asked. She tried to explain in her pidgin English that if the girl doesn't please the client, they get a beating."

"Even if the man is physically abusive?" I asked.

"Yes, that's the lot of a child-whore. The house owns her. She's their slave. She said her parents sold her at thirteen to buy rice for winter after a poor harvest. The buyer raped her, sold her to an exporter who sexually exploited her and resold her to the whorehouse here."

"How can she get through customs and immigration here? She's clearly a minor?"

"She says they claim she is the Chinese wife of a male emigrant living here.

"And since no one here speaks or reads Chinese, immigration officials accept the story and pocket a tip if offered," I added.

"It's not that much different for the Chilean girls from what Teri tells me. Their pimps bring them here where they don't speak the language, pay bribes and claim they are wives. The girls are housed in cell-like cribs like the Chinese girls and have to service all takers. When there are several ships in port Teri says the poor girls have to service up to a hundred clients a day. It's disgusting and degrading. They, too, are no better than slaves," said Manon.

"Why was the first girl in tears?" I asked.

"She was afraid I would tell the madam I didn't want her or she didn't please me. She would get a severe beating. I told the madam both girls were very satisfactory and I would refer business to protect the girls. I would have liked to slit her throat and rescue all the slaves," Manon, said her eyes blazing and nostrils flaring.

"Where do you want to go next?" I asked as we finished our meal and laughed over Wah Fong's sour look.

"I would like to see a Chinese gambling hall and an opium den," Manon said without hesitation.

"Oh boy, you're gonna make this Wah Fong's most miserable day as a tour guide."

"He deserves it. He just wants to whitewash all the ugliness," Manon asserted.

We paid the food tab which was surprisingly reasonable. I told Wah Fong that "Silvio" had promised the sawbones aboard his ship he would buy some opium for use as a pain killer in the ship's dispensary. He reluctantly led us to a Chinese herbalist located in a back alley.

The shop was full of pungent herbs and animal parts dangled on strings from the rafters. After an animated discussion with the herbalist, Wah Fong showed us a small tin box with Chinese characters on the lid.

"This opium from China," he said. "Velly expensive, so maybe you no want."

Manon picked up the tin box that looked only big enough to hold 30-50 lucifer matches. "What's it say on the lid?" She said pointing to the characters.

"Say 'Gate to Heavenly Dreams,'" Wah Fong said.

Manon pried open the lid and looked inside. She shook out a small, gummy, sweet smelling substance that looked like a tar ball.

"How do you use it?" She asked.

"You heat it and put in opium pipe," he replied clearly frustrated with her inquiry.

"I want to buy an opium pipe as well," she demanded.

Wah Fong addressed the herbalist in a high-pitched tone that betrayed his increasing annoyance with Manon. The herbalist, a tall, thin man in his forties with a stringy beard and taciturn expression listened to the barrage and shook his head no.

"Medicine man no sell pipe. Just sell remedy," Wah Fong asserted.

I decided to try to defuse the growing power struggle between the two before it escalated. "Ask him if he has opium for sale in liquid form. It would probably be easier to use as a pain killer that way," I said to Wah Fong.

When asked, the herbalist produced an assortment of small bottles with cork stoppers filled with a white, hazy liquid. I pulled the stopper and smelled. The sweet opium smell had been diluted with alcohol just like the many pain remedies in vogue at the time. This was the same concoction sold as "laudanum" in many pharmacies and patent medicines. I had even seen ads for a preparation called "Mrs. Winslow's Soothing Syrup" to be given to babies when they were teething or would not stop crying. It was considered a "baby killer" by some due to the number of babes given too strong a dose to shut them up.

"We'll take two of the dark green vials shaped like tear drops," I said to Wah Fong.

Manon gave me a quizzical look and I signaled her to back off as I paid for the opium. Giselle had been having severe cramps with her monthlies and maybe the pain killer would help. She'd like one of the tear-shaped bottles in any case and Manon would probably like the other. I'd make sure our babe didn't get any of the contents.

Wah Fong was unhappy with the request to visit a Chinese gambling establishment. I assured him we just wanted to compare it to the gambling palaces on the Plaza where many Chinese also gambled. I indicated we would only observe and not participate.

As we made our way from the herbalist and through the rabbit warren maze of bustling alleys full of vendors and hawkers, Manon suddenly darted down a series of small steps and disappeared through a doorway covered with beads. Wah Fong was horrified to see me bound after her.

The sweet smell of burning opium had alerted Manon to the existence of an opium parlor. She was already on her way out as I poked my head into the den. A startled attendant was seated cross-legged on the floor coaxing a small flame in a glass bowl to soften an opium ball, or "gow pill," like the one we'd seen in the tin. A long opium pipe with a colorful ceramic bowl lay beside him. Several clients were stretched out in a series of wooden bunks three high. Some puffed on opium pipes and others lay prostrate in a somnolent state of bliss.

Manon's Cheshire-cat grin said it all. She was pleased with her little escapade and initiative. We rejoined our now thoroughly distraught guide and he hustled us along at an ever faster clip. He led us into a large wooden building near the eastern end of Dupont Street. The interior was crammed with Chinese men in various native costumes though all wore the long, traditional queue that generally reached to the end of their smock-like outer garment they wore over silk leggings or pantaloons. All wore distinctive caps from their native provinces.

Our entrance created no stir among the gamblers, though a few of the merchants and shopkeepers paused to appraise Manon, the sailor boy. It was evident by their rich attire the gamblers represented the affluent class in the city as there were no coolies or slaves present. The men crowded around four tables or "banks" heaped with brass counters and directed by the croupier for the house. There was no bar as in the gambling palaces on the Plaza. A group of Chinese musicians played odd shaped instruments that emitted high-pitched and unfamiliar music at the far end of the room. The walls were decorated with scrolls depicting Chinese myths and sagas.

While one table played poker with cards, the other tables played fan tan, a form of lotto. Fan tan was played on a table square marked 1-4 on each side. The croupier selected a pile of brass tokens from a large bowl, quickly placed them on the table and immediately covered the tokens with a metal cover like a top to a casserole pot. The gamblers had to guess how many tokens would be left over after all the tokens on the playing surface were stacked in piles of 4. Bets were placed on 1 to 4 tokens. The gambler bet that only 1-3 tokens would be left after the stacking. The bet on number 4 was a wager that all the tokens would stack in piles of 4. The gamblers who guessed correctly won 4 times the amount they bet less a commission to the house. The gambler could bet on only 2 numbers at a time.

We had seen merchants, hawkers and even Chinese laundries selling paper lottery tickets called "the white pigeon," so named for carrier pigeons used in China by professional gamblers to carry results, communicate and evade authorities where lotteries were illegal. Here, even non-Chinese played the "white pigeon" lottery where you bought $1.00 tickets, ticked off 20 of the 80 characters on the ticket and gave it back to the seller. The lottery center picked 20 characters each day. If you got 5 of the characters selected, you won $2.00; with 6 you won $20.00; with 7 you won $200.00 and if you picked 10 you won $3,000.

Here in the gambling palace, the Chinese gamblers were so intent on their quest to win that we could pass almost unnoticed among them as we observed their play, joy at winning and stoicism at losing.

Since we were near the Italian quarter, we paid off Wah Fong to his great relief and made our way to Little Italy.

"CHINESE GAMBLING HOUSE" c. 1851.

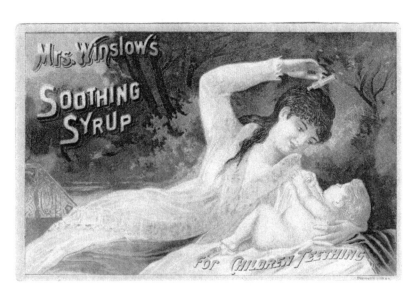

A trade card for "MRS. WINSLOW'S SOOTHING SYRUP."

"CHINESE RESTAURANT," San Francisco.

California Gold Rush Journal
CHAPTER THIRTY-TWO
San Francisco — June 1851

We popped out of Little China on the eastern side of Dupont Street and headed up Broadway toward Telegraph Hill. "Little Italy," like the French quarter, was a hodge-podge of merchants selling fruits, flowers, vegetables, wines, pasta and traditional Italian "salumi," the delicious sausages, salamis, and cold cuts they used for their "primo piatto" antipasto starter course and "panini," sandwiches filled with cold cuts.

Like the French, Spanish and Chileans, they stick together in a tight-knit but small community. They, too, had fled poverty for the promise an emigrant could pick up gold out of rock crevices along the river with his knife. They sought their fortunes in the southern gold fields in Calaveras, Mariposa, and Tuolumne Counties. Most returned disillusioned to Italy while some stayed to farm the rich Sacramento Valley or to fish.

Manon had considered the Italian fishermen for her suppliers, but their prices were much higher than the Chinese. The Italian fishermen were Genovesi from Liguria and very clannish. The failed miners were mostly "contadini," poor farmers from Toscana. After the high-pitched chatter of the Chinese, the sing-song lyricism of Italian dialects was music to our ears.

We headed for a "trattoria" called "Bella Toscana" and ordered a bottle of Chianti Classico and a platter of "salumi," Italian cold cuts and sausages.

As it was the slow, late afternoon period, the proprietor, Luigi Salterini, a small, full-fleshed man with rosy cheeks and a bulbous nose that attested to his love of good wine, served us personally. We were delighted that he spoke French.

"Have you heard that the vigilantes hung the Sydney Duck they tried last night?" the proprietor said.

"No, I heard the Committee of Vigilance had him and were going to try him," I replied and invited Salterini to join us for a glass of wine and a chat.

"How did it end up in a hanging?" I asked.

"Let me see if Pasquale can join us. He was there last night."

The proprietor returned from the kitchen with his cook, Pasquale Lupino, who brought his own wine glass and served himself a full glass of wine after stuffing a slice of dry salami and several olives from our dish down his craw. Pasquale was a short, portly, jovial fellow in his early fifties with a huge belly and like his boss, a nose that was no stranger from the pleasures of hearty Italian red wines.

Salterini asked him in Italian to recount what he had seen and heard the previous night after Pasquale stated shyly with his luminous eyes on Manon, "Io non posso parlare franchese." Salterini was more than willing to translate the cook's account.

"We had patrons who lingered over their desert wine and cigars, so I wasn't able to close my kitchen until they left. As I was locking the restaurant, I heard the bell of the fire station clanging away. People started running to the station and I joined them. Everybody was afraid of another big fire and that the Sydney crooks would set it."

Pasquale took time out for another foray on the antipasto plate and to refill his glass. "When I got to the fire station, there was a big crowd heading for the office of the vigilantes. They said they had caught a thief from Sydney Town red-handed and were gonna try him and hang him that night. I followed the crowd."

Our translator paused to fetch another bottle of wine and a plate of olives before continuing.

"We stood around in front of the vigilantes' place for over an hour and the crowd kept getting bigger and bigger and hollering for the hanging."

"Were the police there?" I asked.

"Yes, there was a Captain Ben Ray and other police. Ray knocked on the door of the vigilantes' building several times demanding they open and hand over the prisoner. This went on for a long while. Finally, a vigilante named Schenck came out and addressed the crowd along with Sam Brannan. They said the Sydneyman, who gave his name as John Jenkins, had been tried and found guilty of premeditated theft and was sentenced to hang by a unanimous jury."

"What did the police do?" I asked.

"Couldn't do nothing. The fellow Jenkins was still inside and the crowd was all armed and hollering to throw up a rope and hang him from a window of the building. Must have been nearly a hundred vigilantes inside and an angry mob outside. Brannan came back out and told the crowd, 'the prisoner will be executed on the Plaza within the hour.' The crowd gave a big cheer and most headed for Portsmouth Square on the double to get a good spot to view the hanging."

"Did the police wait for the prisoner to come out?" I asked.

"No, they also headed for the Plaza. Word of the hanging was spreading fast. They even rang the bell of the California Engine Company again to alert the people of what was happening. I stayed put to see what would happen when they brought this fellow Jenkins out. Some was saying the Ducks would come and free their countryman."

"What happened next?"

"We had to wait a long while. Rumor had it the prisoner decided to ask to see a clergyman. One went into the building anyway. Finally, the vigilantes came out with the prisoner who was yelling foul-mouthed expressions and trying to escape. The vigilantes surrounded him and marched him off toward the Plaza. They all had their pistols out."

"Did the Ducks try to rescue him?" Manon asked.

"I was told they did, but I was so far in the rear I didn't see it. It's about a half mile to the Plaza and some Ducks was waiting to jump the vigilantes but there was too many of them and they couldn't get to Jenkins."

"Did the police try to rescue him?" I asked.

"Yes, they actually got a hand on him as they crossed the Plaza for the old Spanish adobe, but they also got beaten back. The vigilantes said they'd shoot the police if they interfered and they meant it. The police backed off after two vigilantes put a pistol to Captain Ray's head."

"What did this fellow Jenkins do?" I asked.

"He was still smoking the cigar he'd asked for when they marched him to the Plaza. The vigilantes had him surrounded four deep with pistols still drawn. One of them threw a rope over the cross bar of the flagpole at the old adobe. Then they put a noose around his neck. Jenkins started hollering for his mates to save him, but the vigilantes just hauled on the rope and soon he was swinging from the pole. Once they were sure he was dead, the vigilantes marched out of the Plaza and back to their headquarters. They just left the thief hanging up high for all to see."

Manon and I exchanged sober looks and she nodded toward home.

We had planned to stock up on Italian delicacies and pastas while in the area, but the story of the hanging unnerved us.

Sydney Town was only a few blocks south of the trattoria and we didn't fancy running into any Ducks hell bent on revenge. We thanked our hosts for the info, paid our bill and scooted back along Dupont Street for the safety of the French quarter where we could find sanctuary if trouble erupted. It was close to sundown when we skirted the Plaza and made a beeline for the Eliza.

Next morning I bought the Alta California from a street hawker and headed to my new office. I nodded to Sophie who was stocking shelves and retreated to my desk in back to glean the latest developments in our lawless town.

The coroner had taken Jenkins' body and ruled he'd died of strangulation. At the inquest, the Sheriff identified by name six members of the Committee of Vigilance who were present and took an active role in the hanging. The newspaper supported the Committee's action and its editorial reported that Jenkins had $218.00 in his pocket — proof the members were not thieves like the dead man. The paper also noted that under California law, the premeditated robbery of a business premise was a capital offense if the jury sought to impose the gravest penalty.

Apparently, Jenkins had dumped the stolen safe into the bay before being cornered in his skiff, but fishermen had recovered it. The newly elected mayor, police, defense lawyers and judges wanted members of the Committee arrested as they were afraid of retribution by the Sydney gangs. The newspaper claimed the people were on the side of the Committee and Jenkins had a fair trial.

Witnesses testified at the trial before a jury of twelve Committee members in the Committee's building they'd seen him steal, chased him and recovered the stolen property. Jenkins hadn't denied the crime and had even asked for a glass of brandy and a cigar after the verdict, confident his mates would rescue him. Miners routinely held impromptu trials of thieves and claim jumpers and had no qualms about stringing up a criminal after a speedy trial.

To counter the legal authorities and justify their actions, the Committee called for a meeting in the Plaza to reconfirm their actions and solidify public and newspaper support. They even sent the newspaper a list of 183 members of the Committee who condoned their action and opposed police or political interference.

I was determined to stay well away from the increasingly confrontational dispute between the warring sides for control of the city and its justice system. All the newspapers supported the action of the vigilantes and had been fueling public passions for a hanging on the Plaza since the big fire of May 3-4. Some editors were bold enough to name the Sydney Ducks as the arsonists even though there was no proof.

Manon was pestering me to get our marriage license and legitimize our babe. So, I put my worries aside and made my way to City Hall near the Plaza. The Whig party won the recent election and took office the day of the May fire, so all the faces had changed but the fees were as high as ever. I forked over my $20.00 and was told to see the clerk of Judge Parsons to arrange a date for a civil marriage.

I bypassed Judge Parson's courtroom. He had disbanded the grand jury and quashed an indictment against an alleged arsonist, named Lewis. His actions guaranteed no criminal cases could be tried until a new grand jury was empanelled and in session and that couldn't happen for a few weeks. His actions fueled the charge that the courts failed to function to prevent crime and justified the creation of the Committee of Vigilance in the public's eye.

I went over to the civil division and filed my action for civil embezzlement and request for seizure of wine inventory against Raoul in behalf of Teri. The clerk read the complaint and chuckled at my legal maneuver.

"The judge is gonna like this case. Is your client a good looker?" He said with a leer.

"Oh yes, and she's a fiery, hot-blooded she-demon to boot," I exaggerated to the clerk's delight. Now that I had him convinced he'd see a red-hot mama and hear some juicy testimony, I requested he get the judge to sign the wine attachment order.

"No need to bother his honor." The clerk signed the judge's signature and affixed the court seal with a flourish of authority. I'd have Georges serve it on Raoul later today. As the clerk was in such a good mood, I showed him the marriage license and requested a date with his judge. He consulted the court calendar book.

"You in a big hurry?" he asked with a knowing grin.

"My lady is," I replied.

"Typical woman. We see our share of gold-diggers here in a hurry to get their hands on the money and name on the deed. Hope you know what you're getting into," he said.

I ignored his chauvinistic remarks. "She finishes work around 3 P.M. Perhaps the judge could squeeze us in at the end of his day," I said and dropped a $5.00 gold coin on his desk. "What about tomorrow at 4 P.M.?"

The clerk made as if to consult the court calendar again before replying, "Sure, the judge can fit you in tomorrow at four."

As I left city hall, a maintenance man was busy plastering posters on bulletin boards announcing a $2,500.00 reward for information leading to the arrest and conviction of the arsonist(s) who torched the financial district May 3rd.

On my way back to my office, I bought a dozen red roses

for my bride-to-be and new box of cigars and some special champagne to celebrate welcome events in the next few days. Giselle's husband was sailing on the afternoon tide. I'd file her divorce petition with the court when we arrived to be married. Teri would want to celebrate her victory over Raoul and Manon and I had the most to celebrate of all.

Georges met me at my office with a huge pile of mail from the French Consulate. I sent him to serve the order of attachment on Raoul at his new mistress's bordello while I perused the undelivered mail from France. I needed help sorting all these letters. I'd ask Georges to run the bar and Teri the canteen in the afternoon so Giselle could help me screen the correspondence.

"HANGING OF JENKINS ON THE PLAZA," 1851.

California Gold Rush Journal
CHAPTER THIRTY-THREE
San Francisco – June 1851

Manon was thrilled that I arranged a civil wedding so quickly. All the ship's women had cause to celebrate. Our dockside canteen and bar was flourishing and profitable. Each woman was putting money aside for her nest egg. Teri had convinced Giselle to put away the severe, high-collared spinster-like clothes and bonnet she had been wearing to hide her figure and charms. Like Teri, she now let her rich auburn locks flow freely down her back adorned with a flower over her ear to signal she was a single woman at last.

Men flocked to their stands. Only in the gambling palaces could they see such attractive women. Here they could flirt and gossip for the price of a bowl of soup or a glass of wine. In the gambling houses they had to pay $16.00 an hour or more for the attentions of a hostess and risk their gold poke on games of chance. Slowly, Giselle was coming out of her shell. The shadow of Robert had left on the evening tide. While still shy and re-served, she'd learned from Teri that she could sell more and earn generous tips by engaging in friendly banter with her clients.

Georges' presence and Teri's ability to set limits kept the peace when men sought to go too far. She wouldn't serve drunks or tolerate crude language or behavior. Even our fellow merchants on the wharf kept a protective eye on our women. They also enjoyed the sight of vivacious women at work and earning their keep on a wharf with few women or attractions. Our dog, Fido, was probably the best deterrent of all. Giselle was his mistress and he'd do battle with man or beast if need be to protect her.

Our ship was a beehive of activity as we prepared for our wedding and celebration to follow. I had booked the private dining room in Pierre-Louis' bistro for the evening. He'd promised me he'd find enough escargots, by hook or crook, for our first course. Manon loves them as a starter and to date, we'd not seen them offered on any menu in the French quarter though I'd seen some on my tour of the mines.

The main courses we'd asked for specially were rolled veal scallops with fresh vegetables (paupettes de veau à la jardinière,) and flamed veal kidneys (rognon de veau flambés.) We'd selected veal dishes as we couldn't get lamb from our hunters unless they poached. Pierre-Louis wanted to make a special wedding cake, but Manon preferred his rich, creamy chocolate soufflé. We compromised and ordered them both. Giselle would provide the best vintages from her newly acquired wine stock.

By late afternoon, everyone was atwitter with excitement and anticipation. Our women were dressed to the nines but sought to hide their charms under long, hooded cloaks they'd worn at sea. Fortunately, city hall and our date with the judge was only a short walk and the chilly afternoon breeze blowing through the golden gateway justified the cloaks.

We made quite a sight in Judge Roberts' court as the two women on Georges' arm threw off their cloaks and cowl-like hoods. No monks these two gorgeous women. Teri's flaming red dress with daring décolletage dropped the jaw of the pimply-faced clerk who'd signed the judge's order yesterday. Giselle was stunningly elegant in an airy, mauve dress fit for the opera.

Her jeweled tiara atop her wavy, tumbling locks gave her the air of a fairyland princess.

Judge Roberts made his appearance just as Manon doffed her cloak to reveal a radiant, ravishing bride-to-be in a cream colored gown.

"My, my," he tutted with a welcoming smile. "Que vous êtes très jolie, mademoiselle," he uttered in his hesitant high school French.

When he saw the two stunning bridesmaids and the beaming Georges, he asked, "Is it to be a double wedding?"

"Non, seulement moi," Manon said proudly.

"Well, if that's the case, there's going to be two more very happy bachelors getting hitched soon with such beautiful ladies to choose from. My compliments to the bride and her groom. We are delighted you have chosen to marry and become American citizens. It is our gain and France's loss," the judge said perusing the marriage license and citizenship petitions for all five of us.

For those of us who have attended French nuptials in France, the ceremony was over in a few short minutes. No priest or Latin rites. No lecture on the duty of husbands and wives to produce kids and for the new wife to be subservient to her new master. We promised to love, honor and cherish each other until death do us part. After saying our "I do," and exchanging rings, the judge pronounced us man and wife.

"You may kiss your lovely bride," the judge said. He signed the certificate of marriage with a flourish of his pen. "When these two captivating ladies decide to marry, please bring them to my court as well," the judge said with a twinkle in his eye. "I will have the citizenship applications processed by the appropriate authorities," he added.

We all beamed with pleasure and shook hands with the judge. Only the court clerk stood unmoving, his greedy eyes glued to the subtle movements of Teri's bosom. After thanking the judge with a bottle of French cognac to cement our new Anglo-French relations, we donned our cloaks and headed for Pierre-Louis' bistro to pop champagne corks and start our festivities.

We had planned our wedding festivities on a Saturday night so we could all sleep in the next day. Teri and Giselle fixed breakfast trays and served the newlyweds in bed. We had no intention of getting up before noon on Sunday, June 22nd. Suddenly, the gentle pealing of church bells calling the faithful and sinners to church changed abruptly to harsh and frenetic clanging that signaled fire.

We jumped out of bed and struggled into our clothes. Teri, and Giselle stood by the rail of the poop deck peering intently toward the plume of heavy, ominous black smoke blowing from Broadway towards Stockton and Dupont Streets.

Georges was in the crow's nest of our ship with our spy glass watching the fire. After a few minutes he came down.

"It do look really bad. Wind's a blowin' somethin' fierce and the fire's just jumpin' from house to house. People are running with valuables towards the Plaza," he said.

"Good lord. Not again," I exclaimed to no one in particular.

"Maybe we better see if Pierre-Louis needs help. The fire looks like it's headed for Dupont Street," Manon said.

I was conflicted. I, too, was worried about our friend and his bistro, but reluctant to risk Manon getting caught in the panic of fire-crazed people and animals. I knew Manon would not settle to be a spectator when our friend was in need, so I asked her to change into her sailor boy costume and arm herself. I asked Georges to organize our wharf's fire defenses and for our two other women to defend our ship from looters if need be. They were to draw the gangway aboard after Manon and I departed and ready our two shotguns with bird shot.

Our cat, Gamelle Boy, had found a new mate, a calico colored female, and they we sparring with each other about who'd be boss on board. I was rooting for the calico as she and our dog combined to keep our boat rat free, while Gamelle Boy hung around the galley waiting for scraps when not on snooze patrol on his favorite chair. Fido raced back and forth between Giselle and the gangway barking up a storm and feeding off the commotion and anxious energy that pervaded our ship.

Manon and I headed up Clay Street toward the Plaza. The scene at the Plaza was total chaos. Frightened citizens heaped valuables in piles, and then raced back toward the conflagration to attempt to salvage more goods. The wind off the ocean howled and blew acrid smoke our direction that made us cough and our eyes tear. Some refugees looked like minstrel actors with their soot-blackened faces and frayed clothes.

We darted around startled horses, carts and even stretchers loaded with sick and injured persons dumped on the square alongside the heaps of goods. We felt the heat of the fire and heard the ominous popping and cracking as flames gutted and exploded through buildings and ate up the wooden sidewalks.

We raced left along Dupont Street toward Pine Street where Les Bons Amis bistro is located. Just last night we'd celebrated our marriage here and now all was pandemonium. Fire wagons retreated behind us, their horses shrieking and rearing with fright to escape their harnesses and bolt for freedom.

Pierre-Louis sounded like a drill sergeant as he barked orders to his scared staff. "All the silverware, candlesticks and good serving plates to the cellar. Put them in the iron chests. Vite! Clear the bar. All wine and hard liquor to the wine cellar."

He did a double take at Manon's sailor boy disguise, and then smiled ruefully. "This time it will probably be us by the looks of the fire and wind direction. Damn the Sydney bastards. They want revenge for the hanging of Jenkins. The Committee of Vigilance should hang them all," he shouted and pointed to his kitchen. "Help me save my kitchen," he said as he dashed through the serving door with us on his heels.

Manon needed no instructions. She gathered the copper pots and skillets and told me what to take. The three of us soon stripped the kitchen bare leaving only the stoves to face the approaching inferno. Once all the valuables were stowed in the cellars and the heavy iron trap door to them locked, Pierre-Louis brought a bottle of pastis, the licorice flavored alcohol of the south of France, and placed it on a table with a view down Dupont Street. "Merci, mes amis. We've done all we can. Now we drink and wait."

Pierre-Louis dismissed his frightened staff who scurried off as fast as they could away from the approaching fire-storm. Pierre-Louis poured three shots of pastis into glass tumblers and added water that made the liquor turn a milky gray. He quaffed his glass in a fluid motion and poured another dollop. Manon took a dainty sip and I waited to light the cigar Pierre-Louis passed me. I have never liked the licorice taste of pastis, so I concentrated on my cigar while we watched the street nervously.

A Hook and Ladder company of firemen worked feverishly to dismantle buildings on Dupont Street near Clay Street and the Plaza to stop the fire's advance just three blocks from where we watched.

"I think you two should get away now. The fire could jump the fire lines and spread faster than you can run," Pierre-Louis said soberly. Ash from the fire drifted down the street as he spoke.

"We'll go when you go," Manon replied as the firemen down the street blew up a tall building hoping it would keep the fire from jumping the block.

"Why aren't they hosing the fire with water?" Manon asked.

"There's never enough water in the cisterns to fight a fire of this magnitude," Pierre-Louis replied.

The smoke suddenly cleared a path so we could see a line of fire marching from Powell Street down Jackson Street all the way to Montgomery Street, five city blocks in length and nearing a wharf. Pierre-Louis poured himself another shot of pastis as we observed the macabre scene. The fire continued its advance towards us, but more slowly. The block on Dupont Street bordered by Washington Street now caught fire.

"My god. It's going to burn Portsmouth Square where all the goods were piled," Manon exclaimed with horror.

"Let's hope they get all those hospital patients they put there to safety before the Plaza goes up in smoke," I said bitterly.

We watched soberly for another hour as the fire crept ever closer. Suddenly, Pierre-Louis stood up. "Look, the wind is dying. The smoke is blowing back towards the fire. If it turns back on itself, it may burn itself out," he said hopefully.

We watched as the flames became less intense until some item being consumed exploded and sent a cascade of fire streaming into the air like a fireworks display. The firemen on Dupont Street reversed directions and now attacked the fire in the direction it had started. We all drew huge sighs of relief. Unless there was a new flare up, Pierre-Louis' bistro was saved.

Pierre-Louis disappeared into the bistro's pantry and returned with two baguettes, olives, a salami, a hunk of cheese and two bottles of previously opened red wine. We'd eaten nothing since our coffee and croissants on the ship hours before. Suddenly, we were all ravenous and attacked the food like birds of prey.

We invited Pierre-Louis to join us for dinner on our ship, but he declined. "We have only won the first round. The criminals who torched our city again won't stop until they succeed in burning us out or we hang them. They got away with the

May fire. No one was caught or arrested for the arson. Jenkins hung for premeditated thievery not arson. I must stay here and guard my business against looters and more arsonists."

"We'll stay and help you guard the premises," Manon said.

"No. I'll be fine. You two need to get back to your ship before there's more trouble. It will soon be dark and the streets will become treacherous; opportunistic criminals like Jenkins will look to rob, loot or assault the unwary. I'll lock up the bistro and sit upstairs by the window with my faithful shotgun. I would love to get a bead on a burglar or two to even the score."

"Are you really sure you don't want us to stay? We could take turns guarding during night," Manon offered.

"No, you may be needed on the ship. I hope to get sponsors and join the Committee of Vigilance as soon as possible. Only they can patrol the streets and bring the arsonists to justice. Hopefully, they've been able to catch some of the incendiaries in the act. I'll help them tug on the rope," Pierre-Louis said pounding the table with the knife we'd used to slice our salami and cheese.

We took our leave and scurried down California Street to our wharf. We'd inspect the damaged part of the city tomorrow when the sun was shining and the clean-up underway. Pierre-Louis was right. It would soon be too risky to be on the streets alone.

Georges and a group of others who lived or had businesses on the Long Wharf milled around the entrance as we arrived. We informed Georges that the bistro was safe and that they should blockade the entrance and organize a night patrol to guard it. Sentiment among those present ran high against the Sydney Ducks who they suspected of firing the city again. I pointed out that we needed to protect our property and our women. We had been lucky that the fire losses to the commercial district were few. The Ducks and Chinese would be looking for new places to squat as the fire had burned in their residential and business areas.

All was well aboard the Eliza. Everyone was relieved to hear Pierre-Louis' bistro survived the fire and we were safe. It had been quite a climactic first day of marriage. After splashing the soot from our faces and arms, we shared a light dinner of soup, salad, and crepes stuffed with strawberries and cream with our friends. Georges took the leftovers to the citizen patrol guarding our wharf. We pulled up the gang way for the night and Manon and I tumbled exhausted into our bed. We were too tired for more lovemaking, so we just cuddled and soon were sawing logs.

"FIRE OF JUNE 22, 1851."

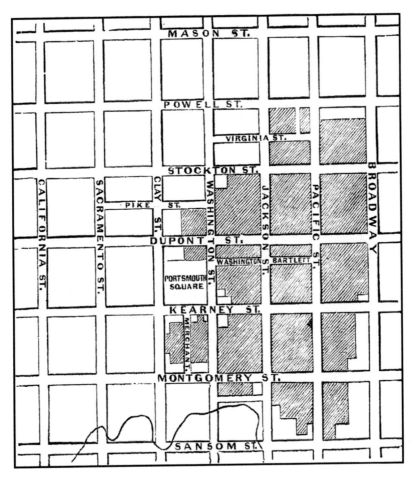

"DIAGRAM OF BURNT DISTRICT OF JUNE 22nd FIRE."

California Gold Rush Journal
CHAPTER THIRTY-FOUR
San Francisco — June - July 1851

We woke early with renewed energy and celebrated our nuptials in bed the way we'd planned the day before. I lit the cooking stoves in the galley and the wood stove in our stateroom. I brought my queen a basket of freshly delivered croissants and a mug of steaming hot coffee to start her day. She eyed me with that "you're gonna be a naughty boy" look.

"So, while your so-called 'queen' slaves in the galley to pay the rent and put food on the table, you're gonna gallivant around town to listen to the gossip, read the papers and view the fire scene, yes?" Manon said wagging her finger at me.

I gave her my best innocent little boy look and dropped my eyes in false modesty. Manon crooked her finger and motioned me to approach the bed. She pulled me to her by my cravat. "So, Big Boy. Now you're married, you have more responsibilities at home, yes?" She whispered in my ear.

I nodded affirmatively. She took my hand and placed it on her belly under her night shirt. "You feel that, Big Boy?" Manon whispered.

"I feel soft, lovely skin that is starting to grow," I whispered back. She was just starting to show her pregnancy and complaining she would soon not fit in her clothes. "Maybe I should get you one of Teri's ponchos," I teased.

"Hah. You wish. You're gonna get a big fat bill for Manon's new wardrobe. Fancy smocks for pregnant ladies in the latest Parisian style. Giselle and your queen bee are going shopping this afternoon, so you better be home early," she said biting my earlobe just hard enough to get a reaction.

"Is that why you were so worried about the fire getting past Pierre-Louis' bistro? That it might burn the women's mode shops on Dupont?" I said to get her goat. She yanked me onto the bed and won the tickling match that ensued.

"You better drink your coffee before it's cold and your clients start to complain," I said tongue-in-cheek as I scooted for the door before she could nail me with one of the croissants on her tray.

I left the ship feeling chipper as I headed down the wharf. Despite recent events in the city, I felt on top of the world to have such a funny, spunky and sexy woman to build a future with here in the New World. My upbeat mood took a hit once I reached Montgomery Street from my route up Clay Street to the Plaza. All the way down Montgomery Street to Broadway was a jumble of burned out buildings and smoldering heaps of rubble. Firemen were hosing the hot spots from their pumper wagons.

The scene only got worse as I approached the Plaza. The stench was unbearable. The coroner's wagon was parked in one corner of the square.

"What happened?" I asked a by-stander who was surveying the scene and shaking his head.

"The fire was so hot that burning cinders ignited heaps of goods piled here helter-skelter. Apparently, some of the sick folks from the hospital were brought here on litters and caught fire like the goods," the man said with a grim look, pointing to the coroner's wagon and two attendants who were loading a stretcher onto the wagon.

I could see that about a third of goods on the Dupont Street side of the Plaza had burned along with the buildings. The Post Office had escaped along with most of the gambling palaces on the Plaza, but the Jenny Lind Theatre had burned again. As lots of police and firemen probed the wreckage, I decided to buy all the local newspapers and learn what I could of what had happened and who was responsible for the conflagration. I stopped at a news kiosk on the way to Les Bons Amis bistro to buy the Alta California and the Herald newspapers.

"Where's the Alta?" I asked.

"Burned to the ground this time," the newsboy said.

I bought everything in print. The Herald had gone to press while the fire still raged. Pierre-Louis looked pretty haggard after his night of of vigilance, but greeted me with a grateful smile and joined me for strong coffee and slices of fresh baked brioche. I figured I'd learn more from him about events than the broadsheets, whose headlines claimed the Sydney Ducks as the arsonists.

"Any truth to the allegations the Ducks set the fire?" I asked.

"Not yet. But it's on everybody's mind. Some of the firemen who took their coffee here this morning said that it was definitely arson."

"Any evidence to support their claim?"

"They said there were several attempts to set fires in the commercial center, but most were thwarted by vigilant citizens and police."

"Did they mention any arrests?"

"Not for arson, but the police shot and killed two looters and apparently angry citizens beat two looters to death and injured several others. Members of the Committee of Vigilance had to save some looters from the mob. They took several persons into their custody to interrogate."

"Aren't they going to hand them over to the police?" I asked.

"Well, the police are homeless. City Hall burned to the ground, so they lost their offices, the municipal courts and prosecutors' headquarters. There's just the prison ship in the harbor."

My god, I thought. Judge Robert's court was destroyed and probably the record of our marriage, as well as the case against Raoul and our citizenship papers. We had our marriage certificate, but the rest probably went up in smoke. "Did they save the records at City Hall?" I asked.

"Don't know," Pierre-Louis replied.

I scanned the broadsheets for details of City Hall's demise, but other than saying it burned, there were no specifics. I decided I had better investigate.

The walk down Dupont Street was sobering. Merchants and property owners vied with opportunists to find valuables in the still hot and smoldering rubble. Some owners had hired armed guards to protect their lots and few police were in evidence. They wouldn't be able to tell who owned what in any case. Once again, possession and a gun determined ownership rights.

At Pacific Street, I turned east and walked to the corner of Kearney Street where City Hall once stood. It had burned to the ground along with every building in the area. A couple of workers raked through the piles of trash.

"What happened to the records?" I asked.

"Got 'em all out afore she burned," the one leaning on his shovel observed in his Irish brogue. "Hell of a job it were. Cart horses kickin' and tryin' to bolt. Jamie here, got a bruise to show for it. Damn horse nicked his leg with a hoof."

It would be months before a new facility could be built and records assembled. Once again, we'd been lucky. We had our marriage certificate and I had a signed order to put a lien on Raoul's Chilean wine when it arrived. We'd escaped both disasters with no losses and would probably see Manon's catering business grow now that more competitors had been wiped out.

A vast area of Little China, with its cribs, opium dens and restaurants Manon and I toured had been consumed by the firestorm. Also gone was much of Sydney Town with its cheap dives and rude tenements. The crooks would have to flee the wrath of the Committee or risk swinging like Jenkins. With the legal establishment hobbled by the fire's destruction of their premises, the role of the Committee of Vigilance would increase and perhaps become more relevant.

It was sad to see that a good portion of Little Italy fed the flames. The wonderful trattoria Manon and I had visited was no more. Still, I was confident the hardy pioneers who'd built this part of town would resurrect it again just as the merchants in the commercial district had done after the May fire.

If there was any blessing in these two events, it was that the same parts of the city had not burned twice. It was the sixth major fire since 1849. Lots of gold still made its way to the city's banks, merchants and governmental coffers. There'd be money to loan and every incentive to rebuild. Hundreds of ships were on the sea bringing goods to sell, more emigrants, and building materials. Those who were wiped out or discouraged would leave. Those who stayed would rebuild and prosper.

As I made way back down the ruins of Kearney Street to my office, it was hard not to reflect on how much had happened in three short months since we'd stepped off the Flying Cloud in Chile and San Francisco. We'd secured a home and place of business on the busiest wharf in the city; we had loyal, compatible workers and friends; Manon's business was flourishing; we had money in the bank and a line of credit; Manon and I were committed to each other, our babe and our new country. We were happy and city life was exciting and no more dangerous than certain areas of Paris.

There would be significant changes on the horizon with the arrival of our child, Georges' sweetheart, and Teri and Giselle's immersion into the social life of the city. Could the next three months be more interesting, exciting or controversial than the preceding three? Food for thought.

Whatever the future here, we would ride the cusp of history. We were Americans now and would actively partake in the commercial, social, and political life of our city. With its beautiful bay, fertile valleys to the north and south, rich forests and gold bearing gravels and mountains, and its thriving inland trade through Sacramento and Stockton, San Francisco could become the gem of the Pacific coast and perhaps the New World. With its energetic emigrants from all corners of the world, it would surely become the most cosmopolitan city in the western hemisphere. We would all work to make it happen.

End of Part One
of Pierre Dubois' Journal

July 4, 1851

California Gold Rush Journal
AUTHOR'S NOTE

As with most historical novels, writers often rearrange or introduce aspects of the historical record out of sequence in order to accommodate the story line or make it more interesting. The same is true for this novel.

The Clipper Flying Cloud did set the trip record from New York to Valparaiso to San Francisco in 89 days in the Spring of 1851. However, it was the ship's maiden voyage. Other Clippers were transporting tea, spices and opium to Europe from China and the Far East and then sailing on to New York before heading around Cape Horn for San Francisco as described in the novel.

In order to introduce the small cast of characters we would follow throughout the novel, it was necessary to increase the number of passenger cabins from three to five. Clippers were designed for speed of cargo delivery and profits and not passenger comfort. The choice of an American Clipper allowed for a quick passage to the New World, a visit to New York, a chance to learn English for Georges and Giselle, Pierre to study American common law principles and pleading as well as American values, and an opportunity to introduce Manon's culinary talents.

The idea for the novel came from the author's long involvement as a dedicated bottle digger and amateur archeologist both in the San Francisco Bay area and in France. The French pharmacy, food and wine bottles, bear's grease pots and lids, pottery food containers, opium bottles and paraphernalia, torpedo soda bottles and other artifacts described in the novel were dug or acquired by trade with other bottle diggers. The author's entire collection of French artifacts from the San Francisco Gold Rush Era along with the maps, books, engravings, lithographs, tin types, etc., were donated by the author and his wife and are on permanent display in Le Musée du Nouveau Monde (Museum of the French in the New World) in La Rochelle, France. The museum has published a complete, color-illustrated catalogue of the collection which includes the author's introduction in French and English and historical vignettes by Annick Foucrier, Professor of History at the Sorbonne in Paris. The catalogue, entitled Les *Keskydees*, my be purchased from the museum. See their website.

The publication of the French broadsheet, *Le Californien* (which the author purchased from an antiquarian book dealer in San Francisco) provided a convenient and interesting way to expose the fraud and manipulation of poor Europeans by unscrupulous promoters and a practical way for the French government to rid itself of political undesirables and others in light of the violent events in 1848 that saw King Louis Philippe deposed. Years ago, the author dug a champagne bottle from an 1852 dump site in San Francisco with an applied seal bearing the arms and blazon of King Louis Philippe (one of only 5 known and on display in Le Musée du Nouveau Monde). What was the bottle doing in San Francisco? Was it from the French consulate's cellar? Drunk to celebrate or mourn his deposition? More intrigue to motivate the author to write this novel.

The decision to use French protagonists allowed the author to explore the ethnic rivalries and rifts that separated the English speaking miners (American, Irish and English) who banded together to oppose the non-English speaking miners (principally the French, Chileans, Mexicans and Chinese). The tensions between the rival groups for access to the best diggings led to the discriminatory $20.00 a month tax on foreign miners, which though soon reduced, continued to fuel animosity between the factions over who had the best right to the gold.

All events in San Francisco and the northern placers portrayed in the novel occur between the two great fires of 1851 — a short two month period. That the city would be rebuilt again, there would be more winners and losers as with all the fires, and more fortune seekers would keep coming despite the slim pickings in the placers argues for a continuation of the narrative. The author is writing the sequel to the adventures of Pierre and Manon and the changes in their lives brought on by a new birth, Pierre's new business activities and the changes in their associates' lives who are now free of feckless men and must engage in the social and political life of their adopted city.

The author would like to give special thanks to a number of important individuals who encouraged the book project from the start and contributed to its success. Thanks to Professor Annick Foucrier, who contacted the author after the first display of the historical artifacts in France at our local historical museum in the Allier. The migration of French to the New World is Prof. Foucrier's area of scholarship. I am indebted to her for sharing with me her wisdom, vast knowledge and resources on the French in California. The book's accuracy on historical detail and events is due to her careful reading and critique.

Thanks as well to Annick Notter, Conservator of Le Musée du Nouveau Monde in La Rochelle, France for making the exhibition of the author's donated collection such a success in France and her continual encouragement on the book project which she is bringing to print in France.

Special thanks also goes to Suzanne Maéso for her lively

prose and faithful French translation of the author's novel. Mme Maéso is the author of several books and her most recent work, a novel entitled, *LUCIE PANTALON, Lettres de Californie* traces in journal form the life of Lucie Pantalon, a French emigrant and feminist during the California Gold Rush who refused to wear skirts in favor of jeans and carved out an independent life for herself in California. Her portrayal is based on the life of Marie Pantalon, who emigrated from the Haute Savoie around 1850 and died in California.

And lastly, the author wants to thank the following individuals, Joe Miller and Anneliese Armstrong and others, who read the novel in draft form and provided valuable proof reading and critiques.

California Gold Rush Journal

BIBLIOGRAPHY

Allende, Isabel, *Daughter of Fortune,* Harper Collins, 1999.

Ashbury, Herbert, *The Barbary Coast,* Alfred A. Knopf, Inc, 1933.

Bancroft, H.H., *History of California,* Vols. 1-7, San Francisco, The History Co., 1884-1890.

Beilharz, Edwin A. & Lopez, Carlos U., *We Were 49ers — Chilean Accounts of the California Gold Rush,* Ward Ritchie Press, 1976.

Borthwick, J.D., *Three Years in California,*1857. Reprint, Oakland, CA, Biobooks, 1948.

Brock, Leo, *To Harness The Wind,* Naval Institute Press, Annapolis, MD, 2003.

Calhoon, F. D., *COOLIES, KANAKAS AND COUSIN JACKS,* Cal-Con Publishers, Sacramento, Ca, 1986.

Clappe, Louise, *The Shirley Letters from the California Mines 1851-1852,* New York, Alfred A. Knopf, 1949.

Clark, Arthur, H., *The Clipper Ship Era,* G. P. Putnam's Sons, New York & London, 1910.

Dana, R. H., Jr, *Two Years Before The Mast,* P. F. Collier & Son, New York, 1909.

De Russailh, Alfred Bernard, *Journal de Voyage Californie — 1850-52,* Aubier Montagne, Paris, 1980.

Fohlen, Claude, *La Vie Quotidienne Au Far West (1860-1870)*, Librairie Hachette, 1974.

Foucrier, Annick, *Le Reve Californien. Migrants Francais sur la cote du Pacifique* (XVIII-XIX siecles), Belin, Paris, 1999.

Guming, Deanna Paoli, *The Italians of San Francisco — 1850-1930*, Center For Migration Studies (in English and Italian), New York, 1978.

Holliday, J.S., *Rush For Riches — Gold Fever and the Making of California*, Oakland Museum of California & University of California Press, 1999.

Heizer, Robert F. & Almquist, Alan F., *The Other Californians — Prejudice and Discrimination under Spain*, Mexico and the United States to 1920, University of California Press, 1971.

Kemble, Edward, C., *A History of California Newspapers — 1846-1858*, Edited by Helen Harding Bretnor, The Talisman Press, 1962.

Lydon, Sandy, *Chinese Gold — The Chinese in the Monterey Bay Region*, The Capitola Book Company, Capitola, California, 1985.

Marryat, Frank, *Mountains and Molehills*, Longman, Brown, Green and Longman, London, 1855.

McMullen, Jerry, *Paddle Wheel Days in California*, Palo Alto, Stanford University Press, 1944.

Monaghan, Jay, *Chile, Peru and the California Gold Rush of 1849*, Berkeley, University of California Press, 1973.

Nasatir, A.P., *A French Journalist in the California Gold Rush — The Letters of Etienne Derbec*, The Talisman Press, 1964.

Nasatir, A. P., *French Activities in California*, Stanford University Press, 1945.

Paul, Rodman Wilson, *Mining Frontiers of the Far West, 1848-1880*, Holt, Rinehart & Winston, 1963.

Soule, Frank, John H. Gihon and Albert Nisbet, *The Annals of San Francisco*, New York, D. Appelton & Co., 1855.

Stewart, George, R., *Committee of Vigilance — Revolution in San Francisco, 1851*, Ballantine Books, Inc, 1971.

Weston, Otheto, *Mother Lode Album*, Stanford University Press, 1948.

Windler, Adolphus, *The California Gold Rush Diary of a German Sailor*, edited by W. T. Jackson, Howell North Books, 1969.

White, Stewart Edward, *The Story of California*, Halcyon House, 1940.

ABOUT THE AUTHOR

KEN SALTER is a professor emeritus in Communication Studies at San Jose State University, San Jose, CA where he taught critical thinking and persuasive writing courses, and directed pre-legal studies. He is also an international attorney specialized in international real estate and mining. He directed a placer gold mining company for 15 years in Mexico and Chile. He is the author of several books on famous trials including the *Trial of Dan White*, who killed San Francisco Supervisor Harvey Milk and Mayor George Moscone. He and his French wife live in Berkeley, CA and in the Auvergne, France.

3 1901 05413 0911

CPSIA information can be obtained at www.ICGtesting.com
Printed in the USA
BVOW080250010713

324691BV00002B/12/P

9 781587 902406